VINNIE
The Autobiography

Vinnie Jones was born in Watford in January 1965, and grew up in the Hertfordshire countryside. After a brief spell with Wealdstone, he was given his chance in League football, signing professional terms for Wimbledon before his trial period was over, immediately making his League debut in November 1986 and scoring the winning goal a week later against Manchester United.

He went on to gain an FA Cup winner's medal in 1988, helping defeat Liverpool in one of the biggest Cup final upsets of all time. The following year, he was transferred to Leeds United for £650,000, helping them to promotion in his only season at the club. In 1990 he moved on to Sheffield United, where he spent another year, and then on to Chelsea. Eventually, for a fee of £700,000 in 1992, he moved back to Wimbledon, for whom he played around 250 League games. He went on to captain the club, and win nine caps for Wales, captaining the side against Holland. In March 1998 he signed for Queens Park Rangers as player/coach, retiring from the game the next season.

His first film *Lock, Stock and Two Smoking Barrels* was a huge critical and commercial success. He is now working on his second film, *Gone in Sixty Seconds*.

VINNIE

The Autobiography

Vinnie Jones

headline

First published in 1998
by HEADLINE BOOK PUBLISHING

First published in paperback in 1999
by HEADLINE BOOK PUBLISHING

13 15 17 19 20 18 16 14

ISBN 0 7472 5914 3

Typeset by
Letterpart Limited, Reigate, Surrey

Printed and bound in Great Britain by
Mackays of Chatham PLC, Chatham, Kent

HEADLINE BOOK PUBLISHING
A division of the Hodder Headline Group
338 Euston Road
London NW1 3BH
www.headline.co.uk
www.hodderheadline.com

contents

DEDICATION

To Granddad Arthur: I just hope I am everything he hoped I would be as his eldest grandson.

ACKNOWLEDGEMENTS

My thanks to Derek French, Dave Bassett, Don Howe, Bobby Gould, John and Wendy Moore, Howard Wilkinson, Mick Hennigan, Leeds United supporters, Joe Kinnear, John Fashanu, Sam Hammam, all other supporters I have played for and the players I have played with.

And thanks, of course, to Mum, Dad, Nan, Ann, and the rest of my family including the Lamonts, Steve Davies, all my friends from Bedmond and my good friend Brian Hall, and to John and Jo Sadler for their help in writing my autobiography.

And special thanks to Tanya, Kaley and Aaron who are the three most important people in my life.

CHAPTER 1

devil or angel

I was seven years old. Just another kid in the street, an ordinary kid apart from the fact that I was already pretty experienced with a shotgun! Shooting was in the family – my dad, Peter, spent just about every spare minute he had out in the countryside with his mates and their guns. Just another kid with hopes and dreams, often lost in his own little world of make believe, longing one day to be as good as the Brazilian footballers we pretended we were. Our goalposts might only have been a couple of jumpers chucked on the ground at the local 'rec', but to us, it was the World Cup finals and just as serious as the real thing.

But one day I shattered my own childhood peace of mind. I remember it as vividly as if it happened yesterday, because bad things, really bad memories, stay with you for a lifetime and this mistake, at the age of seven, taught me a painful lesson that still hurts whenever I remember it – the first good hiding from my dad.

He was a builder and had done a hell of a lot of work improving our new home at 147 Lower Paddock Road in Bushey, Hertfordshire. He'd even put in a spiral staircase and not many kids could boast they had one of those at home. My room was in the loft. Dad had converted it specially for me, all wood panelled and reached by its own ladder from the second floor. I was proud of that room and so grateful he had taken all that trouble just for me. I never wanted to let him down.

He had his office in the house. Nobody else was supposed to enter but we did go in occasionally for odds and sods and one day when I went in, I picked up what I wanted – and hesitated for some reason. I can see it now, that wooden desk, and it still sends a shiver down my back when I remember what I did next. I opened one of the drawers.

It was stacked full of money. Loads of money, dough like I'd never seen. Around £5,000 or more, I reckon, all in banknotes. I closed the drawer and tried to forget about it but it played on my mind. All my life I've had this thing about carrying an angel on one shoulder and a devil on the other. That was where it started, where one would be saying to me, 'No, don't touch it' and the other would contradict: 'Go on . . . all that money, no one would ever know.'

For those few days I was in a state. Keeping away from dad's office as the angel kept saying 'No' and then wandering back to it as the other voice repeated 'Go on.' I regret to this day that I gave in to the little bugger who kept urging me to help myself, but I took one, a tenner, right from the middle of one of the piles. Can you imagine what that must have been like – a tenner to a seven-year-old? It felt like £100,000. But the crazy thing is that I didn't nick it for me – and that was my downfall.

I took all my mates down to the sweet shop, but instead of buying penny chews and stuff like that, I bought the whole box. I bought them penknives and all sorts of presents for a couple of days until the money ran out. So I just went back for more, more notes taken from the middle of other piles. The game was up, though, the day one of the teachers at Oxhey Infants School raised the question of little Jones's generosity and how he was coming by the money for the boxes of sweets, blocks of chocolate, knives and other gifts spread around the classroom. I told her my mum and dad knew about the money but I froze to the spot when she called my bluff and said: 'All right, then let's go home and talk to them about it.'

I don't think any statement from anybody has ever frightened me more than that one. My first thought was 'Oh no, how do I get out of this?' when I knew full well there was no way out. I was in it, right in it up to my little neck, and deserved everything that was coming my way. By the time we reached Lower Paddock Road we were greeted by a scene that would now look as if it came straight out of *The Bill*.

As we got out of the teacher's car, my mum, Glenda, was just stepping out of the house. There was another car parked nearby and although it was unmarked I knew by some kind of instinct where it was from. At that age you feared getting on the wrong side of the police.

Mum must have thought I'd been brought home to talk about some routine thing at school because she told the teacher: 'We haven't time for this. We've been robbed. The fingerprint experts are here.' My parents had discovered some of the money had walked from dad's desk and they'd called the police.

'Well, that's what we're here for,' said the teacher. I was a tiny lad for my age and, right then, as I stood by her side I was trying to look smaller by the second.

'What on earth do you mean?' Mum shot a glance from the teacher to me and back again.

'Vinnie's coming to school with all this money in his pocket.'

Those words hit me like a hammer. I went cold and hot and cold again. There was no way out, and later that afternoon the lady from the sweet shop rang mum to say I'd been buying up half the stock.

Mum was a proper mum – one who cared and who put discipline high on her list of priorities. She'd sometimes clipped me round the backside when I'd done wrong and it's strange, now, recalling how dad used to take her to task for it. But she remained the disciplinarian. This time was different. What I'd done was more serious than a prank and she stuck me in that beloved bedroom of mine, not only while things cooled off downstairs but to wait until dad came home from work. That wait lasted a lifetime: I had to sit there waiting, stewing and hating what I'd done. But never in a million years did I think he would hit me because he never had before.

My stomach churned when I heard his voice downstairs. He went absolutely ballistic and 'lost it', really. He was completely appalled by what I'd done. He gave me such a hiding – only with his hand, but it was a hiding all the same and I think the shock of it had more effect than the hurt. It really brought home to me what·I'd done and it made me ashamed of myself for a long time. It certainly cured me of theft – I could never have turned into a bank robber after that!

It didn't end with the hiding, either. He grounded me for the entire summer. It's the only time I've ever seen the Olympics because it was during the time of the '72 Games in Munich. I couldn't play football or cricket and that was terrible because my bedroom window overlooked the park and I could see all the lads, my pals, playing 'World Cups' and 'Test matches'. It was even worse at first because they'd come round for me but my dad stood by his decision and there was no shifting him. It all had a profound effect on me. My isolation forced me to think. I had always regarded myself as a strong kid but I'd given in to the wrong voice from the shoulder. What troubled me most was that I'd let my mum and dad down and I knew that what I had done must have been awful because I had never seen dad in such a state. It had shaken him badly. He'd done everything for me, taken me trout fishing, shooting and so many other things and, with my sister Ann, believed he had the perfect children.

To make things worse, at about the same time, Ann, who was three years younger than me, needed a bone-marrow transplant. It was an extremely difficult period for my parents. 'How could I have done such a thing?' I asked myself over and over in that bedroom I treasured, during the hours I spent alone. I was desperately ashamed and sorry. We talk about it now sometimes and dad knows I didn't take the money for myself but to treat my mates. Nevertheless, it was me who'd nicked it.

I never did such a thing again, but I did falter once – only slightly, though. Like all youngsters, the group I knew played marbles and one lad, Ray, had some real beauties. Mine were scrubbers by comparison, plain and dull and mostly chipped. His were clear and bright and with every colour you could imagine swirling through the middle. We used to have a little camp in the woods, a 'den', with branches and leaves as a kind of camouflaged roof and a carpet on the floor. Ray used to hide his marbles under the carpet in a little canvas bag and I was so envious of them that I nipped up there one night and took them. But it was pointless: my conscience wouldn't allow me to keep them, and they were so good I couldn't have used them so I took them back the next day. I put them in a slightly different place, though, just to make sure he knew we knew where he kept them.

I have never knowingly taken anybody's property since and never could. I had learnt one extremely important lesson. Other lessons have taken longer to learn. I know I hurt my parents deeply but they, without intending to, were to hurt me a few years later in what was the most traumatic time of my life, a life that's had more than its fair share of controversy, but I've worked bloody hard to make the most of it and something of myself. I'll leave you to be the judge but it's been a long, sometimes lonely, but always fascinating road.

CHAPTER 2

the first shot

Life has been full of ironies, premonitions, coincidences – call them what you like – but some experiences are beyond my powers of explanation. It all began for me on 5 January 1965 when Vincent Peter Jones took his first breath in Shrodells Hospital. If I'd been tall enough to peep through the window, my first view would have been of nearby Vicarage Road, home of Watford Football Club who, years later, rejected me and turfed me out saying, among other things, I wasn't big enough to be a footballer.

When you think back to your childhood the memories are black and white, good or bad, happy or sad and there doesn't seem to be anything much in-between. My early days must have been a bit cramped as my folks and I shared a house in Queen's Road, Watford, with another family – two rooms, shared bathroom and shared kitchen. And how is this for coincidence? Years later I discovered that Joe Kinnear, my gaffer at Wimbledon, owned half of Queen's Road including that first house of ours. He also had The One Bell in St Alban's Road, the pub where my mum and her current husband trained as publicans and were eventually to take over. And my sister went to the same school as Joe.

The first house I actually remember was in Coldharbour Lane, Watford. I suppose I was about three years old. We had shared accommodation again, rented from the bloke who lived there. There were two other members of the 'family' by then: Titchy and Perky, a couple of Jack Russells, the first dogs we had but by no means the last. I've been living with them ever since! Titchy was the male, all white, and the first character to teach me the meaning of panic. He used to bugger off on regular occasions and we'd spend hours looking for him. I never wondered why but I was a bit bemused by the fact that every time we brought him back, Titchy would fight like hell with the other one.

Mum didn't have the best of starts in her life. She was one of eleven children, and they lived in Trowbridge, Wiltshire. I don't know how she ever got over the nightmare that happened to her as a teenager. She was taking two of the younger ones to school, holding their hands, one on each side, and they stopped to cross the road. Just then, one of the little girls saw a pal waving from the other side. She tugged out of mum's grasp and ran straight out. She was hit and killed by a lorry.

My dad had started out in the heating and plumbing trade and was striving to work his way up. He was such a workaholic that it had cost him a whole string of his mates because while they were out doing what blokes do, drinking and chasing crumpet, he was grafting to get the business going. Parties and the like didn't appeal to him. He was into his shooting and fishing – the interests he had followed from a young age.

It was a regular sight for me, I can see it as clear

as day even now, dad coming home, sitting down and cleaning his gun, getting ready to go out into the countryside again. It was his passion and it became mine as well. The great outdoors has had a terrific influence on my life, so much so that, even in recent years when I've known real success, I have often thought I would have given it all up, forfeited the lot, just to be a gamekeeper.

Mum had been a nurse, but when I was born, that was the end of her working days outside the house until my sister Ann and I were older. She was the one who brought us up, mainly, because she was always around. Dad set standards, too, but we didn't see that much of him because he was working so hard, and when he wasn't working he was out shooting.

That's how I got into it so young. Dad had built a pigeon hide and you can't begin to imagine the excitement, the wide-eyed wonder of a five-year-old being taken by his father into that secret little place – all netting and camouflage and 'Don't say a word or make the slightest noise'. If I think about it long enough, I can still tremble with the anticipation, the tension, the thrill of that first time sitting in the hide with the old man and the gun at the ready. Brilliant!

We had decoy pigeons set out on the ground in front of us attracting the real birds to come down and feed. Dad whispered, 'When one of them sits, boy, you fire.' We had a flask with us. I was on a stool, he had his shooting-stick and we were enjoying a cup of coffee. As we looked up, a pigeon came curving in and landed. This was it. Dad rested the twelve-bore on the ledge of the hide. I knew what to do next because he'd talked to me about guns, using

them and the respect I must have for them, as he sat
and cleaned them in the kitchen.

He helped me position my body properly around
the gun and I took aim . . . squeezed the trigger . . .
Boom! I flew backwards off the stool and the coffee
went everywhere, but it wouldn't have mattered
even if it had been scalding. 'Have I got it, have I got
it?' I was screaming and dad was crying with laughter. I'd got it!

That hide was down by Chorleywood. The M25
now runs straight through the field but the little bit
where the hide stood is still there and I pass it once a
week or so. I wanted to have the pigeon stuffed and
mounted, as my first trophy. That never happened,
but it spent a hell of a long time in the freezer.

Ann was born after our move to a council house
in Newhouse Crescent, Garston, on the edges of
Watford. The old man had two green vans for his
work, all old-fashioned with big round headlights.
They looked a bit like hearses painted the wrong
colour. The house had bushes outside, with big,
mauve flowers that attracted butterflies by the score.
That was another part of life as a kid, and the joy of
it, catching butterflies, all shapes and sizes and
fantastic colours. There don't seem to be as many
nowadays and that should bother us.

I'd started kicking a ball, the way five- or six-
year-olds do and I was always competitive, always
wanting to be top man at every activity, and it was
the same with butterflies. I spent hours trapping
them with my little fishing net when they settled on
the flowers and sometimes plucking them out of mid
air. They were the real catches, the ones you made
when they were in flight, because that took skill. We

kept them in jamjars long enough to judge which kid had caught the most before releasing them. I remember always wanting to be the one with the fullest jar yet getting as much pleasure from letting them go as from catching them in the first place. Some of the other kids would get bored after a while and went off on their bikes but I'd stay there, catching more. There'd be hundreds of them: peacocks, red admirals, cabbage whites and lots I couldn't name.

Wasn't it best when youngsters made their own entertainment? I don't want to sound old-fashioned, but I'm certain we had more fun and developed greater imagination than if, like many kids today, we had sat in front of the television or computer screens, gazing at videos and playing electronic games.

I don't recall any television sets. Everyone lived in each other's houses. It was kind of communal living for kids, house to house, just turn up and sit down and join in. All the houses were in a row with alleys in-between. You went out of your front door, down the alley and you were straight into somebody else's garden. Their bikes and scooters and other toys and even their dogs all muddled up together and we all used to share. I remember one Christmas present that really thrilled me was a space-hopper, a kind of thick plastic inflated balloon with a face on the front and two handles. You sat on the thing with your legs to the front and bounced around like a human kangaroo. Oh, the fights that broke out because all the other kids in the neighbourhood wanted it. My first fights, come to think of it, though there have been one or two others that have been more widely publicised since!

We had a policeman, PC Parkinson, a big man with glasses. He lived on the corner and they had a couple of girls and a boy. I'd go round there virtually whenever I wanted. Over the fence and into their house and I'd end up having tea with them. I was mental for boiled eggs and PC Parky's wife did me them all the time – with soldiers! I was little and hyperactive, never still, but easy and comfortable in anybody's company. So I have happy recollections of house-hopping as well as space-hopping, and I was never put off, scared or even wary of the policeman on the corner of our street. As long as PC Parkinson's wife had eggs in the fridge, he was all right by me.

I was even more 'all right' after the next transfer of the Jones family to the house in Lower Paddock Road, where from our gate only a small road separated us from the recreation ground.

There were lights all along the road that bordered the 'rec' so we could play football at any time because we had our own 'floodlights' financed by the local council. Eight o'clock was my 'in time' when mum or dad used to come out and make the dreaded call that took me from the mates who were allowed to play longer: 'Vin—cent!' I was always thankful that I wasn't the first to have to leave, as there was a bit of a stigma about that, but it was an Irish lad, Timothy, who had to go in at 7pm. My first best mate was Peter Burder whose house was right on the corner of the 'rec'. I had one of my first pictures taken with him on a day out at the model village at Beaconsfield.

Our life was dominated by football. And when

my dad brought me back my first proper ball, from holiday in Rimini, well, I was king. Black and white and genuine leather. None of the other kids could believe it. It was as if something had dropped to earth from Mars and landed in our street. I felt proud and privileged and special, the envy of the area. All the lads, 'Bird', Tim and Ray, couldn't bring themselves to play with it at first, because of the thought of getting it scratched, removing that lovely new look that lasts only until the first time you make it meet its purpose. We just sat around it and stared at it.

That ball was so precious to me and those friends that for ages we'd use it for nothing more damaging than a goalpost. The old man wouldn't let me take it to school where I was longing to show it off as he explained that playing with it on concrete would ruin it. But even worse, somebody nicked it, my football, a real ball. My pride and joy was lifted out of our back garden where the big hedge stretched all the way round to the pub carpark next door. We never got it back and whoever stole it ought to know that they left a little lad and his pals heartbroken. That person has not been forgiven.

My first real game of football was at Oxhey Infants, nothing grander than one class against another during a PE lesson but your first competitive match is the one you never forget. Fortunately for me somebody had forgotten something. Having no boots of my own I went to the school's 'Lost and Found' and found a pair. They were white Alan Ball boots, and advertised as used by our World Cup winner of '66. What a stroke of luck, what a find! No matter they were slightly on the big side, I was in business. I also did Bally proud because we won the game and I scored a hat trick, with one of my goals perfectly steered through the goalkeeper's legs. There were goalposts but no nets, which was a pity as goals always seem better, more satisfying when you can see the ball nestling in the net as if to prove it beyond doubt.

Strange things can occur in the mind of a child and something horrible occurred in mine when I was about seven. I had a real panic attack when it first dawned on me that, eventually, everybody dies. Maybe it was because I was having such a great time that this thing about dying had such an awful effect. I couldn't sleep. It was a genuine feeling of panic. I cried almost nightly, wanting my mum to be able to tell me I wouldn't die, wondering where and when I was going to die and have this wonderful life and all the good times taken away from me.

I have to admit that, although I don't really know where this phobia came from, I still suffer from it quite a bit, even now. As I grew older, the fear calmed down and I can control it but as a child I had a real hang up about dying.

I also went through a terrible time when the family decided to move on, to 'Woodlands', a bunga-low dad had bought at Bedmond, near Hemel Hempstead. He was intending to improve it over the years and it was perfect for our shared love of the country, being just off a little lane with about three-quarters of an acre of land. A wood to one side of the house, a forest was visible to the left, and at the back and round the other side were disused gravel pits that attracted the local youngsters.

The trouble was I couldn't come to terms with leaving Bushey and Lower Paddock Road. I was nine. All my mates and my football were there in that familiar patch. It was my empire. It was me. I went crackers at the idea of moving away and thought that the more I played up the more chance there was of the family deciding to stay put, so I went berserk. I slashed all the curtains and bedspreads in mum and dad's bedroom and in mine, and the front-room curtains as well. Mum and dad tried to explain that whatever I did would make no difference, but I was emotionally upset and the more they tried to calm me the more I screamed and cried. The biggest wrench about leaving was my sense of security. I reckon I'm tribal, then as now. For instance, if my wife Tanya suggests going for an evening meal together, the party will have stretched to six people within minutes. I find it very hard to go for a meal, just Tanya and me, even though we are an extremely close couple.

On reflection, at the time of the house move I probably felt closer to my mates and to my football than to my family. I was being told I had to leave behind everything that to a little boy was precious. I thought my life was going to cave in and I'd never be able to get it back.

Then one of those weird happenings occurred in the middle of all the turmoil. We were half packed, a lot of the furniture and larger items had gone and the rest was being moved on the Saturday. I looked round the place where I'd been so happy and it was like a ghost house. That night, I had a dream.

Bear in mind I knew nothing of the new place and its surroundings. I think I'd been there once when mum and dad were considering buying but I didn't want to know, and I can't remember giving that bungalow a second glance. But I dreamed of a place where I walked up a lane with no one around, crossed a big main road and walked round a council estate with little walls. Round the corner and down a narrow lane and there it was on the left: a football pitch. A green, chain-link fence all down one side and the gap where you walked through had a single concrete bollard with a round top. I walked through the gap to the clubhouse and saw, across the pitch, a hedge and goalposts beyond. I saw all that, in the clearest detail, in the dream.

We moved the next day and I had a strange feeling that I was being led and told not to worry, that everything would be all right and my life would resume where it had left off. (If strange or reassuring things happen to me now I believe it's my late granddad having an influence, but he was alive then.)

When we got to the new place, everybody was busy unpacking and my dad said to me: 'Go into the village, son. Go round the estate and meet the lads.' So off I went . . . up the lane with no one around, across the main Bedmond Road, past the little walls on the estate, round the corner and down Tom's Lane. By then I knew what I was going to find: the football pitch on the left, the green chain-link fence, the single bollard with the round top, the clubhouse, the hedge and the goalposts beyond: the posts on the pitch at my new school.

I can't account for all that. Nowadays I still look back and see it all twice – first, the dream and then how it was in reality. I headed back to the bungalow and it was like darting through a maze. I was thinking on the run, contradictory thoughts. 'I shouldn't be here at all, this is too scary.' And then 'Yes I should be, it was planned, it was meant to happen.' The way my life has turned out, I am convinced that that house move was intended somehow. The whole area proved to be football crazy.

As for that hedge beyond the football pitch . . . a couple of years later a professional footballer came to coach us. He had us all chipping the ball over that hedge. He pointed in my direction and said to John Cornell, the bloke in charge of us: 'That boy is head and shoulders above the rest. Let me know how he gets on.'

That footballer was Dave 'Harry' Bassett, the man who signed me for Wimbledon and gave me the chance of a career in the professional game, the man who has had an enormous influence and effect on my life. See what I mean about premonitions and coincidences? Weird.

CHAPTER 3

a fight for recognition

I wasn't to know it or appreciate it immediately, but it was here in Bedmond and at 'Woodlands' where my life really began, where my passions for football and the country life blossomed until, for a wonderful few years, I thought I'd arrived in paradise. But I had to endure some setbacks along the way: I had to 'qualify'. That process began within minutes of turning my back on the football ground I had seen in my dream.

I was so unnerved by it, so confused and unsure whether it was a good thing or a bad omen that I set off running back to the house where the family's future was being unpacked from cases and boxes. I came to a kind of green where a group of local lads were playing football, so I stopped and watched. The inquisitive banter started and I was suddenly made to realise what it was like to be the new kid on the block. I suppose I'd been looking on and joining in the verbal to-ing and fro-ing for about half an hour when it all 'went off' and a fight broke out. Three of us, all banging away swinging fists and feet. It was two against one with another kid just watching but it wasn't deadly serious. They were testing me out, seeing what the new kid in the neighbourhood was made of. For my part, I was proving to them that the Jones boy was not to be messed around or taken for granted. I think it was the need to be accepted that meant I couldn't afford to give an inch. I can't remember which of us looked worst when it all calmed down, but I came out of it all right. In fact, I came out of it with three new pals – Cal Jenkins, Seamus Byrne and his brother Fran. Cal and Seamus have become lifelong mates. I was best man at Cal's wedding!

School was the next problem. It was all a bit much for a little lad who hadn't wanted to move in the first place, finding himself in a strange house on the Saturday and at a new school on the Monday morning. I'd been at Bedmond Juniors less than a week when my parents were called. I'd been threatening to hurl bricks through the windows and had told one teacher that I wouldn't be at this school much longer because I was going to burn it down.

The headmaster, Derek Heasman, took my dad to one side and told him: 'Your boy, Mr Jones, I'm worried I've inherited a nutcase.' Or words to that effect. Dad did his best to explain the situation, the house move and my dismay at thinking I'd lost my friends and he must have done a good job because Mr Heasman reassured him: 'Right, leave it to me. I fully understand the boy's problem.' As it turned out, he was the most fanatical football fan, a Queens Park Rangers supporter no less – he even had the school team turn out in QPR's blue and white hoops. He was also the best PE master you could ever wish for and it's a good job for me that he was.

'Does he like sport?' he asked dad.

'Crackers about it. Well, mad on football.'

And that was the line the headmaster took. I think he decided to pacify and encourage me through football and he couldn't have chosen a better therapy. I was in!

In PE lessons Mr Heasman and I would take on the rest of the class – about fourteen or fifteen others. We had a lad in goal but just he and I as outfield players and I don't recall us ever losing a game. I'm not kidding – we knew how to pass it and run off the ball and get it back but all the others did was boot it forwards. I learned from him how to pass and move properly. I must have learned quickly as well because I'm still the youngest ever to play for that school team. Just as I'm still the youngest to play for the Bedmond first team in the Herts County League.

All my life I've ended up playing with the older kids, and Mr Heasman put me in the school football team even though, at nine, I was two years younger than all the rest. I played midfield at the very start.

I was always in trouble in the Juniors, forever involved in fights for one reason or another, and being sent to Heasman's office for the familiar punishments: grabbed by the hand and whacked across the arse with a white plimsoll. The first time Heasman did it I yelled at him: 'Right, I'm telling my dad and he'll come up here and kill you.' Dad went to the school all right but told Heasman: 'Well done. Do it any time you like.' 'You bastard,' I thought.

It seems odd, looking back, that many of my school fights were with Cal. We were always at one another's throats and yet always friends in the end. During playground kick-abouts the ball was forever finishing up on the roof and you can guess who went to retrieve it. If I wasn't chosen, I'd volunteer, and I can't remember how many times I was caught either on the way up or on the way down. A teacher nearly always appeared at the wrong time and all the other kids knew my immediate fate – the 'Black Seat'! It was a black armchair that stood outside Heasman's room. It stood there unoccupied and threatening because of what it meant. When you were caught out doing something against the school rules you were sent to the chair. To sit and wait and to stew. Again, like the delay in dad coming home after I'd been caught nicking the money, the waiting was the worst part, despite knowing that once the headmaster returned the routine was the same – whack, whack, whack with the white plimsoll. With laces. The other kids said they tucked books in the backs of their trousers for protection but I never seemed to get round to that.

I wasn't interested in anything at school if it wasn't connected with sport, although I did quite like drawing. But there was one thing, one small period that persuaded this hyperactive little so-and-so to sit down and sit still. The half-hour storytime in the library. I was transfixed by that brilliant Roald Dahl tale, *Charlie and the Chocolate Factory*. I'd sit there hanging on every word, probably with my mouth wide open. It is the only book that has ever fascinated me. To me, when the teacher was reading that story, it wasn't a story at all, it was absolutely real. I went through a pretty lengthy spell of good behaviour at the time because I knew that if I stepped out of line I'd miss the next reading. It still gives me a good feeling inside when I think about it.

I always wanted to be Charlie.

The local estate, quite close to our bungalow, was where most of my mates lived. Only a couple of us were 'outsiders'. Basically we all belonged in a nice little patch: the council estate, the school, the football pitch and that was us. All tucked into an area so everybody knew everybody and that suited me perfectly. I was known by the kids as a good little scrapper but I was regarded even more highly for my football.

I might have been small but I was ahead for my age in terms of ability. I think it stemmed from the time at Lower Paddock Road where all the others were older than me and I had to try and reach their level. I was strong, I was quick and I could pass the ball. You can watch a team of Under-10s, compare them with a side of Under-14s and the difference is obvious. The younger ones all tend to kick the ball and chase after it. I was different – I could control it, dribble round people and ping an accurate pass, short or long. I wasn't dirty – I couldn't afford to be against bigger lads – but I learnt how to look after myself.

So when my dad and a couple of the other dads got together and formed a Sunday morning side, I turned out for the older team. It wasn't long before people from Watford, Hemel Hempstead and the like had all heard of Vince Jones, the lad in the Bedmond team. By the time I was thirteen or fourteen, I was doing things that blokes of eighteen or twenty were trying, like chipping the keeper from the edge of the box.

Proud moments? None more so, I suppose, than winning the first of the medals that now have pride of place in the cabinet at my home. A match was arranged against Garston boys, a village about five miles down the road. They arrived along with a big video camera. I still feel a little glow inside when I think about that day – being presented with the man of the match medal at the age of about nine. It's only plastic and I've lost the little base it stood on, but it's right there next to my FA Cup-winner's medal!

From then on, they all wanted me to play for them but I stuck with the boys from our patch all the way through. For the next few years I'd usually play games twice a day at weekends, for the school or the various Bedmond Sports and Social Club teams, beginning with the Under-10s. The guy who really got us going was John Cornell, whose son, Jimmy, played as well. John ended up as manager of Bedmond. He became my biggest fan – and still is. That infamous photo of me grabbing Paul Gascoigne by the balls – John Cornell told me how to do that. When I was about eleven he taught me three tricks.

'Three tips for you, boy,' he said. 'When you knock an opponent over, go and pick him up, be all matey and smile. Pick him up and pull under his armpits at the same time, because the others are all older than you, and when they squeal just act all innocent. When a ball goes through to their keeper and he's standing there with it just run up to him and knock it out of his hand.

'And the third one, if you are being marked too closely just reach back, grab him by the balls and twist. They won't mark you too close next time.' Yes, that's where the Gazza incident originated. John wasn't teaching me to cheat. I can see now that he was only suggesting how I could protect myself because I was a small lad competing with much bigger, older players.

Eventually, like many I played with and against, we were chosen for Watford Boys and trained after school at Vicarage Road on Mondays and at Watford Leisure Centre on Thursdays. When I signed the blue schoolboy forms for Watford at the age of twelve Graham Taylor was manager. I wasn't carried away by the thrill of joining a professional club even though, as you might imagine, I was chuffed. However, I stuck with Bedmond and my old mates – I've always been one to stay with his roots. There was a kids' Sunday team, Ember Echoes, whose manager went round recruiting the best players in the area. It didn't matter how many times he tried to tempt me, I stayed with Bedmond where my old man was manager of the Under-12s.

These really were idyllic times. The football was going well, I believed I was developing into a good player and there was the perfect contrast of the country pursuits: fishing for hours on end, shooting or snaring rabbits. I suppose it became something of an obsession because there were times when I cried my eyes out when I couldn't be outdoors again the next day because of school. School never did strike me as a decent alternative!

The disused gravel pits by our house attracted local kids like bees to a honey jar. I have fabulous memories of warm summer days building rafts, shooting snakes with our air rifles and catapults. And in winter, when it all froze over, ice-skating. You don't appreciate danger at that age. We couldn't have done because our antics on the ice got more and more daring until the lads were tearing around on motorbikes or pushbikes.

Bird-nesting was another favourite pastime – great fun, with real excitement finding the nest and identifying the different types of eggs. I wonder if youngsters, nowadays, ever learn the fascination of all that outdoor stuff. We made all our own entertainment, that imaginative gang of us around Bedmond. Sometimes there'd be thirty or forty of us playing tag in Beechwood Forest. A simple enough little game by normal standards but there was nothing normal about the way we did things. We played tag in the treetops – great big trees. Boys and girls alike, leaping like monkeys from tree to tree and you weren't allowed to touch the ground. What a time we had!

Dad was into shooting in a big way, though mum preferred bingo. Her only involvement was cooking for the shoot dinners – she didn't know one end of a gun from the other. He rented some land and put pheasants down. He was what they called the shoot captain for a syndicate based near St Albans and on a Saturday morning, in the holidays, a group of us would go beating for him. We were paid about £3 apiece which was really good money then. And at the end of the day, as dusk crept in, the men all went on to the duck shoot and took us with them. Wildlife was a great fascination to me. Some of us spent hours with a budgie cage baited with nuts, holding the spring door open with a long piece of cotton. Once a squirrel or a bird was tempted inside you'd release the cotton and trap them. Nothing sinister – we just tagged them and let them go.

But I can't say I'm proud of some of my antics as a nipper when dad wasn't around. It horrifies me, now, to think of some of the dreadfully cruel things we got up to. I suppose I could conveniently forget what I did but, if this book is to be the proper story of my life, the bad bits need to be known as well as the good.

Sometimes we took the chickens to Cal's house where there was a wall and a see-saw. We'd put the chicken on one end of the see-saw, then one of us would hit the other end having jumped off the wall. Not a simple manoeuvre, this. The timing had to be immaculate, not only by the one jumping off the wall but the one letting go of the bird on the see-saw. They were the highest-flying chickens you're ever likely to see. We didn't do it that many times. It must have struck even two tearaways like us as cruelty beyond all reason so we soon packed that in.

But we also played tricks on others, too. Around that time the skinhead fashion was in and a crowd of us often gathered outside the church hall waiting for the old ladies to emerge from bingo. They obviously thought the worst of us, because of how we looked, and I was usually the chosen victim of a mock good hiding as the lads waded in leaving me spreadeagled on the floor. In came the old girls, flailing their handbags as the boys scattered. 'Are you all right, love?' they'd say to me, crouching down, really concerned. They were not amused when I staged the miraculous recovery, laughed and ran off to join the rest.

Another popular stroke was splitting into two groups, either side of the main road, waiting for a car to come along and then pretending to tug on a rope suspended from one verge to the other. It was all imaginary but our timing was so good, so split second that the cars pulled up with screeching tyres.

Those motorists weren't amused, either, but they never caught us because we had our escape route and were experts in losing ourselves among the nearby gardens.

By the time I moved into secondary school at Langleybury half my mates, including Seamus and Cal, were with me and the other half went to another school, Francis Coombe. They lined up on the opposite side of the road to us as we all waited for the school bus. I was never fussed which bus I caught and half the time I hopped on to the Francis Coombe coach and went to school with them. Well, their school was a little less strict than ours!

Two of my best mates were Mark and Paul Robins – like brothers, they were. They went to Francis Coombe, so every now and again I went to school with Mark and Paul, explaining to the teacher that I was their cousin, just visiting. No problem – I sat in on the lessons and the school didn't have a clue. I even played for their football team once! Travelling on their bus was no bother, either, because we fiddled the passes.

I had two tasks to carry out at home. One was filling up the coal bunker for the boiler, which meant going down to the bottom of the garden behind the barn in the pitch black. Then on Fridays I had to clean out the dogs' kennels. These jobs had to be done without fail.

Work, proper work, found its way on to my agenda when I was twelve or thirteen. Dad had lost some of his patience with me, sick of my scrapes, of finding me in trouble here, there and everywhere so he set me to work in the building game during the school holidays and I hated it, but I worked for five days a week, with my own time-sheet and dad handed me my money in cash. I remember wishing he'd give it to me in a proper wage packet like the other builders. I might have hated working but I felt a bit special going down to the youth club with fifteen quid while the others had only about two pounds pocket money. It was dad's attempt to get me back on the straight and narrow because I was forever in bother. Never really serious trouble, no nicking cars or burglary or that kind of stuff. Pranks, basically, constantly involved in fights and generally upsetting the neighbourhood, pissing people off I suppose. Occasionally there'd be a copper at the door but usually someone's mum or dad. If something had gone wrong or something had gone missing, Cal, Seamus or I were the first suspects.

I earned a bit more some Saturdays at the builder's yard in Garston, which was owned by Russell Hensard's dad, Colin. Russell is another lifelong friend – you will lose count of them by the end of this book. Colin had his own greyhounds and took us to the races at Wembley, Henlow, Walthamstow and such. All the kids loved Russ's dad because he was so generous. As we walked to the greyhound track he would give me a fiver to have a bet. We went along to watch him play Sunday cricket and it was there that I first set eyes on Tanya, now my wife. She was watching the cricket with another family.

I still had that instinct for flitting in and out of other people's houses, some kind of desire to have another family as well as my own. I always fitted in with no trouble at all. With Mark and Paul Robins, for instance, I had Sunday dinner on a regular basis. If I was out in the estate feeling hungry, rather than get back to my house I was straight round to 'Auntie Chris's' – I still call her that – and Basil's. I'd just walk in the back door, shout 'Is there anything to eat?' grab a handful of biscuits and be off. Or I'd go round with Paul and Mark and Auntie Chris would say, 'Put the kettle on and make us one of your nice cups of tea.' So I made the tea. There was a real sense of community, a feeling of warmth, everywhere. Steve Robinson's was another family I joined regularly. I'm now godfather to his daughter, so that's another of those childhood friendships that have lasted to this day. Steve and I had a paper round for a while and there was a spell of about six months when I virtually lived at his house, going there straight from school.

I went back home for a bath and bed, basically. My mum, apparently, was forever asking, 'Where's Vince?' but she knew I'd be safe. Perhaps my staying elsewhere so often had something to do with the half-mile lane that led to our bungalow. There were woods either side and the trees met overhead in some places so it was like being in a long, dark cave or tunnel. And if I didn't have my bike with me, I ran. I never walked up or down that lane. But nothing was going to catch me, I learned to run like the wind.

I also learned how to fight, one-handed. We had one pair of boxing gloves between the lot of us and made a ring area by putting our jumpers down in a circle. You were allowed two rounds, three minutes with the glove on one hand and three more with it on the other, and you could hit only with the gloved hand. I'm not sure what it taught us, exactly, apart from how to get maximum use from the minimum of equipment!

It was going to secondary school that began to open up my life. Secondary school is where you become an adult – in my eyes, anyway. That's when you first confront responsibilities although the first responsibility I had was remembering to take my football to school. These days, if I'm on the way to training and realise I've forgotten my mobile phone I have to return home to get it. It was the same with my ball at school. Unless I had it under my arm or in my bag, normal life just couldn't go on. We had half an hour's break at dinner-time but I wasn't interested in eating. I'd grab a quick handful of something and be straight out into the playground getting a couple of sides together. We played every single day, always with my ball.

I don't know whether it was a case of leadership potential showing itself early, but even in my first year they all came to me to get the match set up – even the fifth-formers and there were some tough nuts among them, believe me. There was a lad called Dave May who eventually died, tragically, as a teenager with some other friends roaring about in a motor that hit a bridge. He was taken on Chelsea's books at one stage. I loved him. He lived in a council home and he was a right wheeler-dealer, into this and that, a real rogue but get him playing football and he seemed to change character. He was a few years older than me and, like the other lads from the care homes, was regarded as a hard case. But even they would run up to me and plead: 'Give us a game. Where do you want us? Which side are we on?' Dave May hated school and never really wanted to be there. It was as if he plucked up the courage and endured everything else just so that he could play football at dinner-times.

I had started watching big-time football with my pal, Russ. He was an Arsenal fan and my team was Tottenham so we alternated between the two. It didn't last long, though, because one day on the Underground we were confronted by a bunch of lads waving knives. Once was enough – we didn't go again after that!

CHAPTER 4

what happened to paradise?

You're always comfortable as a kid providing you have a routine and it is not disturbed. But something strange started happening to mine when I was thirteen. For Vince Jones, thirteen was worse than unlucky, it was a total disaster. My world caved in, paradise was lost. Most of the things I held dear collapsed around me. Nothing and nobody can prepare a child for what was about to happen to me at a time when I thought everything in life was just wonderful.

Friday night was disco night at the youth club. Russ's mum and dad always took us on their way to the dogs and picked us up in Abbots Langley on the way back, dropping me off at the end of our lane, normally at around eleven o'clock. It seemed such a long way up that lane in the pitch dark, but I knew the lights would be on and that there was always somebody waiting to see me safely in. Until the bewildering, frightening first occasion when I ran down the lane to discover there was nobody at home. It was never explained why there was nobody in on Friday nights.

Months earlier, when I was still twelve, something strange had happened one Thursday evening, the night dad usually went out for a meal with some mates. I answered the phone and a woman's voice said: 'Is Peter there? He's got my car and we're waiting for him.' I didn't understand. I came off the phone crying, panicking that something was going on. It turned out that my dad had been out with one of my uncles who was a right womaniser and it was the uncle who had the woman's car. That was the first upset I recall and I suppose it was when the trust began to wear a bit thin.

I'd never heard my mum and dad have a row or much of a difference at all. I thought my secure home life would just go on for ever and ever. You learned about other parents splitting up and being divorced but never expect such things to happen in your own family. At that age, the thought of your parents divorcing seemed as horrifying as if one of them had died. Then the impossible dilemma of having to choose between them – how could a thirteen-year-old properly solve something like that? But it was something I was going to have to face, because the arguments started and went on and on for about a year. I retreated to the comfort of my room, my sanctuary, but there was no escape from the sound of anger, the raised voices downstairs. I can still hear dad's voice to this day, protesting over and over: 'It was a one-night stand, nothing more. And I'm sorry. It wasn't love, it was lust and it doesn't mean a thing.' The proverbial had hit the fan, right out of the blue, when a woman had appeared without warning and knocked at our door. I wasn't at home at the time but apparently as soon as mum answered the door the woman came out with the lot: 'I'm getting married but first I want to clear my conscience, get this off my chest, wipe the slate clean. I slept with Peter ten years ago. Just the once, just a one-night stand but I had to tell you.'

The woman wasn't unknown to mum. Wouldn't you have thought, after ten years, she'd have let sleeping dogs lie? Maybe she would have done if she'd known the trouble and the heartbreak she was causing to us. Dad had made just one mistake, that's all, but little did he know what lay in store as he arrived home from work whistling, happy as a sandboy. Until mum met him at the door!

Mum and my sister Ann can be quite hard in certain circumstances whereas dad and I are pretty forgiving. If something upsets us we react, full blast at first, but time is a healer with us. With mum, certainly in those days, it wasn't. The rows between my parents seemed to flare up whenever they were face to face and they got more intense. It makes me shudder when I think of all that stuff, them going at it hammer and tongs, Ann and me cringing upstairs trying not to listen, wanting to shut it out but knowing it was hopeless.

If you walked from the front room, up the stairs, Ann's bedroom was in front of you and mine was along the landing on the right. I must have made that little journey from my room to my sister's a thousand times. The hardest part was when the arguments raged on later and later into the night, sometimes until four o'clock in the morning. I felt helpless. The rows were fierce, and I would be at the top of the stairs, just sitting there, longing for it all to stop and occasionally running down into the room, crying.

I'd still be crying when I went into Ann's room. I felt that it was up to me to protect her, to try to take responsibility for her. She was my little kid sister. I'd never had much time for her before. In fact, we fought like cat and dog. Suddenly, though, I felt like the big elder brother. I sat in her bedroom and cuddled her and tried to reassure her as the arguments blazed away downstairs. Sometimes I found myself on the stairs, torn, not sure whether to charge down and grab hold of my mum or dad, or run and take hold of my sister.

I nearly always opted to put my arms around Ann. It's easy to say, now I'm an adult, that I did it all for her benefit but I suppose I was crying out for Ann to cuddle me as well. We never really bonded together until later on in our lives but at that troubled time we shared a dreadful feeling of insecurity, made worse by the fact that mum was now sleeping upstairs and dad downstairs. It turned my guts because it proved that they were no longer really together.

The rows became intolerable. The Friday nights took on a familiar pattern as I'd come home from the youth club to find both parents out and Ann down at my nan's. I'd always spent a lot of time at her house, enjoying endless hours kicking a tennis ball against the wall. Nan – my dad's mother, Ann – was always my favourite and still is. On those terrible Fridays, finding nobody in, I had to run the four miles to my nan's at half past eleven. Mum or dad picked us up next morning or sometimes I'd go straight to football from there.

Eventually, it was a good thing when mum left, even though the timing was a bit unfortunate: the day before my fourteenth birthday, that's all! We were back from school when she came in with her black bag, knowing my dad was at work, and gathered together all her things. It couldn't have been more obvious what was happening and I begged her not to go. I was clinging on, both arms wrapped around her legs, begging. She was trying to explain why she had to go but she wasn't herself. It's a bit of a blurred picture, that awful scene, but I remember vaguely that she had people with her, who I yelled at: 'Fuck off! Leave my mum alone. Get out of our house!' It was no good, though, I finally released my grip. I had to let go.

When relationships are going well and everything is rosy it is easy to take it all for granted. But immediately a couple break up you soon find out who your friends are. In our case, the trouble was that those who took my mum's side never seemed to have the view that things had gone wrong but maybe they could help to save the marriage. Instead, they were telling her, 'Sod him. Leave him. Don't go back.'

Because of the trouble at home, my prospects of a career with Watford Football Club were put in doubt. The pattern had been for mum to pick me up from school and drop me off wherever Watford Boys were training, though I had a train journey and a long walk home. After training, I had a half-hour walk to the station, got off at Kings Langley and had a good four-mile walk from the station to the bungalow at nine or ten o'clock at night. When things were fine at home, it was no sacrifice at all. I would have done anything to go training with a proper club. But home life began to have its effect. I missed training sessions here and there. I could feel things slipping a bit because I was often so tired, having sat up until the early hours listening to the arguing.

I must have been knackered because missing training meant missing out on the 50p expenses Watford gave me for my train fare. They thought I travelled both ways but, in fact, as I had a lift in it only cost 22p for a single – the other 28p bought my fish and chips on the way home.

You are never properly prepared for bad news even if you half expect it, and that's how it was when they kicked me out of Watford. For the first time, I was told I wasn't good enough, not good enough to be kept on as an apprentice. My best mate was Graham Coles, even though, with him living in Hemel and me from Bedmond, we only really met through Watford Boys. I was captain of Watford Schools at the time and we both played for the Hertfordshire county side. We thought we were the bees' knees.

There was a group of about twenty of us who went to Watford all the time. In the first team were players like Nigel Callaghan, Kenny Jackett, Steve Terry. They were the ones we eventually hoped to be. On the decision day about who would be taken on and who would be released, there were all kinds of rumours about, but I came to the conclusion that we were on our way out. All those nights training with Tom Walley, who was in charge of the kids, all those dreams. Was this the end? All the other lads went in one by one but they called Colesy and me in together.

Bertie Mee, the former Arsenal manager whose team did the League and FA Cup Double in 1971, had overall responsibility for the youth set-up. He was clutching his folder. What happened next was what all starry-eyed, would-be future stars dread most: that shattering moment that says you are not as good as you thought you were and the pro game, or at least this pro club, doesn't want you. Bertie peered over his glasses but didn't say anything for a second or two. I was praying he'd get it over with. At last he said, 'Well, lads, as coaches and scouts we make mistakes when we let players go.' I'm still thinking: 'Well, go on then, spit it out, you old bugger,' when he finally reached the point. 'We have decided, rightly or wrongly, that we are going to release you both from your schoolboy forms at Watford. We are not going to take you on as apprentices.' He explained to Colesy, first: 'Graham, we think we are making a mistake with you. It was very close, we've spoken to various coaches but decided to release you although we appreciate we may be making an error.' Colesy was a midfield player, tucked in behind the front two, or a winger. A bit of a Peter Beardsley you might say. 'But it's not all lost,' Bertie assured him. 'Several clubs have told Tom Walley that they wanted to be contacted if ever we release you.' Colesy was told West Brom, Coventry and Leicester were interested.

Then he turned to me. 'Vinnie, you treat life as one big joke. Unfortunately, we think you are going to be too small. Nothing wrong with your football, your ability, but your size is a problem. We've retained other boys ahead of you because of your height.' I couldn't take that in. I thought that if you could play, you could play. Size shouldn't come into it. But Watford seemed to have a thing about it. Tom Walley had told my dad a fair time earlier that I needed to fill out, that he should give me a bottle of Guinness or Mackeson each dinner-time and make me sit for half an hour to absorb it properly. No chance and my dad knew it. After every meal I was out with a ball in the back garden on my own, or out with the lads.

But dear old Bertie tried to soften the blow with me as well, saying I had the chance to go to Coventry, like Colesy, and that Tottenham had also shown an interest. I didn't bother with either. It didn't seem to matter as much as before. Colesy went to West Brom but hurt his ankle in training and nothing materialised. We both had a spell over at Hertford Town, but it seemed miles to travel so we packed it in and went our separate ways.

If mum and dad had been together, maybe I would have pursued the so-called 'interest' from a couple of clubs. But dad had started to see another woman, and was still trying to run a business and the shoot, and there were continuing problems with my mum. If it hadn't been like that, I'm sure he'd have said, 'Right, let's get those numbers off Tom Walley and we'll take you training.'

Worse was to come. We had to leave the place I had feared so much but where I had found such contentment. I was to lose everything, in fact, when the split came at home. Not only my family and my football dream world at Watford but my close friends as well because my dad was forced to sell the house to give mum her share of the money.

So we had to leave a beautiful house that dad had worked like hell to get just right, and move into an old, semi-detached, labourer's house he bought from a farmer. Dad, my sister and I moved into the place in Colney Heath, St Albans, and mum took a job in a nursing-home where she lived in. My life had been building up nicely, brick by brick, but now it felt like a bulldozer had driven straight through it. As far as I was concerned, the day we left 'Woodlands' and moved to the little house in Colney Heath, my good life was in ruins. That was the day the bulldozer came.

CHAPTER 5

life in a bin-liner

Like any kid in his early teens, I needed my mates, and in the circumstances, with home life shattered, I needed that feeling of belonging even more than ever. The move to Colney Heath meant that Ann and I had to go to a new school – Chancellors' in Brookmans Park. In one way I didn't mind, because it provided a bit of excitement in that at least *something* was happening, although the dominating feeling was that of losing my family, my mates and my school. I felt I was good for nothing. My mates were living over near Watford and I was on the other side of St Albans. Gone, the lot.

Starting a new school is never easy but I can tell you that my circumstances made it bloody hard. It wasn't long before one of the self-styled tough guys of the school made himself known and forced a hell of a fight with me. If this was intended as a challenge to the new boy then I wasn't going to let them down. I gave the bully a good pasting and bust his nose. He must have had something of a reputation because when the headmaster took me into his office I wasn't punished, I was more or less commended and virtually told that I'd done a good job, as he'd had it coming.

However, after I'd been at the school for about six weeks I'd had enough of the place. I didn't really know anyone and I was desolate. I did manage to get on with a couple of lads, but I didn't give a toss about anything much, apart from biology which I quite liked and did have a bit of a go at it, putting in some effort. I was interested in evolution, how things were formed, the development of the bird from the egg, and so on. It was the only thing that held my interest. I'd even stopped playing football at break times. Not even football, the thing I loved as passionately as the outdoor life, took my mind off the awful pain of the family break-up and the upheaval it had caused.

I didn't tell anyone about my football background, that I was pretty good at it, that I'd played for Watford Boys and the Hertfordshire county side but after a couple of games during PE other boys started taking notice and urged me to play for the school team. I refused to begin with but relented and played once or twice. You'd have thought the football might have eased the situation, tempted me back on track, but it didn't because I was to leave school early.

The time came when I had to declare which exams I would be taking. It was an easy question for me: 'None. I'm taking no exams. In fact, I'm out of here.' The teachers knew my mind was made up and that there was no point in attempting to change it. They suggested I went to work for my dad on the buildings, turning the last months of my schooling into a kind of work experience. They released me from Chancellors' and I've still never taken an exam in my life.

Dad had his problems, as you might imagine. He was seeing another woman, trying to get his life going again. But he was kind of hiding away with her. Not surprisingly, he needed love and comfort and he found it with her. The trouble was there were times when he wasn't home until three or four in the morning, or not until the next day. It wasn't his fault, he'd just lost the plot. We communicated by leaving notes for one another. It was as if Ann and I were in the way. My dad was torn apart, emotionally. Not that he ever stopped loving us but his new woman was pulling him as far as she could. I never thought, though, that he would find his shoot a burden. He was the captain, he handled the money and he reared the pheasants. It was his passion. Looking back, he must have been on the verge of some sort of breakdown. He passed the shoot to the farmer next door, who he'd bought the house from and told him to run the shoot until he could get his head right.

They had a gamekeeper, Neil Robinson, who with his wife Andrea lived in a rented cottage up at the wood. I spent much of my time with them, helping rear the pheasants but, generally, just wanting to be there. They didn't have children of their own and being there started to feel something like a home again.

Mum arrived once a week to take us out. How I hated that. It was all so forced, with so little genuine emotion. I refused to go after a few occasions but Ann felt a bit guilty, I think, and went each week. Ann stayed pretty close to mum but I didn't have a lot to do with her for some time and when she rung up, I was always busy . . .

The divorce was terrible, too. There was me, dad,

nan and my auntie sitting on one side of the room and my mum and a couple of her mates on the other. Horrible. She knew I wouldn't leave dad, that my football and shooting would keep us together, but she wanted custody of my sister. Eventually and thankfully dad pointed out to her that all this was crucifying the kids and about a week after the court hearing she decided not to pursue her custody claim.

Little wonder that school could not sustain my interest and concentration! I had to get out and do something different, so it was off to the building site. Up in the morning at the same time as my dad and away in the van. He dropped me off to join his other blokes building house extensions. Humping bricks in a hod, digging, mixing cement – general builder's labourer, that was me at sixteen. And the fact that I could drive came in handy!

The old man needed some time off work when his hand went septic, so he gave me the keys to the van and there I was driving all round the Watford area, without a licence. I wasn't old enough to drive. Some days I even took the lorry – anything to keep the firm ticking over while dad was out of action. I'd be picking up supplies, having a laugh and a crack with the boys, working a fiddle here and there. Ten bags of cement on the back of the truck and they'd bill us for five! I was really enjoying this little lot but if dad had been sound in his head at the time he would never have let me do it.

Time heals some wounds and dad got better after he'd met Jenny Ambrose, who is his wife today. She screwed his head back on and helped him start to get his life back together. Mum got rid of all her lousy friends and met a fella, Dave

Hockey, who is now her husband. All of a sudden life had started to get better. At least, that's what I thought. We spent the best part of a year building my dad's large new house. He had bought some woods off a shoot with planning permission years earlier. I wasn't driving any more, so I had to walk about half a mile over fields to the plot every day. He paid me £100 a week.

I liked Jenny, liked her a lot, and still do. I accepted her because she was such a lovely person but I couldn't have anyone else as my mum. She was living at her own house, constantly backwards and forwards between her place and ours but she didn't stay over. Peace, real peace, rarely seemed to last very long. I started mucking about at the building game to such an extent that dad told me: 'You'd better go and get a job, son.' When the Youth Opportunities scheme was introduced, Vinnie Jones was one of the first involved. Stacking supermarket shelves at £23.50 a week. Some bloody opportunity!

I started staying overnight at Neil and Andrea's cottage, sometimes because we'd be up all night rabbit shooting or on the lookout for poachers. I think my dad began to resent the fact that I was spending so much time there. Perhaps he sensed that I was looking on Neil as a kind of father figure. I remember the two of them had a blazing row on our doorstep and, in the middle of the argument, with me standing at the kitchen door and yelling at the old man, he spun round and gave me a right-hander. It was the last time I ever went into that house. I went upstairs to my room, gathered together my gear and football medals and stereo and stuffed them into a black bag. I jumped into the Landrover with

Neil and went to his cottage – my life bundled up in a black bin-liner!

I stayed with Neil and Andrea for three or four days. I told him I wanted to get out, to clear off and make a fresh start somewhere. So he rang his father to see if he could get me a job. And he managed it, but not in gamekeeping as an underkeeper or something of that kind, something I longed to do. He got me in at the boys' public school, Bradfield College, near Reading. Neil's dad, Tom, was the hairdresser who called at the college a couple of times a week. He went to see the bursar and he got me a job: washing pots and pans!

Tom came from Newbury to pick me up. I stayed one night in his house and he drove me to the college on the Friday. Me with all my worldly goods in a black bin-bag. I felt lost, alone in a strange, big posh school wondering what was going to happen to me, what the future had in store. Tom went off to cut hair and the bursar took me to my room.

I didn't see much of my surroundings in those few minutes, at least I didn't take it in at the time because the bursar was trying to explain how they did things at the college, what was expected, but the only words that really sank in were: 'You will be paid £42 for a six-day week. Sundays off.' I don't even remember dumping the bin-liner in the room before he took me to the kitchens and introduced me to Mick, the head chef. He was tall and clean looking and turned out to be a really nice old boy. That was it. I was left there with the chef and the two sinks where I was to spend just about all my time.

'You wash the pots and pans,' Mick said to me.

'Wash them, then sterilise them in that tank, dry them and then put them away. I suggest you do it like this.'

He gave me a demonstration and I just stood there, looking and listening. On one side of me were all the racks, crammed with the pans and all the other gear they use in a kitchen. On the other stood a guy called Harry. He was the potato peeler – at least the bloke who cut the spuds in the big machine that peeled them for him! He turned out to be a good pal, Harry – always willing to say, 'Go on, son, you get off and I'll do it' if I needed to shoot off early.

Mick took me back to my room, showed me every step of the way – out of the kitchen, up a staircase and turn right along the longest corridor I'd ever seen. It was spooky. I had an uneasy feeling about it all that first day away from home and everything I knew best. There's something scary about finding yourself in unfamiliar territory with strangers, and that feeling wasn't helped or eased when Mick pointed out the first door on the left – home to a bloke called Reg. He was in his mid to late forties, I'd say, had only one leg and never seemed to leave that room 365 days of the year. Apparently, he had worked as a groundsman or something and there had been an accident involving lime that eventually led to the amputation. The school had looked after him, given him a room with his own little kitchen and bathroom. And that's where he stayed in his wheelchair.

Next door along was the shared bathroom, very basic and with paper peeling off the walls. Out of the bathroom, two steps and into the shared kitchen with its Baby Belling. Opposite the bathroom was Harry the caretaker's room. And a bit further along was John's room – the college maintenance man.

Then mine. It was built on a corner and overlooked the gardens and the sportsfield, which was lovely, and there was a river at the bottom. It was almost bare – just a bed and bedcovers and a carpet. My wardrobe was outside the room in the corridor. This was to be my home, but I didn't have much in that bag to make it feel that way though I did my best. I unpacked my few clothes and then, one by one, took out my football medals and mementoes and set them out on the window-sill and mantelpiece . . . medals from the schoolboy matches, Watford Boys, Man of the Match, Player of the Season, Top Goalscorer. I put out my stereo and a few records and that was the lot. That really was all I had.

I sat on the bed. Suddenly it dawned on me that it was Friday, that I wasn't due to start work until seven o'clock on the Monday morning so I had the whole weekend to get through. It was horrendous. The nearest shop was about three or four miles up the road and I had only a tenner to my name so I opted for an early night, which seemed fine – until all bloody hell broke loose. Harry and John, the two piss artists, went to The Queen's Head, the nearest pub, after work on Fridays and then got stuck into the whisky when they got back to their rooms. That was their weekend: down to the bookies together, into the pub together, back to their rooms and into the scotch. And spark out on their beds having forgotten all about the beans they'd put on the Baby Belling – burned beyond recall. God knows how I got through that weekend before Neil's dad called and took me to his place for lunch on the Sunday. However bleak things appear at first, however unfamiliar and frightening, you do adjust. Especially when you have to! Monday morning arrived – down to the kitchen, seven o'clock sharp and suddenly I was a lot happier, occupied, off and running. And eating properly for the first time in ages. Boy, did I eat.

It was a great routine. After breakfast for the boys and the masters, what was left over was ours! Honestly, we could take our pick of the stuff that hadn't been eaten. I was having four or five boiled eggs in a morning plus the bread rolls that went with them. A big roast at dinner-time, three cracking good meals a day with everything fresh. Washing up three times a day didn't seem such a sacrifice after all! And in the evenings it was off to The Queen's Head. Work done, I'd cadge a lift, stay at the pub all evening then walk home. I was such a regular, killing time at the dart-board, that they put me in the pub team.

They had a football team at the pub, too, but I didn't tell them I played. I just played darts. I didn't want the hassle or the responsibility. I just looked forward to doing simple things that appealed. Football, then, was something I avoided because, if I'd started playing again it would have constantly reminded me of what happened before. I would have been reliving the time when I built everything up, when I was blissfully happy, and then that bulldozer came along and knocked everything down. To play football would have meant me going through all of that again. And I couldn't.

I remember having another thought. I'd always

played football with my mates and they will tell you that I was rated the best player most days. To have played again would have meant putting myself to the test, trying to rediscover the high standard I'd achieved. Having not played for quite some time I think I was a bit scared of failing. Better just to be known as Vinnie, the bloke who worked at the college, played darts, had a drink at the pub.

I was a bit wary of Reg, that first Friday he was pointed out to me. But I shouldn't have been and soon realised it. He was a sweet man and I sort of befriended him. I started doing bits of shopping for him and he'd give me a pound for going. I used to sit with him, just chatting about this and that, what was going on around the college, where I'd come from, what had happened to him. He got to me after a while and I started thinking about his situation, and how awful it was for a great fella who'd been used to the outdoor life to be confined to one small room all year round. I thought how sad it was and that it wasn't right that he was on his own and decided to do something about it, just on the spur of the moment. I'd been at the college about a fortnight, so I suppose it was out of my second week's wages that I went out and bought him a budgie and a cage. He loved it dearly . . . it became his life.

The summer break arrived like a win on the pools. The pay in advance amounted to close on £500. My transport problem was solved at a stroke – and at a cost of almost half my sudden windfall – £200 on a beaut of a motorbike, a white 250cc Kawasaki. That was me, then, roaring around Berkshire full blast on my mean machine. No licence, no insurance, no tax – irresponsible, downright bloody crazy I suppose, looking back, but you did things like that as a young-ster. I'd had my left ear pierced by now. It was the latest fashion and I didn't want to feel untrendy. Actually, I didn't *have* it pierced like others do, by an expert, I did it myself in my room at Bradfield. I'd got hold of an ordinary sewing needle from somewhere – I don't think I sterilised it – and just sat slowly forcing it through my earlobe. I don't know whether the needle was extremely blunt or whether I had particu-larly tough tissues but it took ages until it eventually made it all the way through. The whole process must have taken twenty minutes. I know I put a poxy little fake stud in the hole and it turned my ear grey and green. I have a £1000 diamond in it these days.

After the holidays, I didn't mind being back in the old routine with pots and pans for company, twelve hours a day. But there was trouble. One day I found my wardrobe damaged and my clothes every-where and I had my suspicions who was the culprit. I was angry, but wary as well. Next it was my motorbike, my prize possession, which was tam-pered with too. After that I left my bike unattended as rarely as possible.

Despite this trouble, life had become a bit of a breeze. I was ticking away nicely, being paid, roar-ing around on my bike and had no shortage of pals. It all changed on one of the little country lanes between college and the village. I was belting along, when suddenly, round one of the bends, there was a great lorry heading for me. I turned the bike, went hurtling up a bank and through a barbed wire fence. The lorry continued on its way, but I ended up in the college hospital with cuts and a badly injured wrist that meant having my arm in a sling. When the school came to inform my nearest of kin the only person they knew was Tom Robinson, Neil's dad. He came to the hospital and phoned Neil who then phoned my mum.

Something changed when mum turned up. I just said: 'I can't take all this any more.'

She said: 'Come on, collect your gear and we'll get you in the car.' I don't know whether everything dawned on me all of a sudden, that, despite new friends and what seemed like a pretty good existence, the reality was working long shifts, washing pots and pans and my bike being sabotaged, but I had the thought that I was really getting nowhere and that perhaps I was kidding myself. Anyway, as soon as mum said that I packed up, left a note and went.

CHAPTER 6

fights but no war

Mum was still living in at the nursing-home and I hadn't spoken to my dad in nine months or more. I used to ring my sister Ann from a phone box on a fairly regular basis and she would nearly always cry even though I always told her I was all right and not to worry about me. I sent her a radio-cassette player for her birthday in an attempt to convince her how well I was doing, even though I wasn't.

The question, on the way from Bradfield, was where to go. Neil and Andrea Robinson no longer worked for dad. They were gamekeeping near Hitchin and mum took me straight there. With my bin-liner, medals, clothes and record-player: my life. I went straight out and signed on the dole. I tried to get a job, going from interview after interview wearing Neil's gamekeeping gear because I'd never had a suit and tie in my life. Maybe it was a struggle to get work because of the 'vision' I presented at the interviews decked out in Neil's tweed jacket and trousers several sizes too big. I went for jobs at Homebase, B & Q, places like that, answering advertisements for shelf-stacking and the like. There'd be twenty other people after the same job and I had only one reference, from Neil.

So I stayed on the dole and worked with Neil as a kind of underkeeper and I loved it. I was me again, doing what I liked most again, known and acknowledged by the head gamekeeper, beating for the shoots and generally helping out and hoping that if a genuine job came up on the estate I'd be able to put in for it. If that had happened, it's a reasonable bet that professional football would never have seen Vinnie Jones. I would be a gamekeeper now, with many years' experience.

Not long after moving in with Neil and Andrea, a spooky thing happened, fate, if you like. Cal Jenkins bumped into my mum. They'd had no contact for ages but, of course, he asked about me. He had just passed his driving test and he drove over, in his new Escort estate, to see me.

'What are you up to with your life?' he asked. 'We are all into the nightclubs and pubs, having a great time of it.'

'I spend my time watching for poachers, feeding the pheasants, that kind of stuff,' I told Cal and I could see kind of a sympathetic look settle on his face although he didn't actually raise his eyebrows.

'Come and spend the weekend at my house and join the rest of the lads. You'll love it.' I knew I needed to ask Neil and Andrea if it would be OK and they encouraged me to go.

I went to Cal's home for three or four weekends, returning to Neil's during the week. I began to get a taste for the night life, the clubs, the pubs, seeing my old mates again and getting out and about in Cal's car. While I'd been away they'd all been getting fixed up with jobs as carpenters, mechanics and so on. Being on the dole I began to feel I'd missed out a bit. But I was back, one of the lads again, nightclub-bing and fighting, often running from the police after various bust-ups. And all the time that regular job I wanted remained elusive.

There was another price to pay for my new-found freedom. Things became too much for Andrea and Neil, we had a row and I had to leave. The wanderer was off again, this time to live with Cal. It wasn't their fault, it was mine. The pressure of my coming back and the fact they could see that I was changing before their very eyes. No longer up at first light and out tending the pheasants. I was lying in bed. It was hardly surprising that the arguments followed.

Still, things move on and I had the life of Riley at Cal's place. I was still on the dole, still hadn't spoken to my dad, but I was with familiar faces again and that alone gave me a sense of security.

We went into business. Well, the nearest thing to a business we were capable of setting up. There's a big roundabout at Watford called The Dome. We borrowed £25 off Cal's dad, bought six buckets, a long hosepipe, an eight-foot by four-foot sheet of plywood and painted 'Cal's Car Wash' in big letters and stood it on the roundabout. We connected the hose to the water supply at the nearby garage, borrowed a corner of their forecourt and were on our way. We spent the whole summer washing cars but didn't save a penny. Everything we made, we spent – on the piss in the clubs.

Washing cars every day throughout the summer, wearing Doc Marten boots and a pair of shorts and lying out in the sun during any spare moments, it was one of the best times of my life. Cal and I knew just about everybody in Watford so they all used our car wash.

On returning from the garage one evening we found Cal's dad in shock. 'We're at war,' he told us. 'This country's at war.' Cal and I thought it must be World War III, nuclear weapons and all that, but the Falklands became the big talking point as the build-up went on and one night Cal and I decided to join up! No joke. We discussed it for quite some time and became totally serious about volunteering. We were always up to something and agreed it would be a great idea to put ourselves to some proper, worthwhile use. So we headed for the Army Recruitment Office in Watford and told them we wanted to sign on for the conflict in the Falklands. We filled in all the necessary forms and once mine was completed, the moment I put down the pen, I felt certain I'd done it. I was going to war!

'What about this criminal record?' I heard the bloke in charge ask Cal. He'd had to declare on the form that he'd been in court and been convicted for a breach of the peace. Whatever it was, it was enough to wreck our plan. The Army wouldn't accept Cal and we had made a pact that if one of us didn't get in, the other wouldn't join. But we never thought we'd fall at the first bloody hurdle.

You do some daft things at seventeen. We were serious about joining the Army and going to fight a war somewhere in the southern Atlantic because we didn't particularly fancy washing cars in the winter! To think . . . from Watford to Goose Green. I reckon one punch-up that found its way on to Cal's record did me one of the biggest favours of my life.

Punch-ups were a regular occurrence, every

Friday and Saturday. We didn't go looking for it but nearly always ended up involved in one – occasionally needing a few stitches for our trouble. The pattern was familiar – about thirty of us meeting up at The Three Horseshoes in Garston. It was like a religion. Always there by 7pm on the dot and drinking bottles of Skol Special. Loads of people around, acquaintances, girlfriends, strangers.

We'd reached the stage where not only Cal but a few others had cars and we'd all pile in and steam off to another pub. Bosh! Bother! Something would trigger a row and a fight would follow so often that it eventually seemed like normal behaviour. There was always a ruck, at The New Penny in Watford, or Bailey's nightclub, we were fighting all the time. The Friday night punch-ups were the talk of Saturday afternoon and the Saturday night punch-ups were the talk of Sunday dinner-time. It went on like that for months and I have to confess that, yeah, I loved it.

There was one night when I lost the rest of the lads. I thought they were in a bar where there was a notorious bloke on the door, one you didn't mess with. I ran up to the door and all I remember was the end of a snooker cue coming out of the end of his jacket, feeling a sudden pain and seeing stars. Next, I was up on my feet and gone. I must have done a mile in under four minutes. My dad always taught me that if you ever got hit and went down you had to roll into a ball the moment you felt the pavement, to protect yourself against the kicking that invariably followed. But I didn't wait for any of that with this bloke!

Parties were popular with us even though we

weren't always popular with them. We'd turn up at the venue, somebody's house, be told 'You lot aren't coming in here' and end up climbing through a window. Wallop again, a free for all, the Old Bill summoned, the usual story. I don't think we did anything really bad, I didn't ever go to court, although a few of the others did, but fighting set me on the road again.

Cal's dad, who thought the world of me and still does, was waiting up for me on one occasion after a bit of a 'set-to' with the occupants of a car we'd cut up. As I arrived home he came out brandishing a golf-club and yelling: 'There's your bag. Now piss off!' He'd had enough of the late nights, the scraps and the worry. I couldn't blame him, but luckily for me, my Auntie Margaret lived nearby. I just walked round to her house with my worldly possessions in a green football-kit bag this time and set up my latest base, on her sofa.

I knew I couldn't exist like that for long so eventually I phoned my mum to explain my latest dilemma. One of her friends, now dead, had a son, Colin Bushby, and she suggested I went to see him. He was a strange bloke in some ways, Colin, single and in his forties, I suppose, but he was brilliant to me. He took me in. He had a two-bedroomed flat in Summerhouse Way, Abbots Langley. I was back near my old patch, less than a couple of miles from Bedmond. As I was still on the dole, I would cook dinner before we used to sit and watch television together.

But it wasn't to last long because the lads were urging me to take up football again. I hadn't played since Watford, but I was still eligible to play for

Bedmond's Under-18s. My mate Russell Hensard came to me and said: 'Listen, Vinnie, the team are crap. We're getting hammered every week. All the boys are involved so why don't you join us?' I thought about it and, well, what would I do with my Wednesday nights, otherwise? And it is nice to hear you're wanted. We were lucky because, years before, he helped raise the money to install flood-lights and an all-weather pitch. That's where we trained and that's where I got the buzz for football once more. My getting involved was thanks to the support of all those friends like Cal Jenkins, Mark Robins, Russell Hensard, Dave Johnson, Jimmy Cornell, Mark Tanner, the local boys. They took me training and made sure the manager, Johnny Moore, was there to see me.

'This is Vinnie Jones and we want him to sign on,' they told him.

'Well, let me have a look at him training, first.' Johnny hailed from Rickmansworth, so he didn't know me. He'd only heard that I was a good player. We hadn't been training for long before he couldn't believe his eyes, or that's what he said. He wanted me in the team and, somehow, I think I realised the time had come to start doing something with my life. I had wasted time but now those mates had steered me round another corner and made sure I didn't waste everything.

Before long it seemed that every team wanted me and I was playing for the lot. Starting with the Under-18s who, in fact, were the whipping boys for the rest of their league. It wasn't long before I was in Bedmond's first team, playing men's football on Sundays, for the Glenn in Watford and St Joseph's from Bushey. I couldn't get enough, all of a sudden, and couldn't understand how I'd managed to get along without the game. The pattern was to play for the reserves on Saturday mornings, the first team in the afternoons, St Joseph's, Glenn or Leggetts on Sunday mornings – three matches each weekend and a midweek game for Bedmond thrown in!

Although I was still on the dole, I earned a tenner or so a time by doing some gardening and odd jobs for Johnny Moore. He felt sorry for me and one day, out of the blue, he arrived at Colin's flat with his wife Wendy and their children. I noticed they had a couple of black plastic bags with them so I suppose I should have known I was on the move again.

Johnny said simply: 'Get all your stuff together. We've had a family meeting at our house and we want you to come and live with us.' Coincidences? I became part of their family living in Tom's Lane, Bedmond, so close to where my life had been bulldozed and only a decent volley from the house to the football pitch. I shared a bedroom with their son, Sean. As I keep saying through these pages, when I make friends I tend to keep them, and Sean and I are still close to this day. I regard him like a brother. John and Wendy really are incredible people and with Sean and daughters Debbie, Michelle and Victoria make up what must be the perfect family.

That's the way it was when they so kindly took me in. Their generosity seemed to have no limits as far as the local kids were concerned. There was a lot of hardship around at that time, no shortage of one-parent families, but if any of the lads from the football team were in danger of going without Sunday dinner they were encouraged to come round to Tom's Lane. Sometimes there would be ten or fifteen of us and everyone loved being there. After Sunday dinner we'd watch television together and later Wendy would come in with the tea. They have never changed and they are still as kind and generous with their time and effort even today.

Johnny had lost his father and he kept telling me that it wasn't right for me not to be in contact with my dad, as I hadn't seen him for almost three years. Johnny and Wendy kept chipping away, encouraging me to break the ice, so it was inevitable I would agree and give in.

It was Cal and I who went to see him in the end and it was a difficult meeting, both of us finding it hard to choose the right words. In fact, we just talked about this and that as though nothing had happened. It was reassuring to realise that the separation hadn't done any lasting damage and, nowadays, we couldn't be closer.

Our reunion wasn't exactly blissful to begin with. It wasn't long before dad had me working back on the building sites – in fact, I was part of the team that built his new house in Colney Heath. But it didn't really work out initially. The rows began again – nothing major but enough to be unsettling. I was that bit older and wanted to show him that I could stand on my own two feet, so I left to work for other building firms, returned to my dad for a while and then was off to do some labouring for others again – including digging out footings with a mate of mine at weekends, Mark Atwood. He lived just up the road from Johnny's, where I continued to live, and had spent all his life in Bedmond. Mark was about three years older than me and we became really close and went everywhere together. His brother was a builder and he gave us work preparing the ground so the brickies could move in and start on Monday mornings. But it was meeting Mark and becoming such good friends that began a transformation of my life. Basically, this was where my life actually started to take the shape that developed far beyond anything I ever expected.

CHAPTER 7

say a little prayer

Mark's dad, Peter, was head groundsman and gardener at the Masonic school in Bushey, the International University of Europe, and he found me a job there. At last, Vincent Peter Jones – hedge pruner, hoer, sweeper up of leaves – joined the legions of British taxpayers!

Gardening was the worst job in the world in the freezing cold and pouring rain. If I close my eyes, I can see myself clear as day trundling around eighty acres of grounds with a wooden rake, tractor and trailer and the two boards that you used to pick up the leaves. Hour after hour, day after day. But at least it was work and although it didn't pay all that much this was the place that was to lead to the greatest opportunity of my life.

I started playing football with the students. Peter had told the sports master I was quite a performer and I was allowed to take Wednesdays off work to turn out for the college football team. One team led to another, and they formed a Sunday side, the IUE Flyers, and would you believe we made it into the Watford and District League? It was some team for a Sunday morning outfit. Mark Atwood and I found ourselves in a side with players from

Nigeria and all over the place. Saturday mornings with Bedmond, Sundays with the Flyers – football was growing in importance, dominating my thoughts.

I was basking in my own little bit of glory one afternoon, cutting the grass in front of the large college house on a great big motor mower. I kept thinking ... I was doing pretty well, one of the youngest ever players to make it to the Bedmond first team, and I had a write-up in the local paper as well, once, for two free kicks against Cockfosters. I made the headline on the match report. Two screamers, both from outside the box, one in each half – wallop, through the laces, top corner.

I was mowing away, in my green overalls and lost in my own thoughts. And suddenly I was praying – a proper prayer. It was to my granddad, Arthur, dad's father. My prayers were always to him and still are when I find the need. He and nan were always special. Granddad was kind of head of the family in many ways: his word ruled. He had a walking-stick but didn't use it for walking – it meant he could keep everybody in order and give us the odd jab or two if necessary without having to jump out of his armchair.

He died in October 1977 and it had a deep effect on me. It was the first time I'd experienced a death in the family, the suddenness of it, the abruptness and the awful emptiness of the space granddad used to occupy. How does a kid reach the favourite old man who isn't there any more? How can you forget the dreadful slow death that reduced such a strong, finely built man to something like seven stone as cancer took thirteen months to kill him after he'd been told it would take six?

Yes, granddad was special. So special that, since we lost him, I've always believed he was still in touch. I am convinced he is my spiritual guide. Nobody needs to ask why it was granddad I spoke to, quietly, that day I was cutting the grass, convinced he could hear every word despite the noise from the mower. I remember saying out loud: 'I'd love to be a professional footballer, granddad. Fourth Division, anything. It's a footballer I want to be, granddad. A footballer. One chance. Anything, anywhere – but one chance. I don't know how we can do it but one chance is all I need. If you can help . . .'

Maybe it was a week or two later when Alan, the sports master, came over to me in the grounds one morning and said: 'We'll have to get this football pitch in proper shape because Wealdstone are coming to do their pre-season training here.'

Wealdstone! The top boys from the Gola League, now the Conference, with their ex-pros from Fulham and Chelsea and all over. This was a big-time football team to me and they were coming to practise right there where I worked. When their manager, Brian Hall, told me: 'You can join in with us if you like' there was only one thing to say: 'Thanks, granddad.'

Previously, when Wealdstone came to the school two or three times a week, I'd sit there on a grass bank in my green overalls, gazing at them longingly. I didn't need to be asked twice when Brian Hall invited me to take part. And I soon thought of something that would take the eye, make them notice. It's something I've repeated at every opportunity throughout my career. When it came to the long training runs, cross-country, I told myself: 'Go and win it – it's the one at the front they'll remember most.'

It must have worked because I was soon travelling with them to other training venues. One of them, on Epsom Downs, took place just after Stuart Pearce had left to join Coventry City and that was the big talking-point among the players. But the big moment for me was sitting down with the rest of them for lunch. I thought I'd made it there and then.

Wealdstone's reserve side played in the Capital League where professional clubs like Wimbledon turned out their own reserve teams. I travelled with them for some time, desperate to be a substitute. I had a spell training and travelling but not playing. Working at the Masonic school and dreaming at the same time, I was longing for my chance to prove I could pass the test.

Which brings me to the day of my driving test. I took it at nineteen, borrowing the fee from my mum. I'd applied for the test while I was working at the school but I hadn't had a lesson. Well, I'd driven as a kid and used Cal's car a few times in the days of our car wash, and that seemed like experience enough. So I announced it among the boys in the pub: 'I've got my test tomorrow, lads. Anybody lend me a motor?'

Michael Conway, a year or two older than me, answered the distress call: 'My sister-in-law's got a Mini-traveller. I'll give her a buzz.' No further question was necessary. We had a bond between all of us that somehow seemed to carry a guarantee. Whatever was said and promised would be carried out.

We could take it for granted.

'Right,' I said, 'I'll meet you down at the test centre in Clarendon Road.' He was as good as his word. And, as you might have guessed, most of the other boys turned up as well. It was quite an event – me taking my driving test with no insurance, no tax, nothing, in a vehicle I'd never seen before, let alone driven. No wonder they promised me: 'If you pass today, we'll all show our arses in Harrods' window.'

In I went. 'Mr Jones.'

'Yes,' I blurted. 'Yes,' came the same reply from somebody else within a split second. 'What?' I said, looking round and feeling a bit of a prat and thinking I'd made my first mistake already. Then this bloke in heavy black-rimmed glasses stepped forward. Mr Jones, the examiner!

The Mini-traveller was on the other side of the road as the two of us emerged from the centre to be greeted by the lads sitting on the bonnet giving me the treatment, with appropriate hand signals. They were still giving it plenty as Mr Jones and Mr Jones pulled slowly and illegally away from the kerb.

The driving itself was no bother, hardly a mistake, as I remember. Then the question. 'Where in the road do you think you should be driving?' I paused for quite a time, half wondering about the question but mostly hoping that the other Mr Jones didn't notice what this Mr Jones already knew – that the tax was out, that right there little more than a foot from the end of his nose was nothing more than a home-made disc insisting that the disc was 'Applied for'.

'That's a hard one,' was my immediate, brilliant

response to his question. 'Where should you drive in the road? In the middle.'

I thought I had blown it because he jumped on my answer. 'What! You mean you should straddle the white line?'

'No, no. I mean you should drive in the middle of your own lane to give enough room to cyclists when overtaking.'

'Mr Jones,' he said. 'I'd like to congratulate you on passing your test. Well done.'

I wanted to yell 'You what?' but controlled the urge until I'd left the car and been greeted by my familiar welcoming party all fearing the worst and totally gobsmacked when I let it out: 'Yeeeaaahhhh!' They all started shouting and we headed straight for the pub. Mikey wouldn't even let me drive the car there, either, but once inside I couldn't hold back: 'Right, you tossers, up to London and let's see your arses in Harrods' window.'

Patience, all the travelling around, paid off for me when I was given a few reserve games here and there. Nothing spectacular but I gave it everything at every opportunity, training and playing for my life. There were to be many memorable days at Wealdstone but none has stayed with me clearer than the call from Brian Hall, the manager, to tell me: 'You've done brilliantly, you've stuck at it and done well in the Capital League. We want you to be part of the squad now.'

I'm a semi-pro, on £28 a week plus the odd £20 to cover expenses now and then! Not only that, but they gave me a club blazer and tie. That was my pride and joy: to be able to wear the official gear. I'd stopped playing for Bedmond's first team having signed for Wealdstone, but I went back every Saturday night with my blazer and tie on and often told a fib, that I'd been substitute when I hadn't. It was nice to hear everybody saying: 'Brilliant, well done, keep it up.'

It was around this time that mum married Dave Hockey, while dad got married to Jenny, too. It's nice to be able to say that they are all still together. I continued living at Johnny Moore's and working with dad in the building game. House extensions, mainly, with me doing the labouring – digging out, loading, mixing cement, hod-carrying. To be honest, there were times when I really bloody hated it – most of the time, come to think of it.

But dad had caught the football bug again. He was happy to let me go off training a couple of times a week, and he and Jenny started coming to watch me in matches. I was flying – happy to have finally made things up with the old man and really determined to make the most of the big chance that came my way through somebody else's appalling misfortune. Tragedy paved the way to a first-team place.

A dreadful thing happened to our first-team centre half, Dennis Byatt from Northampton. He lost his wife and baby during childbirth in hospital. Dennis is another whose friendship I've kept over the years. Who could ever forget that such terrible circumstances offered you the chance to take the first steps of a career? During Dennis's time away from the club I was put in at centre half. It was the season Wealdstone were going for both Gola League and FA Trophy titles – aiming to be the first non-League side to do the 'Double'.

One of my first games was away to Frickley Colliery. What a name that is! There was a fire in the dressing-room with a bucket of coal to keep it going. Outside, beyond the ground, were all those little houses, row after row. It was a night game with a crowd of around a thousand. There was that strange smell in the air that seems to come with fog. We were winning the game 2-0 and the mist was getting worse, so bad that it became difficult to see the Frickley goal.

The home fans clearly didn't like the thought of their side getting beaten and took extreme action. They lit a great fire behind one goal, doubling the effect of the fog that already had us worrying that the game might be abandoned. You could hardly see anyone in the other half of the pitch but the attempted sabotage had the opposite effect because the referee told us: 'Right, that's it. We're going to finish this match now at all costs.' Brilliant! We had vital points in the bag and he refused to call it off even though, at a corner kick in the last couple of minutes we couldn't even see the geezer taking it. We finished as two-goal winners. It was the first time I ever shook a referee's hand and meant it.

I fixed myself up with a set of wheels not long after convincing the other Mr Jones I was capable. I bought myself a blue Mini-van from a friend for £110. Again, no tax, no insurance, nothing. I used it the night some of us visited a nightclub and arranged to meet a couple of birds at one of their houses. One of the lads threw a wobbly and wanted to go home, and I volunteered to take him. It was only about ten minutes away by car. My pal, Dave Jefferson, came with me. On the way back a police car drove past us in the opposite direction along the High Street in Abbots Langley. I glanced in the mirror and saw the car turn round so I put my foot down and shot off. Not because I'd had a load to drink – I'd taken it steady with a few beers because we had a match next day, but I was worried about the lack of tax, insurance and so on.

I turned into a cul-de-sac and saw a big caravan in one of the driveways so I parked behind it and sat there. We were just opposite The King's Head, an old watering-hole of ours. We sat for what seemed like ages, probably half an hour or so, rolled a fag and chatted. We could have left the car and walked home in fifteen minutes across the fields. On reflection we should have done exactly that, but we thought we were in the clear. I reversed out of the drive but as we reached the end of the cul-de-sac two police cars eased out of the pub carpark. Wallop – they were on me.

It turned out that an electrical shop in Abbots had been turned over – the window caved in and televisions nicked. When the police saw a gash on my foot, I became prime suspect. I've had this thing about socks all my life. I don't wear them, unless I have a suit on or I'm out shooting. I wasn't wearing any that night and during a bit of aggro at the nightclub a glass had dropped on my foot and cut it. The cops believed me, of course! Not a chance, they dragged us out of the car, slung Dave into the back of one of their vehicles, handcuffed me and chucked me into the other.

I thought that if they don't find the car keys on me I could just say I wasn't driving, so with my free hand I managed to stuff the keys behind the seat.

We were taken to Watford nick and they kept us there all night. I was breathalysed and registered 43 on the scale where 35-40 was supposed to be OK. At least, that was my understanding of it.

But it was the lads from CID who kept coming into the cell and waking us and roughing us up a bit and insisting: 'Come on . . . tell us.' They were convinced we'd done the electrical shop. I was done for drink-driving and they released me at ten o'clock in the morning. I had to be at Wealdstone for eleven o'clock to leave for a match at Maidstone. I'd had to tell the police about the keys and they brought them from the back of their car. In just one hour, I had to take the bus from Watford to Abbots to pick up my van, then belt to Bedmond for my club blazer and tie and get back to Wealdstone for the coach.

The coach was just about to pull out and behind it, seeing me arrive looking like dog muck, were my dad and Jenny. 'Where the hell have you been?' they asked. It wasn't easy explaining how my preparations for the big game were a night without sleep, in the nick, getting done for drink-driving.

I managed to delay the inevitable suspension from driving. One of my mates tipped me off that if you turned up for the first hearing without your licence they'd adjourn the case. So I did, and they did. It gave me a bit of extra time behind the wheel. It was three months after the offence that I tried to represent myself in court. I can't claim to have made much of a debut as a lawyer: fined £180 and disqualified from driving for eighteen months.

So I had no licence from then on, but I had no *boots* when I clambered on to that coach for the trip to Maidstone. I borrowed a pair from somebody, size nines instead of eights, and one of them flew off into the crowd with my very first kick in the pre-match warm-up! I got it back, persevered and we won the game. If all wasn't well on the day, at least it ended well for Wealdstone who were on course for their double.

Trouble followed me to Gateshead on a weekend where we stayed over, playing two games within a few days. After the Saturday match the local boys didn't exactly take kindly to the sight of me walking around a club with a couple of local girls. There was a rumpus outside among the locals who were furious at being kept out by the staff. Some of them were even armed with bricks. Our lads were in the hotel bar but I went outside and battered two of the 'protesters'.

The fight was kept quiet from Brian Hall because, only the week before, at Maidstone he'd told me I had to watch myself. In the morning, as we prepared to board the coach for training, he noticed the blood on the forecourt. 'What the hell's gone off here?' Hall asked, probably knowing it must have involved me. The skipper, Paul Bowgett, pulled him to one side and said: 'There was some trouble last night. It wasn't his fault. He didn't cause it, but he ended up giving a couple of lads a terrible hiding.' The other players seemed to love it and made up their minds: 'You'll do for us.'

The Gateshead incident was remembered by Hall the day we played away against Stafford Rangers. I was due at the station at eight in the morning. No bleeding alarm clock! A friend took me to the station only to find that the train and the team had long since gone. Sheer panic. I'd never been out of

Hertfordshire on my own before, but knew I had to make it under my own steam.

'What platform for Stafford?' I yelled out the question for anybody, everybody within earshot. In fact there were two trains at the platform they mentioned and I jumped on the wrong one. By the time it was pulling out, a bloke who had noticed my club blazer asked where I was heading. He was off to play rugby somewhere – somewhere miles from bloody Stafford! I jumped off at the first stop and, somehow, thanks to a couple of other trains and a taxi, made it to the Stafford ground by one o'clock.

I got there *before* the Wealdstone team coach and Brian Hall made no bones about the importance of that journey. It had been well worth the sweat and the fares. He'd just about had enough, what with my trouble with the police and the bloodshed at Gateshead and he told me straight: 'You were finished if you hadn't turned up here. I would have cancelled your registration. You'd better sort yourself out.'

It gave me the fright I needed. He could have bombed me out, anyway, but he treated me fairly, to say the least. And I knew that by making it to Stafford I had saved my chance of a career in the game.

I was nowhere near established in the Wealdstone side, having had only a few Gola League games at centre half as Dennis Byatt's deputy, and when he came back I was actually preferred to a lad called Brian Greenaway, who had been a pro at Fulham. In fact, I was chosen for the right-wing job in the FA Trophy semi-final second leg against Enfield, which was far from my most memorable game, and I was pulled off. It didn't matter too much that we lost by the only goal at home because we'd done them 2–0 away, when I hadn't played. Wonderful! The team had made it to Wembley, but I was destined to be no more than a sub for the rest of the season.

When it came to the final against Boston, with only two substitutes allowed, I was part of the squad but not really part of the deal. I was not chosen in the starting line up, nor as a sub. They involved me, which was kind. I was part of the crack in the dressing-room and watched the game, in my track-suit, from the Wembley benches. The boys duly completed the job to become the first team ever to win the Gola League/FA Trophy double.

That night they held a celebration 'do' back at Wealdstone. During the evening they stopped the disco to make presentations to those of us who had not played in the game, as the players had already received their winners' medals at Wembley. I couldn't properly enter the spirit of the occasion. I must have had twenty-five of my mates there and it felt, I don't know, strange and somehow awkward to be stepping forward for a presentation. There were three of us and we were each given a handsome-looking carriage-clock. But none of this felt right. I kept telling myself: 'I can't be involved in all this. I had nothing to do with it except for playing in the semis.'

So I went straight into the toilets, taking the clock with me and hurled it against the back wall. It smashed to smithereens. I wasn't being a spoiled brat or anything, I was just so gutted I had the hump. You see the clock didn't mean anything. I knew it was a nice gesture to present it to us, but the boys had beaten Boston and collected their medals at

Wembley and I was walking about with a clock. Although they tried to make me feel part of the occasion, people coming up and saying, 'Don't worry, you're the future of the club,' none of it felt right. So when the clock scattered across the floor of the gents I just left it there and walked out.

With a new season coming, the driving ban was a pain. I still felt like a kid compared to most of the Wealdstone players but a kid who was bloody determined to break into the side. I needed to impress in training but to do that, I had to get there. One of my mates had a brainwave: 'Get yourself a little moped and a bleedin' great crash helmet so when you drive through the village, the local copper won't know you.' Wicked! That's exactly what I did. My Honda 90 (deposit paid by mum as usual) was a kind of cross between a pedal-cycle and a motorbike – maximum speed 28–30 mph. Flat out. Downhill. With a following gale! It took me the best part of an hour to get from Bedmond to Wealdstone in all weathers, a parka jacket and the biggest, blackest crash helmet you've ever seen. What a 'trainspotter'!

It did the job though. The local copper didn't recognise me. In a helmet that size and on a bike of that type, nobody recognised me! It was pretty grim, biking to and from training and matches at little more than jogging pace in pouring rain and freezing cold but I was determined to keep going. A slight crisis occurred the Saturday the skipper, Paul Bowgett, suggested I made my own way to a meeting-point near the Watford junction of the M25 and he would take me by car to the away game against Slough. At first, it went as smooth as you like – parked the bike, played the game, was driven back to where we started. Off he went in his car, but with my crash helmet still on the back seat!

I daren't ride off without a disguise. I just stood around wondering what the hell I could do when, would you believe it, thank you God, along comes this little kid with his skateboard. And his *helmet*. One of those dodgy-looking things cyclists used to wear that looks like a bunch of bananas linked together. You wouldn't want one but I needed one and for £3 to the bewildered kid I bought it. It got me home unrecognised, but what a sight I must have been. I looked bad enough before, and not surprisingly the Wealdstone boys regularly took the piss out of me on my moped.

My perseverance and determination to get to training whatever the handicap seemed to make an impression on Brian Hall. For instance, there were times when, as the other players arrived in their smart suits, I'd turn up in my building clobber – all mud-stains and cement smears. If I'd been working in London, say, I'd catch a train and then a bus to Harrow and Wealdstone station and walk the rest of the way. Sometimes I'd get there an hour and a half early. More often than not I'd spend the time until 7pm sitting in a little caff down the road where the local winos gathered so I just chatted with them while I had a meal.

I was completely taken aback when Hally told me there were League clubs taking an interest in me. I wondered 'Is he just saying that?' because I knew he quite liked me for being a bit of a lad. I knew, as well, that my enthusiasm had impressed him, that he knew I was as keen as they come.

It was around the time I came of age. At least, that's what's supposed to happen when you reach twenty-one, isn't it? Party time. What a stroke of luck that mum and Dave had set themselves up as landlords at The One Bell in St Albans, the perfect venue for a party. It would be the first time mum and dad and Dave and Jenny would all be together at the same time, so it was a bit tense to begin with.

Prior to the party I'd had a giggle with dad about coming along and meeting Dave. I knew the circumstances would be difficult but told him it would be good for my sister Ann and me and, in the long run, for everybody involved. That's the way it was to turn out. The party broke the ice but I can't say that ice was the only thing broken that night.

A group of blokes gatecrashed my twenty-first. The party was held at the back of the pub and this lot must have filtered through from one of the other bars. They were completely out of order. My uncle Martin, dad's brother, was on the dance floor when one of the intruders just barged him out of the way. I went over and that was it. We sorted them out. Dad, uncle Martin, Dave and I set about them in no uncertain terms. There were around a hundred invited partygoers, my mates from Bedmond, a few from St Albans and some of the lads from Wealdstone as well as the family. But it all ended a bit ahead of schedule – people were screaming, throwing punches, there were blokes tussling all over the shop and tables flying – the full monty! The police were called and order was restored, but the party was over.

I remember thinking afterwards, though, that there was one important consolation from the night that ended in a complete shambles. I had my dad and stepdad fighting on the same side!

My FA Cup debut was marked by something similar. Well, not as violent and not as many involved, but it 'went off' in the away tie at Reading. I was sent on as sub and my very first tackle triggered a fifteen-man set-to in the centre circle. I just went in on this fella and swear to this day it was a good tackle but he got up and went berserk at me. There were a lot of senior pros about, quite a few well into their thirties and I was twenty-one, playing in the FA Cup for the first time, but I wasn't going to be shoved around by anybody. It all blew over, fortunately. We lost 1–0 but I wasn't sent off.

That happened in a match at Weymouth who had a goalkeeper who was supposed to be a bit of a loony. I went for a 50–50 ball as he tried to grab it. Woosh! He took exception to the way I'd gone for the ball and I didn't like the way he reacted. Wallop, wallop, other players dived in – a few fists and a lot of handbags. We were both sent off. It was my first time. Not that it ended there . . .

We had to walk through part of the crowd on our way off and I noticed my mate Steve Perkins, the nutcase of our team, sitting in the stand. As I made my way through some of the Weymouth supporters, one of them moved towards me and spat into my face. Shades of Eric Cantona! I was into the crowd after him and Steve (or Polly Perkins as we called him) was down from his seat and jumped in with me. I think we managed to whack the bloke a couple of times before we were pulled away and calmed down. They always say that it's a long walk to the dressing-room when you've been sent off.

CHAPTER 8

holmsund sweet holmsund

Despite those little distractions I did hold down a midfield place in the Wealdstone side during 1985-86 season. I was happy enough with my progress, in fact, still having difficulty believing I'd made it to Gola League level. But then I heard some dressing-room chat that pricked up my ears. The lads started talking about a player called Dibble and another called Nigel Johnson. It seemed strange because they weren't around and I didn't take that much notice until I went training one night and they were there, practising with us, as if they'd never been away.

It turned out that during the summer months they had been playing in Norway and Sweden. 'Hey,' I thought, 'there could be a chance here. Sod the building game, this could be football full-time.' So I asked them a few questions. They told me they went over in April and came back at the end of November. They had had a terrific time. And guess who was the bloke who arranged it all? Call it coincidence again, if you like, but it was only Dave Bassett, the one who had us chipping balls over the hedge at Bedmond. Now the highly successful manager of Wimbledon.

I went to Brian Hall and asked him if there was any chance I could be fixed up with one of those numbers abroad. Me! I didn't really know where 'abroad' was! But I'd heard the banter ... cash in hand, flat provided, free food and a car and thought, 'This'll do me.'

Harry Bassett had heard of me. Derek French, Wimbledon's physio, had lived in our village years earlier and taken me down there to train alongside the apprentices for a few days. But I later discovered Wimbledon had watched me. Frenchy had informed Bassett I was playing for Wealdstone. As luck would have it, we were building an extension opposite Tom Walley's house and I saw him for the first time in years. We had a bit of chitchat about when I'd played under him at Watford, and I struck a deal with him.

'See all those leaves on your front lawn, well, I'll rake them up and clear them away into our skip if you'll come and watch me play a game for Wealdstone.' Deal done. Tom was as good as his word because Watford sent their scout John Ward to take a look. What I didn't know was that Wimbledon sent Dave Kemp, now their assistant manager, to watch me in the same game and he reported back to Dave Bassett that I had something.

So when Brian Hall contacted Bassett about me he knew a little about who I was. I went to his house where he was sitting with his wife, Chris, and the kids and he said: 'I hear you'd like to go out to Sweden and I can arrange it for you. Providing you give me your word that there will be no fighting, no aggro, nothing.'

I couldn't get the words out quick enough: 'I

really want this, I really want it badly. I won't mess it up, that's my promise.'

A couple of weeks later, with my first passport in hand, I'm down to London and gone. I flew for the very first time. My skinhead days behind me. There I was with a mop of curly hair and only the clothes I stood up in, out from Heathrow and into Stockholm on 2 April 1986. With some jeans and my boots in my old, familiar piece of luggage – the black bin-liner. I must have been expecting something different because I was a bit puzzled to find the weather just as I had left it in England, or maybe even colder. But I knew I was in a foreign country when a geezer came up to me and said: 'Winee Djones? Winsent Peter Djones?'

I must have looked a right picture and he must have been thinking whatever the Swedish is for 'What the bleedin' hell do we have here?' as I walked off with him in my poxy sheepskin jacket, tracksuit bottoms (well-worn), well-worn trainers and the black bag that was obviously almost empty.

'Winsent Peter Djones,' he said again. 'I am Burt Bustron, chairman of IFK Holmsund. We need, now, to catch the aeroplane.'

'What? But I've just got off.'

'No, you do not understand. Now we must fly to the north of Sweden.'

It was a small plane heading for Umea, a tiny airport. Once on board he assured me: 'Yes, we are a very nice football club and we have big ambitions.' In fact, Holmsund were in the northern section of the Swedish Third Division. It turned out that I was about to play for the equivalent of Bedmond first team! Well, maybe a bit higher than that, but nowhere near Wealdstone standard.

I thought we were still above the clouds as the plane landed, because there was snow everywhere, four feet deep in most places. But that was only part of the shock because after we'd walked across the tarmac somebody opened a door and I saw the welcoming party: fifty or more media people waiting for us – reporters, interviewers, cameras of all kinds, lights, the works.

I was invited to sit down and had already started thinking: 'Don't let this be happening. This lot believe I'm something I'm not. Bassett has done a right sales job, here.' He'd told me to say I was on Wimbledon's books but I didn't realise they were expecting a star. I told a string of porkies – I was in the Wimbledon side and, as a young player, had come to Sweden to get experience and keep myself sharp. All the time that press conference was in progress I was feeling guilty and regretting every minute of it. There it was, next morning, all over the papers – the long-awaited arrival of Vincent Peter Jones. And that's how they referred to me in print and on TV throughout my stay.

My regret about those little white lies was soon replaced by a sense of wonder, as I was driven to my apartment. We went through a large town and beyond, up a road into the country for about twenty minutes. The scenery was stunning, with rivers and lakes, and there I was in the back seat thinking: 'This is bang on.'

And it all got better and better. There was another lad still to come out a few weeks later, Steve Parsons (of non-League pedigree with Wimbledon connections!), but I was to live with Mark McNeil, a centre forward with Orient. The apartment was beautiful – the ground floor of a typical, large Scandinavian house built of timber and overlooking the sea – three bedrooms, massive lounge, kitchen, a nice little garden. Oh, and a brand new Saab saloon to share between the two of us. I thought I'd won the pools.

'We were told you like to go fishing,' the chairman announced. 'Well, we have a nice boat for you, with an engine.' The money didn't seem that important all of a sudden but it was still handy to learn I'd be paid £300 every fortnight, cash in hand.

Whatever sportswear I needed I was simply to choose at a huge store and charge it to the club's account: the full kit, boots, tracksuits, even Astroturf boots. Choose them, try them on, admire yourself in the mirror and just sign for the lot. I knew, there and then, that I had to make football my life. I stopped wondering what to make of my future but, having had a quick taste of all this, the thought of returning to work on the building sites was terrifying . . . So was the dread of not doing well with Holmsund and having to be sent home ahead of schedule.

They don't mess about in Sweden. I was met at the airport, changed planes, did a press conference, checked in at the apartment, kitted myself out at the sports shop and made my debut all on that first day. 'We have our first pre-season game tonight,' they said, 'and we want you to play.' I could hardly refuse.

The venue was a bit like a leisure centre. A grey, gravelly all-weather pitch under floodlights, which looked pretty spectacular once they'd bulldozed the snow into piles eight-feet high all round the place. I thought we were about to start a training session but no, they insisted, this was an important pre-season fixture before the league started a week later.

It was a freezing night, but I wasn't prepared for the sight that greeted me when Mark led me into the changing-room to meet the lads. They turned out to be a terrific bunch of guys but they looked a right bloody picture to me, first off – all done up in tracksuit bottoms with long socks over the top, double shirts, gloves and thick bobble-hats. That was our strip for a pre-season fixture. We won 6–0 and had only one player not wearing a bobble-hat, the bloke in the middle of our defence, the centre half of Wimbledon (supposedly) who was out there keeping in good nick!

There was no players' bar after the game, but we did get together, our boys and the opposing team, in the sauna. Cosy! It was a bit of a culture shock for me in the beginning: game over, into the sauna, then back home with Mark to cook a meal and watch a video. No pubs as I knew them, only bars with hardly anybody in, so there was no socialising in winter, though we did have barbecues at the players' homes on warmer evenings. That was the big night out for them and their wives and kids. We normally played on Sundays so there was no going out on Saturday nights. The university disco was about the only place to have a drink, so I didn't bother – I gave it up. The culture shock was a pleasant one and I welcomed the new routine despite finding it hard getting used to twenty-four hours of virtual daylight. No wonder the apartment had curtains as thick as duvets.

I took stock: I'd had a free flight out, then free

(ABOVE) In the party spirit at an early age.
(LEFT) I was about twelve when this picture was taken, and already very keen on shooting.
(BELOW) The dream house, Woodlands, where my childhood happiness fell apart.

(LEFT) In my first season at Wimbledon, we reached the sixth round of the FA Cup before losing to Spurs (*Allsport/Dave Cannon*), but a year later

(BELOW) we went all the way after we beat Luton in the semis (*Action Images*).

We had decided that one of the key battles in the FA Cup final was who could impose themselves on the match, me or Steve McMahon. I was determined that I would let him know I was there from the whistle (*Allsport/Dave Cannon*).

Our 1-0 victory over Liverpool in the 1988 final was one of the greatest moments of my career (*Colorsport*).

(ABOVE) The celebrations are just beginning as the Wimbledon team line up with the trophy (*Colorsport*).
(LEFT) On the team bu parading the FA Cup, though I nearly didn't make it in time – and the it was on to The Bell wi the Bedmond boys for y more partying (*Allsport/Pascal Rondeau*).

For once I was up against my old friend John Fashanu when I was in action for Sheffield United in the 1990-91 season (*Allsport/Dave Cannon*).

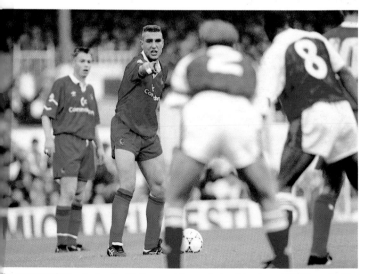

The next year I was playing for Chelsea, and it was during this game at Highbury that I was fined for making 'obscene gestures' to my friend Tony O'Mahoney (*Action Images*).

(ABOVE) When I rejoined the Crazy Gang at Wimbledon as captain, the cameras all turned up, but (BELOW) it was great to be back with mates like Fash (*Allsport/Anton Want*).

My time at Leeds was one of the best of my career – I still get a great reception whenever I go up there. Here I exchange a few words with Shane Westley of Wolves (*Colorsport*).

It's a tough job but someone's got to do it. As judge of a 'best bum' competition, I got an early glimpse of Scary Spice (bottom (!) left). When I next met her, at the Brit Awards in 1997, we had a long chat about the occasion, but my lips are sealed as to who won (*Jeff Ross*).

(ABOVE) Although our form slipped late in the 1989-90 season, we were able to win promotion to the top division as champions with a victory at Bournemouth on the last day of the campaign (*Action Images*). (BELOW) The party began immediately in changing room – such a big club was back where it belonged (*Colorsport*).

apartment, club car and free sports gear. It took some believing by the boy from Bedmond. And one of the club directors owned a supermarket and we could just fill a trolley with whatever we wanted, all brilliant fresh produce. I'll never forget the rolled fillet steaks, two-feet long. Load 'em up, in with the veg, all the stuff for breakfasts – off to the check-out and sign the lot to the club again. Was I in paradise or what?

We trained every night. The players were part-time pros, most of them employed in 'dolly jobs' organised by the club. While Mark and I were on £150 a week, the others were paid thirty to forty quid for their football. It was still a good life for the local lads, being paid for playing and being handed the best jobs in town. Put it this way, I never heard any of them complain.

Getting to sleep after training was difficult at whatever time you tried, but we developed a handy alternative. If Mark and I couldn't sleep, we'd go off for a round of golf at three or four o'clock in the morning. Then back to the apartment for some kip, tidy up and out again down to the river, pike fishing. Twenty-four-hour daylight has its advantages if only you're smart enough to adjust!

I became friendly with a cod fisherman, Tom. Often I'd join him at 4am to help put out the nets. I made another pal who, if we didn't have a game, took me camping and fishing in the mountains. So I had the sea, the rivers, the mountains and the football. As close to perfection as I could get. The only thing missing was the shooting!

Apart from fishing, Sweden gave me another experience I'll never forget. The father of one of my team mates promised me a special day and he didn't let me down. Having stayed at his place overnight we were up at 5am and off in his motor . . . to the Baltic. We turned up at this sort of farm. Nothing else to see but snow, everywhere and reaching every horizon. We were kitted out in the kind of gear the Eskimos wear, climbed astride a couple of snow buggies and roared off across the snow and ice. We were driving over the surface of the sea!

About a mile or so out we stopped and he drilled a great hole in the ice. I'd seen this kind of thing on nature documentaries but this just blew me away. He took a short rod and lowered the baited line in the hole. I watched as he waggled the rod in a simple, up-and-down routine that brought a fish to the surface within minutes. Then it was my turn. We must have caught about a dozen before buggying on down, home to his place and having them for supper. Amazing!

Looking back, it's hard to remember I was out there to play football because there were so many aspects of that unforgettable experience in Sweden that fascinated me and still do. The game gave me a wonderful time as well, though. Mark and I turned into minor celebrities. The various divisions in Sweden have 'player of the week' awards and I won it more times than anybody. In fact, at the end of the season I was the winner of the Third Division trophy, nationwide, top choice from all of sections north, south, east and west. As Holmsund enjoyed the glory of being top of the table, I was lapping up the recognition. Signing autographs at the supermarket was a new experience and I liked it.

The simplicity of our little ground just added to its appeal. It had a smashing pitch and clubhouse, the obligatory sauna and somewhere to have a cup of tea. Its capacity was about 2500, mostly accommodated on wooden terraces. This was the venue for a mighty cup game against Djurgaarden, one of the country's major clubs from its top division. This was like, say, Manchester United playing Wealdstone away.

I'd been allowed to fly home for a few days during the club's two-week break earlier in the season, and I asked Dad and Jenny out to Sweden for a week. My old man couldn't believe it, me signing autographs! He loved it in Sweden and even played in a specially arranged match between the players' fathers and the club coaches. Him and his skinny little legs, with my boots on scoring with a thirty-yarder. The bloke who'd been on Watford's books as a kid revelling in another moment of glory!

Djurgaarden's centre forward was Brian McDermott, the lad who used to play for Arsenal. As centre half, of course, I was the one who would mark him. The press had us both together for pictures the night before the game and I actually remember feeling starstruck.

They should have beaten us 10–0, especially after they took a 2–0 lead, but they reckoned without the centre half and the centre forward from the same apartment. I marked McDermott out of the game and my mate Mark McNeil just went bang . . . bang . . . bang . . . wallop. He scored all our goals in a 4–2 win that seemed to confound the entire country. It took time for it to sink in, properly, because there were no obvious places, pubs and nightclubs, to celebrate as they do in England. For us, the team and the directors, it was round to the captain's house for a barbecue.

It was only the next day when we fully appreciated what we had done, when the national papers said we had pulled off one of the greatest giant-killing performances of all time in Swedish football.

We went on to meet one of the leading First Division sides, a team already in the promotion play offs, in the quarter finals. They had a geezer up front who was six-foot-seven, and, as the regular centre half, I was instructed: 'Vinnie, you have to mark this man. You stop him – and we win.' After losing the home leg 2–0, we beat them by the same score in Stockholm and it went to penalties.

No, Mark and I wouldn't take one because we didn't want to be the blokes who cocked it up. We left it to the Swedish boys and they did the business, taking Holmsund into the cup semi finals in what was, without doubt, their best season for many years. Not that the journey home was anything glamorous. Nine hours on a coach – correction, on something more like a school bus – with upright seats and hardly any room for your legs let alone tables.

Holmsund were knocked out in the semis, but by then Mark and I had returned to England. I had met three of the club's bigwigs sometime earlier to negotiate a new deal for the following season. They were offering me a £10,000 signing-on fee to be paid in instalments. If there had been such a thing as the lottery in those days then I'd have won it. That's the way it felt and I couldn't stop thinking about it while they took some time to sort out the details.

When I was next called in I was expecting to sign the contract on the spot. No hesitation. Especially when they said I could have the ten grand *and* £400 a week, tax paid! I was highly regarded at Holmsund, having played every game since my arrival and always at centre half. I got a load of bookings but there was no totting-up of points over there. One yellow card in a game was forgotten at the end of it. Two yellows in a game and you were off, then suspended, but I'd given Harry Bassett my word that I wouldn't get into trouble over there and I always had the feeling I had everything going for me.

But I didn't sign that contract. As soon as I stepped into the office they handed me a letter. It was from Bassett, handwritten, saying: 'Heard that you're doing brilliantly and that you're coming back next week. Link up with French on your return and come into Wimbledon for a month's trial.'

CHAPTER 9

booted and suited

I returned to England with £1,200, which I'd saved in a drawer. And one of the first things I did, back home, was buy my first 'posh' car – a Cortina Estate for £900. Those six or seven months in Sweden had changed my life yet again.

I went straight back to John and Wendy's and rang Bassett within an hour. I told him how well things had gone for me abroad and that I hadn't had a drink – a record I was to keep up for almost a year after returning. Wimbledon had just been promoted to what was then the First Division. They had completed that amazing leap from non-League to the very top level in such a short time, and now I could be part of it.

'Get yourself settled,' Bassett told me. 'Give Frenchy a ring and come in on Monday.' So much happened over the next three weeks and I still can't fully understand some of it. I never played for Wealdstone again but I did spend two or three training sessions with them and had a confusing little meeting with Brian Hall.

As I planned, I went in with Frenchy on the Monday morning to Richards and Evans, otherwise known as the public playing-fields just off the A3 which is Wimbledon's training ground. With a transport caff, full of lorry drivers in the mornings, just off the changing-rooms. We'd read the papers and tuck into a pre-training breakfast: eggs, chips and a fried slice. That was the scene on my first morning – all the lads together, first team included. 'This'll do for me,' I thought, 'a good old bacon roll for starters.' Find a table, two lorry drivers and four footballers, most of them smoking their roll-ups.

Frenchy took me to see Sid Neal, the kit man, and I have to admit to being lucky with my start at the club because I was already mates with Wally Downes. Wally had been the first apprentice at Wimbledon and was regarded as top man. He was a sort of combination of shop steward and piss-taker, and was regarded as Bassett's son. I'd got to know him at Wealdstone where he often came to parties and other dos. Straightaway he put his arm around me, and no other initiation was required. The new boy was a mate of Wally's: I was accepted. I was in.

We had a practice match and finished with a cross-country run which you had to complete in under seventeen minutes. Right up the side of the A3, through the woods, up hill and down dale and back again and a lap round the public playing-fields, with Alan Gillette, the assistant manager, standing there stopwatch in hand. Yes, as you might have guessed, I was at the front. I just bombed out there and left the rest behind.

On the way back, past the physio room above the caff I could see all the heads at the window. Frenchy opened it and yelled: 'Go on, our Jones boy!' It gave me a wonderful feeling, just to win that little race for Frenchy, the man who had urged

Bassett to give me a chance. I knew he'd be, well . . . over the moon.

My first match was at centre half for the reserves at Orient and nothing special, then a night game at Feltham in strong wind and driving rain, which was bloody horrible. I was over-enthusiastic, wanting more than anything in my life to succeed, but not daring to hope too much. Frenchy, bless his heart, kept telling me: 'Listen, just show them how fit you are. The gaffer knows you can play.'

After two games at centre half and still doing well in the cross-country races three times a week, I'd struck up a friendship with John Fashanu, mainly because I sat next to him in the changing-rooms. Then there was Wally and Mark Morris and Glyn Hodges. I felt really settled, as though I'd been with them for years, and I think Bassett liked that.

There was an afternoon game during the third week of my trial against Brentford reserves at the training ground and for some reason they stuck me into midfield – probably because I hadn't been doing all that well at centre half. I took that as a bad sign. I thought I was down the road, out of there with the words all players dread: 'Well done, lad. We don't have an opening right now but we'll keep an eye on you.' In other words, don't ring us, we'll ring you.

And then I went and scored two goals in a 3–1 win. I just felt so comfortable in midfield, enjoying more freedom to run, winning all the headers. I learned, later, that Frenchy was urging Bassett to play me at midfield. And something else happened during that match when Bassett and the others were sitting upstairs, watching through the office window. I took a throw-in. For no apparent reason I ran over the touchline, picked up the ball and launched it almost to the far side of the penalty area. I heard a kind of gasp and several of the players all letting out the same words at the same time: 'Fu . . . cking hell!' They'd never seen anything like it before and I didn't know I could do it either. Little did any of us know, then, that it was to become part of my trademark.

David Kemp, one of the coaches, had shown a lot of faith in me. We used to travel home together on the train and he'd give me a little pep talk every day. That was my new routine – home at night with Kempy, back with Frenchy next morning and into the caff with the truckers. Until Alan Gillette came down one morning of that third week and announced: 'Jonah, Harry wants to see you.' The cry went up immediately from the other players: 'Go on, my son. Contract! Contract! Contract!' I went up those stairs not daring to even wish, just expecting him to say something like 'You're doing a bit better in midfield so we'll play you there a couple more times.'

Bassett came straight out with it: 'Jonah, you're doing well, son. Gonna take a chance with you. I'm gonna sign you.' It's hard to describe the feeling that came over me at that moment. I imagine it was a bit like dying, when everything goes, just seems to evaporate. I couldn't get a word out, never mind in. I stood there, stunned and gobsmacked, so grateful but completely bewildered all at the same time. I finally managed to gasp, 'Yeah, yeah, yeah.' And nodded my head repeatedly.

'We're going to give you the rest of this season and next season. Two seasons, then. And make sure you bloody well work hard.' Then he explained something about me having to go and see Brian Hall and sign contract forms for Wealdstone because Wimbledon were paying £8,000 down and £7,000 more if I managed to make twenty-five appearances. The details were flying over my head as Bassett explained the deal. I couldn't think clearly ... I couldn't think at all.

I went to see Hall that night, signed a contract at £125 a week, picked up £250 for two weeks' wages and so took care of the technicalities allowing a fee to be paid for my transfer. Next morning I signed for Wimbledon with Bassett saying: 'Right, I'm putting you on £150 a week plus £50 a goal and £50 per appearance in the first team.'

'Right,' I said.

'Go on then, son, you've done well. See you tomorrow,' was Bassett's parting shot. But, as he could see me hesitate slightly, he said, 'What's up? Something you want to ask me?'

I'd heard about signing-on fees at Wealdstone and I'd been offered one to return to Sweden so I asked Bassett: 'Any chance of a signing-on fee or something?'

'No,' he snapped. 'I've given you your chance. You get in the first team and I'll look after you. Now fuck off.' End of contract negotiations. But Vinnie Jones was a full-time professional footballer with a club in the top division of the English game. Thanks again, granddad.

Thursday was Bassett's day for picking the team. The only things going through my head were the thrills of training alongside professional players and having been rewarded with a contract a week before my trial period was up. I looked around me and saw lads who had been with Wimbledon for years but had never trained let alone played with the first team. For somebody who had been in and out of the Wealdstone side, well, it was enough for me just to be there.

The session finished with a game between the reds and blues. Those in the blue bibs would be the team for Saturday. That's the way it was, that was Bassett's routine. Everybody stood and looked at one another when Steve Galliers, a stocky little midfield player, was told by the manager: 'Right, you swap with Jonah.' Other players stood and scratched their heads and, like me, were obviously thinking what the hell was going on as I was handed a blue bib and told to play in midfield. Bassett didn't make a thing of it, he was matter-of-fact and I'm not sure how I felt. I didn't worry about Steve Galliers' feelings at that moment because I couldn't fully appreciate what was happening, the significance of it. I was just training.

But as we were about to start, the chitchat began. Wally came up to me and said: 'You're in.' In? Me in the Wimbledon side to play at Nottingham Forest two days later? I thought they should have put Wally in a straitjacket!

But it was true. Bassett named me in the side. It was like somebody saying: 'Right, you are now King of England. Get on with it.' I phoned my old man and my uncles who were all to come to the game but I couldn't tell them, then, about tickets because I didn't know how to arrange them. I just had to phone a mate.

The first thing my old pal Mark Robins asked when he answered my call was, 'What are you doing on Saturday?'

'I'm playing for Wimbledon against Nottingham Forest.'

'You're having me on!' Mark shouted. Who could blame him? I couldn't believe it either. It even affected my speech!

I still look back and cringe at my first TV interview. London Weekend came to see me at John and Wendy's and asked the obvious question: 'How has all this happened?' And I couldn't get the words out. I developed a sudden stutter for the first and only time in my life and spluttered something about 'W-well, B-Bassett was g-giving out these blib . . . lib . . . blibs . . . bibs. And he g-gave m-me a b-blue one.' Glyn Hodges took the mickey out of me mercilessly. Even now, when I phone him, he cracks up if the conversation ever involves TV.

Bassett had lent me £150 to buy a suit. He insisted the players wore them on match days and I didn't have one. I dashed into London and bought a dark-blue suit and a nice white shirt to go with it, and treated myself to a new pair of football boots. And the first thing I did when I got home to John and Wendy's was put on my new gear with the official club tie and looked at myself in the mirror. I didn't want to take it off – ever! If you went to my wardrobe, nowadays, you'd find ten or fifteen suits, most of them hand-made. And twenty to thirty shirts bought in Jermyn Street. But that day, the eve of my First Division debut, my one and only suit was my pride and joy.

I don't remember much about the journey to Nottingham. We stopped at a service station on the motorway. Bassett wandered across and told me I was rooming with Wally Downes. Even with

Wealdstone we used to stop at a nice hotel and have a light meal such as scrambled eggs on toast. But here I was in the big-time, with Bassett handing Wally a fiver for the two of us: grub money. And you were not allowed to spend more than £2.50 each. I just followed the rest of the lads . . . the full grease up, sausage, egg, beans, chips and anything else within the cash limit.

Wally had become my minder. He knew that I could handle myself and was a bit of a rebel. He'd also been told that I was a good pal to have. But I couldn't understand why he kept urging me to hurry up as we checked into the hotel in Nottingham.

'All right, all right,' I said, running to the lift. Once upstairs, Wally rushed me into our room and all I could hear along the corridor was laughing and the sound of running taps. The other players were filling their wastepaper-bins with water and those who were slow into their rooms copped it. Whoosh! It was what the lads called 'having a crack'. Seven o'clock and down for dinner. Wally was up to something. Most of the pranks seemed to go through him and I sensed he was up to some mischief. There was a bit of sleight-of-hand under the table followed by the sudden departure of Glyn Hodges and Mark Morris, who were away for about ten minutes.

We sat and had a coffee after the meal and the players started drifting off to their rooms. Bedlam. Two of them came back down and they were blazing. 'You rotten bastards!' The boys had struck, nicked the key and obliterated their room. Messages written in shaving foam on the mirror, bed-linen tied in knots, towels and clothes dumped in the bath with the water running. This was the law of the jungle with Wimbledon. The first time I'd seen it in action but I was to experience it hundreds of times more.

Wally leaned across and said to me, quietly: 'That is why you guard your room key, our key, with your life.' That was the crack with the Dons. You guarded your key more closely than any other possession. The moment you put it down and turned your back, it was gone. Everybody in the squad saw it as a challenge. And if you had your room turned over, you were expected to sleep in it as it was. No calling the chambermaid, you had to sort it out as best you could and get on with it. You're with Wimbledon, now.

CHAPTER 10

an amazing start!

Wally's warning of what I was like, how I loved a punch-up at Wealdstone, delayed the 'initiation' that welcomed all newcomers at Wimbledon. There had been the odd wisecrack and mickey take during those first three weeks but no 'official ceremony'. So I thought I'd escaped. It was a happy and contented but extremely nervous twenty-one-year-old who eventually wandered off to his bed that night. They'd made me feel as comfortable as any lad could, facing his debut within days of signing a contract. I hadn't been singled out for mischief. I felt part of the scene as I settled down in my bed.

It was about 11.30pm. No chance of dropping off straightaway because my mind was in a whirl, wondering what tomorrow was going to bring and remembering the specific instructions Bassett had given me about marking somebody called Neil Webb. I'd never heard of the geezer, didn't know him from Adam, but Bassett had pulled me to one side and advised me in his own inimitable fashion: 'Listen, son, this bloke could be the next captain of England. He's the dog's bollocks. Don't worry about playing football, just run around and stay with him and stop him playing.'

Yeah, I was thinking as I lay in bed, hands clasped behind my head. Just stop him playing, don't let him get the ball, don't give him time to pass it. The thoughts raced on until they were suddenly broken by the phone ringing. Wally only heard one word before he put it down again: 'Wankerrrrs!'

It rang again and again and again. Wally said the call was for me a few times and passed me the phone to hear the various good luck messages: 'Lucky sod. First Division player, are we? Tosser. Shitting your-self, yet?' They came from several rooms, even Bassett and Frenchy were kind enough to call!

Wally was smiling that knowing smile of his. It must have been the bewildered look on my face. This was not the night I expected before the biggest day of my life. I was even daft enough to think that the long pause since the last phone-call was the sign for me to turn over, close my eyes and dream on.

It rang again. 'Yeah?' Wally replied. 'Yeah? No, no . . . *no*!' Nothing to concern me, he said, just the boys mucking about. Five minutes later – bang, bang, bang. I thought our door was about to be forced off its hinges. Wally jumped up, opened it and in they piled. Four of the players not involved in the match and they had with them this old bird who, I learned later, was a well-known if not legendary Nottingham Forest supporter nicknamed Amazing Grace.

I'm lying there, not able to believe my eyes and muttering: 'This can't be happening. Somebody please tell me this ain't happening.' The boys knew they wouldn't have made it into any of the other rooms but were sure that Wally would let them in. They'd all had a good few drinks on a lively night out in Nottingham and recruited the 'Amazing One' somewhere along the way.

'Come on, Jonah,' they started. 'This is your initiation.'

'Piss off,' I told them. They were making a hell of a din and I could imagine Harry Bassett storming through the door at any moment.

'Go on, go on Jonah,' Wally chipped in. He was rolling about on his bed, laughing like the rest of them. It's hilarious, looking back, but I was suddenly a very frightened young man. There was anger mixed with fear because I thought of Frenchy, all the faith he had in me and I imagined his face and his words: 'How could you do such a thing on the biggest night of your life?'

I pulled the bedcovers up to my chin but there was no stopping the cabaret. The boys sat 'Amazing' at the end of the bed in front of the mirror and started helping her shed her gear. Off came her top, then her bra and I started shouting: 'No, no!'

'Come on, come on!' the others were yelling.

'Leave me alone. Fuck off the lot of you.' I was close to panic but suddenly relieved when the lady in the looking-glass announced: 'Let's have a drink. I've got to get a drink.' Surely that was the sign for them to get the hell out of there, but no chance. Two of the lads said they would go and get a couple of miniatures from the hotel machine while the other two stayed behind to 'keep her warm'.

The drinks duly arrived in style. Not a couple of miniatures but the entire bloody machine wheeled into the room! I was ready to quit, to leg it to another room, anybody's — anywhere but there. Wally could see the panic on my face. He wasn't just laughing any old laugh by this stage, the tears were rolling down his face.

Amazing rose to her feet and peeled off her remaining gear, stood in front of the mirror and then looked at me. 'If you come anywhere near me—' I said from my bed. She didn't. She turned, sat on the end of the bed completely starkers, facing the mirror. And then she started to sing. 'If you're happy and you know it clap your hands.'

I'm terrified, wanting them out of there, desperate to sleep. Because it was my debut later and I had to make sure that somebody called Neil Webb didn't get the chance to play!

'If you're happy and you know it and you really want to show it' she sang and stared at herself bouncing in the mirror and the lads were clapping and singing along as well. That's when something snapped. I'd reached the point where something just 'goes' with me. I was shaking as much with rage now as fear. I gathered up all her gear, thrust it at the lads and told the lot of them to get out of that room. They must have realised I meant it, that the show really was over, because out they went.

I couldn't sleep, though. It was 1.30 in the morning, perhaps a little later, and I was still shaking. I'd imagined having a plate of pasta for dinner, a nice early night to prepare for my big day. And I ended up with a naked bird in the room and several choruses of 'If you're happy and you know it'. That was no way to prepare for a match, never mind your debut appearance, surely.

'But that's the chaps,' Wally said to me before we finally turned in. 'That's us. That's Wimbledon. We have players at this club like Dennis Wise, a free transfer. Lawrie Sanchez, twenty grand from Reading. We're not superstars, we are still lads off the street, playing in the First Division. And this is our spirit.'

From that day, or night, I knew the score and how I was expected to carry on. It was the first time I'd ever thought of that old saying: if you can't beat 'em, join 'em. Although, in the early hours of that particular morning, I'm glad I didn't!

So I got a few hours' sleep, had breakfast with the boys, read the papers and watched a bit of telly and phoned the old man. There was a small reference in the papers about 'Vince Jones may be making his debut for Wimbledon' but I knew my name wouldn't get a mention in the Forest match programme, as they wouldn't have heard about me. We got off the coach and were heading for the dressing-rooms when we all suddenly stopped in our tracks. There, standing in the corridor, was the legend himself, Brian Clough. Nobody moved.

It was as if the Wimbledon lads, crazy as they were, had found themselves confronted by a forty-foot wall and didn't know how to get beyond it. Cloughie, in his green sweatshirt with the white collar turned up, unnerved all of us without saying a thing. Nobody seemed to want to go past him. A few voices were heard in whispers: 'Go on, go on, some bugger go first.' Still, no one made the move until Cloughie broke the ice by turning to Alan Cork and saying: 'Good afternoon, young man.' Corky was a right lad in his way but then he turned almost to jelly.

'Hello, Mr Clough,' he replied in a gentle little voice that was hardly audible. But he walked ahead and the rest of us followed in a hurry. Once inside the dressing-room the banter started: 'And what were you like, Corky? What a tosser. You were scared of him – crapped yourself.' That was rich, coming from team mates who hadn't dared move a muscle. If Clough could bring Wimbledon to a standstill without moving or saying a word, what damage would his team do to the First Division newcomers?

When we trotted out to warm up I was hit by a weird sensation. The nearer I got to the pitch the smaller I felt I was becoming. I was like Alice in Wonderland. The further I went up the tunnel the more I seemed to be shrinking, both physically and mentally. When I actually stepped on to the grass I felt no more than twelve inches tall. As if I had gone from six-foot to one-foot in a matter of seconds. It was strange and it was scary.

Then the shakes started. I turned from the touch-line and looked around: the two dugouts, the tunnel entrance, quite a few spectators scattered around the stadium. I began to tremble, slightly at first but then more exaggeratedly and beyond my control. For some reason I started to run, not to anywhere or anyone in particular, just running, headlong, round the sides of the pitch. Like Forrest Gump. The shakes don't show when you're running and I was hoping it would work the fear out of my system. Eventually I could feel myself coming together, I started to take in the scene around me, and then one of the boys pinged a ball in my direction. I pinged it back. It felt OK. So I trotted across towards a corner flag and joined Andy Clement, knocking balls to and fro.

Clemmo had just got into the side himself and was probably as terrified as I was. For me, though, the whole mood and atmosphere changed the moment I pulled that first team shirt, that No 4, over my head. It was a feeling I will never forget. The only time I matched it was at Wembley in the FA Cup final the following season. I tucked the shirt into my shorts and smoothed both hands repeatedly down my chest. God, did I feel proud. Everybody seemed to be willing me to succeed.

Sid Neal, the kit man, the physio, the other players and Bassett all saying: 'Good luck, today, son.' From feeling one-foot tall I now felt twenty-feet high. I thought: 'yeah, this is me. And we're invincible.' It was a kind of inner spirit, a sudden sense of real belief that burned and swelled inside. We'd walked into that dressing-room like mice but we thundered out of it like giants.

Our lads knew next to nothing about the Forest players. Wally Downes was up-to-date and knowledgeable about his football but eighty per cent of us in the squad didn't really know. We were aware of Nigel Clough, their centre forward, because of his old man but as for Neil Webb and players on the verge of England honours, we hadn't a clue and didn't care. Funnily enough they didn't know any of us, either. We were the surprise packets who had suddenly made it to the top level and that was our strength.

Intimidation was part, a big part, of the ploy. Imagine Webb's feelings when, with me standing alongside him, he had Wally yelling at him: 'You're going to get it today – right in the mouth.' Webb spread his arms as much as to say: 'What's all this?

I'm just here to play football.'

'You're going to get it anyway. First chance and we'll do you.' You turned round and John Kay would be saying the same thing to, maybe, Franz Carr. You'd be defending a corner and keeper Dave Beasant would be saying something similar to a couple of their players in the goalmouth. The looks on their faces said it all: 'What are this lot about? What *is* going on, here?'

Not that it worked particularly well, that day. I was chasing Neil Webb everywhere and couldn't get near him. I kept thinking: 'I'm in the wrong place here, well out of my depth. This is not for me.' I couldn't believe the speed of Carr, whipping down the touchline at what seemed like even time for the hundred metres and taking the ball with him. I honestly feared I was out of my league even though Carlton Fairweather put us in front after two minutes.

The rest of the Wimbledon side thought I was off my trolley twenty minutes later when, after Carr and Webb had swapped passes, the ball was swung high into our goalmouth. Beasant was stranded and I could sense Webb next to me at the far post. 'Don't let the bugger score. This is the one who's going to be the next England captain, mark him out of the game.' The thought rushed through my head. But instead of jumping and heading the ball I was so determined he shouldn't get it – I punched it. On my league debut. Twenty-two minutes into it and I punched the ball. Needless to say the young Clough put away the penalty!

And we were losing by half time after Andy Thorn deflected the ball into his own net. I don't think I touched the ball with my plastic-coated boots during those first forty-five minutes. I do remember going in for the interval and being thankful it was over. As we reached the mouth of the tunnel I tugged at Glyn Hodges' shirt and asked him: 'How am I doing?'

'Yeah, yeah, great. Just keep going.'

I wasn't convinced. We sat down and Joe Dillon, assistant kit man and general helper for the players, was doing his rounds. Bassett was busy talking: 'Let's do this, second half . . . let's get the ball wide . . . let's get among them.' Sid Neal, who must have been in his seventies, came round with the tea in white plastic beakers. I'd never dream of having a cup of tea at half time these days, but I took one then. I was desperately in need of some reassurance as well so I asked Sid: 'How am I doing?'

A little hard of hearing, Sid tapped his earpiece and said: 'What? What you saying?'

I was trying to ask in a whisper but he was replying with a shout. 'How am I doing?' I repeated my question quietly and slowly. I sensed the dressing-room had gone quiet and dreaded what was coming.

'How are you doing?' Sid boomed as if the crowd outside were expected to hear him. 'Well, let me put it this way, you might as well give me that bleedin' shirt 'cos I could do a lot better than what you've just done!' I just thought that was that. The old stager could see I'd had a nightmare so that was me. Done. Finished. Back with Bedmond next week, probably.

The second half wasn't much of an improvement. I was still chasing Neil Webb who was playing the ball to Cloughie who swept it out to Franz Carr who returned it inside leaving me to set off again chasing Neil Webb. Glyn Hodges' equaliser for us broke their rhythm for a while but I was to start my career in a losing team after all.

I was pulled in to be part of our defensive wall when Forest were given a forty-yard free kick in the fifty-eighth minute. Another new experience was in store as Johnny Metgod, a tall balding Dutchman who was a very gifted footballer, stepped forward to take it. In fact he stepped back, and back, and further back still. I thought 'Any further and he'll fall in the Trent.' Metgod appeared to have massive feet. They must have been size twelves and looked even bigger as he thundered forward and met the ball as clean as a whistle. It screamed past us and I whipped my head round in time to see it flying in. I saw Beasant dive but thought 'Don't bother, son. That's in the top corner and I think I'm on the wrong planet.'

I was on familiar territory that night when the coach journey back to south London was broken at Bedmond. We all trooped into The Bell, something that became a routine on the return from matches up north. Joe McGilliat was with us, a big friend of Bassett's. You could have taken him for a director and he had a posh voice compared to most. Squeeze your nose with your fingers when you talk and you'll have some idea of how it sounded when he told the manager: 'Harry, Harry, how could you play a prat like that? Playing Jones, you must have lost your marbles.'

I heard it. I thought I had little more to lose considering the way I'd performed at Nottingham, so I stormed across to the bloke and gave him the verbals, full blast. End of conversation. End of debut. Thankfully, it was not to be the end of the world.

The only good thing that came out of the Forest game was that throw-in of mine, the long launch that I didn't know I had until I produced it, out of the blue, in training. When I launched it again, in the second half at the City Ground, everybody took notice. Maybe, again, it was the adrenaline that propelled it.

Bassett seized on it the following week. He had me throwing it and throwing it and throwing it some more for up to an hour on the Thursday and Friday until I was putting it straight on to John Fashanu's head or anybody else's who charged into the box. The week had started with me thinking I'd blown my big chance. Gerry Francis, later to be manager at QPR and then at Tottenham, coached the back four and at the end of training there was the cross-country run so I kept on winning them. It was a tough regime at Wimbledon. We became super fit. Other teams would cringe at the routines we accepted as normal. We'd have a match every day against the reserves or the kids but it was so monotonous I don't think I could face it nowadays. The coaching was basic to say the least, a simple strategy that went roughly like this: if the ball comes near you when you are facing the opponents' goal kick it into the channel straightaway. If it reaches you with your back to the goal, hook it over your head. The plan of attack was to get the ball as far away from our goal as possible.

The one thing that would send Bassett mental

was to play a square ball. No 1 rule at Wimbledon: 'We do not play square passes.' You were not allowed to pass to a player supporting you. You could knock it back for a team mate to hook it forward, whoosh, the pressure ball. Fashanu and Andy Sayer would get after it and the whole side would squeeze the opposition in their own half. That newly discovered long throw of mine was to become part of the Wimbledon weaponry.

It was probably because of that long throw that I was in the squad for the next game. It must have nagged at his mind. He had seen another way of getting the ball into the opponents' penalty area in one fell swoop, another way of setting up goals. He must have thought that if we practised it long enough the routine would begin to bear fruit. Those long sessions, hurling the ball as far as I could from the touchline and from different angles, must have saved my career. It was to produce 10–15 goals a season and at Plough Lane, our tight little home ground before the switch to Selhurst Park, I could throw the ball into the box from the halfway line.

Oh no, the big teams didn't like facing us at our place. Least of all, Manchester United.

CHAPTER 11

from hod to hero

I must have had to get thirty tickets for my second game, my home debut. Everybody wants to see Manchester United anyway, and you can imagine the fascination among all those mates of mine ... Vinnie playing against Alex Ferguson's mighty men from Old Trafford. Fascination? Disbelief, more like, until they actually clapped eyes on me coming out of the tunnel.

They were all there: mum, dad, the boys from Bedmond, everybody. Afterwards, it was as if that match changed something. It was different at the pub on Sundays. We all met for our usual drink but they would keep asking: 'Couldn't you hear us? We kept shouting at you, trying to attract your attention.' Suddenly I was made to feel different, as if I had flown the nest and found myself at another level. Not higher or better than any of them because I always wanted to feel the same and still do, but different, certainly. I really tried to stay one of the crowd but events were going so fast and overtaking me. They had never been out of the Watford area, but I was to finish up going to the likes of the Hippodrome and Stringfellows. But to this day I still manage to be Vinnie Jones, the pal who grew up with them, fought with them, drank with them, went out with them and worked with them. It was just that after I played against Manchester United, well, it underlined the fact that I had become a player.

I couldn't stop looking around me, that afternoon. I looked at the crowd and saw my friends and family. I looked at the opposition and had to keep reminding myself that all this really was happening at a time when I should have been just completing my month's trial. That I was part of a team about to play against the likes of Paul McGrath, Kevin Moran, Jesper Olsen, Remi Moses and Frank Stapleton. And Bryan Robson if he managed to get off the substitutes' bench.

I was nervous but I was also keen to get started. No feeling small, this time, but with a sense that Bassett had kept me in the side for some reason and whatever it was I had to justify it. I had to say thanks in a way that was obvious to everybody. And with that need came a feeling almost of confidence.

That's how I started the match. The quality of the opposition, the reality that it was Manchester United, didn't matter any more. When the whistle went, it was about me and what I could do to make sure my team won. And it all began nicely. I felt comfortable and strong and I wanted the ball. A few successful tackles and winning headers always help and they went my way. About midway through the first half I went for a volley and caught it, sweet as a nut, only to see the ball come back off a post. I wanted some more of that!

Bassett hadn't restricted me this time. He encouraged me to go and do more of my own thing rather than having to track an individual opponent.

So I felt free to go looking for chances at free kicks and corners without ever even imagining what was to happen to me in the forty-second minute.

Some books are boring, I know, when players drone on about countless goals in countless matches. But I make no apology about describing, in as much detail as I can recall, the goal that sank Manchester United at Plough Lane, because it was mine!

We won a corner on the right. We knew Glyn Hodges would whip it in with his left foot and where he was likely to put it. We had players ready to attack at the near post, the far post and in the middle. I just stood there somewhere beyond the box when Brian Gayle said to me: 'You go first.' Me? Go first? This was my second game for Wimbledon, right? And I was facing players I'd only ever seen before in books or on the telly.

I started to make a run but then realised I'd gone miles too soon and would probably be alongside Hodges by the time he struck the corner! I stopped, began to walk back and realised Kevin Moran had gone with me. I was actually being marked by Kevin Moran, Manchester United's Irish international. So I ran again, really ran and as the ball flew in from the right I thought it was coming for my head. My head! In the box against Manchester United. I held Moran off with my left arm and threw my head at the ball. I didn't know where I was putting it, just thought, 'There's the goal, head towards the goal . . .'

Bosh! Perfect contact. Remi Moses was guarding the post that I'd hit with that volley earlier. I remember he still had his hand on the post as the ball sped for goal. He tried to head it and I thought he was going to knock it over the bar but the power of my header knocked him back. The ball hit the roof of the net and poor old Remi landed on his bum. I had scored against Manchester United!

I didn't know what to do, how to react. I just ran and shook an arm in the air and looked for family and my mates in the crowd. I managed to see most of them before I disappeared under the pile of team mates who leapt on me from all angles. It might seem strange, but at that moment I said another little prayer: 'Come on granddad, come on, please let it stay at 1–0.' And he did. United did bring on 'Pop' Robson, but there was nothing Captain Marvel could do to spoil my incredible day.

Afterwards, there was bedlam in the dressing-room. I had the next peg to John Fashanu and all the other players came over and took hold of me, yelling: 'Yeah, you've done it, Jonah. We've done Man United.' I could actually see the Wimbledon spirit everybody talked about. It was all there in that dressing-room and created a sensation of complete togetherness, which is why I couldn't understand Bassett's mood when he walked in. I expected him to be buzzing like the rest of us but it was as if nothing special had happened. 'Well done, but you should have done this . . . what were you doing when so and so did such and such?' All that stuff was above me.

Next thing, a steward put his head round the door and asked if I could go and talk to the press. I looked at Fash, for his approval, I suppose, a nod from the bloke I was growing pretty close to, a friendship that developed into a real bond. The press boys rattled off their questions and there were plenty of them because nobody had heard of me.

—'What job did you do before turning pro?'

—'I used to work with my old man on the buildings.'

—'What sort of building work?'

—'Well, digging out footings, hod carrying, things like that.'

It was out. The hod carrier was the label from that day. It was something I had to live with, the fact that the critics would seize it like vultures and shake it for all it was worth. When Jones became the target, up went the cry: 'Get him back on the hod where he belongs.'

I haven't liked that because, in their attempts to rubbish me, they have degraded many decent people. There is nothing wrong with carrying a hod for a living and I have been proud to have retained the links with my background and my roots. When supporters look at me I'm pretty sure many of them think: 'He's still just one of us.' Kevin Keegan, Bryan Robson, Alan Shearer, people like these were known only as footballers but I want people to say of me: 'He was nearly twenty-two before he became a pro footballer and he remains one of us.' I have tried to be their torch bearer in a way – working in a different world but knowing and appreciating where my world is.

Talking of worlds, I was having difficulty coming down to earth. Not just after scoring the winner against Man United, either. We played Chelsea away and won 4–0 and I scored again. Watford, the club who had turfed me out as a schoolboy, came to Plough Lane and were beaten and I scored again. Sheffield Wednesday, seen off 3–0 at home and I scored again. I was on a roll. I'd been in my first punch-up as well, although all my headlines were about the goals I'd scored rather than my bad behaviour in the beginning.

The trouble occurred at Chelsea but it was not of my making, I just joined in like everybody else. At Wimbledon, you see, everything was done with an attitude of 'all for one and one for all'. Doug Rougvie, Chelsea's big bruiser of a defender, a Scottish international to boot, went in on Dave Beasant and sparked off a free for all. There was mayhem at Stamford Bridge with about twenty players involved in a right old bundle. Fash ended up on the floor, apparently head-butted by Rougvie and I ran in and went whack. Mine was not the only right-hander delivered into the general ruck. It seemed that everyone was in.

We'd played only seventeen minutes and Rougvie was sent off for the incident with Fash. It was all over the papers, next day, and Bassett had us watch the video of the game in the office and warned us: 'It's good that we all stick together but we can't be doing this, lads. That was out of order.' Yet we were all caught up in the tempo of life at Wimbledon, in training sessions where we would run round shouting 'Power!' and punching the air with Bassett encouraging us because he argued that those on the outside looking in would say: 'They're invincible, this lot. Have a go at one of them and you'll have to take on all eleven.' He even had us practising surrounding and badgering the referee.

I sometimes think that Bassett took out my brain, reprogrammed it and put it back in. I was so grateful for the chance he gave me, so keen to justify his faith, so terrified that it would all be taken away overnight, so bloody determined to win every tackle, every ball, every advantage possible. And certainly every game. I became a different person when I stepped over the touchline. That weird shrinking sensation at the City Ground never returned. I was feeling bigger and bigger but was also conscious of this Jekyll and Hyde thing deep inside me. If I put my hand on my heart I have to admit I have never been able to fully control it. My agent, Steve Davies, worries when things get on top of me because he says something is going to give. Something snaps and ninety-nine per cent of the time I regret it.

We understood his warning after the Chelsea punch-up and yet, as we watched the video, somebody noticed a couple of figures right in the corner of the screen. John Kay with his arm round Pat Nevin's neck, walking off with him while whacking him in the head. Completely separate from the main squabble. There were a few sarcastic 'tut-tuts' from the players but, deep down, there was approval again.

I used to think everything was luxurious and smooth-running for the professional footballer until I found myself, the player who was making all the headlines for scoring goals, shoving Frenchy's Jetta for a bump start on the M25 going to training. That might not have been life at Man U, Arsenal or anywhere else but it was part of life at Wimbledon and part of the reason why they have survived for so long at the highest level. Also, reminders of tougher days can be good for you. I peered from Frenchy's car one bitterly cold morning and noticed a group of builders. It took my mind back to desperate mornings when I arrived on the site wearing my balaclava. Everywhere frost-bound. The sand was so hard that we built a fire in an oil drum and stood it in a hole in the heap to start a thaw. As the sand gradually softened we could then begin to mix it and get on with the job – providing you could free your hand from the frost on the handle of the shovel.

As I looked out from Frenchy's motor it was like gazing at my own past: déjà vu. Those builders, with the oil drum in the sand heap, were doing exactly what we had done. They were in the real world, a world a darned sight harder than mine, but the building boys didn't moan. They worked their hands to the bone for £300-£400 a week but were as happy as any people I have ever seen, enjoying a few pints for a couple of hours on Friday nights.

Now I'm able to get up in the morning with a smile on my face that was first put there twelve years ago. Even if I knew we were going to have to do the Richmond run, eight to ten miles cross-country, it was a fantastic feeling. I'd been blessed.

I felt that way about the goals I was scoring right from the start. I couldn't stop. Or that's how it seemed until we played Charlton at our place. I was through on their goalkeeper, one on one. Another goal was a mere formality, but I put it wide. Another chance passed me by. Then I made a run that was timed to perfection, beat the offside trap and set myself up with another chance. Missed again. The goals dried up as quickly as they began with that wonderful moment against Manchester United.

I didn't score another goal that first season.

That part of my game, the attacking part, was gradually coached out of me. Once I had stopped scoring I was made more aware of the other aspects of the game, the defensive rather than the positive. 'When the ball is directed at our right back, with the opposition attacking, you've got to drop back and double up,' Bassett started to urge. That side of the game hadn't particularly concerned me before. All I was interested in was getting forward in support and hoping to get a goal.

I was getting into the opposition penalty area less and less. It seemed that my job was now to win the knock-downs, the key tackles and to support the players with the ball. Gerry Francis took care of that part of the coaching with our defenders and central midfield players, including me. I didn't particularly enjoy it at first. Bryan Robson was a pretty regular goalscorer for Manchester United and hit quite a few for England as well, and I thought I was more suited to that kind of role.

The whole feeling at Wimbledon was so intense and frantic. It was hammered into us that we were playing for the very survival of the entire club. We felt under threat all the time – that if we were relegated then we would all be finished. Everything was done at an amazing tempo. We lived and played at 100 mph. Hardly surprising that trouble, big trouble was just around the corner: Arsenal at Plough Lane. Graham Rix, now assistant manager at Chelsea, said something to the effect that we shouldn't even be sharing the same pitch, not in the same league as Arsenal. I thought: 'Right, smart arse. You might be Graham Rix. You might be Arsenal. But now you're going to learn about Wimbledon and about me. You're going to find out who I am.' And I whacked him. At the first opportunity, I just lashed out and caught him. I was so caught up in the emotion of it all that I actually believed the other lads would think it was great. Not a bit. The referee came across and said: 'What do you think you're doing? There's no room for that on my pitch. Get off!' The reality of it all hit me like a sledgehammer. Get off. Early bath. I could see Bassett going berserk on the touchline and his anger was not aimed at the referee, either. I was in disgrace.

I walked off and headed for the dressing-room on my own. I've always thought that somebody should accompany a player sent off if only to show him he's still wanted, still 'one of us', instead of being isolated because of one mad second. But nobody walked with me and it seemed a hell of a long way.

Once in the changing-room I just sat on my own. A dressing-room, in those circumstances, is the loneliest place in the world. One minute you're out there with all the boys, the opposition, the crowd and the next minute you're in there on your own and nobody wants to know you. It's a horrible experience. I just sat and wished a hole would appear in the floor so I could jump right in. I would have given anything to slip back in time for the chance to ignore Rixy's wind-up, to be able to just run past him and get on with the game.

I didn't go out to watch the rest of the match. I stayed inside that dressing-room knowing I had let everybody down and I kept going over it, time and again, in my head: 'Why? Why did you let him get to you? Why did you do that? What the hell happened?'

It was not to be the last time I asked those questions of myself and I've never come up with a satisfactory answer. It is easy to say it was the excitement, the adrenaline, that caused me to take leave of my senses, but there is also a question of control and I never managed to fully achieve that.

People have asked me countless times and I have asked myself what happens to me once I get out on that pitch. I see other players 'lose it' and I think to myself: 'What's he doing? He's a far better player than that – doesn't need to resort to that kind of stuff.' Yes, I've been asking myself the same question for ten to twelve years and still haven't found a proper answer.

There was no sympathy from any of the Wimbledon players and staff that day. They washed their hands of me after the game and repeated the words of the referee: 'What did you think you were doing?' I knew it was partly the adrenaline, the fact that Vince Jones was actually playing against Arsenal, but it was made clear to me that not everything would be regarded as acceptable. Wimbledon had their limits.

Part of my problem was that I underestimated myself. There I was, making my debut at Nottingham Forest and thinking: 'What am I doing here?' In my head it was as if I was telling myself I shouldn't really have been there at all. But then there is the pride, the self-respect. I'm not really sure how the 'hard man' thing started but I began to get the feeling I was going to be the one the opposition looked at and chose not to mess with.

One thing I've never been able to stand is the thought of people looking down their noses at me. They do say you can take a man from the gutter but you can never take the gutter from a man. I think I've been rebelling against people with the attitude towards me throughout my football career. I adopted an attitude that said: 'I am from Watford, I'm off the building site and I'm representing ordinary working-class folk of this country. I know all about the Eric Cantonas of this world, with all their dosh. Great players but we're not all born like that. We've not all been so lucky. Some of us have had to work bloody hard to make it this far.'

Harry Bassett didn't offer the kind of encouragement that said 'What a great pass' or 'The way you brought that ball down was brilliant.' He was more a 'Get in there' manager and I've never seen any player at Wimbledon shy away from a challenge or a tackle. He knew we could all play a bit but concentrated on the 'through the brick wall' attitude. Motivation was everything. He loved a bundle, a physical set-to. You could be on the treatment table and he'd run over, dive on you, wrestle a bit and land a punch or two. He encouraged it among the lot of us.

There is a big rugby pitch at Wimbledon's training ground and one day, in thick snow, 'Harry-ball', a primitive form of rugby, was born. You pick up the ball and chuck it or run with it towards the try line. All he was after, in fact, was a 'bundle' among the players. One crashing tackle and everybody piled in. Harry would love it, yelling: 'Look at you lot – poofs!'

Frenchy was jogging along with a couple of injured players, on one occasion, when Bassett said to me: 'Jonah, he's just given you the finger. Go get him.' No sooner said than done. That's the way it was. I set off full tilt after Frenchy, launched into a rugby tackle and smashed him down into the snow. The other players charged over to take the mickey out of the poor old sod, but it all quietened down a bit when Frenchy climbed to his feet and we discovered that I'd broken two of his ribs. But he took it like any of us would have been expected to take it. It was part of the motivation and the expression of the spirit of the whole set-up: togetherness. On Friday mornings before home games, 'Harry-ball' became the routine warm-up.

CHAPTER 12

changing managers, losing heads

Harry was as much a part of the mischief-making as the players who were eventually to become known, nationwide, as the Crazy Gang. Tony Stenson, sports reporter with the *Daily Mirror* and a Dons man through and through, came up with the nickname that described us perfectly and was then used by all the media. Stenson coined the phrase after a whole series of pranks, so-called initiations and general mayhem. It was no surprise, for instance, to return to the team hotel and find your bed hanging outside the window, suspended by its sheets.

I don't think we had been officially installed as the Crazy Gang when we went to Portugal for a few days before an FA Cup tie against Portsmouth at Plough Lane, but every time I recall what happened out there, it creases me up.

I was rooming with John Fashanu, but it was Wally Downes and I who spotted that golden moment: a room key in a nickable situation. Bassett turned his back for just long enough – now you see it, now you don't. The other players weren't in on it. You didn't go round bragging about the key swipe. The important surprise element was part of the intrigue.

We came up with a beauty this time: whatever wasn't screwed down in Bassett's room, we removed. The bed, dressing-table, television set, chairs, lamps, the lot. All to be neatly assembled elsewhere. And everybody was there for the climax as the lift doors opened and Bassett stepped out . . . to find his room laid out before him, in the lobby! It was set out exactly as it had been originally. Bed, here, dressing-table, there, telly to one side, towels neatly folded and all his belongings just as he had left them. His match notes were there as well, detailing players with specific tasks at set pieces, but the notes had slight adjustments: the kit man and Pat from the caff were substituted for Bassett's original choices.

A few days later, before the Portsmouth game, he really wound us up, telling us we were going to get beaten and constantly calling us 'poofs'. We were so keyed up and ready to go against Portsmouth. On the Friday, Fash and I daubed our faces with the whitewash used for marking out the pitch. It was our warpaint although, as I said at the time, it showed up far better on Fash than on me!

We slaughtered Portsmouth to such an extent that their manager, Alan Ball, said he was ashamed of his own team. We were on BBC's *Match of the Day*, for once, and I was having an absolute blinder, winning the tackles and the headers and feeling absolutely inspired. I wanted to be in on everything, part of every move. I was really bombing and not long into the second half I caught Mick Tait with my arm in a pretty hefty challenge and was booked. I was so up for this match, so determined to respond to all the build-up during the week and knew I was doing really well, until, with less than half an hour to go, Bassett crucified me. I must have been man of the match but it made no difference – he pulled me off and sent on the sub. I was blazing, my eyes were standing out of my head. I must have looked as if I was on cocaine or something.

I went stomping round the dressing-room yelling: 'Why's he done that? How could he bring me off? Why, why, why?' Alan Cork was in there and came to put an arm round me but there was no calming me down. I charged across the room and head-butted the wall. Bang, bang, bang! I actually put a dent in the surface. Corky just said: 'Bloody hell' and ran out. Apparently he went straight to Frenchy and told him I was nutting the wall, wrecking the dressing-room.

I sat there for what seemed ages but the anger wouldn't subside. I was thinking, 'You bastard, Bassett. You spend all week pumping us up and I go out and give you everything and then you take me off.' Even when the game finished and the others came in I was still at boiling point. My fists were clenched and I was yelling: 'Where's Bassett? Bring him in here. Just let me get hold of him.'

Frenchy realised what was about to happen, what I intended doing. And this time, there was no quiet, fatherly advice. He went absolutely mad at me. He regarded me as his boy, his prodigy, and he knew it was time to blow his top. He was screaming louder than I was and he dragged me into the showers and said: 'Now you bloody well listen to me. He's the manager. He's the one who gave you your big chance in the game. He makes the decisions and you can't do this to him.'

I had never seen Frenchy freak out before and

the shock of it calmed me down immediately. He made sure he acknowledged that I had played very well but also made it crystal clear that if I whacked Bassett I'd be throwing everything away. And what happened when Harry walked in? Typical of the man: 'Hey, Jonah, Jonah,' he yelled across the dressing-room. 'Brilliant today, son. You had a real go at them. Brilliant.'

It was like putting a pin in a balloon. He just flattened me. If that dressing-room had been quiet enough I swear we'd have heard the hiss of the anger escaping from my ears. My arms relaxed, my fists uncurled. What else was there to say but, 'Thanks, boss.'

That match was one of the first times I'd ever been in action on TV so I couldn't wait to watch the highlights that night. The commentator (I'm sure it was John Motson) suddenly announced: '... and there's going to be a substitution. Yes, it's Vinnie Jones and that's a sensible move by Bassett because if he hadn't been brought off he could well have been sent off.' That was when the message got home, like putting the letter in the envelope and sealing it up: received and understood. I'd been substituted for my own good and for the benefit of the side that could well do without needless suspensions, although the manager himself never explained why I'd been subbed.

Dave Bassett has been a kind of God in my life. I couldn't be critical of him because he brought me into professional football and gave me the massive opportunity all kids beg for. I have nothing but admiration for the man, not only for what he got out of me but for the way he inspired everyone and everything at his disposal. I admire him more than anyone I've ever worked with and he will tell you, even now, that if ever I have a problem, I dial his number. He remains an important father figure to me. He created me, gave me the chance and encouraged me to make the very most of it.

Wimbledon had survived in the First Division, which was a fantastic achievement for a little club that had been elected from non-League into the Fourth Division only ten years earlier. Bassett's priority was to make sure they stayed up in that historic first season at the top, to lay the foundations that have kept them there, against all the odds, to this day. I honestly believe that if he'd stayed, he would have changed Wimbledon's style of play. He would have switched from that basic, get it forward strategy commonly known as 'Route One' to a more constructive and subtle passing game, but it was not to be, not with Bassett, anyway. One morning during the summer break, it was all over the back pages: Bassett goes to Watford.

I thought it was the end of me and the end of my world. Nobody but Bassett would put me in their team. I truly feared I would not be able to play for anybody else. He had left us to go to Watford but hadn't taken me with him. He knew how I felt about his managerial style, he knew I was a Watford boy, but he hadn't asked me if I fancied going with him and I couldn't understand why.

In fact, he was to invite me a couple of months later, asking me down to watch the game and have a chat. I went eagerly. I think they played Swindon that night and afterwards Bassett took me into the boardroom and said: 'I'd like you to meet Elton John.' If only the boys could have seen me, shaking hands with Elton John! Standing there, large as life, having a chat with Elton John! It was my ambition to play for Watford and I still hold out hopes that I might be involved there, in some capacity, some day.

'So you're a Watford boy,' Elton said. And we talked for some time. I told him how my granddad had been a supporter at Vicarage Road and we nattered on about Wimbledon's successful first season at top level and, of course, about Harry Bassett. I was at ease with Elton because I could see he was so in love with Watford and that he liked Bassett's reputation and attitude as an all-out winner. Graham Taylor, the manager who had inspired Watford's transformation from Fourth Division to First and to the 1984 FA Cup final, had left the club after an amazing decade of success to take over at Aston Villa. It was the start of another era, just as it was to be at Wimbledon, and I sensed they would quite like me to be part of it.

'Right,' Harry said. 'I'll have to go through the proper channels and have a word with Sam Hammam about buying you. I'll do it during the week.' (Sam Hammam was Wimbledon's owner.) As I was about to leave, Elton asked, 'Vinnie, what are you doing now?' I came out with the sort of thing you are not supposed to say to the chairman of a football club about to try and buy you: 'I'm going up the pub.' And immediately thought, 'Mistake, Jonah. Clanger. Shouldn't have said that.'

'Which pub?'

'The Bell. I drink at The Bell in Bedmond.'

'How far is it? How long to get there?' I couldn't

believe this was happening. Elton John, world megastar, asking me how long it would take to get to my local boozer. Somebody wake me up.

'About fifteen to twenty minutes,' I said, still believing he was only making polite conversation.

'All right if I come with you?' Was he being serious? It was only a fleeting thought. Nah, this must be one of Bassett's wind-ups, with Elton more than happy to be part of it.

With no more ado he arranged for his driver to come round and pick him up in the Roller and follow me up there. A few of the boys were in there as usual but I didn't say anything the second I walked in because I wanted to wait until Elton had had time to park up. But as he walked into the bar I announced: 'Meet my new mate, lads!' There were more open mouths than in a mass audition for *Oliver*. Nobody said anything for a few seconds but Elton broke the ice, began the football chat as if he had been a regular among us for years. He was just one of the chaps. Brilliant. Within ten minutes the pub was jam packed. He stayed for about three-quarters of an hour until the usual problem: everybody and their aunt wanting autographs. He obliged umpteen times before coming across to me and saying: 'I think I'll shoot off. Thanks a lot.' It was only after he had gone that we discovered he had left £50 behind the bar. Drinks for the boys – what a star!

The proposed move to Watford didn't meet with Wimbledon's agreement and, as things turned out, it would probably have been the wrong time for me to go there. Bassett got the sack, Elton sold the club and I didn't see him again for many years until we met at the Brit Awards. Watford were struggling and

I told him to make me the manager but he appointed Graham Taylor again, so I don't suppose he had any regrets.

Bassett's departure from Wimbledon gave me a chance to jump in. It was the first time I really got to know the club's owner, Sam Hammam. Harry had gone, we didn't have a manager at the time and I fancied my chances of a new contract, so I went straight to the top, to Sam's offices in London's Curzon Street. He upped my wages from £150 a week to £350, and this time there was a signing-on fee of £7,000 a year. But when a new manager arrives at a club you just don't know what the future holds.

Our new man for 1987-88 turned out to be Bobby Gould, who had called at a few places both as a player and manager. He was 'unveiled' by the chairman, Stanley Reed, who first of all gave his welcome back speech to the players before revealing the identity of the new gaffer. What now?

It was not an easy situation for Gould. We were all Harry's boys and none of us thought there could be much of a life after Bassett. Wally Downes was among the first to get the axe, and it was soon obvious that one or two more would be on their way, that we had reached the end of an era.

Gould made an immediate impact by signing Keith Curle from Reading, for £500,000. Half a million quid for a defender. That was unheard of for Wimbledon. This was a slice of gateau arriving in the middle of the custard-pie brigade. Not only that but Gould made it clear right from the start that he would do things his way, stamp his authority on the club and had no room for anybody who wanted to live in the past, in the Bassett era. You were to be a Gould man or you were out of the door.

Gould was a different character from Bassett. There was no more 'Harry-ball', no more mock punch-ups between the manager and a player stretched out on the treatment table. There were to be times, though, when things weren't going too well and he attempted to revive some of the Bassett influence. I remember one particular row with Dennis Wise who had become miffed and was ready to leave. Wisey had started playing up a bit, complaining of injuries and not training. Gould came in one day with two pairs of boxing gloves, ordered all the players to form a circle, chucked Wisey one pair and put on the other pair himself.

'Come on, then, get it all off your chest,' said the manager. And he did. A few blows were struck, a few missed, but there wasn't a clear winner of that particular contest. Just another reminder that no player should be bigger than his club.

The new arrivals came thick and fast: John Scales, Terry Phelan, Clive Goodyear, then Eric Young. And somebody else, somebody who caused a lot of eyebrows to be raised not only at Plough Lane but throughout the country: England coach, Don Howe. Wimbledon had adopted a kind of 'them and us' mentality and Howe was certainly regarded as coming from them. Nobody thought for a moment he would want anything to do with us. It was Gould's attempt to change the club, to alter its controversial image and introduce an air of respectability and professionalism. We soon realised that Gouldy was pretty useful at promoting himself, that he wasn't frightened of being in the papers. In fact, he loved it.

There was some resentment among the more senior players as Gould brought in new personnel and made his changes. During Bassett's time we didn't have much respect for anybody. That was part of the Wimbledon spirit and culture. Gould's introduction brought the culture shock but Howe's arrival had us thinking, 'There is going to be life after Bassett, after all.'

Don was sensible but he was fun, as well. He enjoyed the banter, the crack, and that surprised us. All of a sudden, he wasn't Adolf Hitler, he was a football man who could be extremely funny. He came to me one morning at training and said: 'I think we'll have one of those army songs. Come on Vinnie – up to the front and start it off.' So there I was, leading the jogging, chanting the way the American troops do with the other lads echoing the words, sentence after sentence. They felt like prats at first but Don got them at it: 'Come on, lads, all in it together.'

He introduced small-sided games in place of Harry-ball. We didn't think it was quite us in the first place but it grew on us and became more enjoyable until we thought the training routines were fantastic and Bassett's ghost had been exorcised. It was Don who did most of the training while Bobby would stand and watch.

Don was trying to teach us that you can respect your opponents without offering the initiative to them. You can have fun without being irresponsible. There is a line that should not be crossed. His and Gould's hardest task was making sure we stayed on the right side of it. We were rebels and I have to say that some aspects of our football pushed the rules right to the limit and often beyond it. Don Howe insisted that we could push only as far as was acceptable.

Personally, I was feeling a bit more grown up and responsible, anyway – not that many would have noticed! I left Johnny Moore's place shortly before Bassett left Wimbledon. I bought my first ever house – a three-bedroomed semi in St Agnell's Lane, Hemel Hempstead. It was a joint venture with my mate Steve Robinson who split the £48,000 asking price with me on a joint mortgage and, before long, Kerry Coles – Colesy's dad – moved in as well. He'd been on his own for years and we were glad to have him. At least he kept a bit of order in the house.

As opposed to trouble in the camp. There was plenty of that, a couple of months into the new season, when I did my first newspaper interview that involved a fee. We were due to play Liverpool at our place on the Saturday and Steve Howard from the *Sun* linked up with me. The deal was that I would be paid £250 for the piece.

I'd talked to journalists before. The casual, quick chat after matches but nothing on this kind of scale. Bear in mind I was still a novice in many ways; I didn't even have thirty games under my belt by then so I was a bit green. It was all going nicely, nothing particularly controversial, how was I approaching the Liverpool game and what it had been like to play against them at Anfield the previous season. That kind of thing. But then came the question that taught me a lesson about dealing with the press. Steve suddenly hit me with a question about something that had happened at Anfield, something I didn't even know the other Wimbledon lads had been aware of, that I thought was known about only by me and Kenny Dalglish. It was a legitimate question, all right, but I'd no idea about the impact my answer was going to have. Goodbye to my £250 fee – and that was the least of my worries.

'What's this I heard about you and Dalglish?' Steve asked. 'Something about you telling him you'd rip his head off?'

I was staggered. I thought: 'Where the hell's he heard that?' It must have come from the Liverpool end, somehow, because I was certain our lads knew nothing of it. Being naive, I trotted out the details . . .

Dalglish had been playing up front for them at Anfield and when I went in to tackle him he caught me a treat – studs first, right on the shin. It really shocked me. I just looked up and said: 'What's your game?'

Then the verbals. 'Oh, shut it.' Dalglish said and began belittling Wimbledon. The man was supposed to be a legend. I couldn't believe what I was hearing. He was the one who had caught me with a late tackle, not the other way round. And yet he was threatening.

So I told Dalglish: 'Oh yeah? Well if I get near you once I'm going to rip your head off and crap in the hole.'

I had to come back with something and it was the first thing that entered my head. It was something I'd heard in a film, a smart reply in the heat of the moment. Nothing much happened in the rest of the game. I was sure nobody had heard our little set-to. Match over, I couldn't particularly remember the result, all part of the game and I thought no more about it.

Steve phoned me later on and warned there could be bother in the morning. He told me the reporters had no control over the way stories were displayed. The 'ripping off the ear' remark was being picked out in large letters. Of course it was. It had been toned down a little, having me threatening to remove the ear rather than the head and spitting in the hole, but it was still the story. I'd know that, now, but I hadn't a clue, then. I hardly slept a wink that night, I was almost in tears and my stomach was turning over and over.

By the time I arrived for training, next day, there was bedlam. Journalists and cameras everywhere. I was called in to see Bobby Gould and he went ballistic. All over an interview I thought was going to be about me and my football, hod carrying, scoring against Man United, playing at Anfield and Bassett having gone. I'd been getting along quite nicely and then, wallop! I'd dropped my guard and got caught with a beauty.

I have had some right run-ins with Steve over the years and he still giggles about that one. He's got skin thicker than an elephant's. Once Gouldy had calmed down a bit and mentioned leaving me out of the side that weekend, he tried to warn me about the press, about taking great care in what I said. He made it clear that I couldn't be doing things like this.

Don Howe doesn't get hot under the collar in situations like that. He said he understood how and why it had happened but it sounded like a stern policy statement when he said: 'You have to learn your lesson from an experience like this. We have to show people we're not tolerating it at this club. We have to show we're not a non-League side any more and that Wimbledon isn't run by a load of idiots either.'

Sam Hammam was there as well. He had said his piece to the management before I was summoned and I was later told that things were said such as 'He's got to go.' It was probably done to put the frighteners on me as much as anything but there was a genuine attempt to improve the image of the club. They wanted the Crazy Gang bit, the antics, the crack, but not if it went too far. Sam turned up at my house, later, with his 'look Jonesy, boy' fatherly advice that was to be repeated quite a few times. He was always the first to stick up for me because he understood me and argued that the good I did could not be undone by one incident – unless it was something completely indefensible.

Although I hadn't appreciated or expected the impact my own words would have, I was made to feel guilty about what I had done. I told myself, 'They are not going to stand for much more of this' but, at the age of twenty-two, I was still going to find it hard to keep control. By the end of the month, I'd faced my first charge of 'bringing the game into disrepute' and been fined £250. So the interview brought no reward at all – only a bloody nightmare and a load of old hassle.

CHAPTER 13

a whole new ball game

I had become John Fashanu's regular room-mate soon after Bobby Gould took over. Maybe he saw some significance in the fact that we had both endured difficult backgrounds, me having left a broken home to try to find my own way and Fash, of course, being a Doctor Barnardo's boy along with his elder brother, Justin. Mostly, though, I think the manager hoped that some of my passion and fanaticism for the game would rub off on him.

You see, Fash was never a great lover of football and Don Howe just couldn't understand that, even though he acknowledged that Fash would go out prepared to die for his team and his club on match days. The big lad was becoming deeply involved in his other interests, his TV work which was developing into an important part of his career. Howe found the likes of Dennis Wise and me, in fact most of the boys, easy to work with because we loved every second of our involvement every day. But the game wasn't everything to Fash as it was to us. They clashed on a number of occasions but it made little difference to the gap between them. Fash was the first one to have an agent, Eric Hall, who eventually represented quite a few of us. The problem remained for Howe. It was as if Fash was saying to him: 'You will never beat me.'

There was also friction between Fashanu and Lawrie Sanchez. A sort of power struggle grew between them. Sanchez hated the fact that Fash seemed able to come in and train on Friday, play on Saturday and that was that. He would sometimes be unwell on Monday, complaining of a painful back on Tuesday, then have a bit of treatment and a walk around until Friday when he'd join in the five-a-side. Sanchez, one of your actual intelligent footballers, used to seethe about it.

Looking back, I doubt whether they spoke more than half a dozen words to each other in five years. Even in Spain, where we'd go for occasional trips, the rift was obvious, Sanchez complaining: 'Same old faces doing their training. The blue-eyed boy only trains on Fridays.' For Fash's part, he stayed pretty quiet about the resentment. I roomed with him but never knew him sit and slag off Sanchez. It was just common knowledge that they didn't get on and it was expected that one day it would end in confrontation.

I don't suppose it helped when, on one notable occasion, Fash put all our drinks and other extras on the room of Sanchez and Dave Beasant. Normally the Wimbledon boys would accept that kind of thing, get on with it and retrieve their money later in some other way. But those two made a real fuss. Gouldy discovered what had happened but was shrewd enough not to let one incident drive a wedge. He didn't insist on any individual owning up. He spread the responsibility for room charges among the lot of us and had the money deducted from our wages.

We all looked forward to those trips abroad for a few days' training with the old sun on our backs. On one occasion Fash installed himself as official spokesman for the rest of us. He was going out with Marie Sol, a lovely Spanish girl, and insisted to the lads that he could speak the lingo. Until one of them made a request at breakfast: 'Ask the waiter for some Kellogg's Cornflakes.'

'Excuse, señor. Cornflakes por favor.' That was Fash's fluent Spanish, the subject of some fluent piss-taking. We learned about proper Spanish when Laurie Cunningham, the former West Brom and England international – later killed in a tragic road accident – joined us from Real Madrid. Cunningham at Wimbledon! It was like having a Derby winner among the workhorses.

Those breaks abroad did a lot to foster team spirit, that feeling of togetherness that was vital to Wimbledon's success. It was a trip to Spain that gave birth to the Ju-Ju Band. There had been an item in the newspaper about these thin little leather bands worn around the wrist. Fash loved everything to do with black culture as did Eric Young, Carlton Fairweather and me. Because I was always with Fash, and Wisey was generally with the two of us, we became part of the black brigade. About half of us started wearing the Ju-Ju bracelets in matches. We were known as the Ju-Ju Band and the more the team won the longer we kept them on. All the way through the rest of that incredible 1987-88 season.

Any excuse for a tear-up, as well. We reached a stage where, within the club, it turned into a case of the Ju-Ju Band against the rest. Five 'black' players, including Wisey and me, against five of the others. Fists flying, bodies piling in – Fash, me, Wisey, Brian Gayle, I remember, in a right tangle with Beasant, Corky, Terry Gibson and Andy Thorn.

It wasn't just a half-hearted bit of horseplay. It was heavy. Tempers snapped and the whole thing was heading so far out of hand that Don Howe was forced to jump in and stop it. I know it sounds bizarre but that flare-up was the first time since Harry Bassett left that we had seen a really fierce rekindling of the Wimbledon spirit. It went too far but, suddenly, we were buzzing.

We were in business and I began to think: 'We're going to do something amazing this season. We're going to get there.'

There was a young lad up on Tyneside who was making a lot of headlines and exciting all the good judges of the game. At twenty, Paul Gascoigne was on the brink of the full England side – commonly regarded not only as an outstanding midfield player but potentially one of the greatest footballers this country had ever produced. Yes, Gazza was really making his name.

The season had been going brilliantly for us even though I'd had a few run-ins with referees and totted up the bookings, here and there. In fact, I had missed our league game against Newcastle at St James' Park, which we won 2–1, but Gascoigne had completely torn Wimbledon apart. Something clearly had to be done about him for the match at Plough Lane and the fifth round FA Cup tie that was to follow, at Newcastle again, two weeks later.

The routine in training on a Thursday was for our reserves to play the part of our next opponents. So this time they pretended to be Newcastle. Don Howe took Andy Clement to one side and told him: 'Right, you're Gazza.' Andy was a neat player, technically sound and obviously the nearest to the real thing on our books. The practice match hadn't been going long when it was clear to everybody that Andy was ripping us to bits.

Don had told him to do exactly what he wanted. Go anywhere, pick up the ball, run at defenders and take them on. After about fifteen minutes Bobby Gould went spare. I thought he was about to explode, he was wound up so tight with a face that had gone from blazing red to purple. He stopped the match and marched straight across to me.

'I want you to play man to man. That means you follow him everywhere and make sure you mark him out of the game. You don't have to worry what's going on around you. There's an art in this.' He was talking at a fair old rate of knots, really excited as he explained the detail of the 'art' he had in mind.

'When he gets the ball, you don't have to tackle him every time. But when he's looking for a team mate to pass to you just get yourself in the way and prevent him doing it. The art of being a good player is to do it genteelly. Just be there.'

'All right,' I said and we started again. I wasn't really sure what to do and was only half doing what he wanted. Don stopped the action again and went berserk at me. I lost it. 'Bollocks to this. You can stick your man to man.'

'If you can't do it, you might as well sod off,' Don said to me.

'All right,' I said, fuming by now. 'Bollocks to you – I will piss off.' And I did. I stormed off. I had the greatest respect for Don Howe. A real football man from head to toe, a great background as an international-class player and a coach of the highest quality respected throughout the game. It was typical of him that he should come and talk to me later, despite my outburst at training. There was a job that needed doing for the good of the team.

'Look,' he said to me quietly, 'this boy Gascoigne is something special. For this one game we want you to forget about your usual role in the team and simply mark this player. I know you are capable of doing that job and it has to be done or, otherwise, we lose the game.' And that was it. OK, message received and just about understood. See you tomorrow.

It was nearly all set piece work on the Friday. Nothing over-strenuous or over-complicated and no mention of me having another practice run at shadowing Gazza. Don pulled me over again after training and said: 'Get yourself home, son, and put your feet up. Just think about it carefully, get it into your head that you simply have to mark the one man, Gascoigne. No 8.'

I'm not sure I had ever thought about anything quietly, as he put it. But I did some thinking and had pretty much sorted it out in my mind by the Saturday afternoon when I pulled up at the ground and saw a hell of a lot more cameras than usual outside. Gazza was coming! And Mirandinha, their Brazilian import. So there was going to be a bigger crowd than average at Plough Lane and those were the players the people had come to see.

I ran down the tunnel for the pre-match kick-about and Gazza must have gone out just ahead of me. He didn't know me from Adam – yet. No sooner was he in the middle than he was surrounded. The photographers couldn't hold back. They were all over him. It was the first time I'd ever seen that during the warm-up.

All of a sudden something went ping in my head. I thought to myself: 'I'm going to do him – genteelly!'

As I warmed up I watched him constantly. Doing little tricks, flicking the ball up, catching it on his thigh. The photographers kept following him about and I thought, 'Yeah, well I'm going to spoil your party, pal.' It was clear that this kid was special – double special. So I made up my mind that he was going nowhere. From the first whistle I was there. I eyeballed him and he eyeballed back. He started making silly runs to wind me up but I didn't need any winding, I was pumped up anyway – teeth gritted, veins standing out in my neck. We hadn't been playing more than five minutes when he turned and asked, sheepishly: 'Are you all right, mate?'

'I'm all right, pal. But you'd better get used to this 'cos there's another eighty-five minutes of it coming your way.'

'We'll see about that.' Gazza grinned. 'We'll see.' But every time he got the ball I was on him. Every time they tried to pass to him I jumped in front. Every time he tried to run past me he was shoving, using his body. Quite physical, but I could tell I was doing OK, I was preventing him from doing his stuff. There were a few verbals as there usually are in the course of the game, although more has been made of it over the years whenever I was involved. I told Gazza he was 'bloody fat' and he told me I was 'bloody thick'.

The referee, Mike Dimblebee, spoke to the pair of us occasionally, and gave me a couple of hasty lectures. But there was nothing vicious. The only time I was allowed to leave Gascoigne's side was to take my throw-in. But I had my doubts at the very first one. My instinct said, 'No, I'm not straying over there, daren't abandon him.' Even when I was signalled to go and take the throw I shouted across to Gazza: 'Fat boy! Wait there. I'll be back in a minute.'

I was flying. Other players heard it and there were a few chuckles but I don't think Gascoigne could believe his eyes and ears. I noticed him glance across to the Newcastle bench with a bemused expression on his face as much as to say: 'Where's this geezer coming from? Fruit and nut, him.' The longer the game went on, the more deflated he became. Instead of trying to get away, he began marking me, standing close up at set pieces. It was then that I remember what John Cornell, my first-ever manager, told me as a kid. Remember?

'If an opponent is marking you a bit tight, reach behind you and give him a little squeeze. He won't get that close to you next time.'

Gazza was becoming frantic, at least that was how I saw it because he was doing his utmost to get away from me, then get as tight as hell on me. He was trying to show that I wasn't bothering him but I knew I was. My chance came with a free kick to us. I was facing the ball, he was right behind me, so close that he whispered: 'Hey, shouldn't you be marking me?'

Just reach behind you . . . I moved my left arm backwards and grabbed his knackers. As he tried to pull away, startled and shocked, I held on and gave a little squeeze. Genteelly, of course. Gazza didn't squeal. Well, not a lot. I think he tried but no sound came out. He got on with the game after we 'parted' and I'm certain that, like me, he thought no more about our little get together. The game ended as a goalless draw and although there might have been a gesture or two out of place I felt happy that I'd done my job. Happier than Gazza at half time, apparently, because I was told later that he'd gone in shaking and in tears. He must have been frustrated.

I was still full of myself, still hyper, as I reached our dressing-room. All the lads were lifting me off the floor and saying, 'Brilliant job, Jonah.' The row with Gouldy and Don two days earlier was all forgotten when they marched into the room, looked at me and said: 'What a great job you've just done!'

A few minutes later I was heading for the bath when somebody shouted, 'Jonah, Jonah,' and a steward came through clutching a red rose: 'Mr Gascoigne would like you to accept this.' Excellent! Where the hell he'd found the rose I had no idea, but it was a fine gesture worthy of response. I immediately looked round for something to send in return. I spotted the toilet brush on its stand so I grabbed it and said: 'Take that back for him with my compliments.'

It was an amusing end to a bloody good day and I'm sure there were no hard feelings between Gazza and me. In fact, I know there weren't because we have met and had a laugh about it since. It had been a spur-of-the-moment thing, not done with malice.

What I didn't know was that the photographers had captured the moment. Something that happened in seconds was frozen for all time – and plastered all over the back pages. The reaction staggered me.

There had been all the publicity about the Dalglish issue. I was developing a reputation as something of a tough guy although I didn't like it. But after the photograph of me grabbing Gazza, which looks far more severe in a still shot than it was at the time, people started to say: 'This bloke is a brick short of a barrowload. This bloke's a complete hoodlum.' It wasn't so much that I was being portrayed as a hard man but more as some kind of monster who was out of control. A law unto himself. Not really a footballer, and anyway, he came off a building site so what do you expect? That kind of attitude. What killed me was that I'd done such a good job in marking a skilful player out of the game for the benefit of my own team. I didn't regret doing it because I knew I had pleased Gouldy and Don Howe and that they appreciated the contribution I'd made from the footballing point of view.

It was only because it was Gazza that the response, elsewhere, was so hostile. How could somebody like me dare to stop a talent such as his? There I was, being congratulated and slapped on the back in the dressing-room yet about to be hammered in the newspapers. Not just the Sundays either, but for the rest of that week. The subject was brought up for months.

That shot of me grabbing Gazza by the short-and-curlies was the second 'classic' confrontational football picture for many years – possibly of all time. The first was that wonderful moment when Dave

Mackay seized Billy Bremner by the scruff of his shirt, lifting him virtually off the ground as the little Leeds skipper protested his innocence, arms spread wide. I suppose it symbolised one of football's fiery characters receiving his come-uppance at the hands of a truly hard man of football, a legendary figure who stood no nonsense from anybody.

Honestly, I was shocked at the headlines that greeted the incident with Gascoigne. 'Psycho!' 'Nasty!' 'Crazy Vinnie!' 'X-Certificate!' 'The Ugly Face of Soccer'. Was it really that serious? Was it all that bad? Whenever I look at that picture, it gives me a giggle and I'm certain Gazza also sees the funny side.

Bobby Gould tried to put it all into perspective when he told the press after the game: 'I asked Vinnie to look after Gascoigne and he did. He did one hell of a job for the team, so let's not be making him out to be the villain.' Gouldy wasn't just being biased, because he did admit: 'Perhaps Vinnie did some silly things at times, as well. We'll discuss those – but he also showed a wonderful spirit out there.'

Gouldy did take me to task for what he regarded as unnecessary risks and provocation. The eyeballing antics, the gestures and some of the verbals. But he was equally keen to applaud and encourage the aspects of my football he regarded as valuable qualities within the side.

It was never my football that would make me famous, it was that picture with Gazza. I was carrying a stigma, I suppose. I also carried a few bookings that totted up into a one-match suspension that kept me out of a game at Anfield but, funnily enough, Merseyside saw my first match back. Well, seventy-two minutes because that was all I lasted at Goodison Park before referee Jim Rushton sent me packing. So no sooner had I returned from one ban than I was facing another. And out came the headlines once more. I'd made it easy for the press boys.

Again, there had been a bit of a build-up to the match. With my return from suspension and speculation that Peter Reid, Everton's and England's midfield player and a renowned right little hard nut, would be waiting for me. The usual newspaper talk and build-up to a game. It was the same when we played against Millwall and Terry Hurlock, another with a reputation for being able to 'look after himself' as they say. Lawrie Sanchez had taken me to one side and said: 'Vin, you've got to start being more careful out there.'

'What do you mean?' I looked blank.

'You are diving into tackles without thinking. It's reckless and you're going to get your legs broken.'

I was so naive. It was done out of an honest will to win. I just wanted the ball, I was 110 per cent committed to winning possession from every single tackle. And it developed into an inevitable routine. Tackle . . . booked . . . tackle . . . sent off. I became carried away by what I read in the papers, the build-up turned into sort of a wind-up with me, and I went into the Everton game believing Reidy was aiming to sort me out. It was the kind of mentality that said: 'If you want to come looking for me today then I'm ready.'

I think my first tackle on him came after a few seconds, maybe thirty. I involved myself in a bit of a skirmish with Adrian Heath because I didn't like the way he had challenged Sanchez. None of my business, I know, apart from the fact that Sanch was a team mate and whenever I wore the shirt I was ready to do anything for those who wore it alongside me.

Most of the game had a bad-tempered air about it that night. Four others, including Heath, were booked in a 2–2 draw but it was my sending off, *my only* dismissal of the season, that dominated the sports pages once more. The thug nailing a class player again. Reidy was never noted for his angelic approach to the game and we had come together a couple of times before, but yes, I went too far. We tangled going for the ball, a challenge described next morning as a 'shuddering clash'.

I was so wound up as usual that I went in again with Reidy on the floor. I should have held back and stayed on my feet but I dived in. My boot hit Peter's face and as he rolled over and my bum hit the ground that was the moment I thought, 'Oh no. Bloody hell, I've done it again.'

Bobby Gould didn't defend me on that occasion and nor should he have done. He said he was disappointed for me and for the club, and pointed out that my only suspension that season had been the disciplinary points totted up over a period. That was as kind as he could be. There was no question of trying to prove innocence. The case was open and shut. Reidy and me in a right tangle and I caught him. But there was no deliberate attempt to put the boot in. I've never done that and never would. No putting the boot into somebody who is down. I believe people who can do that are not worth a light. That isn't brave, it's cowardly.

Out came the critics, all the same, and I was

especially annoyed at being slaughtered by Ian St John, the former Liverpool and Scotland player. He gave me such a sorting out you'd have thought he had watched me from the day I started, but it transpired that this was the first time he had seen me play. If he could be so accurate in his judgement of somebody on the evidence of seventy-two minutes' play then he must be more of an expert than I believed. And he should certainly have been far more successful in his attempts to become a manager!

It wasn't all bad news, though. Something else had been ticking along for Wimbledon. A nice run of results from matches that featured the familiar cry from Fash: 'Put it in the mixer' as keeper Dave Beasant prepared to clear the ball by aiming to drop it deep in the opposition's half. In the mixer and everybody in after it, the hairs on your neck standing up with the excitement and your opponents thinking, 'We don't need this. Let's get it over and done with and out of here.' The mixer was stirring up a Cup run. It couldn't be that Wimbledon, scruffy, hard-up little, under-talented, over-physical Wimbledon with that hod carrier who grabs people by the crutch, could be on their way to Wembley. Could it?

CHAPTER 14

getting there . . .

Most of the publicity seemed to centre on Big Ron Atkinson prior to the start of our FA Cup adventure. The flamboyant, popular manager of West Brom was bringing his side to our place, but most experts preferred to wonder whether it was going to be Big Ron's year for the trophy. Nobody gave a second thought to Wimbledon's chances.

Well, we didn't need any help. We were expecting a tough old game against Albion but didn't get it. We trounced them 4–1. Ron and his players had a right old moan afterwards, accusing Dennis Wise of exaggerating the effects of a challenge on him by Bobby Williamson. It happened just after Wisey had smacked in a glory goal from thirty yards and although he was carried off he returned a few minutes later. But the real reason for Albion's defeat was down to Wimbledon's good play and our refusal to be distracted from the job in hand.

Even I managed to keep in mind Don Howe's insistence that we played more football and cut out the irresponsible behaviour. It would have been easy for me to crack that day because David Burrows spent just about the entire game trying to rattle me, pushing my temper to the limit. I was caught by his elbows and his boots but somehow managed to keep the red mists at bay. If only I had always been able to summon up such self-control!

In fact, at one stage I offered Burrows a word of two of advice. He had clattered into me with a couple of wild tackles and I said to him: 'Don't waste your time, son. If you don't calm down you'll get yourself sent off.' He looked at me a bit funny, but I just smiled and said: 'I'm not joking. I used to be like you last season, but I've learned!'

That victory gave us a good feeling. We deserved it and there was a fresh mood of optimism in the dressing-room as the whole place vibrated to the rock 'n' roll of Little Richard. There was a lot of yelling and singing and somebody, I think it was John Fashanu, began the chant: 'The Dons are on the march again.'

The ghetto-blaster rocked the room as we showered and changed, and celebrated a cracking win. It's funny how the memory plays tricks but I'm not dead certain when the blaster was first introduced. Fash and I bought it, pre-season, and after first letting it rip in the dressing-room before a game it just stuck and became a Wimbledon tradition. Full blast, heavy-beat disco music – anything that took our fancy. Paul Clark, a DJ pal of Fash's, made up all the tapes for us and although we first provided the blaster it eventually became a vital part of the kit and the club replaces them now.

I didn't have any gut feeling about the Cup after the West Brom game, but I started to wonder after we beat Mansfield, away, in the fourth round. Again, there had been the usual talk, beforehand, about what the little club was going to do to the First

Division opposition. Fash wasn't going to get a kick, that kind of thing. There were only 10,642 people at Field Mill on the day but at times it sounded like a crowd loads bigger and all of them screaming their anger at everything we tried to do. Maybe it was the fact that our defender, Terry Phelan, scored his only goal of the year, or maybe it was Dave Beasant's penalty save that secured our 2–1 victory, but something certainly set me thinking.

Where next? Where else but Newcastle. St James' Park for a massive Cup tie exactly two weeks after that match at Plough Lane. It was between the tie at Mansfield and the next round at Newcastle that we had that explosive tear-up in training that was so severe Don Howe moved in and somehow restored the peace. That was the time I felt the 'old Wimbledon' had joined forces with the new regime, that something special was beginning to develop. Yes, I began to have a feeling that all things were possible.

Unfortunately, I discovered it was impossible to make my peace with Newcastle before the Cup game. I had planned to fly up to Tyneside and have a photograph done: Gazza and me, all smiles and no ill feeling. Just the way it had been after the game at Plough Lane when the two of us walked off arm in arm accepting that what had gone on between us had been taken as good fun. I was keen to go up there on a day off but the idea was killed off by Newcastle's manager, Willie McFaul. Apparently he wanted none of it and somebody said he had threatened his players with fines if they joined in pre-match publicity.

Ah well, get up to Tyneside and get the job

done. Most people believed it was the end of Wimbledon in the Cup, anyway, even though the tie was billed as the big re-match between Paul Gascoigne and Vinnie Jones. Those Geordie fans can certainly make themselves heard especially when there are almost 30,000 of them up for the Cup. Their passion for that old silver pot is fiercer than anywhere else in the country. They really love the FA Cup at Newcastle and some opponents could be intimidated by their intensity.

We weren't. We loved every second of it and were lifted, inspired by the atmosphere of the place. Gascoigne was my responsibility, again, and I have to say, with all due modesty and without wishing to blow my own trumpet, I was ... well, 'magnificent' is the only word that springs to mind! No joking, Gazza didn't get much of a kick and I didn't need to grab him either above or below the waistband of his shorts. Final whistle, 3–1 to us and, bloody hell, we're in the quarter finals.

We had changed in portacabins that day and before the game a little boy wearing Wimbledon colours came to the temporary dressing-rooms and gave me a small bunch of white heather. He said it was for luck and after that result I made sure I took it home and kept it for the rest of the season.

Watford, next. My old club, the one that rejected me but still my club at heart. They'd already beaten us twice in the league but when you are on a roll negative thoughts don't enter your mind. This was the Cup so this would be different. If you can win at Newcastle you can sort out Watford at home. Yeah, even though they scored first and we had Brian Gayle sent off before the break. Biffo the Bear as we called him – the man with the biggest willy in the world – was to pay a high price for that dismissal. Bobby Gould substituted defender Eric Young for striker Alan Cork and it turned out to be a master-stroke. Young had equalised four minutes into the second half and Fash put us into the semi finals.

We had to beat Luton first time around, because I would have missed any replay – suspended for that dust-up with Peter Reid at Goodison the week before. So there were only 25,963 at White Hart Lane – the lowest crowd for a semi – but who cared? It looked and sounded like 100,000 to us. Eric Young had stayed in the side, much to Biffo's disap-pointment, and it was his job to look after Luton's Mick Harford, a real tough nut of a centre forward, a well-respected pro who had scored goals for all his previous clubs and would keep scoring them for a lot more clubs to come!

But what do you know, Harford knocks a goal in and we're on the back foot until we get a penalty. Normal procedure here is that Fash walks up, places the ball, takes a couple of steps and bumps it into the corner, cool as you like. Imagine what is going through our heads, this time. I'm thinking: 'Forget the normal routine, Fash – just smash the bleedin' thing. Smash it straight in.'

So he places it, a couple of steps and dinks it, calm as you like. Nothing cool about our reaction, though. We were screaming at one another: 'Come on, we can make Wembley! The bloody FA Cup final! *Come on*!' I noticed the look on the Luton players' faces as we screeched at each other. It was a look that said: 'This lot are going to go on and win.' And we did, with a goal from Wisey that kind of cannoned in off him as he went in for a tackle. I've never even bothered asking whether he meant it.

There is no sensation to compare with how you feel when the referee blows the final whistle that confirms you're going to Wembley. And I know there's nothing worse than the whistle that tells you you're not – as happened to me and Wimbledon in 1997. I just threw my shirt into the crowd at White Hart Lane the rest is a blur of total happiness. Wimbledon through to the FA Cup final. The nobodies had made it and proved that if you want it enough, love it enough, work at it and believe in it enough you really can get there.

I drove home with Dennis Wise or at least to his dad's pub, The Bridport Arms in Notting Hill. We had a great drink. Us two at Wembley. Cor, we were millionaires now, weren't we? Wimbledon in the final, the telly on the coach and all the interviews, all the attention. The more we drank, the more exciting it all became. Like two kids in Aladdin's Cave. Of course we were millionaires and we both decided we were going to buy brand new BMWs – black and with a soft top. No, that didn't materialise because eventually you come down to earth and you're not going to be millionaires just then, after all, but it was a lovely vision while it lasted.

But there were still games to play, of course, before the big day, and a warning from Bobby Gould to Andy Thorn and me before one of them that if we got booked today, we'd miss the final. I can't remember who we played on that occasion but I can still see us in our last league game before Wembley – Manchester United at a muddy Old Trafford with everybody in our dressing-room saying the same thing to themselves: 'I'm not going to get injured today.' It began like a pre-season friendly. United had nothing much to play for and we were taking it nice and easy until Terry Gibson changed everything by scoring for us. I only had two words for him: 'You prat.'

United got the hump and with players of the calibre of Bryan Robson, Norman Whiteside and Remi Moses they were more than capable of kicking lumps off us. And for a while they did. It had all been lovely at 0–0 but suddenly it was a different game altogether. They stuck two goals past us but it didn't seem to matter and I attempted to take the mickey out of Robbo a bit by asking him: 'OK, but what will you be doing next Saturday?'

To which Whiteside reminded me: 'And you might not be going to Wembley either. There's ten more minutes of this game, yet.'

We played those last ten minutes on our tiptoes, daintily steering clear of any trouble and any threat of injury. It was the only time we have played like that in our lives. But the one or two of us who thought the week leading up to the final was going to be nice and easy couldn't have been more wrong. The squad was told we were going to prepare properly for this and we were made to train as hard as at any time all season.

We were given a hell of a boost with word from the Liverpool camp after their last game. Garry Gillespie and Nigel Spackman had gone up for a ball and cracked their heads together. They needed stitches and it became the talk of the Wimbledon boys all week. We trained, telling ourselves at every opportunity: 'They're not going to want to head it at

Wembley. They're not going to fancy too much of Fash. There's no way they will be 100 per cent.' Even wearing fancy headbands!

The preparation was a credit to Don Howe and his complete knowledge of the game. Wisey would be employed on the right instead of the left side of the field and held deeper to counteract the threat of John Barnes. Although we frowned and wondered at first there was such a tone of confidence in Don's voice that real belief began to develop and to spread.

Each player was told what was expected of him. In my case it was straightforward: I had to win the battle with Steve McMahon. All week the pages were full of what Liverpool were going to do, how they would dominate midfield, how Barnes would run riot and why Wimbledon would be beaten, possibly as heavily as any side in the history of the FA Cup final. Oh really? The thought of defeat never entered our heads. We planned things down to the last detail and I clearly remember watching goalkeeper Dave Beasant thumbing through his little book on the game's penalty takers and which side they tended to hit the ball. Nothing was left to chance.

We even trained twice on the Friday. We didn't finish practising set plays and things until after six o'clock on the evening before the final and then it was off to the Cannizaro House, the swish hotel on Wimbledon Common. The laughs started out on the patio when Bobby Gould announced he had a little gift for all of us. His mum had knitted us each a doll: Wimbledon colours, all blue and yellow and wearing black football boots. I took mine, complete with the No 4 on the back and we all collapsed when it came to the No 9. She had knitted Fash's doll in black. Brilliant!

It wasn't all laughs on the eve of the big day, though. Fash and I were setting out for a walk after dinner when we were confronted at the bottom of the stairs by a bloke we sensed was a press man even before he spoke.

'What are you up to, mate?' I asked.

'I'd like a word with Fash,' he said. 'We've had a tip-off that you're messing around with this woman.'

This woman, as he put it, had apparently done some story with the *News of the World* for the Sunday after the final. 'Don't know what you're talking about,' Fash told him. And I said, 'You'd better get your arse out of here' before we called our agent, Eric Hall, and Gouldy to sort it out. Fash and I went back upstairs. Bear in mind this is a real classy hotel, no cheap furnishings, no plywood or chipboard. And this was the first time I'd ever seen John Fashanu lose his cool.

I was trying to unlock the door to our room, a really solid door, probably oak, when all of a sudden Fash's eyes went and he let loose a proper right-hander. It left dent marks in the surface of the door and the impact drove his knuckles into his hand. It came up like a balloon and he thought he'd bust it. Panic! I phoned down for the physio, Steve Allen, who was sure there was no break but the damaged hand had to be bandaged, and we had to report to the manager downstairs.

'Listen,' Gould told us, 'this is going to be the biggest day of your lives. Nothing must distract you. Forget the rubbish that's just gone on, it's all part of life and you'll have to deal with these kind of things from time to time. Let's just concentrate on what we're here for.' Don Howe didn't get involved. There was no way he would allow anything to upset his apple cart. The ultimate professional with only football, football on his mind and absolutely nothing was allowed to intrude.

Gouldy was about to move off but then stopped, turned to Fash and said: 'Right, here's a few quid, get all the boys together for a few jars down the road.'

It was a good move because rumours had swept through the hotel and the players were concerned and beginning to wonder what had gone off. It was about eight o'clock and we all joined ranks and walked to The Dog and Fox in Wimbledon. Some had a beer, some had a shandy and, as usual, Fash had a soft drink because he'd never drunk alcohol in his life. There was one absentee as I remember – Terry Gibson. He'd just been sponsored and was walking up and down along the hotel landing in his shorts, frantically trying to break in his new pair of boots. What some of us are prepared to do for a few hundred quid!

Gouldy's bit of simple psychology worked a treat because the crack soon started in the pub and the worry turned to laughter again. 'Hope she's a welldy?' somebody shouted to Fash – a playful wish that 'this woman', whoever she was or if she existed, had been a Page 3 type, well-endowed. 'If she's ugly, Fash, your street cred will be down the drain.' He took it in that lovely way of his when he knows the crack's on him. He's serious and dry but a little smirk appears on his face and he gives a little nod of approval.

'Put a bit of vodka in Fash's lime and lemonade,' I said to Corky. No sooner requested than delivered. At the double! The joking continued, the incident with the journalist was forgotten but the moment Fash took a sip from his glass, he knew. 'Jonesy? What have they done to my drink?' We all cracked up and that was it, back to the hotel where Gouldy greeted us at the door: 'Everything all right, lads?'

'Yeah, boss, everything's fine, couldn't be better.' You could see the relief on his face. We were back on track and it was typical Wimbledon. Somebody had tried to throw a spanner in the works, a touch of adversity, and once more we'd used it to our advantage. Us against the rest. We were bonded, anyway, but that night glued us together. Even Lawrie Sanchez spoke to Fash more than ever before. Their differences were put to one side as he helped to support a team mate.

Sanch . . . the man we called Sargeant Bilko because of the flying jacket he loved to wear. The one who startled all of us on a winter trip abroad by announcing: 'Right, I'll prove I'm a member of the Crazy Gang.' And promptly charged across the hotel foyer, dived headlong at a Christmas tree, rugby tackled it and wrestled it to the ground and ran off through the main entrance with it – all dressed up with decorations and lights. We were all asked to leave but Sanchez had made sure of his membership. Like the rest of us, the night before Wembley, he did his bit to put Fashanu's mind at rest.

Tony Stenson, the *Mirror* man who first dubbed us the Crazy Gang, phoned our room to wish us all the best and typically asked: 'What are you doing?' I said: 'Not a lot. Come up and see us and bring a couple of beers.' A couple to Sten-gun meant several. He brought them on a tray. It must have been after 10pm and we probably had no more than a couple of mouthfuls. It was just nice to see a friendly face and to hear him telling Fash not to worry about the woman story and that it was probably all a load of bollocks, anyway. And he had a word of advice: 'Whether it's in the paper or not on Sunday, just get your girlfriend and shoot off to France. Take her to Paris for the weekend and then she won't even see the papers.' As it turned out, there was a front-page piece on the Sunday, some allegation of an affair, but it was thankfully nothing that caused too much upheaval for Fash and it soon blew over.

Tony stayed only about half an hour or so. We were quite tired so we settled down to prepare for the biggest day of our lives. I had been thinking, all week: 'I'm not going to believe all this until I'm actually there at Wembley.'

I lay there, unable to drop off, my mind racing. All those friends and relatives were going to be there. My nan was going to the first game of her life, all my uncles – dad's five brothers – dressed up in yellow and blue top-hat and tails, mum with her new husband and dad with his new wife. And I was flying Ann, besotted by her interest in horses, home from Italy where she had been working at a riding stables and returned speaking fluent Italian. And all the boys from Bedmond and the rest of Hertfordshire where I had so many friends. More than a hundred people of mine, in all – Christ, I hoped I wouldn't let them down.

Granddad. I lay there at peace with the world.

Everything was together. My family and friends all united and gathering for an event that was to be the highlight of the Vinnie Jones football career which had seemed so unlikely such a short time ago. All the troubles that had affected my life seemed to have settled. Fash had nodded off and the room seemed to go all tranquil. Until I thought of a cup final I played with Bedmond as a kid. I needed a word with granddad.

I had got carried away in that game because everything had been going so well, but I made the mistake of trying to dribble the ball out of trouble and a geezer nicked it from me, the other lot scored the only goal of the game and we lost. I didn't want anything like that to happen to me at Wembley.

I didn't ask granddad for a winner's medal. There were three things going through my mind: I didn't want to cock it up. I didn't want to get buried by Steve McMahon, allowing him to be governor for the day. And, like any kid who dreamed of Wembley, I'd have given anything to score a goal.

I recalled the day I watched Watford in a Cup tie, a big defender took a free kick and his shot was still rising as it flew over my head halfway up the terraces. I thought about that when I spoke quietly to granddad: 'Please don't let me be the one to make a crucial mistake. Please don't let Steve McMahon do me. And if there's any chance of me scoring, granddad . . .'

I fell asleep on the Friday night thinking about that Watford free kick, ages ago, only this time it was me hitting the thirty-yarder at Wembley, against Liverpool. And the ball flew under the bar instead of over it. I dropped off without any complete assurance from granddad. It's not like that when I talk to him, there is nothing guaranteed. But I did drift off to sleep with the feeling that we were all going to be all right.

final reckoning

I was awake and out of bed at 6.30 am. Well, a player shouldn't miss a moment of FA Cup final day. Fash was still sound asleep and I knew there was no waking him. It always cracked me up, looking across at his bed, blankets pulled right up and the only thing showing was this little brown nose. He loved his sleep and always kept the curtains drawn tight until we were leaving to catch the coach. If ever I did wake him he'd go barmy and tell me to get out of the room.

I always say it was the butterflies that woke me so early that morning. It was as if they had flitted in through the window at first light, hundreds of them, and entered my body. Enough of them to fill me from head to toe. The moment I woke, the palms of my hands began to sweat. They were to stay like that all the way through – throughout the build-up, the match, the entire day and through the following day as well. However much I tried, I couldn't keep them dry.

Once washed and shaved, I gave Dennis Wise a ring. It was only about 6.50 and I expected a drowsy voice to answer but, just the opposite, it was as chirpy as a cricket as he said: 'Hello, Jonah – all right, son. What's happening, then?'

'You up?'

'Up? I've been up for half an hour. So, what we doing?'

'Fash is fast out. Any of the boys about?'

'No, I don't think so. Haven't heard from anybody.'

'Come on then,' I said. 'I'll meet you downstairs.'

Wisey, like me, was hyperactive. We needed something to do, anything to occupy us for a while, we were so excited. A walk round the hotel gardens served its purpose but on the way back I said to him: 'I want to get my hair cut. I'm going to have the old short back and sides.'

'Right,' Wisey giggled, 'lovely. That's what we'll do, then.' And we took his car and drove into Wimbledon village, never pausing to think about the time. At 7.30 in the morning, there was nowhere open. 'Right, we'll go back to the hotel, have breakfast and then get our hair cut.' Before I became a professional player I always thought footballers should have a haircut and look smart on match days.

We were full of beans, even before breakfast, and Bobby Gould must have read the warning signs because he insisted that we joined him for another walk around the grounds and told the pair of us: 'Now, you two have got to drop down a gear. You must calm down or you're going to be burnt out before the match even starts. I know you're on a high and you're flying but you have to come down to earth.'

We listened and agreed and said, 'Yeah, yeah, OK, Bob' but we were still determined to go for that haircut after breakfasting on fruit, cereal, yoghurt and plenty of juice. We read the papers and, again, they were full of what Liverpool were going to do to us. The trend seemed to be 'Imagine some of those great players who never won a Cup final medal and perish the thought of Vinnie Jones getting one. For the sake of football, Wimbledon mustn't win.' Nothing new there, then!

At the first chance, as soon as Gouldy turned his back, Wisey and I dropped the shoulder. We were out of there, into the car and cruising through Wimbledon High Street. It was still quiet, probably around nine o'clock, but we noticed a lady walking alone wearing a Wimbledon scarf. We slowed alongside her, wound down the window and yelled: 'Wayhey, go on you Dons!'

Bloody hell, it was June Whitfield, then of *Terry and June* fame. I didn't know it at the time but she was president of the Wimbledon supporters' club. She wandered over. 'All right, boys?' We chatted for a while, asked her to give Terry all our best and she smiled her nice smile and said: 'Good luck to you and the team. I'll be there this afternoon.'

And we shot off, found a little Italian barber's and steamed in. The bloke was startled, saying: 'You're early, lads. First ones of the day.' Then he looked gobsmacked as he said: 'You're not . . .?'

'Yeah, just a quick trim for the pair of us,' I said.

'You're not . . .?' he repeated at least twice and I think he actually pinched himself. On a sudden impulse I asked him if he could do something different. He cut my hair down to a point at the nape of the neck and then shaved up both sides to meet the longer stuff – almost like a Mohican. My old man never let me live it down!

Once out of the barber's, Wisey went up the road to a sweet shop and spent about a tenner on a huge bag of pick-and-mix but it was the nearby florists that set me thinking. I had noticed June Whitfield was wearing a little spray of flowers in her lapel: Wimbledon's colours.

'What about if you and me buy a spray each,' I said to Wisey. 'Blue and yellow and we walk out with them behind our backs and hand them to Princess Diana when the teams are presented to her before the match?'

'Yeah,' he agreed, with that characteristic, impish grin of his. 'Let's have some of that. Brilliant.' So we bought about half a dozen bunches just in case some of the other lads fancied joining the plan.

Back at the hotel, the preliminaries had started. You could sense the atmosphere, the feeling of excitement and anticipation as soon as you walked in. It was electric – the directors and club officials, families, relatives, all sorts of people were out on the patio, every one of them wearing a smile as if to say they were going to enjoy every single second of the day, win, lose or draw.

We roused Fash and brought him down to join the rest, all looking forward to what was to come in the afternoon and the promise of the big party in a marquee on the Plough Lane pitch that night to mark our little bit of history before all returning to our own rooms at the hotel. We were buzzing as we boarded the coach. Chris Lewis, the BBC man with the film crew, was a big Wimbledon fan and a mate of Harry Bassett's anyway, and we'd had some great cracks with him already. He was lapping it up.

On the coach, the customary card school got

underway and we kept glancing at the television screen showing Liverpool leaving their hotel, the Hilton at Watford, I think, and Wisey shouted: 'Look at them – they don't fancy it, lads!' In all honesty, although the TV picture kept breaking up, their players came out of the hotel looking as if they were on their way to a funeral. We saw them clearly as our coach stopped at traffic lights and the picture settled. There was word, sometime after the final, that the Liverpool lads had talked of being bored. I suppose it was a case of having been there before, seen it, done it. And it was written all over their faces.

Everybody decided Wisey was right. Even Bobby Gould agreed that they didn't fancy it. And when Don Howe joined in, it gave us licence to shout it even more because he was obviously enjoying it and that, to us, offered a kind of official approval. So the card school was going strong, the TV camera was moving up and down the coach, we were all resplendent in our new suits – some of us wearing sprays of yellow and blue flowers – when the voice of the agent chipped in with another reminder that we were on our way to Wembley.

'You've got to drink this drink because there's money in it for you,' Eric Hall announced. So down went the Lucozade and we all wore baseball caps, advertising the fact.

Dennis Wise is the worst ever loser I've ever met. At anything. So he was effing and blinding his way through three-card brag, moaning the whole time. In complete contrast to me because I grinned like a Cheshire Cat from the minute I woke up until the minute I went to bed at whatever time of the early hours the next day. Mind you, I also happened to be winning all the dough in the card school – eighty quid on one hand, a fair amount of money, then.

Harry Bassett would never allow us to play for money on the way to a game because of the resentment and bad feeling it could cause. He only okayed it on the way back. But this was the FA Cup final. Nothing could spoil this day for Wimbledon and the fact that Wisey was getting caned made the banter even better. Everybody, even the worst loser on earth, was in a brilliant mood. The boys with no chance were definitely together.

That togetherness was the ace up our sleeve. We had the characters but, most vitally of all, we had the spirit. We knew what was expected of every single one of us when three o'clock came and we were conscious of the hard work we'd put in all week and we had total belief in Don Howe and his preparations.

'This is how you beat Liverpool,' he had told us and drummed it into us for days. You don't want boring with tactical detail, and neither do I, but it was basically about preventing John Barnes particularly and Steve McMahon winning the encounter in midfield. If those two could be restricted enough, Liverpool would not be able to function properly. That was the plan, anyway, and we were at the stage where we believed everything Don told us.

The card school ended as we approached the stadium and the buzz of Wembley Way. We looked out from the coach and the only colour we could see was red. Liverpool supporters everywhere, shouting and clapping as we threaded our way through:

'Good old Wimbledon,' the scousers yelled. It was all good humoured but you knew they regarded us as nothing more than whipping-boys.

Our spirits were probably too high, if that's possible. Gouldy walked up and down as we filed off the coach, frantically trying to calm us down as if to say: 'Keep the lid on it, lads. Keep some of it bottled up until you get out there.' Something did stop us in our tracks a bit. We were all a little bit miffed at being given the away dressing-room. But only until we walked into the place – all tiled, a little bar in the corner with a geezer standing behind the Lucozade and the bottles of water. On the left was what looked like a small swimming pool – a massive bath, really deep – and a little further on, the showers and the medical room. I stood and looked around the place and thought: 'This is out of this world. This is *Wembley.*'

I made up my mind that, as it was likely to be the first and last time I ever played there, I would remember it. I could never understand all those players who had been involved in Cup finals down the years who shared the regret that it had all passed so quickly and they could hardly recall a thing. This was to be the biggest day in my footballing life and to forget any part of it would be a crime.

We virtually knew what the line-up would be, but we didn't know the subs although I had joked with John Scales, who had missed the last three games: 'Lucky bugger. It's a lovely day so you won't be needing an overcoat sitting in the stand.' Bobby Gould told us to sit down and I was next to Bryan Gayle, a Wimbledon man through and through, a product of the youth teams and a first-team regular until he found it difficult to regain a place after his sending off at Watford in the sixth round. Eric Young had got in and done well although Gayle was used while one or two players were rested prior to the final.

I felt certain Scalesy would be left out altogether. I thought this was a day for Wimbledon and its traditions because I knew Gouldy was a passionate and emotional man but he was a hard man that day. Gayle and I were just chatting and then we heard the names of the substitutes: Laurie Cunningham, which was a big shock because, although he had done a good job since his arrival, he was a latecomer, and John Scales.

You could have heard a pin drop in that dressing-room. I thought my old man had more chance of being on the bench than him. Even in the semi-final Gayle had come on as a sub. Even in the Wembley programme, Gayle and Cunningham were the subs. I couldn't fathom it. Scalesy had joined us from Bristol Rovers, Gouldy's old club. He was intelligent and a nice man with a lot of charisma. He was a dedicated professional and at that moment it was confirmed that he was the manager's blue-eyed boy.

There was a deathly silence and nobody could bring themselves to even look at Brian Gayle. I'm sure it lasted only a matter of seconds but it seemed like an age before somebody broke the ice in that room by saying: 'Right, come on, let's get out on that pitch.' I reached across, put my hand on Gayle's knee, gripped it hard and gave him a kiss. To this day I don't know how he dealt with that feeling of rejection. I said to John Fashanu: 'I've a good mind to fuck off straight through that door and out of the stadium. Either that or fly at Gouldy.' A lot of the other lads were hurt on Gayle's behalf as well. The entire atmosphere within the Wimbledon team, the confidence and optimism, could have been ruined just by Gould's decision about the substitutes. Wimbledon could have lost any hope of Cup glory right there and then in their own dressing-room. It was thanks to Brian Gayle and his response that we remained together. He was a lovely fella, a great pro and I got on with him wonderfully. He just looked up and said: 'Thanks, lads, but come on, this is Wimbledon in the FA Cup final!'

I know Bobby Gould respected Fash and me because of the hard times we survived as youngsters. His own father was blind so he needed no telling about adversities. I don't know whether he couldn't make up his mind about the substitutes and just decided on the way to Wembley, but he should have taken Brian Gayle to one side and explained why he was not being included. Or perhaps he realised that if he'd told him any earlier he could have really upset the apple cart.

Whatever, the mood was good again as we strolled out to the pitch. We were out ahead of Liverpool and it was a terrific feeling – no sense of pressure apart from the still sweaty palms. Fash and I strolled together, and I spotted my Uncle Colin in his top-hat and tails, and then my mum and the rest of the family. We saw Fash's brother Philip and Marie Sol so we had a wave with them – Fash wearing the Fash grin, sauntering with his hands in his pockets and constantly giving that little nod as much as to say: 'Oh yes, I do like this.'

Wembley wasn't full at that stage but it was eighty per cent red. There was one small pocket of blue and yellow, singing and waving banners 'Vinnie Bites Your Legs' and 'Corky's Got No Hair – We Don't Care'. That little walkabout did calm us down and on the way back towards the tunnel Fash said quietly: 'This is a bit of us, Jonesy. This . . . is . . . a . . . bit . . . of *us*, son.' The Liverpool players were out by then and a couple of our lads had a chat with one or two. I wanted to get ready.

The buzz was back in the dressing-room and I can remember, vividly, taking off my suit and shirt and hanging it on the peg and thinking: 'The next time I put this lot on I'll have played in the 1988 FA Cup final.' The butterflies were back but they felt more like eagles and they were right up to the back of my throat. I felt myself tensing up as Don Howe was giving last-minute instructions. It was beginning to turn into a matter of life and death. There was one main thought whirling in my head and, after talking to the other players since, it preoccupied them as well: we couldn't get done by five or six goals. We mustn't lose heavily. Hand on heart, we just wanted to come out of that final with a bit of respect. The dread of getting beaten 6–0 frightened us and I think it was the fright that got us through.

The buzzer sounded, time to go. The butterflies gave another lurch. The players stood and Lawrie Sanchez, usually the calmest of individuals prior to a game, started waving his fists and yelling: 'Come on, let's do it. Let's do it together.' We went into a big huddle and you could feel the belief passing between us, the belief that as long as we stood together we could overcome anything, anyone. Don busied himself walking among us and around us: 'Do this, do that. Twenty minutes we work our socks off . . . shut them down, don't allow them to play the way they want. Don't let them dictate. Send them back at half time needing to reshuffle it all.'

As I stepped into that tunnel I felt twice my normal size. My arms and legs felt massive. I knew I could run for a week, never mind an hour and a half. We all knew our preparation had been perfect and that we had peaked at exactly the right time. The Liverpool players were in the tunnel first. They had come out quietly but we came out roaring! Literally roaring. The Liverpool boys looked completely shocked and the stewards stepped back out of our way.

'This is ours today!' one of us yelled. 'Big-time Charlies,' I shouted across at their lot. 'You're going to get it out there.' Kenny Dalglish tried to take the sting out of it all by urging his players not to listen to us. There was no comeback from them, just a sort of nervous half laugh. Spackman and Gillespie were wearing ridiculous headbands and they took some terrible stick: 'Look at them, they daren't head it this afternoon. No chance. This is our day, boys.' The more it went on the more pumped up we became and it was as if we were actually growing physically on that slow march to the halfway line while Liverpool shrank further and further into their shells.

There is nothing to match the sensation that hits you when you walk from the mouth of that tunnel. The first sight is like a horseshoe made up of tens of thousands of faces amid dazzling colour. All those faces, for some reason they all seemed to be white faces standing out, peering among the flags. I looked around and it was a mass of red and white like a wall from the Royal Box right round to the other. Bloody hell! But then the blue and yellow Wimbledon support brought together like never before, bless their hearts. 'Not bad, this.' I thought. 'Not bad at all.'

We had left our flowers for Di in the dressing-room. Don had told us that it was a nice gesture but not the right thing to do, not being properly focused and professional. We weren't sure but we decided, reluctantly, to leave it. And I regret it to this day. As the Princess came along our line I was hoping she would stop and talk to me, though it was odds-on she would talk to Fash, but I think she ended up chatting to Terry Gibson. She just said 'Hello' to me and shook hands and that was it.

As the anthem played we stared straight at the Liverpool players and they looked away uncomfortably. It wasn't pre-planned but a spontaneous thing. They were singing the anthem and looking anywhere but straight into our eyes.

I can't even tell you who kicked off. The first thing that springs to mind was Andy Thorn getting tied up with Peter Beardsley, the referee blowing his whistle but Beardsley carrying on and putting the ball in the net. He probably heard the whistle, anyway, but it was an early scare.

John Barnes had a scoring chance and I knew I had to get there to stop him. I went in shoulder to shoulder, bosh – sheer strength that swept the ball away and barged Barnesy as well. He looked at me as if to say: 'You want it that much, do you?'

For twenty minutes we worked our socks off, didn't let them win the midfield, shut them down, didn't let them play the way they wanted. Don Howe's words were going over and over in my mind and then Steve McMahon had the ball. I always had

...he middle of singing ...party piece, 'Woolly ...ly', with my 'Woolly ...ly' hat on!

...ssie, my Jack Russell ...rier, who proved herself ...fe-saver.

(ABOVE) All smiles as
Wimbledon go through to the
semis of the FA Cup in 1997 –
sadly, there would be no repeat
of 1988. (RIGHT) In action
pre-season in July 1998 for
Queens Park Rangers. Things did
not work out as I would have
hoped (both *Action Images*).

this impression of McMahon in possession – receiving the ball, opening up and switching the play. As he shaped to receive it, I started running at him knowing exactly what I was going to do, picking up pace and saying to myself that I'd never get a better chance. I knew he wanted to stamp his authority on me and rattle me as quickly as he could.

I made up my mind to gamble that he would let the ball come across him and open out with it on the inside of his foot. If he'd just stopped that ball I would probably have been sent off. If he'd just touched it backwards, I'd have buried him. I gambled on meeting him head on with a proper solid tackle on the ball. It turned out just like reading a book. As I arrived he opened up, lovely, and my momentum took me in – wallop! I met the ball and saw his legs go up in the air. I was on the ground looking up at him as he was coming down on his back.

Some pro, Steve McMahon. Even on the way down, he was thinking, and as he landed he caught me with his elbow underneath my left eye. It split and bled and the mark still shows sometimes. My lifelong reminder of a close encounter on the sacred turf!

As I leapt to my feet all our players were shouting: 'Come on, Jonah, get in there.' I had won that tackle but, for some reason, conceded a free kick! But the point had been made because that incident threw Liverpool off their game. After that, they had one eye on the ball and the other on our players every time we went in for a tackle.

Their game plan was to play us off the park but they didn't rise to the physical challenge. I had set the precedent. That was how we were going to play it, making every ball a matter of life or death, and the feeling went right through the team.

Suddenly there was bedlam. Bedlam and disbelief. A free to us from wide of the box and I stood on the edge in case the ball wasn't cleared. Alan Cork made his run, Lawrie Sanchez stood his ground and got in a header. I saw Bruce Grobbelaar transfixed. It was as if he had just been set in stone. There was nothing he could do but look behind him and down. I looked down to where he was looking and the ball was behind him in the net and the roar battered the eardrums. A goal, a bleedin' goal! We had scored! Wimbledon had scored at Wembley. There had never been any talk of us scoring and we were as shocked as anybody in the crowd. But what a wonderful, fantastic, unforgettable feeling it was.

Half time brought panic stations because we were sure the only thing that could beat us would be ourselves running out of steam. Don appeared and told us: 'Get your shirts off and wrap yourselves in these.' He had filled the bath with cold water and soaked a load of towels. Big towels, bloody freezing, but we duly obliged. It was to cool the blood on a steaming hot day but it would have taken more than wet towels to properly reduce the temperature of the Wimbledon team that day.

Especially when referee Brian Hill gave Liverpool that penalty in the second half. We couldn't believe it – just as, I'm sure, Liverpool's players couldn't believe the 'chalking off' of Peter Beardsley's 'goal' early doors. We knew Dave Beasant had done his homework on John Aldridge's penalty kicks. I stood there praying that Beas would go the way he knew, and that

Aldridge would take his normal bloody pen, because if he did it would be a save. I stood a yard or so outside the box as Aldridge ran in because I wanted to be first there in case of a rebound. He hit it the way our keeper thought he would and Dave Beasant made history with the dive that brought the first ever penalty save in an FA Cup final. I was first to him and grabbed and shook him but he was so fired up and instantly preparing to defend the corner.

Everything became frantic. Liverpool sent on Craig Johnston, the Aussie, a right busy bugger and the last person you need against you in those circumstances. Then Jan Molby came on and had a shot that whipped just over our crossbar. We were hanging on, Cunningham came on for Corky to do his little bits and pieces and keep the ball, then John Scales was off the bench as well. I called to him because he was standing in front of me; 'Scalesy! What are you doing? Where are you playing?' He hung his hands by his sides, frowned and said: 'Don't know. He said something like, "just roar about up front".' But time was running out, and we held on to our 1–0 lead.

The final whistle in a Cup final you have won is the most beautiful single sound imaginable. Fash and I were ecstatic. We all were. Andy Thorn jumped on Beasant's back, Gouldy came running on and leapt into my arms and Don was still being Don 'Mr Cool'. The injured lads and those who hadn't played at all joined us and it was great that Brian Gayle came out too, and that all the players made a big fuss of him.

We clapped the Liverpool team as they went up for their losers' medals and Gouldy warned us: 'Now you be gentlemen and do the right things.' Up went Beasant, with Wisey behind him and the rest of us followed. You grab a hat, a scarf, and shake as many hands as possible up those steps. A medal from Princess Di and a kiss from Sam Hammam and, with no disrespect to either, you wished it had been the other way round!

Back on the side of the pitch I thought about all the stick I had taken over the time leading up to that day. I wanted to locate the press and give them a wave!

The Liverpool players were shaking our hands but when I made my way towards McMahon he turned to walk off. Kenny Dalglish grabbed him by the arm and told him: 'Oi, shake his hand.' He shook it, but he didn't look at me. Then there were photographs, the lap of honour, the elation and the joy that you've never known before. And, all of a sudden, the feeling of being drained, totally knackered. But, in my case, not too tired to run up to the photographers brandishing my medal, really aggressive with the veins standing out in my forehead telling the press boys: 'You can't take this away from me.'

On the way round our lap of honour, all dancing and singing and yelling and trying to take in what we had done, a steward stepped in and reminded us of where we couldn't go. But as soon as I spotted the Bedmond boys, all the mates I used to play with, nothing could stop me. I shoved the steward out of the way and roared up to the fence taking the rest of the players with me. All those pals were reaching out, trying to touch my medal and I thought, 'Shit, if I drop it . . .' and stood back a bit.

One of the players shouted: 'Bassett's in the

gantry.' He was doing some TV work and I grabbed the Cup and held it up and as Harry looked down I became all emotional. I filled up but I screamed at him: 'For you, Harry. This is for you, son. This is yours.'

And I pretended to throw it up to him. The very bloke who gave me the chance I had prayed for.

The crack, the banter, the whole atmosphere in the dressing-room afterwards had to be experienced to be believed. People said Liverpool's was deathly quiet but ours was full blast. Photographs were being taken everywhere, BBC commentator John Motson joining in and having a whale of a time. And there were scores of faces in there I'd never seen before. Everybody was reluctant to leave – we just didn't want to let go of precious moments like those.

But all the other players were dressed and on the coach by the time Lawrie Sanchez and I came out of the bath and we were still taking our time when Gouldy came back in and told us to get on to the coach. I only had my trousers, shoes and socks on so I left the dressing-room stripped to the waist clutching the rest of my clothes all wrapped up with my souvenir programme and the hats and scarves the fans had given me. I still have them today. So I finished getting dressed on the coach . . . with another full blast of champagne.

There were people everywhere at Plough Lane. The place was seething and somewhere along the ten-yard walk from the coach to the entrance I was hit by what amounted to a rugby tackle. It was my old man, as happy as I'd ever seen him but crying his eyes out all the same. He spun me round and they were all there – mum, my nan, my sister and God knows how many more relatives and friends. Looking round I saw the other lads surrounded by their families as well. Everybody wept tears of joy – it was like one of those scenes from the old newsreels of troops being welcomed home from war.

We seemed to be swept along on a tide, into the huge marquee where we all had our own table of ten. I'm not sure John Fashanu ever sat down. He was with Eric Hall all night – an article for the next day, business deals, the show must go on.

We hadn't been in there long when a steward tugged me and said: 'Percy's at the gate.' Percy had been a big Wimbledon fan for years. He used to come to every game, a real passionate supporter who would shout 'Give it to 'em, Vinnie' and glow and beam when I spotted him in the crowd and shouted back: 'All right, Perc.'

'He's with his missus,' the steward said, 'and reckons you told him that if Wimbledon won the Cup he could have your tie.' So out I went and Percy was in tears as well, as emotional as the rest. He has a handicapped child who he takes to games and looks after and maybe twice a year he'd phone and I'd get him into the players' lounge. Yes, I'd struck a deal with him so it was off with my tie and I said: 'Here you are, son.' I draped it round his missus's shoulders and I knew I had to do something more. 'Come on, son,' I told him and had the gates opened so they could step through and come and join me among all those at my table for the meal and the entire evening of celebration.

It was good to have Ann there to share it all. Years before, my sister had lived with mum in Watford while she finished her schooling and after doing a couple of jobs went off with a school pal to be a stable-girl in Bologna. We didn't have a lot to do with one another but we never lost touch and I had to have her there for the final and all that followed. I was a bit of an odd man out, I suppose, virtually the only unattached member of the team. I had been going out with Mylene Elliston for quite a time but we had broken up about six months before the final.

Dad had to leave the Plough Lane bash because he had invited everybody in Bedmond to a party in the barn at home. My nan and all my relatives – some from Liverpool – left with him. I knew they were in for a great time. I suppose I always knew I would join them, eventually!

Sam Hammam had several friends in the Royal Ballet. A few had been regular guests at our games and they were there at Wembley and, later, at the banquet in the marquee. One of the top dancers, Cynthia Harvey, wandered across with her friend Gail. We had a couple of drinks and a dance, but I was still thinking about all my mates and family back at my dad's place. I couldn't get it out of my mind so I said to Cynthia: 'I'm supposed to stay with the rest of the team – we're going round on the open-top bus tomorrow, but all my family and pals aren't here. Fancy coming back to my dad's to join them?'

Cynthia agreed, so we dropped the shoulder, into my car, up to the Cannizaro House to collect all my gear and shot off home to London Colney. It was about one in the morning and the party was at full blast. I'd rung to let them know I was coming and the whole place exploded when we arrived. Everybody wanted to see and touch my winner's medal and just about everybody cried again. I'd never seen so many tears in a single day. Funny, but we'd been there less than an hour when I just sagged. I felt completely drained – a bit of a Dying Swan, you could say. So Cynthia and I went back to my place – a new house at Hunters Oak, the place they called the 'Footballers' Estate' at Hemel. Several players lived in the area, from time to time, and I'd moved in a few months before the Cup final.

The crowning glory, as all Wembley winners enjoy, was the bus tour on the Sunday. I was lucky to make it because I was 50–50 whether to go back to the hotel but, having to drop off Cynthia anyway, I drove to the Cannizaro House as the open-top was about to leave. I was glad I didn't miss it, I can tell you. The mayor, the town hall balcony, the thousands of people lining the route and gathered in the centre. Fabulous memories of an event that could never be repeated – certainly not for a lad who once paused while mowing the grass and prayed for just one chance to be a professional footballer.

There was only one way to end a perfect weekend. Down at The Bell with all the Bedmond boys on Sunday night. It was the start of more celebrations that went on and on and on, for the best part of a week!

CHAPTER 16

to coventry by ferry

By contrast, I couldn't have had a worse start to Wimbledon's 1988-89 season as Cup holders, well, pre-season, to be accurate, playing a friendly on the Isle of Wight. It would be wrong of me to say we should never have been there, but I wish we'd never gone. I don't know whether it was for the benefit of one of Gouldy's mates or just a favour or how it came about, but we found ourselves playing a village team in Shanklin at what seemed to be the annual fete. A park like the local rec with side-shows all around.

We had trained hard, as always. The manager allowed us to go out the night before, insisting we had to be back by midnight. We bumped into some of the local players and there was a bit of banter between us. Nothing serious, no trouble, mainly a few remarks aimed in my direction and mostly on the same theme: 'If you have made it as a footballer, I should be a footballer.' I've had that kind of thing thrown at me all my career. If I can make it, anybody can make it. What those people fail to appreciate is that they never had the heart, the passion and the determination that helped me to succeed.

You don't expect to land in it during a friendly

on the Isle of Wight, but it happened. After a corner some geezer gave Dennis Wise a smack. In I went without hesitating and there was a right old bundle. Me and one of their players, Dave Woodhouse, went down, arms and legs flailing. I jumped up and looked round and expected the referee to come over and say something to us, but he stormed over and waved the red card. Get off! Just me! And then there followed another load of publicity about the use of the elbow.

They provided tea and cakes after the game and thanked Wimbledon for coming over and I was chatting with Wisey when Gould came striding over and told me to go and sit on the coach. 'You're not welcome in here.'

Time to reflect yet again. I sat on that coach alone and thought: 'Here we go again ... deep shit.' By this time I realised Bobby Gould was becoming brassed off with me. He had tried to tame me and couldn't and he'd had enough because I was affecting the credibility, the name of the club. And he was quite right. These things keep cropping up – I get myself involved, then hate myself afterwards.

Travelling home on the ferry, I was sent to Coventry. Nobody was allowed to talk to me, although Wisey took a chance and had a word or two. Gouldy gave me a right dressing-down when we got back, not the normal, friendly heart-to-heart, but a clear warning that he'd had enough and wasn't prepared to defend much more of it, if any. To be honest, our days looked numbered then – even though I was to see out another season at the club.

The newspapers made a great issue of the incident, of course, and I believe that the less you say, the quicker it dies. But Gouldy was doing interviews saying he'd stuck up for me enough and announced: 'I'm banning Jones from the club, indefinitely.' To have said that I think he must have given Sam Hammam an ultimatum: him or me. Whatever, it meant I didn't know whether I was going to play for the club again or whether they were going to sell me. The only thing I knew for sure was that if Bobby Gould really meant he'd had enough I would have to move elsewhere and I only wanted to play for Wimbledon. I dreaded the thought of leaving.

Sam came round again. Another of those home visits he always made when trouble brewed, but it hadn't only brewed, this time, it had boiled over. Neither Sam nor I went to the Charity Shield at Wembley – Wimbledon against the champions, Liverpool, in a repeat of the match in which we ruined their hopes of doing the Double. We both went to the BBC television studios and watched it live on the telly. Gould refused to have me with the team. He stuck to the suspension. In fact, he put out half a reserve side so it was hardly surprising that we lost.

These were hard times and even though I can acknowledge my own mistakes I resented what the manager was doing. Having helped to win the Cup I believed I should have been part of that second occasion at Wembley. The Charity Shield should have been our day – an occasion for the lads who had earned the right for little Wimbledon to be there.

The suspension lasted for quite a while but, like most things, time healed the rift. I didn't make the side for the opening game of the season but we lost heavily and I thought: 'Right, Gouldy, now you're going to need me.' I was soon back in. And everything was going well enough until we played at Tottenham, and I got involved in an incident with Spurs' England international Gary Stevens.

I was somewhere around the centre of the pitch when Fash, shielding the ball by the touchline, had Stevens alongside him trying to nick possession. They seemed to be jockeying for ages so I started running over. I was almost there when Stevens did get the ball but he was still half tangled up with Fash. I went in with a block tackle on the ball and went right through with it sending the two of them flying. Throw-in to Tottenham, no free kick. Both players were down on the floor receiving treatment. Fashanu got up but Stevens didn't. He tried to play on, eventually, but his knee was all over the place and they took him off.

There was no way that I went to 'do' Gary Stevens. As I was running over towards the pair of them I was sure I was going to make it and get the ball. I went in strong as I usually do, and the linesman was so close he was lucky he didn't become part of the tackle as well. There was a lot of hooting and hollering, the referee spoke with his linesman but it remained a throw-in, not a free kick.

I still believe Stevens was the victim of one of those things that happen in football. There doesn't always have to be a malicious reason for serious injuries. I think he had experienced quite a bit of knee trouble before and that one block tackle had been too much. It was in no way deliberate, even though the Tottenham bench and fans were going mental at the time. But I still had to make a smuggled exit from White Hart Lane. Don Howe, who lived quite close to me, had offered me a lift but there must have been about 500 Spurs fans gathered outside like a picket-line. He brought his car round to one side and I got in the back and crouched on the floor. Don spread his coat over me and it worked. Those unsuspecting supporters saw only Don Howe in the car and he was able to drive away unhindered and take me home.

I had switched agents by then, and Jerome Anderson was looking after my interests. I phoned him and told him that they were going for me again but that I'd made an honest tackle. Some argued it was reckless, that there was no need for it. Everybody is entitled to an opinion, but if I'd gone in recklessly there would have been as much chance of my injuring Fashanu as Stevens and it's hardly likely I would put my best mate at risk, is it?

We agreed that Anderson's partner, Jeff Weston, should pick me up next morning and take me to the hospital, as I was hoping to go in and see Gary and drop off a few magazines. I called at a newsagents and bought a whole bundle of magazines. I told the lady on the desk at the hospital my name and said that I was there to see Gary Stevens.

She picked up the phone: 'Mr Stevens, there's a Mr Jones here to see you.' A little pause and then she told me he didn't want to see me.

'Have you told him it's Vinnie Jones?'

'Yes, he knows. And he doesn't want to see you. He won't let you go up.'

I thought he'd still got the hump, which was fair enough, but I hoped that in the cold light of day, when he saw the video of the incident, he'd know there was nothing intentional. So I left the magazines and asked the receptionist to make sure he got them. They were just sports magazines I'd picked up at random – all sorts – football, boxing, golf, fishing, I'd scooped almost every kind from the shelves.

I picked up the paper the next morning to find a big piece about Gary Stevens' career being over and look what a sick individual Vinnie Jones is. That I'd visited the hospital and brought boxing magazines to a bloke about to go in for an operation! There was no mention of the other mags, all the other sports, just boxing. The press gave totally the wrong impression and I believe Gary still blames me for what happened.

We met in Mauritius in the summer of 1997. We got talking quite a bit but that tackle still dwelled on his mind. I wish, 100 per cent, that my tackle hadn't resulted in ending his career, but he was still understandably very bitter about it and I don't suppose anything I could say could change his mind. But I do think, rightly or wrongly, that if Gary's knee had been completely sound it would have stood up to my challenge.

Once more, there were some nasty things said about me in the papers. For instance, one of them asked some shrink to do an analysis of me – the kind of bloke I was, what made me do the things I'd been accused of. He did this without even meeting me, letting alone knowing anything other than what he'd read. That really did bloody hurt. I can never understand or accept that one individual can analyse and assess the personality of another without so much as shaking hands.

Just as I still can't accept what happened at Goodison Park in February 1989. It wasn't the sending-off that annoyed me, it was the way it happened that time, and the feeling of being cheated by another professional. I had already been cautioned for a foul on Peter Reid – yes, Reidy again. What a right little hard case he was and what a bloody good player! It was what occurred after I tackled Graeme Sharp that still makes my blood boil!

Sharp is a tough lad as well, a Scottish international striker with a reputation for not allowing anybody to take liberties. My challenge was a stretching tackle – I was reaching too far, not trying to hurt him. Never in a million years. But I caught him late and on the top of his foot and he went over. Other players involved themselves and as I jumped to my feet Everton's Kevin Ratcliffe came charging over and confronted me, close up. So I stuck my chest out and put my head forward and, in the heat of the moment, said: 'Come on then, if you want it, you can have it.' I didn't thrust my head at him. I swear I was inches away and never made any contact.

But he flew backwards, hit the deck and clutched his face as though I had nutted him. There wasn't a touch. If he did that, nowadays, video evidence would put him in deep trouble and in disgrace. I might be many things and have made many mistakes but nobody could ever accuse me of play acting or feigning injury to land a fellow pro in trouble.

Even in this case I could accept the dismissal for one yellow card after the foul on Reidy, because the poor tackle on Graeme Sharp deserved another. Two cautions – and off. No argument. But there was no time for the referee to book me for the Sharp incident before Ratcliffe had dived in and keeled over. So I was sent packing for something I didn't do. It was a joke but it wasn't funny and several of our players called Ratcliffe a cheat there and then. I put my hands up and knew I would have gone anyway after the second reckless tackle but I've never forgotten how Ratcliffe made out I'd hit him with a head-butt . . . him, of all people. I'd always thought he was supposed to be one of the genuine tough guys of the game.

Don Howe went absolutely ballistic with me, and with John Fashanu who had led the protests on the pitch, but particularly with me. 'What am I doing here with you thugs? You're barbarians. This is me finished at this club.' I just sat there and didn't dare open my mouth. I always thought the world of Don Howe. He was the sort who believed you should turn up at the training ground on Monday morning even if you had a broken leg. He had no time for players who were regularly in the physio's room and I have to say, when you think about it, they do tend to be the same old faces.

Bobby Gould was speechless in that dressing-room. In a way, Don was having a pop at Bob as well and I think he was shocked to find all of us under criticism. Bob had his say but I think that was the day Don Howe decided he'd had enough. I tried to tell him that I hadn't touched Ratcliffe but it didn't matter to him. He was even telling Gouldy that he shouldn't have any more to do with us either and to get out. I can tell you that it was a very quiet coach journey home and, if memory serves, I don't think Don travelled with us.

A group of Everton fans were giving me a lot of mouth as we sat on the coach ready for off. Now Fash didn't like it if anybody spoke to me badly. He would take it personally and he did exactly that at Goodison. He managed to sneak off the coach through the emergency exit and waded into the lot of them. And that takes some bottle on Merseyside.

There was no benefit of the doubt for me. I protested my innocence in the Ratcliffe incident, trying to tell people I hadn't touched him, but the headlines condemned me all the same. Sam Hammam was the one person who stood by me through everything. I was dreading him coming round for our usual little chat knowing I had let everyone down once again and terrified that he would say he'd had enough now as well. To this day, Sam will tell you I didn't touch Kevin Ratcliffe. He believed me, because whenever I did wrong I admitted it to him. I was always honest with him.

What a man he has been for Wimbledon football club. And what a character in his own right. Remember the night of Alan Cork's testimonial, following the Cup final? The fans started chanting 'Vinnie, Vinnie, show us yer bum' and we all showed them on the halfway line at half time. It was just a lark but it caused outrage and brought the club a £10,000 fine from the FA. I loved Sam's response – saying he couldn't pay them in money, he'd pay them in camels!

I went to see Sam at his house at the end of the 1988-89 season because I was becoming a mental wreck with all the publicity, the headlines that branded me the hard case. I'd been on the chat shows, Wogan and Jonathan Ross, and it was the

same story: 'Why are you the hard man of football?'
And then, at the end of the interview, a red card.
Things like that were beyond a joke. I detested it and
I told Sam: 'I can't keep going through all this.'

Nothing was ever mentioned about a single pass
or how well I might have played. Hard men, real
nutcases, have something missing somewhere but I
don't regard myself in that bracket. I had 'lost it' in
some situations and gone too far but in my heart I
knew I was an honest lad and not a 'dirty bastard'.
One article, I recall, described me as 'The hard man
hod carrier who couldn't trap a bag of cement.' That
hurt because it ignored the fact that the reason I was
in the side was because I could play a bit as well.

Sam and I talked for hours. I was trying to
persuade him to sell me but he gave various reasons
for saying no. I believed he had to agree because, as
I put it to him: 'I have to wake up to the newspapers
every day. I have to walk into the training ground
and face the lads. We get a great result but it's
always the negative stuff in print and I'm beginning
to think that even the other players have had
enough of it. Maybe, Sam, Wimbledon Football
Club without Vinnie Jones could start to gain a bit
of credibility.'

It was a case of getting rid of the stigma, and I
thought that at a fresh club with a fresh start . . . well,
perhaps I might get a few headlines for the right
reasons. Sam was already in tears and by this time so
was I. But the conversation reached a kind of friendly
stalemate and as I made to leave he handed me my
coat and said he'd think about it. And as I walked out
of the door he added: 'Vin, things like this . . . people
I love . . . I make very quick decisions.'

I said 'OK, Sam' and drove off. I'd made it as far as St John's Wood station, four or five minutes away when my new car phone rang. It was Bill Fotherby, managing director of Leeds United.

'Vinnie, I've just had Sam on the phone,' he said. 'We can meet with you today and he wants the deal done. If it's going to be done he wants it doing today. And no agents. Sam doesn't want any agents involved and if it gets to the press the deal is off.'

I was told to drive to the Oxford Street offices of Top Man, their sponsors, there and then. Sam Hammam, true to form, had made his decision very quickly. I was on my way to Leeds United.

CHAPTER 17

the good, the sad and the bubbly

I phoned my dad from the car, who recommended that I talk to them, but that I should sleep on it and give them a decision in the morning. I didn't think there was much chance of delaying it as soon as I walked into those Oxford Street offices and saw Bill Fotherby, director Peter Ridsdale – now the Leeds chairman – and Alan Roberts, a kind of marketing man at the club, all waiting with a bottle of champagne standing on the table. There were handshakes all round and then the first question.

'How much a week would you want?' Ridsdale asked.

I was on £500 a week at Wimbledon and I didn't really know what figure to go for so, thinking in a hurry, I just trebled it then thought that was a bit much so I knocked off a hundred quid and said: 'I'd want £1400 a week.'

'Yes, all right,' Ridsdale said without batting an eyelid.

'And I want twenty-five grand a year signing-on fee. And a car.'

The words had hardly tumbled off my lips when Bill Fotherby stood up, leaned across the polished wood table, spat on his palm and said: 'Done. Here's my hand, it's a deal.' And we shook on it. Peter Ridsdale, who I was to discover to be a really sincere, lovely fella, opened the champagne. I was a Leeds United player, just like that, subject to the no-problem medical examination the following day.

I should have asked for a fifty grand promotion bonus!

We were given £4000 each for winning the Cup at Wimbledon and around another £3500 from the players' pool. Liverpool, we gathered, were on ten grand appearance money and another ten if they'd won. But all that was behind me as I drove away from the West End. I was at the start of a new stage in my career, although I didn't dare even mention it to my agent that night. I told my old man and swore him to secrecy but I was buzzing. I needed to celebrate with somebody so it was nice that Kerry Coles (Colesy's dad) and Paul Robins (who had split up with his wife) were both living with me at the time. We locked ourselves in and drank to the future.

I know it sounds nuts but for some reason I thought I was signing for Howard Kendall. He was the only Howard I'd really heard of. Wilkinson was still on holiday so after the medical it was Bill Fotherby who completed the forms. He took me into the manager's office at Elland Road and it was plush. Well, plush to me: a television set, drinks cabinet, desk, leather sofa.

On the top of the cabinet was a photograph of the manager and his family. 'Oh, right,' I said. 'Howard *Wilkinson*, yeah, used to be manager of Sheffield Wednesday!' Bill and Alan Roberts looked at me, eyebrows raised. They cracked up when I told them the story, that I'd had Howard Kendall in my mind and had hardly heard of the bloke who was now my boss.

The subject of the sponsored car cropped up later, and I asked Ridsdale if there was any chance of a BMW 325i. Remember Dennis Wise and me before the Cup final? Straightaway Ridsdale agreed. 'And I'd like it that when my three-year contract is up, the car becomes mine,' I said. Mylene Elliston now has that car – G reg, silver. Beautiful.

So it was hardly surprising that I quickly developed a good feeling about Leeds and their people. Alan Roberts told me that they had been trying to sign a midfield player and had even had talks with a lad, but he wanted time to consider. But Wilkinson's view was if a player had to think about signing for Leeds United, then he should be told 'goodnight'.

When I got to Leeds, the thing that immediately struck me was that everybody connected with the club was crackers about Leeds United, even the tea ladies. A bit different from one of the groundsmen at Wimbledon who used to tend to our pitch and then shoot off to watch Queens Park Rangers. As Alan had explained, when I showed I was keen to join them, they made up their mind that I was their man. I had my dad with me and after Alan had taken us for a meal at The Flying Pizza, one of the best known restaurants in town, we went to the Hilton hotel and up to a suite. Alan told me: 'This is where you are going to stay until you get your own place. Eat here, do what you want and put it all down to the club. You have three months to find a house.' No wonder the old man looked at me and said: 'This is the big time, son. Big time.'

He was right and yet, after a holiday and returning for pre-season training two weeks earlier than any other club I discovered an element that was small-minded, to me, and anything but big-time. Quite a few new signings had been made including Gordon Strachan, Chris Fairclough, Mel Sterland and Mickey Thomas. Youngsters like David Batty, Gary Speed and Simon Grayson were on the brink of breaking into the side. But there were others like Ian Baird, Bobby Davison, Mark Aizlewood, John Sheridan and Brendan Ormsby who didn't seem sure about where they stood and they'd formed a bit of a clique. A big change-over in personnel was taking place and I had arrived in the middle of a situation where there were clearly two camps.

Vince Hillaire had become something of a legend at Leeds and it was easy to see why he was so popular. He was one of the funniest players I ever met in football, constantly taking the mickey out of everyone and everything and I loved all that. The training was bloody hard but really enjoyable and I was constantly doing my stuff to the accompaniment of Hillaire's voice: 'See that, lads? Was that a pass? Has he actually passed it? Did you pass that ball ten yards, Jonah?' But I could take that, as it was part of the banter, and was good fun because it was meant in the right spirit.

What I couldn't take was the resentment from the group of players who feared their days were numbered, and who had it confirmed when Howard Wilkinson announced his squad. He then told the others, including Ormsby, Sheridan and Aizlewood: 'You're over there. Do what you want. And you can get yourselves another club. You can go.' They weren't involved with us in training but afterwards everybody ate together – good food, pasta and things. A bit of a culture shock after the full grease-up at Wimbledon.

One day Strachan, who was as conscious as I was of the damaging atmosphere that was increasing between the squad and the 'outsiders', said to me: 'Look, it's a case of us and them.' He gave me the kind of look I took to mean I should do something about it. I had become almost paranoid about eating my food, hearing them whispering and sniggering, and one day I'd had enough. I just leapt to my feet and confronted Davison.

'No, no,' he said, 'you've got the wrong end of the stick.' Like hell I had. That lousy atmosphere had been simmering, building up over a period. I smacked him in the mouth and announced to the other twenty-five or thirty lads in the room: 'This all stops, right here and now. If any of you want to say anything or do anything, here I am.'

'No, no,' I heard one or two voices mumble.

'Right,' I said. And I stormed out and marched off to the changing-room to collect my gear and leave. Gordon had come out behind me: 'You all right, big man? Come on, calm down.'

'Fuck them, Gord. It's us and them. I've not been brought up with this kind of situation. I'm used to everyone being together. I can't handle this, I want out of this place.'

'Hey, hey, hey, big man.' The voice of Mick Hennigan, one of the coaches, boomed from the corridor. 'The gaffer wants to see you.'

'Bollocks.'

'No, come on, son. He wants to see you in the office.'

I thought I'd done it again and was right in it with my new boss, for whacking one of the players and confronting all the others. I walked up there thinking I'd go back to Wimbledon.

Howard Wilkinson is one of the coolest men I've ever met – so confident, so sure of himself and with that uncanny ability to convince others they should believe in him as well. In that blunt Yorkshire accent of his he said: 'Sit down, son.' I sat there thinking I was ready to deal with anything he could come up with. I was steaming about what had just happened. 'You've disappointed me a bit, son.' What? Am I hearing him right? I bit my lip.

'I've just been down to the players' lounge. Can't find one speck of blood in there.'

And then he told me the story of how Leeds came to pay £650,000 for me – the so-called hod carrier with nothing to offer the professional game, the player who had known little other than criticism after almost every match he played. He told me how he had sat in the stand at Highbury with Mick Hennigan at one of the last games of the 1988-89 season. It was when Gouldy had brought in an overseas player, Detzi Kruszynski, a hell of a score at Scrabble, but a pain in the bum that day. Detzi was a Pole, signed from German football, and he was in midfield with me. He was the kind of player who only wanted to perform when he had the ball; he wasn't interested in defending, picking up the runners. I was screaming at him to do his job, to go with his runner but he let another one by and Arsenal almost scored. I flew at Detzi full blast. The other

Wimbledon lads were as angry as I was, but there was a bit of a bust-up and the referee had to separate us. Wilkinson had seen me grab the Pole and threaten him with a right-hander because he wouldn't work back and defend for the team. He had been there to watch Arsenal but he'd turned to Mick and said: 'That's the man we want.' It was my leadership qualities he felt were vital to sorting out the dressing-room and establishing the collective spirit that would give Leeds their best chance of promotion from the old Second Division.

From that moment in the manager's office, the problem was sorted and I was far happier, too. Because for two or three weeks, confronted by the clique at Elland Road, I had found myself desperately missing the togetherness at Wimbledon. I felt safe and among friends at Plough Lane, with a strange but comforting feeling of being protected from the outside world most of the time.

The jolt of arriving at Leeds and into an unhealthy state of affairs in the dressing-room had me returning to my hotel suite day after day and wondering what I had done. I had everything and the training was fantastic, I'd never been fitter in my life, I completely trusted Wilkinson and what he did and the belief in him from his other players was total. And yet I would return to that hotel feeling so depressed and lonely that I often sat there alone, on the end of my bed and cried.

I missed John Fashanu really badly. We were such good mates and had quite a lot in common. There was one night before a match at Everton when I couldn't get off to sleep so I sat on the window-ledge of the hotel room, thinking. Fash, wondering what was bothering me, came and joined me and we sat there and had a real heart to heart until four in the morning – looking out over the city of Liverpool. We spilled our guts to one another. How lucky we were, him from his Doctor Barnardo's background, me having wandered off with my life in a dustbin-liner. 'I can relate to you,' he told me. Apparently, he had a mate at Barnardo's who had looked after him and been the spitting image of me. 'I can see him in you,' he said.

We talked about our lives, the problems we'd encountered and our extreme good fortune in being there, that night, waiting to play against Everton at the top level of English football. Fash, far more of a philosopher than I will ever be, advised me about something else: 'What you have got to do in this game is look after your friends and keep them close. But keep your enemies even closer.'

What he was saying was that you know who your friends and family are and know you can trust them. But you can't trust those who are against you so find out what they're about. Keep your friends close for comfort and reassurance and keep your enemies even closer so that you know what they're up to.

It didn't turn out to be particularly valuable to me because when it comes to helping people I'm a big softie. I keep all my friends close but haven't the time to worry about the enemies. Many a time after a punch-up I'd shake the bloke's hand and that was that. Life's too short. But if you crossed John Fashanu, he'd take it to heart, bear a grudge and bide his time, but he is such a valuable and committed friend.

Missing him so much up in Leeds set me thinking about some of the incidents we had shared. Like the day he put me in a complete panic by turning in for training and telling me he'd been transferred to Tottenham and had called in to say goodbye to the lads. I couldn't even shake his hand. He hadn't given me any warning, I wasn't ready for this. My mentor was leaving – how would I be able to deal with things without Fash around? Happily, it was a total wind-up.

Fash's loyalty was clear on another occasion, but there was no joking this time. We'd gone to train on the Astroturf at Luton in the week of the game at Kenilworth Road. Fash loved a nice hot relaxing bath and as I still had a bit of stiffness in one knee, that had needed an operation some time before, I got in the other bath before training. We were slightly late getting ready to go out and Bobby Gould was in one of his moods.

'You're not fit,' he stormed at me. 'I'm leaving you out on Saturday. You're dropped.'

I lost it and smashed him up against the wall. His head clouted one of the pegs and I shouted at him: 'You're a disgrace. You're just picking on me.' I had suddenly felt unwanted and that's a terrible thing with me. If ever I am made to feel I am not wanted, sensing rejection, I am at my worst. Back at the hotel Fash more or less put it to Gould: 'If he doesn't play, I don't play.' Gouldy played me. But he had the last word – he pulled me off.

Fashanu was upset that I'd left Wimbledon, not at all happy that the club had been prepared to let me go. With such support, such friendship from a team mate, it was hardly surprising that I was missing him at Leeds. I'd lost my big brother and I'd have done anything to go back. It crossed my mind many times to return with my tail between my legs and say: 'Sam, I'm sorry. Please have me back.'

In those weeks of trouble at Leeds, ninety-nine per cent of my phone-calls were to John Fashanu. He started to come up and see me on Wednesdays, our day off. I began eating at a restaurant, La Comida, across the road from my hotel. The Spanish owner, Vicente Rodriguez, a fanatical Leeds supporter, became such a good friend not only of mine but of my family's. I finished up eating at his restaurant every night, sitting there with him, with people recognising me and banging on the window. Vicente eventually became known as 'Vinnie' and it was his friendship and Fash's visits and support that got me through those worrying early weeks.

Howard Wilkinson's reaction to the dust-up that sorted out the Leeds boys gave me fresh confidence as well. I felt wanted and needed and gradually, as a lot of the other players started going to the restaurant – Lee Chapman, Strachan, Batty, Gary Speed – we were becoming a close-knit force. It was like the early Wimbledon days with Wally Downes, Glyn Hodges, Mark Morris and the boys, but without the crazy antics. We were very disciplined and proper at Leeds – you wouldn't go in and turn over Gordon Strachan's hotel room! Dave Batty became my best mate. Like I did as a kid, I used to go to his house for tea even when he wasn't in because he lived with his mum and dad. His dad was a dustman and his mum a supermarket worker and they were both very down to earth, smashing people. I suppose it was the family involvement that

I wanted. They made me feel so welcome.

We had a sign of the professionalism to come the day, pre-season, when we played awfully against some semi-pro side. Wilkinson had torn us off a strip in the dressing-room and then came to the back of the coach and had another go: 'This is Leeds United. You've got to be proud to wear that shirt . . .' And Mel Sterland's mobile phone started ringing. I tell you, talk about wanting a hole to open up. Wilkinson was furious but in that controlled way of his. He didn't need to wave his arms, stamp his feet or bang his fists. He was so good with words – so forceful and capable of cutting you in two. Mobile phones were banned from that moment.

The clique, the outsiders, became known by the rest of us as the Leper Squad. The manager hardly gave them the time of day. They worked separately to the rest of us, did their pre-season training on their own. I honestly think they could have laid back and sunbathed for all he cared.

The first run we did was forty minutes around several football pitches, up a great hill, back down and round again. It was a set course, with the first twenty minutes as a kind of warm-up and then twenty minutes of competitive running and those who lagged behind were allowed to cut across and rejoin the main group to keep everyone together in the warm-up. The race itself became a real challenge for me, as I always liked to be at the front. My dad had wanted me to be a long-distance runner but it was not my game. I hated running, still do, but it gave me that opportunity to be noticed, to make a good impression so I just had to try and get out there in the lead. It hurt like hell. I put myself through agonies but it was something that had to be done. After three of us had shaken off Mickey Thomas I was having trouble catching Strachan and Dylan Kerr, a young lad who really could run. They just kept going and going and as the shout went up, 'Three laps to the finish' I knew I had to go for them. Young Dylan was away and uncatchable but I managed to wear down Strachan and pass him just before the top of the final hill and I came in second. It was bloody exhausting.

As all the others finished there was one poor lad, Chris O'Donnell, who looked several stones over-weight and couldn't run, who still had another six laps to run. There were players collapsing all around the finish but I couldn't see him out there alone, so I went out again and ran alongside him for another six laps to get him round. I did it for the lad himself, but I was told later that the gesture had been appreciated by the other players.

Everybody was wondering whether Strachan or I would be captain for the new season. I thought I might have a shout seeing that the gaffer had signed me for leadership but it was a masterstroke by Wilkinson when he made Gordon Strachan skipper. He was a great player in his own right, had the respect of all the others and he became a great captain. I was to be idolised at Leeds and could do no wrong but there was no doubt that the wee man with the red hair was the right choice.

He pulled me to one side one gorgeous sunny day as we lounged on the grass and said: 'Look, Vin, we know what you're good at, all about your aggression and will to win. Don't ever lose any of it. But we also know that you can pass the ball and that's what we want from you as well. Instead of concentrating just on the tackling, the physical side of the game, think about wanting to pass the ball.'

The 1989-90 season was a massive one for Leeds, they were desperate to get out of the old Second Division and back among the big boys. If we had played that nine-month spell in the top division of English football I would have received accolades. The Elland Road fans loved me and the feeling was mutual. That much was proved after I'd left the club and then returned to play against them for the first time. I was given a standing ovation from the entire crowd. When I came off, the groundsman, John Reynolds, told me: 'Only two ex-Leeds players have ever come back to a reception like that – the great John Charles and now you.'

To this day I get the same reaction whenever I go back. Leeds were a big part of my life and career. They were a club who had been living in the past, still glorying in the achievements of the Don Revie era but Wilkinson, bravely, blew all that out of the water. He took down many of the old pictures because he was determined to build a new, modern Leeds United and turn it into a fortress again, proud of itself, not dwelling on the successful years that had long passed.

I never saw John Charles play, of course, but I learned how great he had been – at centre half or centre forward. The big Welshman was the complete footballer, they said, still idolised in Leeds and in Turin where he made such an impression with Juventus. In fact, I became quite pally with him. He had fallen on hard times, as near as damn it skint. So when I was asked to do presentations up there I took John with me and gave him a couple of hundred quid from my fee.

People have always argued that I was most effective playing for teams who were fighting for their lives. I have admitted to this Jekyll and Hyde thing within me, that I do change once I cross that white line five minutes before kick-off. I am two different animals. But with Wimbledon I actually played my most constructive football when they were comfortable in the table, not scrapping to avoid relegation. I was far more composed, then.

But it was all so different at Leeds. I knew what Gordon Strachan meant when he told me to concentrate on passing the ball more, but I didn't realise how much of an opportunity I would have to do exactly that. I played the best football of my life with Leeds because I was able to perform with a smile on my face. In fifty-three appearances I was booked only twice – against Swindon at home in September 1989 and at Wolverhampton the following March, both cautions for minor fouls. And I scored five goals.

It was different, you see. There was no tension, week-in week-out, no threat of relegation. Every time we went out – and I had the same feeling at times when I was at Chelsea – I was thinking: 'We're going to win this game, no problem.' There was a confidence in our ability, a self-assurance, a sort of aura about the team that I never experienced at Wimbledon, who had so often been the underdogs. The belief and trust in Howard Wilkinson, his preparations and attention to detail had us head and shoulders above other teams.

I used to look around the pitch and see the likes of Chris Kamara, another of Wilkinson's signings (also with a reputation for looking after himself), and Strachan and Chapman and Sterland doing really skilful things and I felt so proud to be wearing the same shirt as them. Strachan once wrote that for everyone involved with that Leeds side it was the best time they had in football. That cannot be coincidence. It was a wonderful, wonderful time and it was there, I hope, that I proved that I could play the game in the eyes of anybody who was prepared to give me any credit at all.

We played Sunderland, away, and they wouldn't give our fans any tickets. Beat them 1–0. We went to West Ham, 1–0 again, and I scored the goal. Wilkinson used to tell us: 'We're going into the lion's den again today and we're going to pull out its teeth.' Leeds were still hated wherever they went. With victory after victory and full houses at home after I had been used to such small crowds at Plough Lane, it was little wonder that I was revelling in it, lapping up every minute.

As to why I received so few cautions, I must say that I found the refereeing far less strict in the Second Division than at top level. I made tackles at Leeds that would undoubtedly have had me in the book with referees a division higher. And those big crowds at Elland Road certainly seemed to intimidate match officials because we were given at least two penalties that weren't penalties at all. I saw some visiting players looking as if they had brown-trousered themselves the moment they heard the Leeds roar.

But I was no longer the bull in the china shop. I

was happy inside, passing the ball more successfully and able to play without all that built-up aggression. I always say my best games are in training because I can do things with a more laid-back attitude.

In many matches I turned into a monster because I wanted to win at all costs. I forgot the football because the aggression, the tackling and the physical aspect of the game took me over completely. But not at Leeds where I was totally content and brimming with the confidence Wilkinson's management and coaching instilled in the side. Believe it or not, he once pulled me off – West Brom, away – because I was overdoing the football! I wasn't getting near to anybody, not winning headers or tackles. I was spending too much time dwelling on the ball. I was playing like the hero of my younger days, Glenn Hoddle, so assured, a beautiful player of passes short and long and a scorer of wonderful goals. I used to go to Tottenham games just to watch him.

It may sound a bit odd but I never consciously felt proud of my improved discipline. Maybe I put it down to the different response from referees but the contentment I felt inside must have had something to do with it. I also knew that Gordon Strachan wasn't going to give me any credit for punching someone or getting myself involved in anything like that. We still had a rugged midfield, mind, Batty and me or Kamara and me – all three tough lads, but the approach was different. At Wimbledon it was a case of avoiding defeat at all costs. We were a physical side and I was completely involved with that. It was 'Let's get stuck into them' from the first day I played with them. I never heard Harry Bassett say we were going to play a neat passing game. All he used to say was: 'Let's smash 'em.'

But my time in Yorkshire was not entirely trouble-free. Howard Wilkinson took a day off and went to see England play at Wembley. I'd gone to a club on the Tuesday night and some geezer got the hump and we ended up having a proper fight on the fire-escape, and I was arrested. I had to make a statement on the Wednesday, woke up to go training on the Thursday and it was all over the front page of the *Sun*. The bloke must have sold his story about what I had done.

Wilkinson rang me up and slaughtered me. I had let him down. It wasn't right, I know, but it was typical of me. I'm quite a proud person and can't stand people being jealous – I've never been jealous of anyone in my life. I'd been standing at the bar having a laugh with a pal, Derek Lowe from Bedmond, when this bloke starts mouthing off, obviously looking for trouble. Unfortunately, it had all coincided with a big effort by Leeds United to eliminate bother from the notorious element of their own supporters. I was ordered to the manager's office.

'Look,' said Wilkinson, 'here we are trying to solve problems with the fans and you go out and do this kind of thing. You've let me down, the players down, the fans – everybody.' That was punishment enough because the thought of letting people down hurts me more than anything. It was a real man-to-man dressing-down and, with well chosen words that were far more effective than any ranting and raving, Howard got his message across. And he didn't leave me out of the side. No, I wasn't charged. I did have a few bruises that hurt for a few days and

I'm sure the other bloke had a few more.

The club had a bit of a dodgy spell late in the season after going about ten points clear. Our luck had run out as well and Sheffield United were catching us. We needed to win at Bournemouth in the last match to clinch the championship, a beautiful sunny day with thousands upon thousands of Leeds fans down there – about 2000 able to get into the ground and what seemed like another 10,000 outside. Chris Kamara did a bit of magic down the right, crossed and Lee Chapman scored. Leeds were champions and poor old Bournemouth were relegated.

For me the feeling was the nearest I'll ever get to the elation of winning that Cup final against Liverpool. Coming home was brilliant. At a supermarket on the way back, the manager gave Mel Sterland and me fifty quid for a few crates of beer and we all had a good drink along the way. With Howard Wilkinson, as usual, sitting at the front of the coach drinking his Glenmorangie and smoking his big Havana, just as he did on the way home every week win, lose or draw. Everything he did, even the clothes he wore, had class.

Leeds was packed that night. Dave Batty, Gary Speed and I all jumped into a mate's car with the sun-roof open and went into the city centre. You'd have thought we'd won the World Cup rather than the Second Division. Fans were everywhere, packing the pavements, clinging to statues, chasing after the car with me and Batty standing up through the sun-roof, waving and cheering as loud as the rest of them until a copper told us to get back inside. We went to a nightclub and word had got out that the whole team would be there because the queue seemed to stretch to the Yorkshire border!

Fantastic memories. A great manager, great lads, great results and great fun. We still talk about the night David Batty, John Sheridan and I had been out for a drink and those two went back to stay at Batty's house, just round the corner from the place I'd bought. I knew Dave used to leave his back door open so I decided to have a bit of fun and borrowed a bird's car, a little Mini, and shot round there at two in the morning. I put my balaclava on, the one I wore when I went shooting, grabbed the dustbin lid and crept in through the open door. The two of them were fast asleep.

I jumped on Batty and clonked him gently with the lid. He was up on his feet in a split second and I couldn't believe it. He was shouting: 'You bastard' and brandishing a bloody great sheath knife. Sheridan was all curled up in another room not knowing what the hell was going on. They realised it was me as I ran out to the Mini and roared off, did a handbrake turn at the bottom of the road, came screeching back and drove straight over the lawn before tearing away up the road.

We were all laughing at Leeds by the end of that season. David Batty's lawn might still have been showing the tyre marks but everything in the garden was rosy. Or so I thought.

CHAPTER 18

giving it both barrels

When I walk down the high street I do get that goldfish feeling, everybody staring, wanting your attention and your time. Sometimes it is too much for me, I get uptight and find myself being rude to people, telling them to leave me alone, but if I walked down the street and nobody recognised me, I would feel so insecure. That's me.

I didn't see my name on my return to Leeds for the start of the new 1990-91 season. I returned only to find the name of Gary McAllister by my peg in the dressing-room. My heart sank. I'd come back in such high spirits, so confident, looking forward so much to playing with Leeds at Highbury, Old Trafford and all the major grounds, and Wilkinson hadn't breathed a word to even hint that I might be surplus to requirements. Not an inkling.

I was carrying my pride at having helped Leeds to the Second Division championship: a £60 tattoo, marking the achievement for life, neatly balanced Wimbledon's one on the outside of the other leg: 'FA Cup winners, 1988'.

The uneasy feeling that greeted me made no difference to my attitude in training, however, I still worked and worked. It must have been pretty impressive because Colin Murphy, manager of Lincoln at the time, came to watch us on one occasion when we were doing 400-metre stints on the track. Afterwards he told me if he hadn't witnessed somebody training like that, he'd never have believed it. He later wrote me a lovely letter saying: 'You have something special – never lose it or become disheartened.' I still cherish that letter.

When the first line-up was announced, Wilkinson didn't even have me among the substitutes. That really broke my heart. I was in one of the sponsor's suites, a new one called the Captain's Lounge. I'll always remember the incident because I was wearing a pair of brown cowboy boots and somebody wandered up to me and said: 'After all you have done for this club, I can't believe you're not even sub.' I filled up. I had to leave quickly because I would have broken down. My mind was confused, part anger, part bewilderment. I couldn't understand what was going on but it didn't take a genius to work out that my days at Leeds were numbered. I had that feeling of rejection again, and was desperate. I always have to feel wanted and needed.

I was longing for Gordon Strachan to say to the manager: 'Vinnie's absolutely flying in training but he's not even sub. What are you doing?' I don't know if it happened but, around the fifth game of the season, away to Luton, I still hoped that I would be back in the side. I'd been doing some shooting up in Leeds and was planning to take my kit on the coach because I was due to stay the weekend at the old man's. Everybody was on the coach before me and, as Wilkinson went to get on board, I said something sarcastic like: 'Will I be needing my boots today?'

He was not amused. When I opened the boot of my car, the idea struck me. The shotgun!

I took it from its sleeve and as the players looked out from the coach I saw their expressions change and everybody went deadly silent. As I stepped inside Howard looked up and I put the barrels of the twelve-bore right up his nose with my finger on the trigger and said: 'Now are you going to bloody play me at Luton?'

I kept a straight face long enough for him to seriously wonder. Of course the gun wasn't loaded, and the safety mechanism was in place but, for a second or two, he looked a bit worried. And then, as I replaced a scowl with a smile and then a laugh, Howard cracked up. He was the first to appreciate the gag and the laughter went through the entire coach even though the lads were saying: 'How dare you pull a stunt like that on the gaffer?' But that's me and Howard knew and he appreciated it more than anybody. And the real laugh was that he played me at Luton, though again had the final word by pulling me off.

Once the team had been named I went to get my usual shirt but Mick Hennigan said: 'Er, Vin, you're not No 4 today, Batty's got the 4.'

'You're joking,' I protested. 'I've worn the 4 shirt all my life, even as a kid. I'm not stopping now.'

'You put the No 8 on and Batty wears the No 4,' Wilkinson said. I was gutted and I wasn't made to feel much better when he brought me off in the second half, although I did have the feeling that I was back in the picture. I trained like a Trojan again on the Monday, with even more of a spring in my step, only to be taken aside by Wilkinson later, and told: 'I don't know whether you're interested or not but I've had Dave Bassett on the phone.' I was speechless. It was like somebody telling the Queen she was on her way out of Buckingham Palace. I had been at my happiest with Leeds, playing proper football and loving the whole professional feel about this place. Now this.

My immediate thought was: 'Right, sod you, I'll go.' So that evening, I met Sheffield United's assistant manager, Geoff Taylor, who took me to Bassett's house, ironically virtually next door to Wilkinson's. I had already made up my mind. It doesn't matter what you have done for a club, how you feel about them and about leaving, you are very much on your own in those circumstances.

Wilkinson had said: 'Look, I don't want you to go. I want you to stay here but it's up to you. You've been great for this club and I'll support you in whatever you decide.' No good – the bull had been let loose in the china shop again. I phoned my dad from the car, like last time, and he was really against the move.

'Sleep on it, sleep on it,' he said. 'Do you realise where Sheffield United are? They're at the bottom of the First Division.' Dad used to come to all the Leeds games and he was well aware of my popularity up there, but I agreed to rejoin Harry Bassett that night. Sheffield were paying Leeds £700,000 but there was a slight snag about my money. Not the wages, they were paying me a grand a week more than at Elland Road, but because I hadn't signed any transfer request, I was due my signing-on fees from Leeds. It was sorted, eventually.

It was only after I'd signed that I looked at the

league table and realised that what the old man had said was a fact. Sheffield United had got off to a rotten start. Bassett wanted me in as captain but dad still insisted: 'You'll always regret it.' In footballing terms I was going backwards. They weren't as good as the Wimbledon side I had left and it was really 'hump and run'. Overall, my season at Bramall Lane was a fairly depressing experience. We were losing a lot of games and I was being made man of the match on a pretty regular basis just for having a go. I was back to the brawn and the aggression and the bookings were flying again right, left and centre. There were spells where the players daren't even go into town because of the bad reaction from the fans.

We did go in one night, to a wine bar, and wished we hadn't. Billy Whitehurst, a big, strapping bruiser of a centre forward and a great lad to have around the dressing-room, suggested the players all met there. I parked my sponsored car 'Vinnie's Vauxhall' on the opposite side of the road only to see, later, a load of Sheffield Wednesday fans jumping all over it. Their match against Forest had been called off so they'd all converged on the city centre. Next minute a load of them marched into the bar and confronted us.

Billy stood up and I moved to his shoulder, noticing the other players getting to their feet as well. Suddenly, a pint glass flew towards us and clouted Dave Barnes, one of our fullbacks, on the head. Billy reacted like lightning. He threw one of the best right-handers I've ever seen – inside or outside a prize-fight ring – and the biggest bloke in the group just crumpled to the floor with somebody shouting: 'Hey, that's my brother!' It stopped the trouble, though. We simply walked out of the place as everybody backed off.

It was easy to see why Billy was so popular with the other players. What a lad! We knew something was up one morning at training, the moment Bassett stepped on to the grass. You could always tell his mood from the way he walked. When there was trouble brewing he moved with a funny little scamper as if his legs were working only from the knees down. 'Right, you bastards,' he snapped. 'Whoever was involved with Billy, yesterday, see me in my office later.'

Apparently, Billy had organised a trip to Cheltenham races with a mate of his from Hull. They'd even organised the transport as well – by ringing up and telling the bus company that a reserve match had been called off but could the coach do a pick-up at a service station. While the reserve players waited for the bus that didn't come, a group of our boys were on their way to Cheltenham in style! The coach driver even waited and brought them all back again. Bassett fined them a week's wages apiece.

Sheffield United were really struggling to make an impression in the First Division and Bassett was getting increasingly worried. He had brought me in as a leader and eventually asked me what I thought we could do, because if we didn't do something, we'd be going down, as we were bottom of the table at the end of January. We talked for a while and he made his decision: 'Go and tell the boys that I'll put a hundred grand in the players' pool if we stay up.' It was all above board – how much you received depended on how many games you played – and maybe it was coincidence that we went on to win seven matches on the trot, which took us up to twelfth, and so we survived.

Not without controversy, of course, and another unwelcome record for yours truly – booked after five seconds of a match against Manchester City at Maine Road. Another of those choice little meetings between me and Peter Reid. I don't know what it was about Reidy, why I landed in bother just about every time we faced each other.

Yes, I was in the book by the time referee David Elleray's opening whistle had barely faded away. I flew straight into Reidy and it not only landed me an instant caution but set the tone for an afternoon in which Whitehurst, Barnes and goalkeeper Simon Tracey were also booked.

We hadn't played ten minutes of the second half when I clattered into Reid again. I was going for the ball, but recklessly. Hands up – I deserved it. My mood wasn't right, I was feeling so low at the time. Those brilliant days, the concentration on passing the ball at Leeds, were well and truly over. I had found myself back to my bashing days again.

Not that I was completely miserable all the time at Sheffield. I rented a cottage close to a golf course. Also, I had started seeing Mylene again after the Cup final but we had grown apart in my time at Leeds. She had a very good job as PA to the governor of a London bank and so we saw less and less of each other. But after the move to Sheffield, I started going back to Watford more, linked up with Mylene again and she joined me at the cottage. There was one particularly good night out we had and the eventual result of it was broken to me in a casino at Luton when she said:

'I've something to tell you.' I half expected what was coming next. 'I'm pregnant.'

I didn't go all gooey and silly. I just went 'Phew.' I was well pleased. Now what's that well-known phrase or saying in our game? Well, it applied, that night: I really was over the moon!

During her pregnancy, everybody was telling me: 'This is what you needed. This will settle you down. This is the best thing for you.' Not in my case. Some blokes do change their personalities and characters, but I still go with the flow.

That close-season we had been to the house Mylene kept in St Albans, loaded everything into the car, including the dog, and were on our way back to Sheffield when she began to suffer what I thought must be stomach cramps. 'I'll be all right,' she said, so we kept driving up the M1. After all, there were six weeks to go before the baby was due. We carried on, until somewhere around Leicester Forest East her waters broke. I didn't know what that was all about but on phoning Jessop's hospital in Sheffield I was put into a right panic because they said: 'Bring her straight here.'

They couldn't contact the gynaecologist at first but the tests confirmed the baby was on its way and when he did arrive he didn't need much of an examination before getting her into the operating theatre quickly. I went in as well and I was really frightened for Mylene because of all the pain she was obviously going through. The doctor was saying, 'No, it won't come,' and all I could see was a small space and what looked like a big head.

'It's never going to come out,' I said, the expert gynaecologist, all of a sudden!

'We'll have to use forceps.'

I couldn't believe my eyes – they were massive things. But suddenly the baby was out: a boy. Covered in blood and as the nurse passed him to me they hadn't separated the cord. I was just motionless. They smacked his bum, put a tube in his mouth and then I was able to hold him for a minute. I didn't say a word, I was completely speechless but I felt ten-feet tall. Until the doctor told me to hand him back to Mylene and my legs began to shake, out of control.

'Come on, then,' I heard the doctor's posh voice say to me. 'Come on, let's go and wet the baby's head while these people tidy things up.' I gave Mylene a kiss and I kissed him – the baby, not the doctor. Within two or three minutes of the birth I found myself in the pub right next to the hospital.

'Another one?' the landlord said to the doctor.

'Yes, yes.'

He had a pint of beer and I had a pint of Guinness. There were one or two locals in, a couple of them saying: 'You the father, then? Congratulations.' It was the doc's routine to go in there following births during opening hours. All the locals knew him and knew the score – brilliant! I don't remember much, only that I wanted to ask him about babies and he wanted to talk to me about football. But I do remember walking back to the hospital and him saying: 'See you later – you'll get my bill in the post.' Mylene had a private room but there seemed to be hardly anything in it. Must have been £200 or more a day and although she was only in a couple of days I went out and bought her a telly. We called our baby Aaron and he still lives with his mother, today, but I pay for his education at Radlett School and see him regularly as he spends weekends at my place.

We went mental at Mothercare buying every toy and item of clothing available. Aaron, being premature, needed special care at first and I was desperate when they told me he had jaundice but was soon reassured as they explained it was fairly normal in the circumstances. Having a child might not have changed my personality but a man does have to make allowances, like the time Mylene sent me off to the chemist's for some women's things. I just gritted my teeth, walked in and got the job done.

Aaron's arrival thrilled me to bits. I went out with a couple of the players and got drunk out of my head. I was so proud, I don't think there was a person left in Sheffield who hadn't heard. I rang the world!

Mylene was always very independent. I had first met her at Batchwood Hall nightclub in St Albans where she worked to earn extra money to pay her mortgage. We were both overjoyed at Aaron's arrival but I hadn't expected the difficulties we would face. Our situation began to change, which wasn't Mylene's fault or, of course, the baby's, but the overall circumstances. A mother under pressure, a baby crying and a professional footballer worried about the lack of sleep. I found myself tiptoeing around her, trying not to trigger off a mood.

Eventually, Mylene started going back to St Albans more and coming up to see me. Then she stopped coming and, in an attempt to sort out the future, I suggested we bought a house and moved in together. Her place was her security, her worldly goods, so that suggestion didn't work. Instead, we reached the stage where I was driving down from Sheffield to St Albans to see her and Aaron, but drastic change was not far away. Sheffield United had played at Coventry early in 1991-92. I went to Mylene's on my day off and while I was there the phone rang:

'It's Dave Bassett for you,' said Mylene.

'All right, Harry? What's going on then?'

'Jonah, how are you? Listen, I've agreed a fee with Chelsea for you.'

And I have to say it came as a huge relief. Relieved to be away from the crash-bang game I'd returned to and excited at the prospect of joining the likes of Dennis Wise again, and Andy Townsend at Stamford Bridge. So, instead of having the day off, I drove to the Posthouse at Heathrow and signed for Chelsea within an hour. Another fee of £575,000 and another 'double your money' contract.

Chelsea were not too clever at the time. In fact, Wisey had told me one or two of the players had been urging manager Ian Porterfield to sign me. I'd started pulling their legs at Bramall Lane, joking, 'This time next week I'll be a Chelsea player.' It was only a gag but I think it actually came about because I was on too much money for Sheffield United's liking and they wanted me out. Even Bassett told me: 'I'm not going to stand in your way. This is a great chance for you.'

I signed on the Wednesday, we were heavily beaten on the Saturday and, would you believe it, we were at Sheffield United the following midweek. I was expecting a nice welcome, if not the standing ovation the Leeds fans had given me, because I had helped them survive, after all, but there wasn't even a burst of applause, just booing and jeering and I thought that just about summed it up.

Within weeks, I joined my furniture at 5 Hunters Oak, seeing Mylene only when I went round to see Aaron. Joe Allon, the centre forward Chelsea had signed from Hartlepool, was at a loose end renting a place he didn't like so he moved in with me, and Kerry moved with me, too. It was a bit like the script from *Only Fools and Horses* – me and Joe with 'Uncle Albert' looking after us.

I seemed to make a habit of living in threes. Kerry lived with me and Steve Robinson at my first house in St Agnell's Lane, Hemel. I remember he was there the day after Wimbledon had won the final and Paul Gascoigne had been transferred to Tottenham. So much for the incident between Gazza and I that people made so much fuss and so many heavy headlines about. We became good mates. Gazza had come round that day and we'd been out shooting. For some reason, Fash had turned up as well and we were all sitting in the front room, drinking tea and watching the box when Kerry walked in.

He just stood and stared as if he had been turned to stone and then said to Gazza: 'What the hell are you doing here?' He couldn't believe his eyes. Gazza was living at the Swallow hotel at the time and I felt a bit sorry for him. He was dead keen on the outdoor life, especially his fishing, and I got him out a bit. In fact, he came down to Bedmond one night and took charge of first-team training. We didn't end up at The Bell but stayed at the club, played three-card brag and Gazza lost fifty quid. I had to lend it to him to pay his corner and, yes, he did pay me back. We lost touch once he moved out of the hotel and bought his own place but I've hated some of the stuff about him that has been made public. I see a lot of myself in him and there have been a few occasions when I phoned him to say 'Keep your head up' or contacted his agent and said 'Tell him I'm thinking about him' when he was going through the bad times.

Joe and I treated Hunters Oak like a bachelor pad – nights out, women, booze, fast cars, training and playing football. Good times – full blast. When Joe had had a beer he got funnier and funnier, a Geordie boy who called himself 'the face of the north-east' and he cracked me up. But it wasn't all laughs.

Not the night we came out of a club and stood by the taxi rank. A couple of blokes were waiting for a cab and minding their own business, it seemed, until one of them started having a go at Joe, saying, 'What are you looking at?' Then he turned nasty so I stepped forward and told him: 'Look mate, if you want to get to him you'll have to go through me, first.' And he did, or at least he tried to, and the two of us ended up in a real street fight. I finished with a big gash in my left ear and a split head that was going to need stitches. In the end we stood up, both completely knackered, looked each other in the eyes and shook hands.

Then, when the first cab did pull up he said: 'Go on, pal, *you* have it.'

'Cheers.'

'Oh, and by the way,' he said. 'Good luck on Saturday.'

Bloody comical when you think about it.

By the time we got home my head was still

ringing. I looked in the mirror and my ear was as black as Fash's. Next morning Kerry was as chirpy as ever: 'Cup of tea, boy?'

'Yeah, thanks. I think I might have come second last night.'

At the training ground there were reporters everywhere – somebody from that cab rank had tipped them off. They told Porterfield they'd heard I had been involved in a bust-up and come out of it with a broken jaw. I'd put a bobble-hat on to hide the gash, kept my left side and the black ear away from them, slapped my chin and told them: 'Seems all right to me.' It killed the story stone dead.

Bob Ward, the physio, was stitching my head at Stamford Bridge when, as luck would have it, chairman Ken Bates wandered in. 'What on earth have you been doing?'

'I came second last night, Batesy.' He muttered something before leaving but I could see he was not at all amused.

tanya

Joe Allon looked out of the front-room window and saw the beginning of the rest of my life.

We were all in there. It was a lovely day and Joe was just lounging by the window that had the phone on the sill. He glanced out into the street and said: 'Cor, what a stunner. Come and have a look at this.' I wandered over, looked out and saw a woman walking past and Joe wasn't exaggerating. She was beautiful. Then I did a double-take.

'It's Tanya,' I said. 'I know her. I'd recognise her anywhere.'

'Oh yeah,' said Joe with the kind of reaction you might expect. 'Course you know her. Don't give me that!'

But it was. It was Tanya, the first time I had seen her in years. And I told Joe the story of how it had all begun . . .

She was among the kids who used to go to the Sunday cricket matches. I went with the Hensard family because Russell's dad played and Tanya was there. We were just kids, about twelve, I suppose. Nothing boy/girl about it, just playmates, knocking around together: Russell and me, Tanya and her pal.

It became a fairly regular outing and we all looked forward to it. And it might have remained just that – one of those nice childhood memories.

She was Tanya Lamont. Her family are Irish, and she went to Francis Coombe school in Garston but I was at Langleybury and we lost contact. I didn't see her for several years until one night I was in The Three Horseshoes and this girl came up to me and said: 'You're Vincent Jones, aren't you?'

I hadn't recognised her, first off. She was beautiful, I recognised that – extremely pretty with long, dark hair. The other lads knew who she was, at least those who had gone to the same school as Tanya and her brother, Shane. When it dawned on me, we stood and chatted for a while, recalling those cricket matches, all that time ago. She also explained that her old man would never let her go to the pub but her mum had agreed on condition that she got back in before dad. I saw her a couple of times in there and eventually one night decided to ask if I could walk her home.

I had taken my motorbike to the pub, so I left it outside as Tanya and I sauntered back, along into her street. Nothing too romantic – a cup of tea in the kitchen with her mum, Maureen, but her dad, Lou, wasn't in. I stayed for the best part of an hour and walked back to the pub. No bloody motorbike! It was the first time I'd had anything nicked.

I didn't really know how to react. It was a case of 'What do I do, what do I do?' running round in circles, looking everywhere, clutching the great helmet they'd left behind, a ridiculously huge helmet for my little Suzuki P100. Tanya had been in the pub with her pals and there were some lads from Garston in the party. She still swears that my bike going walkabouts had nothing to do with her.

There was a phone box over the road by the park, so I thought I'd get one of my mates to pick me up, but as I was dialling I saw and heard a bike roaring up and down the park. I walked over and there was a crowd of lads taking it in turns to ride – on *my* bike. Time for action. I positioned myself to meet the rider who had just turned and as he passed me, roaring like a good 'un, I caught him with a right-hander. Off he came, over went the bike and I was on it and away like a shot before his mates could get near me.

I saw Tanya in the pub the following week and accused her of setting me up. But she insists she played no part in my bike getting nicked and I did, eventually, believe her. But we did have a fall-out because she said: 'And what about you telling Russell Hensard you got off with me in my house!' What? There hadn't even been a kiss or canoodle. Russell had a builders' yard just up the road from her place and had known her for years. I think he was a bit jealous that I'd walked her home so he'd pulled her leg and she didn't see the funny side!

That was it. She blew me out completely and I was sad. There were plenty of women around at the time but she was outstanding. I don't know, there was just something about her, something that made me feel different. I did try to creep back but she wasn't having any of it. Every time I tried to talk to her I got the cold shoulder. If Tanya doesn't like you, she doesn't like you. We didn't set eyes on one another again until 1984 . . .

It was FA Cup final day, Watford against Everton

and Nigel Callaghan, one of the lads who had gone on to sign pro at Vicarage Road and was matey with Russell, got us two tickets. We had a great day, even though Watford were beaten, starting with a bite to eat and a few drinks at a hotel before driving down to the stadium. As we went to park the car, the coach carrying the Watford players' wives and girlfriends breezed past. Another double-take . . . Tanya was on there. I think she was pointing me out to the girl next to her, Suzy Barnes – John Barnes's wife. She didn't know that I had seen her and Suzy must have been puzzled to say the least at having her attention drawn to a bloke who was playing for nobody at the time – on the dole, well before joining Wealdstone or going out to Sweden.

As she was pointing, Russell said to me: 'That's the players' wives' coach and that's Tanya Terry.'

'What are you on about, Tanya Terry?'

'Remember Tanya Lamont, the girl you used to see?' said Russell. 'Well, that's her, she's married to Steve Terry, Watford's centre half.'

I was quiet for a while and then I saw her again walking up the Wembley steps and I stood and watched her. And she was the most beautiful person I'd ever seen. I thought: 'I wish she was going up those steps to watch me play. I wish I was going out there and that she was married to me.'

It wasn't a wish to be playing at Wembley, because that kind of prospect was a billion light years away. I was just wishing she was with me. She was gorgeous. I later learned that when she had said to Suzy 'There's Vincent Jones, there's Vincent Jones', Barnesy's wife, used to having the likes of Rod Stewart pointed out to her, just said

'Who's he?' and looked a bit baffled.

A couple of years later there was a piece in the Watford *Evening Echo*: how she had undergone heart-transplant surgery at Harefield hospital after complications at the birth of her daughter, Kaley. I read it with mixed emotions – so sad for her that she'd had to suffer something so serious but relieved that she had made a complete recovery.

I had last seen Steve Terry when I had a drink with him at Leeds and he was playing at Hull. He remembered me as a kid at Watford and I said: 'You're not far away – why not come over and have a weekend with us.' He said: 'Well, I've got Tanya and Kaley.' So I just asked how she was and told him to give her my regards. They never did come over because Steve was transferred on again.

So you see Joe, I do know her and I would recognise her anywhere.

'Then you've got to go out with her,' Joe said. 'You've got to.'

It was another of those strange coincidences in my life – unless granddad had something to do with it. Tanya was actually living next door but one and I had no idea. I'd seen her pass by in a car and I'd also noticed Steve going to and fro. He'd arrive, we'd have a couple of words, then he'd drive off with the baby and come back later. Then it all fell into place when I bumped into Tanya's friend, Joanne Southern, who'd been at the same school as me. She explained that she and Tanya were living at the house and how Tanya and Steve had split up. Something started jangling in my head . . .

The 'local' was The Venture in Hemel and Joe

was back home early one night because he had a reserve game. When I walked in he stunned me, saying: 'Hey, I've been round to see Tanya.'

'What do you think you are doing, going round there?'

'There was this rabbit in the road, and next door told me it was the little girl's from the house further on. So I took it round there. Talked to Tanya and she told me it was forever getting out.'

'Well, you can stop being a busy bollocks for a start,' I said, knowing he was winding me up. But it made me think. A day or two later I arrived home from The Venture around ten o'clock having had a few drinks. Tanya and I had been sort of avoiding one another, uneasiness and embarrassment more than anything. I sat in the house and wondered how I could possibly talk to her. I sat for quite a while until inspiration struck: "Course – the rabbit!'

Round I went and knocked on the door. 'Hello Tanya, it's Vinnie. Do you remember me?'

Yes, she did, and I said, 'It's your rabbit, George. He was out and I went into the garage and put him in his hutch. You'll have to get that door sorted out.' Then Kaley, who was about four at the time, started crying, upstairs, and Tanya said: 'Can you hold on there a minute, I must go up to my little girl.' So I was left at the door and when it blew open slightly with the wind I could see right through into the front room. There was nobody there, so I went in.

I was a bit merry, to be honest. I was in my skinhead phase and never really lacked confidence, anyway. I put the kettle on, made some coffee, found the biscuits in a drawer and took it through into the main room. When Tanya came down she opened the door, looked outside and thought I'd gone.

'In here. It was freezing out there so I came in and put the kettle on.'

She was really stand-offish. 'Do you always let yourself into other people's houses and put the kettle on?' I could tell she wasn't being the girl I knew from Garston, she was being a bit prim and proper. But we had a coffee and the biscuits and began to talk. We talked and talked and I had the odd Hamlet cigar and we kept talking. Right through the night until Kaley woke up and I left at seven the next morning!

Tanya had asked things like 'What's your situation, now? How did you become a footballer? I thought you were a thug and when I read you were a player I couldn't believe it because I imagined you would be in prison somewhere.' We talked about how she and Steve had grown apart – a bit like Mylene and me – how he had moved in with another girl, and about babies, but she didn't say anything about the heart transplant.

I went home, drove in for training and was back at her house again that afternoon. It was hot and we sat out at the back with her friend Mandy Walker who is my housekeeper nowadays. Jo Southern was living with Tanya to help meet the costs but at weekends a crowd of girls gathered at the house and on summer's evenings I often went round there with Colesy, sitting in the sunshine, chatting and having a great time. Things just progressed and we started going out as a crowd.

Tanya and I were getting to know each other again, growing together, becoming closer but not even holding hands, let alone sealing it with a kiss. There came a day when she said she had to go away for the weekend, to hospital in Nuneaton for laser treatment. It was nothing to do with her heart but serious all the same. Maureen, her mum, and Mandy would be going to visit and she would probably have to stay in there a few days to rest. It started driving me mad, thinking of her in that hospital so far away. So I asked Mandy to come with me. I knew Maureen would be there but that Tanya's dad was away. I also heard he wasn't too happy to hear that we'd been seeing one another!

I drove up to Nuneaton, anyway, and as usual – whatever predicament she might be in – Tanya had made sure she looked nice. She'd already been at the mascara and the lip gloss because she knew Mandy and I would be there. After a little while at her bedside, Mandy and Maureen left us together. I leaned forward, held Tanya's hands and gave her a kiss. Just a gentle, little one. It was the very first time I'd kissed her.

I had already made up my mind that I was in love with her. That was why I had to drive to that hospital. I had never felt that way about a girl before. We had been having such fun and I knew I wanted to be with her and take care of her.

When she'd left for the hospital on the Friday I went round to her house and was looking for something when I came across a pile of letters almost as thick as a phone directory. They were bills and many of them were the red variety. I suppose she couldn't cope with them at the time so, anyway, I wrote cheques for the lot and paid off everything.

At that bedside, after putting both my hands on

hers, kissing her on the cheek and saying 'I missed you' well, that was us, then. She looked me in the eyes and said: 'Vinnie, you've got to take me home. Please get the doctor to let me go.'

I asked, but the doctor said something that amounted to 'You have to be joking.' After Maureen joined in saying that, 'Once our Tanya makes up her mind about something . . .' and Tanya herself was begging the doctor, I said 'I will stay with her if she's allowed home' and he relented and gave permission.

I picked Tanya up and carried her down the corridors of that hospital and out to the car, laid her in the back still in her pyjamas and covered her up with blankets. The car was filled with flowers from her bedside and that's the way I drove her home. And I waited on her hand and foot while she convalesced, staying with her and Kaley who, being so used to having all girls around, didn't seem too struck on fellas.

Tanya was still recovering when we were invited to a wedding. Johnny Watts, a good mate of mine, wanted us there the day his daughter was married. I was in morning dress and Tanya looked absolutely fantastic on what was our first real date, an outing on our own.

There was valet parking at the house, a massive marquee with immaculately laid tables and sparkling chandeliers, and Edwin Starr was the celebrity 'turn'. The wedding was just out of this world. All the chaps from The Venture were there and everybody, probably 300 to 400 people dashed out of the marquee at the sound of a helicopter landing. Tanya and I were in the middle of the crowd as the bride and groom were whisked away with all their guests waving them off. Tanya and I just stood there and watched it go. We gazed until the helicopter became a dot and disappeared and when we looked around us everybody else had gone back inside the marquee. There were just the two of us and I turned to her and said: 'That's going to be us on our wedding day.' We became double-double sloppy then and held one another for ages. That was the first night we ever slept together – at her house.

We'd driven back to Hunters Oak in Johnny's white Rolls Royce. He'd insisted, and it wasn't far anyway, so we jumped at the chance, and parked it in the driveway. I spent that Sunday with Tanya and Monday morning went training. At about one o'clock Joyce, Johnny Watts's wife, came banging on the door asking Chris, our housekeeper, where I was.

'Not here – he's gone training.'

'Oh, I'd just like the keys to the Rolls.'

'But you could be anybody,' Chris said. 'I can't just be giving out the keys to a Rolls Royce.'

Joyce was hopping mad. 'Give us the keys, I've got to go shopping, give us the keys.'

'Sorry. Can't do it. No way.'

When I got home Chris had left me a neat little message saying that somebody called Joyce had been round and could I return her Roller!

I was spending more and more time with Tanya and Kaley, while Joe was still living at my house, and the feeling grew that I wanted to take care of them for the rest of their lives. I wanted to make sure that no harm ever came to Tanya and it was inevitable that I would ask her to marry me. It was quite a formal proposal, when it came. I had become really close with Tanz, having Sunday dinners at her mum's with a few of my mates, my sister and her boyfriend, Tony. It was beautiful. And I decided to go for it. I wanted to marry this girl. I didn't want to leave anything to chance. I wanted to be with her forever.

We had just returned home from a night out when I held her calmly and asked: 'Will you marry me? I want to marry you.'

'Yes,' she said. Well, it was more of a shriek and she went crazy about it. That was nice.

'Don't say anything to anybody, yet,' I asked her. 'I want to talk to your dad first. I want to do this properly.'

I had been to a golf day in Suffolk in aid of SPARKS, the sports aid research charity for kids. I'd been made a patron and was proud of it. I rang Lou on the way back and asked if I could come round. He thought something was wrong.

'No, nothing's the matter. I just want to come and see you on your own.'

He was alone when I arrived and I just said straight out: 'I want to ask you if I can marry Tanz. She has said yes and I want to ask you for your blessing.'

Lou talked quietly and kindly about Tanya's heart transplant and tried to explain. 'Do you know what you are taking on board? This is a hell of a thing, she's no ordinary girl. We sometimes have panic attacks about it all.'

'I know all that,' I said, 'and I want to look after her for the rest of her life.'

'Then I'm over the moon for you.' And Lou gave me a big hug.

He had never forgotten that I had been there to

bring her home early from hospital in Nuneaton. By the time of Tanya's transplant operation Lou wasn't able to enter the ward because of the urgent medical procedures. He desperately wanted to cuddle her, as any father would. He'd been told they weren't sure whether she would make it through the night. Could you imagine, he was standing out in the cold night air when he saw the helicopter bringing Tanya's new heart and only chance of life. And when he arrived, Lou wasn't able to cuddle Tanya. I worship the ground Tanz walks on, but that is nothing to what her father thinks of her. He absolutely adores her and is so glad I'm with her, taking care of her.

The worst part for Tanya is the annual check-up, the angiogram she needs at Harefield Hospital. I'm always there and wait outside. It is a major examination as you might expect and, although she is drugged, she is conscious the whole time. She makes me promise that I'll be there afterwards but the promise isn't necessary. I wouldn't be anywhere else! Sometimes she comes out crying and I just feel: 'This isn't fair – it isn't fair.' It's an immediate reaction to Tanya's discomfort, not a complaint. Harefield is a wonderful place where they perform miracles and our gratitude to the experts and staff there cannot be put into words.

Tanya clings to me after those check-ups and I have said to her so many times: 'I'll always be here for you. I'd move mountains.'

To say we live from day to day is wrong because we couldn't exist like that. We make plans for months and months in advance. When it comes round to Kaley's birthday, Tanz's heart collapsed during childbirth, she does become fragile. In fact, it was Tanz's birthday the day before Kaley arrived so when the anniversary comes around you realise it's been another year but there is love and reassurance in our house and we accept that whether you've got £500 or £5 million, what will be, will be.

I could not imagine being without Tanya, now. She's a great kid, terrific personality, beautiful, and when she's on form she just lights up the room. We haven't had many rows but when we've not been talking she'll say, 'Life's too short' and the making-up is fantastic.

The moment Tanya had said yes to marriage I phoned the old man, told him the news and asked him to find me a plot of land.

CHAPTER 20

out of a nightmare, into a dream

So Joe's casual glance into the street at Hunters Oak really did start something. Meeting up with Tanya again, it's a wonder I was able to concentrate on anything, let alone that 1991-92 season with Chelsea.

In fact, we had a pretty good season. Like at Leeds, I enjoyed that feeling of being with a proper football club. There was that strange kind of aura again and I was strutting about with a chest like a cock pigeon. A few feathers were ruffled along the way, of course, not least my own. You wouldn't believe that record five-second booking could be beaten, would you? But it was. The FA Cup brought Sheffield United to the Bridge and you're always wound up that little bit tighter playing against a former club. I still find it hard to accept there was time for me to do anything in *three seconds* but my first move, my first challenge, produced the yellow card from referee Keith Burge's pocket. I was straight in on Dane Whitehouse. I must have been too high, too wild, too strong or too early, because, after three seconds, I could hardly have been too bloody late!

Strange, though, how you tend to remember defeats as much as victories. Dennis Wise and I, along with most of them in the Chelsea dressing-room, believed we were going to make it to the FA Cup final. Second Division Sunderland at home, although they were going for promotion, looked comfortable enough until a Peter Davenport equaliser forced us into a replay before a full house at Roker Park. I'd heard stories about the famous old 'Roker roar' but, Jesus, only hearing is believing. What a bloody din they made. Especially when Sunderland nicked a late winner. We couldn't believe it. Ah well, I've been knocked out in the fifth round, quarter-finals or semis but I could always say I'd never lost in the final!

There is a blot on my copybook that I still regard as a joke. Literally, a joke. A £1500 fine by the FA for 'making obscene gestures to fans' prior to our match against Arsenal at Highbury. Tony O'Mahoney, my sister's boyfriend, was in the crowd. Mind you, there wasn't that big a crowd in as we warmed up, casually knocking the ball about on what was a lovely sunny day. I spotted Tony in the crowd, grinned at him and gave him the old sign – you know, the one fans use regularly when a player in the rival team makes a mistake. I laughed at Tony as I jiggled my hand and mouthed: 'You wanker.' Just a spur of the moment joke, to a mate. I thought no more of it, but some Arsenal fans made a complaint and I was charged. The FA stuck me with the fine but what actually happened never came out.

Most of the Chelsea lads were card mad – and, no, I don't mean the yellow and red variety. Andy Townsend, Wisey, Tony Cascarino, Kerry Dixon, we were all at it on a trip to Canada for a tournament that also involved Dundee. It was a long haul, must have been eight hours or more, but Gareth Hall managed to get us into first class, as his girlfriend worked for the airline. I took £1000 spending money but I was 'potless', didn't have a dollar left, when we landed. Wisey had won the lot.

As we strolled out of the airport, the Dundee lads were sitting at the back of the coach that was to take both teams downtown. We had collected our luggage but were still playing seven-card brag as we walked along. Wisey looked at the coach and said 'We're not getting on there with them' and Dixon whistled up the biggest stretch limo you've ever seen. We could see our lads on the front of the coach, the Dundee players at the back and nobody talking.

'See you later, boys!' We followed the coach into town, the Chelsea boys rolling about laughing. The 'stretch' cost us about twenty dollars between us – travelling in style can be a snip.

We had great crack, the Chelsea boys. They were a terrific bunch but it had turned out to be a little bit of a holiday camp. At the end of the season I said to Ian Porterfield: 'Look, you need to bring somebody in. Somebody like Don Howe. He was brilliant at Wimbledon and he would bring some order to this place.' He must have taken some notice as Howe was brought in soon after.

But we were only a few games into the 1992-93 season when the wheel turned full circle. I was on the move again. Wimbledon, here I come again, for £640,000 or thereabouts. I was gutted to learn that Chelsea were moving me out. I heard a story – I don't know how true it was – that Eddie Niedzwiecki, their goalkeeping coach, was big mates with Nigel

Spackman and wanted him back at Chelsea. Even if that was true, I'm not blaming Niedzwiecki. What got up my nose was Chelsea thinking they could replace me with Spackman, who couldn't lace my boots at the time!

But he came in from Glasgow Rangers and I was off to Wimbledon and it cost Chelsea an awful lot of money. They had to pay me right up and I look around at my lovely house at Redbourn and smile: 'This is all down to them. They paid for it.' It cost me £105,000.

Coincidence again. I had recently fallen out with my agent, Jerome Anderson, over that notorious *Soccer's Hard Men* video and was now trying to negotiate my pay-off at Chelsea. As luck would have it, one of the lads at The Venture suggested we went to watch our darts team in a tournament and after seeing them knocked out we started my favourite game: three-card brag. I love cards. A bloke was watching us and after half an hour he introduced himself as Steve Davies and asked if he could join in.

He sat down next to my old man who warned him: 'Shouldn't get involved in this lot . . . it's a bit heavy, mate.'

'That's all right. No problem,' said Steve, who just happened to be an extremely successful businessman and legal consultant with a Rolls Royce out in the car park. Perhaps as well, seeing that he ended up losing £800 in that card school and I won the lot.

He came into the pub again the next night and as we chatted it struck me he could help me. I explained about my dispute with Anderson and that I could use some assistance in getting my money from Chelsea and he said he could handle that.

'OK,' I told him, 'you come on board and look after me.' Little did I realise that this chance meeting would develop into such a close and personal friendship in the years to come. I didn't want the problems I'd experienced previously. Some agents spread their loyalty: 'Sorry, Mr Jones is unavailable, that day, but Mr so-and-so will be more than happy to oblige.' That kind of thing. I told Steve he could look after me on one condition: that I was his only client. We shook hands on it. Steve has been brilliant. As things developed, we became close associates, sharing complete personal confidence. On his advice, I am now involved in a sports promotion company with his wife Angela, and have recently made a significant investment in a company in the information technology field – watch this space! Steve is not simply my representative and business partner, but also a very valuable friend who believes he is there to help keep me out of trouble, not land me in it!

Back at Wimbledon in the glittering new Premier League, I had a great welcome on my home debut, my photograph all over the front of the match programme and in it I told the fans they would be seeing a different Vinnie Jones – 'One who can pass the ball, not just hook it on aimlessly. It won't just be crash, bang, wallop.'

So what happens? Bloody mayhem. It was against Kenny Dalglish's Blackburn, the money-bags brigade, and I was to last about thirty minutes before the referee, Martin Bodenham, sent me packing. Two of Blackburn's players, Tony Dobson and Mike Newell, were to be dismissed as well later on, but you don't need telling whose name dominated the headlines.

I did start off by passing the ball, quite neatly and with imagination. But it's when I don't have it but want it that the trouble can start. Kevin Moran, Blackburn's Irish international defender, had it and I challenged him from behind. Moran described it to the press like this:

'I was just bringing the ball out of the box when a huge pair of flailing arms appeared round my neck and I could hear the stamping of giant hooves from behind. Yes, Vinnie deserved to be booked because it was more rugby than soccer.' Bodenham followed his yellow card with an immediate red after I swore at Moran but, as Kevin mentioned: 'The backchat and the verbals aimed at me must have been the last straw. To be fair, Vinnie was using nothing worse than the language that is commonplace in football.'

John Fashanu weighed in, protesting at the decision and Dean Holdsworth had to drag him away otherwise he could have gone as well, insisting to the referee: 'I'm the skipper. I'm not a child, so don't treat me like one.'

I spent the rest of the match watching from Sam Hammam's private box at Selhurst Park and I was blazing. I was convinced my reputation, as much as my behaviour, was going to land me in trouble back at Wimbledon. After all, I hadn't been sent off at Leeds, Sheffield or Chelsea. Manager Joe Kinnear went on record after the match claiming:

'Vinnie sometimes get mistreated. There is abusive language from nearly every player, nearly every week. Referees could send them all off. This one lost control. It's crazy. Vinnie has become a marked man.

Referees have pre-conceived ideas about him. Anything we say, publicly, can land us with a disrepute charge but they're getting away with murder.'

Kenny Dalglish defended his team as well after a 1–1 draw that saw three players sent off and three booked. I was told that Blackburn's manager said to the referee as he left the pitch: 'If my players played as badly as you refereed today, I couldn't defend them.'

A couple of months later, there was more trouble. The shit had hit the fan, big-time, about that desperate video that had me accused of glorifying violence and the dirty tricks of the game. I had been at Sheffield United when the film was made. Jeff Weston, Jerome Anderson's partner or assistant, phoned me and said a video company were making a film about soccer hard men, basically, a few players talking about their experiences and what went on in the game. I agreed to take part in the film and he said: 'It's two grand for doing it, less twenty per cent of course.' So I was to receive £1600.

I sat in a leather chair in my front room with a cameraman and another bloke who seemed to be doing it all. A right cheap outfit, if you ask me. I was asked what went on and I told them, believing other people were going to be involved answering the same questions, and I never bargained for the way it would come out and the trouble it would cause. The verbals, the off-the-ball stuff, studs in the back of the legs.

It was months and months before I heard anything. It turned out that the video had been sold on four or five times, from one company to another until some bright spark got hold of it, went to the papers and said: 'Can you believe a professional footballer has come out with this?'

They say 100,000 copies of that video were produced and sold. I was one of a number of people on it with my picture on the cover. The adverse publicity for me just promoted the video, as it turned out. I never had one, never saw it and wouldn't want one in my home. I wouldn't watch it to this day because I am so ashamed to have been so naive and stupid. The only glimpse I've seen was on the television news – a clip of me talking about lifting up opponents by the hairs under their arms. I just cringed and switched off. The £1600 I was paid originally was sent off to a children's charity.

That November I was hauled before the FA disciplinary people. There were about six FA officials confronting me at Lancaster Gate. I'm tempted to say not one of them looked under eighty but that would be wrong: I could be a year or two out. They didn't seem particularly interested in my explanation of how it came about. I told them I had been naive and wrong, and that I had totally disassociated myself from the whole thing, but all they seemed to be saying was that they couldn't afford another such case and had to make an example. What I said, mentioning a lot of good work I had done for kids and to generate their interest in the game, well, it just seemed to fall on deaf ears. They were going to nail me and nail me good.

'Don't condemn me for one bad, bad mistake,' I said. But it was a record £20,000 fine, all the same, plus a six-month ban, suspended for three years.

The reason the FA came up with that sum was interesting. When I re-signed at Wimbledon, my deal was that I could earn £300,000 – so much in wages and so much in bonuses, including a bonus for every goal I scored. They asked me what my average goal-scoring rate was for the past five years, which was four or five goals.

'Right,' said Sam, 'we will give you five grand a goal.' It was a built-in incentive, like saying, for example, instead of paying you £10,000 a week we'll pay you £5000 but you can earn £10,000. It was the way Wimbledon did things – a potential salary for the year but not guaranteed. It was up to the individual to perform at the level expected of him.

The FA said they were aware from my contract that I could earn that £20,000 fine from my bonuses and were probably disgusted that anybody could earn £5000 for scoring a goal. Yet all these years on, now, in 1998, the Inland Revenue have hit me with an £8000 tax bill! I wanted the fine paid as quickly as possible and told the club to deduct it from my signing-on fee so a cheque could be sent immediately. So it came out of my gross earnings and, after a lot of negotiating, I've recently had to write a further cheque to the Inland Revenue for £4000. Yes, I've been made to pay for that awful mistake.

Thank heaven Tanya and I had grown so close and that there was a wedding to be planned. The old man rang me to say he'd found a place for us at Redbourn. It was an old derelict shell of a bungalow, part of a farm on a three-acre plot. Straightaway, Tanz and I knew it was the place for us. We called it 'Oaklands' and from the front it is virtually an exact replica of 'Woodlands', the bungalow dad had bought for the family and done up.

I don't know whether I was trying to recreate that home from childhood but I even had the same architect, Ken Phillips, who designed 'Woodlands'. I remembered whenever anybody came to that family house they said how beautiful it was, on its own with the fields around, and I just know that when I saw the plot at Redbourn I thought: 'Woodlands. I want Woodlands right there.' And that's what we did. It was just an instinctive thing and Tanya fell in love with the place.

I did most of the demolition and mucked in with the groundwork. But the builders were held up by heavy snow and I became frustrated because it wasn't happening fast enough. We'd already set a date for the wedding, 25 June 1994, and the frustration began to turn to panic because that very special wedding I had promised Tanya was going to take place in a vast marquee on the field next to the house. We had 100 feet of panelled fencing between the house and the field and the final panel was actually hammered into place at about ten o'clock the night before the ceremony.

An extremely sad event was to make a contribution to the happiest day of my life. Around the time Tanz and I decided we would marry, Joe Byrne died. He was the elder brother of one of my closest mates, Seamus. Joe was a big bloke, around eighteen stone. He was regarded as a 'Big Daddy' to us all and was a great crack, into all the Irish ballads and writing songs, but he was a complete pisshead as well. Whenever Joe landed in trouble it was down to the drink, and it killed him in the end.

He had been to the pubs and was finding his way home in the early hours of the morning when he was hit and killed by a car. Only in his thirties. The funeral was in Abbots Langley. Packed – you couldn't get in. I stood to one side with all the Bedmond boys recalling so many memories. Joe had been a postman and there were Post Office vans parked everywhere. I'd never been to the funeral of someone I knew before, let alone a pal I thought the world of.

I just stared at the coffin, thinking of Joe and the good times, the music, the songs, the odd fight. A couple of the lads had stood up and read poems, there had been the customary address, but I wasn't really aware of what was being said until an incredible voice filled the church with the words and sound of 'Ave Maria'. So clear, it was so good that I thought they were playing a cassette. Violet Burn was the singer, an old friend of Joe's who shared his love for music. And she is blind. Her voice jolted me back to reality and I turned to see her standing on a balcony behind us. I knew then, I was about to break down. I held it in and then Violet sang 'Danny Boy', Joe's favourite song, and it was just too much. I saw a lot of grown men cry that day and Mark Atwood, a tough man in his own right, had to steady me as we walked out of the church. The experience was so powerful and so moving that I decided to ask her to sing at our wedding.

My stag night was something else. I went with my pals to Cork for the weekend. Sixty-two of us! There was supposed to be sixty-five but sixty-two turned up including dad, Lou, Steve Davies and Wimbledon manager Joe Kinnear, and we had a great time, lots of drinking, leg-pulling and card schools. Steve had sold the whole stag 'do' to the

Daily Mirror, stories and pictures right through. But during the final champagne toasts on the Sunday there were a couple of blokes sitting in the hotel with a little camera asking if they could take the odd snap or two. 'Yeah. 'Course. Carry on, boys.' We thought nothing of it, until their pictures appeared in the *Daily Star*!

The party spilled outside and into the huge river. The manager of the hotel rushed to me at one stage saying: 'Vinnie, you have to stop them. Many people have died because the current sweeps them away.' A few of the Bedmond boys were jumping in from a bridge and swimming across. I went out, called them back and was inside again within minutes, in time for the last hand of poker. We were still playing, with our taxis lined up outside as the stakes went higher and higher on the last hand: 200 . . . 500 . . . 800. I won four and a half grand on that final game and the cheering was as loud as ever it was at Wembley in 1988.

There was a group of police with dogs when we arrived back at Stansted. They must have been warned there was a boisterous party of lads flying in but there was no trouble. They joined in the crack, managing to smile while the rest of us collapsed as some of the lads squatted, motionless, on the luggage carousel as it went round and round, through the exit flaps and back again.

I had explained to Steve about the wedding I wanted – just like the day Johnny Watts had arranged for his daughter. 'If that's what the boy wants, that's what the boy will have,' he said. And he helped me to plan it. Steve has a solution for everything. If you want a pool-cover, he knows where to get one, if you need special lighting or a bouncy castle for a party, ring Steve. He said to leave everything to him, and I did. We had vast marquees, silver service, the finest food and a helicopter. All in, the wedding cost £100,000.

First, though, we went through a registry office ceremony on the Friday because a marquee wedding alone would not have been legal. The last time I had been in that room was when I gave my mum away at her wedding to Dave. This time, Steve had sold the wedding to the *News of the World* but word had got out and the place was swarming with press people. It was like a circus. The *News of the World* had left nothing to chance, they must have had eight or nine blokes there with cardboard shields, thrusting them in front of all their opposition as they tried to get pictures.

Steve had suggested Tanya and I went in separate cars so we couldn't be photographed together but there was bedlam when we arrived, blokes appearing from nowhere trying to smash the cardboard blockade. Tanz was swamped as she went to get in the car after the ceremony. They were all over her and Lou hit out and made sure at least one of them realised we were not to be messed around. While all this was going on, I legged it out of the back and was pictured jumping over a wall, leaving my own wedding!

The press were all over Redbourn, as well. We hired a security firm for the Friday and Saturday and it was a good job we did. We needed those blokes with their walkie-talkies. I stayed down the road at the Aurbury Park hotel with all the boys on Friday night while Tanya was at the house with all the girls. About a hundred of my pals turned up. So did Tanz about nine o'clock for a quick kiss and a cuddle before she and her friends went out for a meal.

I asked Johnny Moore to be my best man. There were so many candidates, so many mates, I could have chosen any of them, but when it really mattered, when I needed shelter if you like, Johnny was the one who had taken me in and looked after me. He was delighted to accept. He's very emotional, Johnny, a good crier.

If ever there was a perfect day on this planet then it was that Saturday Tanya and I were married in front of all our family and friends at our home. You can see the M1 from where we live and there were people, press people, trying to get across the fields and through the woods, attempting to come from the other village. Yes, we certainly needed that security firm.

My sister Ann was one of the bridesmaids, so was Kaley, with Aaron as a page boy. The entire family was there to share our big day, all close again, forgetting some of the past and looking forward to the future. Yes, the Bedmond boys were all there and Wisey, John Barnes, Sam Hammam, Stanley Reed, the chairman, and Joe Kinnear. Howard Wilkinson was away but Mick Hennigan was there and so was Frenchy. Joe Allon was among nine ushers.

And we had a helicopter. I arrived in one with Johnny – it was lent to us as his wedding present by Kevin Cinamond who has known Tanya all her life. Steve had told me I couldn't buy a wedding suit off the peg but that I should go to Mr Ed's in Berwick

Street, London, where I could choose the cloth and virtually design it myself. I knew the bridesmaids were wearing lilac so I chose purple with gold braid.

It was a blazing hot day – a problem for the 200 guests assembled inside the marquee because, to avoid outsiders getting pictures with their long lenses, we had to pull down all the flaps, which turned the place into a sauna. The guests who had been greeted by a jazz band on their arrival now had to put up with humidity equal to anything they have in New Orleans!

Tanya didn't show it, but she was in awful pain from one of her feet – a temporary side-effect of the drugs she has to take. She told me later, she could hardly put it to the floor on her walk from the house to the marquee, but nobody would have known. When she arrived at my side she looked absolutely sensational. A hell of a lot of tears were shed during that ceremony and the first of them were mine, the second I looked at the stunning lady by my side.

Needless to say, one of the most moving moments of all was when Violet sang after Pastor Warren Tranter had announced: 'Vinnie and Tanya would like this to be dedicated to the memory of Joe Byrne.' Seamus, his mum and all the family were there. It was our tribute to Joe, the memories flooded back and as Violet sang 'Ave Maria' and 'Danny Boy' again, you could feel the emotion that brought tears to the eyes of just about everybody in that marquee. The service seemed to fly by and then it was outside to greet all our friends and the jazz band played right through the meal and on until another couple of hundred guests arrived for the disco in the evening: a black-tie do.

Some of my mates, like the Bedmond boys, had never worn evening dress before. It was great to see them all done up – Moss Bros must have had a field day! I did my party piece, getting up to sing 'Woolly Bully', with Tanz's brother in the backing group and the bride and groom began the dancing by being first on the floor to 'Where Do You Go To My Lovely?' – our favourite song. One of our friends has since made a glorious collage of the day: a photograph of Tanz and me set among confetti with the words of the song set through the middle. I sang a little to my wife during that dance – 'When you go on your summer vacation, you go to Juan Les Pins . . .' And that's exactly where we went for our honeymoon.

We were driven to the airport in my big, seventy-grand Mercedes, Tanya still in her wedding dress, for one night at a hotel then off to the south of France next morning. Steve had booked us into the Juana saying it's the best. It was almost the 'brown trousers' when we strolled in, that feeling when you sense you are completely out of your league! Wonderful food but anything between £200 and £400 for the set menus I seem to remember. We had a Coke each at the bar, plus scrambled eggs for me. I handed the bloke the equivalent of £30 and got three quid change. It was £100 a bottle for champagne, but what the hell. Steve had sent them a cheque in advance, so it was all taken care of.

Even on honeymoon, a week away was long enough for both of us. I can't remember the last time we were away for a two-week holiday. We like being at home, with the kids around and the animals. It's our place, it's what we created together and both of us value our home-life more than anything. As we turned into the driveway I noticed the electronic doors to the garage were closed. Mandy, our house-keeper, ran out of the house with Maureen, asked if we'd enjoyed ourselves – and then up went the doors. The garage was packed. All our families and friends were there again – or maybe they hadn't left after the wedding! Drinks, a fantastic buffet. Everybody sat around while Tanz and I opened the presents and then watched the wedding on video. It was the perfect finish to a beautiful wedding. I was determined that Tanya should have the best.

All the bouquets were handed to the grand-parents – and we have quite a few, between us. I had a cuddle with my nan and whispered: 'It's a shame my granddad isn't here.'

'Oh, but he is, Vinnie.'

'Yeah, I know he is, really. I know.'

I have a real glow now, about the family being so close. I look back on the break-up, all those years ago, and can see it in a different light. It hurt as a kid but you grow up to realise that these things happen and it is wrong to lay blame. Both mum and dad remained supportive, even though there were times when we didn't have that much contact. Dad gave me work, mum paid for my driving test and put the deposit down on my moped. I was the one who gave mum away at her wedding to Dave. We have all been together on many occasions but to see them around us on our wedding day – mum and Dave, dad and Jenny – it just underlined that family feeling that not everybody is lucky enough to experience.

Tanya and I cannot have children together, but I have a beautiful boy, she has a beautiful girl and we both regard them as our own. Tanya gets on so well with Mylene, and Steve Terry often brings his kids to our house to splash around in the pool with Kaley and Aaron. In fact, while the children stay at the house, Steve and I have a day out. There is no awkward atmosphere when we all meet up and that's the way it should be. As long as Tanya is happy and the kids are happy – then I'm content. That is all I want . . . to earn a lot of money to be able to spoil all three of them rotten.

The day I officially adopted Kaley meant so much to me. Mylene hasn't married and Aaron remains Aaron Jones, living in St Albans about ten minutes away. Tanz and I wanted Kaley to go to private school and I said I didn't want her facing questions about why her name is 'Terry' yet her mum is 'Jones', so Kaley agreed and Steve was in favour . . .

Kaley wanted to be part of the family and that made me feel proud. I pay her fees at Abbots Hill and Aaron's at Radlett and I like the thought of the children getting private education. I don't look on it as a status symbol for me and Tanz, but I sometimes allow myself to think 'The children are getting the best education . . . I can't have done everything wrong in my life.' I don't want my kids hanging around the estates. I don't have knowledge about classic plays and opera and so on, but I would like them to be interested in such things. I can't personally give them that kind of knowledge but I've put myself in a situation where I can make it available to them.

I have to confess to spoiling them, especially Kaley who is at home with us. I think I've made her more worldly. I've taught her to drive my Landrover, she's had just about every animal on God's earth although she does suffer badly from an allergy to fur. We went to buy her a white pony but the same thing happened that occurs if ever the dogs manage to sneak upstairs and lie on her bed – her face puffs up as if she's just been hit by Mike Tyson. I was brought up streetwise but always interested and involved with animals. I don't know whether it will be possible, but my ambition for Kaley is that she should become a vet.

A pal of mine from Leeds recently met Aaron for the first time in years. He was tickled pink and rang his wife to say: 'You would never believe this is Vinnie's boy, sitting here. He sounds so posh.' Never mind about posh – if he speaks properly, that's brilliant. His mum has the job of keeping an eye on him, making sure he does his homework, but when he comes here, he lets his hair down, puts his overalls on and just has a great time. He and Kaley behave like any brother and sister. They fight like brother and sister and love each other like brother and sister.

And we're all extremely proud of the pair of them.

CHAPTER 21

this is your captain speaking

My move back to Wimbledon had come out of the blue, as most transfers do. I was playing golf at Watford when the secretary told me there was a phone-call. It was Colin Hutchinson, Chelsea's managing director: 'We've had a bid from Wimbledon and we've accepted it.'

'Oh, have you really?' It came as a tremendous shock. I had been to Leeds and gained some credibility as a player and taken a backward step by going to Sheffield United even though they were in the top division and we managed to keep them there. But Chelsea meant credibility again. Everything was going great, the boys were terrific fun and my first season had been a pretty good one. The thought of leaving had never crossed my mind.

'If you go back to Wimbledon, we'll pay you fifty grand,' Colin said.

My contract, with signing-on fees, was around the £200,000 mark. I was hurt – yeah, properly hurt – to be told they'd accepted a fee and I knew they were wanting to bring in Nigel Spackman so I dug my heels in: 'No way, Col. I love it at Chelsea.' And I carried on playing golf.

About half an hour later, I was called back to the

phone. Hutchinson had doubled the money but I repeated, 'Col, there's no way. I'll only talk to them if you get me all my dough.' I knew in my heart that I should have stayed at Chelsea to improve my status as a player, but when I took another call to be told a deal had been done with Chelsea and Wimbledon each paying me £80,000, I went and met Joe Kinnear for the first time. There was the lure of being back with Sam and the boys, and the fact that Joe wanted me as skipper. Sure, I do like to be wanted – don't we all? But the money ruled my wallet as well! The deal was colossal and it gave me a stature, financially, I hadn't known before.

Wimbledon, the club who gave me my start as a professional footballer, were now providing me with a very comfortable life as a footballer indeed! I immediately took to Joe Kinnear, who I found to be a tremendous fella, and nothing has happened since to lessen my affection for him. There was outrage in the newspapers. How can Vinnie Jones be captain of a Premiership side? But Joe never once batted an eyelid.

'He's my captain and our leader,' he told them all and it was clear, from the start, that we'd hit it off. I had not only found a manager but a new mate who I knew would be completely honest with me. He gave me responsibility and I loved it. Even though Dave Kemp and Lawrie Sanchez were doing the coaching, I was the third coach in line and had the respect of all the players. It was difficult during the first weeks, though, because there were players who had become established in their own right, like Robbie Earle and Warren Barton. I had never played with them and I think my arrival, the return of one of the 'originals', put a few noses out of joint.

I had to be strong, acknowledge that they had succeeded in keeping Wimbledon rolling but I also needed to make it clear that I was there to do a job. Fash was still there, as was Hans Segers, but there were quite a few up and coming members of the 'gang' and we soon became matey and settled things down. But there was more trouble and triumph ahead of me in 1994, an extraordinary year. In fact, it all seemed to be rolled into the space of three crazy months.

It began at home to Leicester in the September and a match that, for me, was to last only thirty-four minutes before the latest of the dreaded red cards. I'd been booked after thirteen minutes for a late challenge on Mark Blake. But it became ten men against ten when the fists flew between me and David Lowe. Both of us let fly, and with Graham Poll, a new referee making a name for himself, it was hardly surprising that we were both sent off.

Walking down the tunnel I was thinking 'Here we go again, I've allowed myself to be sucked in again. I thought I had taken a step forward but I've slipped back ten years. And it's got nothing to do with Wimbledon, it's my own bloody fault.' If anybody has a dip at me my first reaction is to go 'bang' straight away. By the time I've thought about it, it's too late. There is no thought process at all in that split second, it is just an instinctive, physical response.

Two months later and I'd done it again. Not the exact same circumstances but Newcastle's visit to Selhurst Park turned into a bit of a war, with me among the early yellow cards. I was wound up and at one stage Robbie Earle ran across and said: 'You've got to calm down. Don't make another tackle because this geezer's going to send one of us off.'

I listened and I knew Robbie was right, but if there's a ball to be won it's my job to win it whatever the circumstances. Suddenly there was another challenge to be made and although most players wouldn't have gone for it in the circumstances silly-bugger me went straight in on Rob Lee. It looked horrendous and in fact it was horrendous even though, thankfully, Rob was able to carry on after it. I misjudged everything – the height, the speed, the timing. It must have looked more like a kung-fu kick than a tackle and the very second my backside hit the ground with my leg ending up across his back I thought to myself: 'Just walk.' So I climbed to my feet, shrugged my shoulders and held up my hands as much as to say: 'I was fully committed and going for the ball but I made a complete mess of it.' Philip Don was the referee, an experienced official and a man who had my complete respect. I think he was a bit gutted at sending me off because he said: 'Why have you made me do this?' And he was right. No question of the referee prejudging character in this case. It was my fault. Completely.

The Crazy Gang element and influence, the high jinks, had been maintained at Wimbledon although not on the scale of the earlier days. There was still that keen collective spirit among us and a protective quality that saw us close ranks whenever one of us was in trouble. We got along fine with the sports writers generally, it was the news journalists who had to be kept at bay. On many occasions we discovered a group of them waiting at the training ground and Joe would pull me over to ask: 'Who's in the shit, this time?' There were two routines: 'Slip him out of the back before the end of training,' Joe would say. 'Leave his car keys and we'll get one of the boys to run it back for him.' Or the alternative was for Joe to call the reporters together saying: 'Good morning, how can we help you?' as half a dozen of us wearing balaclavas and armed with buckets of water roared from the dressing-rooms and soaked the lot of them. When, later, they protested about damaged cameras and equipment, Sam would explain that it was a group of youth players who seemed to have been involved but nobody was quite sure of their identities. Sam told the papers he would deal with it if they could tell him who they were!

The initiation of new players was far more spectacular in the early days – car windscreens totally coated in Vaseline and then 'stuccoed' with gravel from the car park. All four tyres let down, wipers removed on rainy days, potatoes wedged up your exhaust pipe. 'Right lads, backwards running.' As soon as the order went out there would be a wink as well and one of the lads, often striker Dean Holdsworth, would be down on hands and knees in a flash behind the unsuspecting new arrival. And over he'd go.

I remember Mick Harford joining us from Coventry, a genuine tough guy of the game, and the papers saying that he wouldn't be mucked about by the Crazy Gang but he was tumbled, running backwards, like the rest. Despite all the reports about his back trouble!

New players would come in to find their shoe-laces cut. Even today, if a lad walks in wearing what the others consider to be dodgy gear, like a flash pair of shoes, it would disappear. When defender Eric Young signed he used to have one of those plastic bags that kids carry with the name of their favourite team written on the side. Eric had 'Brighton' emblazoned on his and, despite repeated warnings, he would keep turning up with it. So Wally Downes and I stood it in the middle of the changing-room, dowsed it with lighter fuel and put a match to it. It filled the entire place and the caff next door with so much black smoke that the entire building had to be evacuated.

New arrivals were rugby-tackled, stripped and flung into a patch of nettles, the river or the biggest puddle we could find. It was up to their initiative to sort themselves out with fresh kit, but by the time they'd done it we'd send them on a lap of the playing-fields as punishment for being late for training. I still find it hilarious to recall the day we caned Harry Bassett's underpants with Deep Heat and then watching him sitting there getting hotter and hotter until he fled the place to shower off and change, claiming he had turned as red as a baboon's bum.

The tricks weren't as extreme or regular on my return with the Dons but there were still enough practical joking and initiation to retain the team spirit that has been such a vital asset to them as they have defied the odds for so many years. And in the December of 1994 they had a new international footballer among their ranks – Vincent Peter Jones of Wales!

There had been talk of my qualifying for the Republic of Ireland when Big Jack Charlton was looking for somebody who might do a job at centre half. Nanny Harris, mum's mother, was born in Dublin but despite our efforts to trace a birth certificate it was like looking for a needle in a haystack because, apparently, many records had been destroyed years earlier in a fire.

After the Irish possibility fizzled out, I anticipated more problems when the talk started about me playing for Wales. The national side was having a bad time and somebody did an article saying they could do with Vinnie Jones in midfield. Steve Davies did his homework and, although I was a bit reluctant at first, I went along with it and he eventually traced Granddad Arthur Jones' birth certificate. It had to be submitted in time for me to join the squad for the European Championship qualifying game against Bulgaria in Cardiff. But it so nearly all went wrong.

Mike Smith, the Wales manager, had included my name once the birth certificate had been established but only on the understanding that all the documentation was completed and delivered to meet the rules. It was agreed that somebody from the Welsh FA should sort out the paperwork, and the plan was for me to set off the next morning and drive to Cardiff. I was instructed not to drive over the Severn Bridge before we'd had the official nod.

So that was the schedule for the following day. My phone rang at about two o'clock in the morning. It was Steve. 'Do you realise, boy, we've made all that effort to get this done and we've left it to someone else to actually sort out the procedure in time. What happens if they don't do it?'

'Good shout. So what do we do?'

'I'm not leaving anything to chance. I'm going to get down to Cardiff, right now.'

And he set off. A mate of mine from down the road, one who does a bit of driving from time to time, picked up Steve in the middle of the night and they arrived in Cardiff in time for an early breakfast. Steve waited and waited for the bloke who was supposed to be sorting out my details. Ten o'clock ... twenty-past ... half-past ... nothing and nobody. Steve phoned the guy and found he was in a meeting elsewhere.

Meanwhile, somewhere on the M4, I had cut my speed from 70 mph to 60 mph but I was getting too close to the Severn Bridge without a word. Down to 35 mph and slowing! When Steve has something good to tell me, it's usually the same greeting: 'Go on the super Jones boy.' And finally that call came through.

'You are there, son. You are there. It's all done. You can get yourself over that bridge.'

I had had the words to 'Land of my Fathers' on tape for some time and played them over and over in the car wherever I had been driving. I had learned it phonetically – well, most of it, anyway. Certainly enough of it to be able to ring Steve, once I'd crossed the Severn, and sing it to him full blast. I later learned it properly after Mike Smith brought in a guy to teach us. He didn't need to tell me how important it was for all of us to be able to sing it word for word.

Even when I was driving down there, it still seemed unreal. Me playing for Wales. I'd come through an awful lot, even to win the right to play

Wimbledon spirit, so long the key to the club's success. (ABOVE LEFT) The
zy Gang's Christmas party, 1993 (*Allsport/John Gichigi*). (ABOVE) Go-karting
Joe Kinnear in February 1994 (*Allsport*). (BELOW) Mock celebrations on the
ing field, where so many of our pranks took place (*Action Images*).

Three generations of the Joneses at my wedding to Tanya: me, son Aaron, and father Peter.

My beautiful bride Tanya with Aaron and Kaley. She was in awful pain that day with one of her feet, but you would never have realised it.

(ABOVE) At the register office the day before the ceremony in the marquee, witnessed by my sister Ann and Tanya's brother Shane. Meanwhile the press were swarming around outside. (RIGHT) On honeymoon in Juan les Pins. (BELOW) When we got back, the garage opened to reveal a whole group of friends and we began another party.

... good, the bad... (OPPOSITE PAGE, TOP) Throughout my career, people have [tend]ed to underestimate my ability as a player, but here I beat the Brazilian Juninho [(All]sport/Phil Cole), while (BELOW) I score the only goal of the game to beat Arsenal [in 1]997 (*Colorsport*). But there have been some bad times, and (ABOVE) I've often not [got]ten well with referees (*Allsport/Mike Cooper*). My tackle on Ruud Gullit (BELOW) [got] me sent off and led to me making some comments about foreign players 'squealing [like] pot-bellied pigs' (*Action Images*).

My debut for Wales against Bulgaria in 1994 nearly didn't happen (*Allsport*).

I was chosen by the team to be captain of Wales against Holland in a World Cup qualifier in 1996. It was a huge honour, and I was bursting with pride. Sadly, the game did not go well for us (*Allsport/Ben Radford*).

e Jones family. (ABOVE) Off to Ascot with Tanya. The 'Imran Khan' suit I am aring was stolen at the Arc de Triomphe and held to ransom – I was able to retrieve it hout having to pay! (ABOVE RIGHT) Aaron takes the wheel. (BELOW) With ...ley, aged six.

Two career options - films won. (ABOVE) As Big Chris in *Lock, Stock and Two Smoking Barrels*, my first film, released at the end of August (*Polygram Filmed Entertainment*). (BELOW) In the dugout as coach of QPR in a pre-season friendly against Spurs (*Action Images*).

professionally, so the thought of international recognition still wasn't making much sense in my head. I imagined all kinds of things, including the thought that I would reach the end of the M4 and the bridge wouldn't be there. But it was and I made it and I joined the rest of the squad with my itinerary in my bag. The usual things, training times, accommodation and a list of things to bring. Shin pads, proper footwear, passport, etc. My passport was at home but I thought no more about it as we were playing in Cardiff, anyway. Horror!

Over lunch on the day of the match the boys were asking me if I'd brought my passport and I reckoned I was the victim of a wind-up. But they didn't go on about it for long so I dismissed it. Until I went to board the coach and saw a right old commotion. A lot of shaking heads and frowning faces.

'What's going on?' I asked.

'It's Mark Hughes – he's forgotten his passport.'

I pulled Mike Smith aside and told him, very sheepishly: 'Mike, I haven't got my passport with me, either.'

He only said two words: 'F . . . ing hell.'

Unknown to me at the time, and probably to most people reading this, every player on the team sheet for an international game, home or away, has to produce the passport. Without it, you cannot play. FIFA rules. We had come all this way . . . unearthing granddad's birth certificate, the panic over submitting it in time, the drive from Hertfordshire not knowing whether I would complete the journey, and now it looked as if I was going to miss out, after all, because I didn't have my passport for a match in Wales!

'Sparky' and I boarded the coach, anyway, but it still looked grim when we reached the stadium. Officials running in all directions, including the referee, but the rule book looked like winning. No passport – no cap. Thankfully, common sense won the day. I'm sure Hughesy was more important to Wales than I was and felt certain something would be done to make sure he didn't miss the game. It was all resolved with an instamatic camera. They took a photograph of the pair of us, stamped it and we signed it and date and timed it, as well as arranging for copies of our passport details to be faxed. Luckily, the referee accepted it but I'm certain that 'Sparky' forgetting his passport was the biggest stroke of luck I had with Wales. If it had been me, alone, I wouldn't have been cleared to play and who knows whether I would ever have played for Wales.

It was so important to me, that first appearance. For granddad's sake. He had been born in a workhouse in Wales but lived in Watford with Nanny Ann when I was a kid. We were all mad Watford fans and he used to have his own little patch on the corner of Shrodells, opposite the directors' box and named after the hospital where I was born. I would go down to the front with the other youngsters while he stood with my dad and my uncles and their mates.

I used to long for the call from dad saying we were going to Watford. We'd pick up granddad on the way and then file into the ground to be surrounded by familiar, friendly people including the bloke who always had his transistor radio, filling us in with all the results from around the country. Being Welsh, though, granddad's main passion was his rugby. He also enjoyed a little bet from time to time on the horses and the dogs and it's no coincidence that, like him, I now own a racing greyhound.

I didn't ask granddad for his help before that first game for Wales. It was enough for me just to be there. All I had to do was step out on that pitch and hear the sound of the first whistle and I was an international footballer. I had taken my ghettoblaster to Cardiff, playing the Welsh anthem at every opportunity and singing along with it. Most of the players yelled at me to pack it in, but Gary Speed and Dean Saunders sang it with me. I sang it as loudly as I could before the kick-off against Bulgaria and I knew that granddad would be watching and feeling extremely proud.

I know people have a laugh and a joke about it, but it hurts me when they say that I'm as much Welsh as a rarebit. I have no time for people like that because I feel Welsh and regard myself as Welsh. Things in my house are Welsh – ornaments and furnishings – and although Kaley is English with an Irish background she is being brought up as Welsh as possible. So being part of it in Cardiff on that occasion was like having watched a Welsh barge pass by on a canal, day after day, until the skipper eventually noticed me and shouted: 'Come on, get yourself on board.'

The excitement of it, the massive honour of being picked to play, somehow overwhelmed detailed memories of the match itself. I did OK, I know I enjoyed it, wearing that red shirt with the three feathers. I haven't known many prouder moments in my life. What is it they say, pride comes before a fall? It did in my case.

It was in Cardiff again, a night game in June

1995, another European Championship qualifier, this time against Georgia. The match was won by Georgi Kinkladze with a glorious chip from twenty-five yards about twenty minutes from time. But I wasn't on the pitch to see it – I'd been sent packing about twenty-five minutes after the start. At Wimbledon, Bobby Gould always used to say the worst time for me was when things were going well and I would knacker it. A bit like Gazza, I suppose. I had started off soundly against Georgia with good, clean tackles, winning the headers, passing the ball well. I put a brilliant block tackle on a geezer who was about to score and the timing and the accuracy were perfect as I took the ball at exactly the right split-second.

Suddenly it was as if my heart and my guts overruled my head. There was this feeling that everything was going my way and I could do anything at all. I clattered into Mikhail Kavelachvili. He went down in front of me and I trampled all over him. I remember trying to make it just look a clumsy challenge and I can't say I purposely trampled on him because I didn't think about doing it. I should have jumped over him and out of the way but I trod through him, and he was on the floor as if he'd been shot. He rolled and rolled. I couldn't argue at being sent off but it might not have been more than a caution if the bloke hadn't reacted like that. As soon as I was red carded he was up again and flying. People say you should stop, pause or at least think before making a reckless challenge and they would be right if it was possible. It wasn't with me – I was trying to stop myself but although there was no intent to hurt the guy I knew I was doing something

I shouldn't. By the time you fully realise it, in the heat of the action, it is too late and you are staring at the red card.

That was my worst ever sending-off. Wales were a sort of early-days Wimbledon – striving against the odds, always seeming to be up against it and I had been honoured with a place in their team – and had let everybody down. Nobody came off the bench to walk in with me and when everybody else came in, at half time, I might just have well been something a dog had left in the middle of the floor. Nobody put an arm round me, nobody said anything to me, not a word. And then, to lose 1–0 with only ten men – I was made to feel even bloody worse.

It cost me a five-match suspension and, in the meantime, Bobby Gould was installed as the new manager of Wales. As soon as I heard, I feared my international days were numbered, if not over. I just had the feeling that now he was an international manager Gouldy wouldn't want to make too much of his old Wimbledon connections. Some of the other players argued I would be OK because he was my mate and I tried to tell them that we weren't that close – Gouldy and I had had more wars than love affairs. True enough, I wasn't selected for his first couple of games.

And yet Bobby Gould was to give me the opportunity to do something precious few footballers, not even some of the truly great players, have ever done. I was not only to play international football again – but with the distinction of leading out the Welsh side as their captain!

It was in Holland and the usual skipper, Barry Horne, was out injured. I never saw a piece in the papers explaining how the Welsh players were each given a piece of paper to write down the name of the one they wanted as their captain that night in Holland.

At the hotel Gouldy announced: 'Look, the fairest way to do this is for me to leave it to you. You are all men. Just write your own choice as skipper. That includes putting your own name on paper if you think you should be skipper.' I put down my own name and I think one or two others did the same. But when the manager read out from the slips of paper it was: 'Vinnie Jones . . . Vinnie Jones . . . Vinnie Jones.' I was voted captain of Wales by secret ballot!

Funnily enough, I don't think Bobby was expecting it. I wasn't part of his equation. In fact, when the result was clear, I swear I heard him sigh: 'Oh no.' But there was a spontaneous round of applause from the players. Johnny Hartson, a good mate of mine now, went mad, and I ran straight upstairs, rang Steve Davies and said: 'You'll never guess what's happened.'

'You've been made captain.'

'How do you know?'

'Because,' he said, 'your story just never ends.'

I was the governor, then. And all those people who argued that I should never have been an international footballer now had to say I certainly shouldn't have been an international captain. And I had beaten the lot of them.

Welsh recognition warranted another tattoo, a third to complete the set and I had a beauty put on my chest – the dragon and the feathers. It took three hours and cost £150. But after nine caps my international career ended almost as abruptly as it began. I was right to wonder how long I would survive after Bobby Gould took over. He made it clear he was going to rebuild the team and although he retained some of the older players he put me on stand-by. No explanation, not even a phone-call. The first I knew was when the press contacted me.

I've had good and bad times with the press but this gave the knockers the chance to put the knife in again and turn it. 'How do you feel? You were captain not so long ago and now you are only a stand-by player.' Gould had brought in somebody from non-League and yet here I was, skipper of Wimbledon, waiting for somebody to drop out. The phone never stopped with calls from the papers but it never rang with a call from the manager. I still haven't heard from him. I do think he should have called me and explained.

I used to contact Gouldy, years ago, and ask for his advice because I do respect him. He is a good talker and thinker. I nearly picked up the phone and rang him over the Wales business and realise now that I should have done. Who knows? I might have ended up as his No 2 with the international side. I could still end up as Wales's manager, and believe that one day I probably will.

CHAPTER 22

the darkest hours

Without a doubt, 15 February 1995 was a black day in the history of English football. It marked the terrible occasion when the international match between Terry Venables' England and Jack Charlton's Republic of Ireland had to be abandoned after twenty-seven minutes because of rioting by visiting yobs who called themselves supporters. It was also the night when I did something that almost had the gravest consequences.

I was sent out to Dublin to write a piece for my column in the *News of the World*. We were staying at Jurys Hotel, only a short walk from the Lansdowne Road ground. A few of us had gone over to Dublin, Steve Davies, Tony O'Mahoney, my sister's boyfriend at the time, and one of my best mates Richard 'Click' Clarke, a gamekeeper at Newmarket. There had been a little incident in the morning, when I came across Gary Lineker at breakfast, the bloke who had given all the lads the hump by saying on telly that he'd rather watch Wimbledon on Ceefax than actually see them play. I can't abide people who put others down when they don't have the chance to defend themselves. I'll bet the last thing Gary thought was that he'd bump into one of us in that Dublin hotel, especially me. I went straight across to his table: 'Big ears, you're a disgrace. Not so big-time now, are you, big ears? Not as brave as when you're sitting and talking on the telly.' Then, from my table about ten feet away I chucked my toast at him, hitting him on the side of the head and shouted: 'Put that behind your ear!'

I had a right bee in my bonnet about him putting us down. All the Wimbledon lads had worked their socks off to achieve what most people accepted was a remarkable success, and I couldn't stomach what I considered to be unfair or snide criticism. I was up for an argument with Lineker but the people with him were telling him to leave it.

'Say it to my face,' I told him. 'What is it about us that gets up your nose?' I was goading him because it was my chance to have a crack back on behalf of the Wimbledon players. 'Haven't you got anything to say for yourself? Here I am, just me, say it to me the way you've said it to millions.'

He didn't really say anything in reply. If he'd said, 'I just happen to think you're a crap side and I hate the way you play the game' I could have handled it. But he tried to ignore me completely. Maybe he didn't know what to say, maybe he couldn't back up his own words, or maybe he just didn't want a row in a restaurant, which I can appreciate now. Still, I felt I'd made my point.

I hadn't really started making my way to the match before our plan had to be aborted. We grabbed our coats to leave for the stadium about a couple of hours before kick-off but there was quite a crowd of boisterous Irish supporters outside, big fellas who were keen to let me know they hadn't exactly welcomed the thought of me playing for their country. They had obviously read of our attempts to try to establish my qualification, even though I was in the Wales team by then.

There were one or two provocative comments – the only time I've ever had any stick from the Irish – and Steve rightly decided it was unwise to run the gauntlet, not a good idea to get involved. So we stayed in the bar, settled in front of the box and were appalled, like everybody else, when those idiots following England started breaking up the seats and hurling their missiles from the stand after the Irish team had scored.

It wasn't long before everybody was back at the hotel, supporters and loads of press men frantically milling around, doing their stories. We were sitting having a bottle of champagne when a bloke came over and said somebody wanted to meet me. I went across, there was a bit of fooling around and everybody knows what happened, then. Ted Oliver, a news reporter from the *Daily Mirror*, was sitting at a table with a few other people. I'd had a good drink – I wasn't 'steaming', but I was in high spirits. Oliver said something quite innocuous really but I felt he was belittling me. Then there was a bit of grabbing and tugging, so I got his head in my arm and took hold of his nose with my teeth.

I thought it was completely in jest. Unfortunately, I didn't realise my own strength. Perhaps I got carried away with the drink to some extent. That was it, he told me to clear off and I went back to my friends. Next minute, somebody came over and said: 'You've bit his nose.'

I thought it was all over and done with, so I went to apologise to Oliver and found him pressing his nose with a white handkerchief that had some blood on it, but I still didn't realise that it was quite serious.

'Bloody hell,' I said, 'I'm sorry.' Some time later, on my way to bed, I spotted him having a drink and went over again.

'Look, I am sorry about what happened.' But I wasn't able to make any progress, so I went to bed.

The next morning I was with my pal, Jimmy Creed, on the early flight back from Dublin. I felt I'd equalled the score with Gary Lineker on behalf of all the boys at Wimbledon and the only concern was for English football and the damage done to its image by the terrible hooliganism at Lansdowne Road the night before. But at Stansted airport we walked into chaos. There were media people everywhere. I looked behind me wondering who the hell was on our plane, then I was swamped as somebody yelled: 'You bit off a bloke's nose in Ireland.'

'Oh my God.' The word was that I'd amputated his bloody nose. I was straight on the phone to Tanya and she was crying. I was saying, 'I haven't done what they're saying, it wasn't like that, it was nothing' and explaining that I hadn't phoned earlier because I'd caught the early flight, but she was terribly upset. There were cameras and reporters at the house, and radio and TV people constantly on the phone.

I got home, gave Tanya a cuddle and the sight of her, so distressed, made me cry as well. I just went upstairs and lay on the bed and cried. I couldn't cope with everything that was happening around me. It wasn't a nervous breakdown, as such, but it was some sort of emotional collapse, I suppose. I just lay there. My mouth was wide open, my eyes staring into space and I couldn't move. I couldn't feel my legs or any part of my body. I was gone, wasted. What on earth was happening to Vinnie Jones?

Steve came upstairs and sat with me and held my hand and told me to get myself together, that Tanya would be up with a cup of tea in a minute. But Tanya was in tears again and I just thought: 'This is it. This is the end of the world.' They left me alone but must have checked, periodically, because Steve has since told me I was lying in the foetal position, sucking my thumb.

I had always faced and handled everything before. Always held up my hands for whatever I've done. This time, I couldn't. There was me thinking that what happened in Ireland had been nothing more than a bit of horseplay that got a little rough, yet I found myself being pursued as if I had murdered somebody. If life had been a dream, before, well now it had burst wide open. I must have laid there for about four hours. Then I felt freezing cold, icy from head to toe even though the central heating was on. Sweat poured off me. I forced myself off the bed, came downstairs and found Steve still there. I was in a daze, just moping around.

There was worse to come, next day. A great deal worse.

I was up at 6am and went straight to the shop to fetch the papers. There had been so much hassle from the media, so much speculation about what was coming out, that I braced myself for the worst. And there it was, splashed all over the front page of the *Daily Mirror* – 'Mirrorman's soccer riot agony' – with a picture of Oliver and his damaged hooter. Inside the paper there were more pictures and the heading 'Vinnie fixed me with his teeth and shook me like a dog with a dead rabbit.'

Although I was expecting to be the centre of controversy yet again I didn't anticipate the story being given quite that kind of treatment. Coming as it did alongside all the aftermath of the violence at Lansdowne Road, the timing could not have been worse. It wasn't long before reporters descended on the house again and the phone rang continuously. I decided to go in for training. Often it is a tremendous help just to get in there among the other players, hear their reassurances, put up with their leg-pulling and get out into the fresh air and run and run. That day, though, the press were there before I was and, although I trained, my mind wasn't totally on the job. I had one eye constantly on the car park, wondering who and how many were going to turn up.

Steve had been in regular touch with the *News of the World*. Sports editor Mike Dunn had said it looked as if the editor, Piers Morgan, was going to sack me, believing he would be ridiculed by the newspaper industry if he continued to publish my column. Eventually, we seemed to have settled on a compromise. Piers Morgan demanded that I should do my side of the story with a photograph suitably confirming my regret while, at the same time, offering my own version of events, putting it all into some perspective and pointing out that 'it takes two to tango'. That is exactly what I did and I believed the problem with the *News of the World*, at least, had been resolved.

I was still uneasy, though. I felt strange, having

returned home from training. The longer I thought about it the more worried I became that the *News of the World* would have a change of mind that wouldn't, exactly, be to my advantage. I began to feel awful, again. I went upstairs and back to my bed and Tanya tells me I was in an even worse state than the day before. I was back in that half curled-up position, unable to concentrate on any particular thought, unable to clear my head of the turmoil and the pressure that squeezed and squeezed the longer the day went on.

Then the answer struck me – the answer to it all . . .

Steve was downstairs with Vince Needham, another of my friends. Vince, looking concerned, suggested: 'Come on, boy. Let's go and have a pint.' I wasn't even capable of doing that.

'No,' I said. 'I'll stay here. I need to settle down a bit. Clear my head. Don't worry – I'm going to be all right.'

I persuaded Steve and Vince to go. It was somewhere between four and five in the afternoon and I reassured them again that everything would be OK. Then there was Tanz.

'I've got to have something to eat, love,' I said to her. 'Can you go down to the shops and get me something? I'll be fine. I'm going to have a bath.'

She agreed, but I recognised heartbreak written all over her face. I remember thinking, right there on the spot: 'She has found herself married to a monster. I *am* a monster.' I know all about my image and reputation. There are some who think I'm just a thug, somebody who doesn't know how to hold let alone use a knife and fork, violent, uncouth, bad-mannered. Yet those who meet me and get to know me always say the same thing, that I'm really a nice bloke, soft-hearted and generous.

In our house at that moment I felt like the monster others had portrayed. Having returned home to find Tanz in tears as she held me I thought: 'What am I doing to this beautiful woman? I can't keep doing these things to her.'

So I said I would have a bath as she left for the shops. I went to the window and watched her go. Then I put my shoes on, went and unlocked the cabinet and took down my twenty-bore shotgun, loaded it and walked out of the house.

I had made up my mind what I was going to do, but had wanted to say goodbye to Tanya without raising her suspicions in any way. Before she left I held her tight, kissed her and said: 'Look, I love you. You are everything in my life.' That was to be the last time I ever saw her.

There is a wood at the back of the house, a few hundred yards away. With the gun under my arm I walked up the path and headed for those trees. It was a terrible early evening – dark, bitterly cold and it was spitting with rain as I lowered my head against a strong, biting wind. I knew exactly what and where I was going. There was a little spot in the corner of the wood where I used to go pigeon shooting. It was the place where the bluebells grew in the spring. I had my own little seat, an old oil-drum, and I knew it would still be there. I was going to sit on the drum, put the gun barrel in my mouth . . .

I was about a hundred yards from that place when, out of nowhere, Tessie, my little Jack Russell, came bounding up to me. Then she went running and bounding all over the place as she had done so often before on all those occasions I had adored – being out there in the openness of the countryside. She was hopping and skipping about. She had attracted my attention, distracted my intention and I must have stood and watched her for between five and ten minutes. It began to change my mood – the blackest mood I've ever had, a cold and calculated mood that I never want to experience again and would never wish upon anybody else.

The madness that had taken place earlier, the circus of media attention, began to fall into place and the threat of it receded. I thought: 'Out here, just me with my dog, there's not a lot anybody can do to me. If I do what I came to do a lot of people might be happy. But it will break my wife's heart.' It could well have killed Tanya, too.

Just that lucky distraction of Tess, hopping and skipping, gave me the chance to break my thoughts and so think again. I thought of Tanz returning from the shops and coming and finding me. I couldn't do it for that reason. I couldn't die knowing what I would do to her. I turned round, walked back, went into the garage and removed the cartridges. I put the gun back in the cabinet because if Tanz had seen it standing in the corner she would have known, straightaway.

It was about a month later that I told her what I had planned that day I asked her to go to the shops. She said: 'Whatever happens, whatever we have to go through from now on, never ever contemplate doing that.' I promised her there would never be any repeat. And we both broke down in tears.

I made a conscious decision never to put Tanya and the family through such a thing again. But I also decided to pack in football and become a full-time gamekeeper. I told myself that the only way to stop them writing about me and jumping on my back when something goes wrong is to jack in the game completely. I was serious, but my thinking still wasn't completely straight. As Steve said to me, over and over: 'When God made time, he made a lot of it.' And time really does heal. I know it does.

People still ask me, today, if I've changed, mellowed, eased off the pedal. It's not a question of changing, particularly, but I did calm down on the slow walk back from that wood. It taught me something about perspective – what is really important and what is not. Tanya and our kids are the most important aspect of my life.

I think I have spent too much time and effort fighting other people's battles or, at least, believing I needed to go steaming in on their behalf. I came to realise that part of life was about me, as well. I've had players come to live with me when they were in trouble, without a pot to piss in. They were very grateful at the time, living rent free, and when they left I never heard from them again. I thought of those people, those kinds of things, how I thought it was all down to me to try to keep the Wimbledon spirit going but now I decided: 'Let it take care of itself. If it's that important, the other lads will keep it going. It's not down to me, alone.'

If I wasn't married to Tanz I think I could still take everything on the chin without a problem. I wouldn't have calmed down or grown up as much. But breaking her heart breaks my heart into even more pieces. Other people's wives would be affected differently, but I have to remember what my wife went through and that she is on medication, so I can't afford to put her through such things.

After Dublin, some time after, I realised that Steve would be OK. He'd get over it; I'd get over it. Joe Kinnear and Sam Hammam would get over it, but I can never take for granted that Tanya will get over it so I had to face it. What was I doing? I was going to put her in her grave. Yes, there has definitely been a change in me since that weekend.

Something else changed. Wimbledon were due to play a Cup tie at Liverpool on the Sunday and I travelled with them for the overnight stay at the Lord Daresbury hotel in Warrington on the Saturday. I had gathered myself together a bit by then and was sure I was going to be able to play. After dinner I went for a game of snooker in the leisure centre, partly to keep my mind off things and partly to keep well clear of a couple of reporters who were stationed in the bar.

About nine o'clock I took a telephone call from Steve. 'Jonah? We've got trouble.'

'What now?'

'Just had a call from the *News of the World* – Piers Morgan's sacked you.'

It was like somebody booting me right in the pit of the stomach. I suspected something all along, but still didn't want to believe it when it happened. I'd already had a meeting with Sam Hammam and Joe Kinnear over all the Dublin business and been told I had to 'be a man' and 'deal with it properly'. After Steve's phone call I went to see Joe again and his response said a lot for his professionalism.

'Listen,' he said, 'we've had this for three days, now. You've got to be honest with me, Vinnie. Are you going to be able to play tomorrow?'

I told him I would be. I was sure I was going to be OK. Until I went to my room and tried to sleep, and couldn't. I didn't get a wink throughout that night; I was just tossing and turning or lying there unable to think of anything but the problems caused by that bloody stupid incident in Dublin. I went to see Joe and Sam first thing on the Sunday morning and told them: 'I'm sorry, but I'm no good to you today.'

Sam passed me the keys to his green Volvo and I drove straight home to Tanya.

The *News of the World* ran my version of the Dublin story – together with a picture of me, head in hands. But they also ran one right across the back page announcing they had sacked me. They did pay me for my piece and, as far as I recall, settled any outstanding payments. Not that Piers Morgan and I remained at loggerheads. Funny, but when he later became editor of the *Daily Mirror* he actually took me on again as a columnist. Time had healed yet again!

This time there was no FA disciplinary action as it had nothing directly to do with football, but as players we do have to remember that, while we're in it, the game is everything. I could have pulled the trigger. I could have said 'Sod football and everybody in it – I'm going gamekeeping and I'll read about myself in twenty years when somebody does a feature in a newspaper wondering whatever happened to Vinnie Jones.' Or I could scramble out of the brambles again, face the world and get on with it and win back some credit and respect. That's what I decided to do.

I have never been back to those woods since that day little Tessie mercifully distracted my attention. I think that if I ever walked back there, my mind might change again. I never like going over old ground. I don't mean I could ever go through with what I had in mind that bloody awful day but it could bring back the old thought process and set me off fighting everybody else's battles, trying to sort everybody else's problems.

CHAPTER 23

fouls, fakers and my future as the boss

Despite that conscious decision to let some things take their course without my involvement, the old competitive instincts survived. That fierce will to win and the resentment of anything that struck me as an injustice never left me and probably never will. It all surfaced again, that November 1995 when I only lasted forty-four minutes against Nottingham Forest at the City Ground, a match 'Click' Clarke had travelled to see. I'd been playing well, too. After the Dutch international Bryan Roy had put Forest in front inside the first ten minutes, I was in the thick of action and enjoying myself. I brought Wimbledon level with a cracking equaliser – struck on the volley as I ran in to meet the ball from a corner.

It was a decision by referee Paul Alcock – or the lack of one – that brought down the old red mists again. I knew there should have been an off-side decision against Forest and couldn't resist telling him so in no uncertain terms. Yellow card for yours truly, free kick to Forest on the edge of our box, a tap from Scot Gemmill and one of Stuart Pearce's trademark blockbusters. We were behind again. I was even more incensed and a minute from the break I was back in the dressing-room.

When Roy knocked the ball past me and tried to beat me for pace I swear, hand on heart, there was no way I could get out of his path. I was sent off for body-checking him and I was absolutely gutted. And not only because the team went on to lose the match 4–1. All the lads were saying my dismissal was a disgrace. I just said 'I'm going' and didn't even stay for the second half. Click drove me back and we listened to the rest of it on the radio all the way down the M1. I didn't feel I'd let the team down, that day, because the Roy incident wasn't a booking in a million years. I thought Andy Gray and the Sky television team would point it out and raise a fuss but they didn't.

A lot of bookings, for many players, occur after referees have made a mistake and the last thing they need is for someone to point it out. You try to tell them so that they don't make the same error next time around but some of us never learn that once you start having a pop at the man in charge, he's only human and more likely to react against you. I am certain that is what happened to me at City Ground. Alcock might not have booked me if I hadn't already rubbed him the wrong way with my protests over that off-side claim.

The circumstances were different a month later when the eleventh red card of my career was waved at me by Dermot Gallagher. This sending-off was to become infamous because of the remarks I made about foreign players and the FA 'disrepute' charge that followed. It was a wet pitch at Stamford Bridge, really slippery, and I expected Gallagher to make allowances for the conditions. He didn't. In the fourteenth minute when I went in on Dan Petrescu, he booked me.

I had another chat with Gallagher as we took the field for the second half but you can't win with referees when you insist they should be doing things differently. The match had only been resumed ten minutes or so when I challenged Ruud Gullit near the corner flag. Admittedly I went in from behind, but I did also get a touch on the ball. The big Dutchman went over in a heap and I thought his reaction was excessive to say the least. However, we ended up winning the match 2–1 – a terrific result for Wimbledon.

I was still wound up about that red card when I returned home to find a couple of press lads sitting outside the house. I wondered why they were there. They'd been tipped off that I'd had a go at Gullit, verbally, on my way off. I was still buzzing. I could have handled it more calmly and better the following day but in the heat of the moment I opened up, so the next day – wallop! A big show in the paper with me complaining about foreign players 'squealing like pot-bellied pigs'. It created a huge outcry but, if I had thought longer, considered it in quieter moments, I could have made my case without particularly offending anybody.

I felt, and still do feel, that a lot of foreign players roll over several times and make too much of the slightest touch. If I had tackled Dennis Wise instead of Petrescu, for instance, would I have been booked in the first place? Wisey wouldn't have done the theatrical bit. If I had tackled Steve Clarke instead of Gullit, would I have been sent off? My opinion was valid but I expressed it emotionally and too colourfully for the liking of the people who run the game. Diving and such-like are condemned by managers and players one minute, but the same people rejoice when somebody in their team does it and gets a penalty the following week. I think it's great when referees book the divers and the ones who feign or exaggerate injury. There are too many cases of double standards applying in English football. The same with agents. Managers and directors say they detest agents – until the value of the agent suits them and their cause. I once gave Detsi Kruszynski, my own team mate, a right bollocking for rolling over and over when he didn't need to and the opposing fans loved me for it.

People are not honest enough, sometimes. Managers, players, referees, all of us. Even journalists, because when they see it they should hammer it as managers and players should. We can't leave it all to the referee who has enough problems to cope with, anyway. I know it is part of the game on the Continent, part of the culture overseas, but that doesn't mean we should have to accept it or condone it and see those cheating antics creeping into the English game and being copied by our own players.

The following season, 1996-97, was to see Wimbledon in reach of Wembley again – making the semi-finals of both the Coca-Cola and FA Cups. But it all started in familiar fashion for me with another red card as we chalked up our first Premiership victory of the season, by the only goal at home to Tottenham. I was booked first of all because of my fury after I caught Darren Anderton spitting. Something had happened, I was walking away and turned round just as he spat. He maintains that he was just spitting, but I had the impression that he was spitting at me, and I went for him.

It wasn't long before I got involved, off the ball, with Colin Calderwood. We had a bit of a skirmish and referee Steve Dunn waved the yellow card at me. I was still wound up, in fact I was bloody blazing about the Anderton incident, and it was to get me sent off. I spent the rest of that match – or the remainder of the time I survived – trying to get my own back, although I almost scored with a 'David Beckham', a shot from the halfway line that Ian Walker only just managed to flip over the bar.

I couldn't get the spitting incident out of my head and I pursued Anderton all over the place. I was determined to get even and eventually caught up with him and clattered him. It was enough for referee Dunn to reach for the yellow and then the red card and I didn't give him much option. I had been certain Darren had spat at me even though he insisted he was spitting at the ground. I am happy to give him the benefit of the doubt.

We were having one of our best seasons in the Premiership and the press were being generous to us for a change, but our progress in the cup competitions spoiled our year in the end. Manager Joe Kinnear, like the rest of us, was confident of qualifying for Europe through one of two doors: our final league position or in a cup. The Coca-Cola disappeared down the drain when we lost our two-leg semi against Leicester even though we didn't really lose at all. It was goalless at Filbert Street and 1–1 at Selhurst Park when I was voted man of the match, but Simon Grayson's headed equaliser took Leicester to Wembley on the away goals rule.

Still, it enabled us to fix both eyes on the FA Cup, which was always our main target anyway. Unfortunately, because of the weight of fixtures, Joe had to chop and change the side, resting players here and there, and our form in the league suffered. It cocked us up. When Arsenal won the Premiership title in 1997-98, and did it in real style over the final few weeks, some people argued that Alex Ferguson made a mess of it with Manchester United, breaking their rhythm by taking some competitions more lightly than others. And there has to be a lot of truth in that.

The worst day of the season for me was in the semi-final against Chelsea at Highbury. We stayed the night before at a hotel that didn't suit us, not that I'm looking for excuses, but nothing seemed to feel right. A bit like Liverpool the night before we beat them in the FA Cup final. John Barnes has often talked about the way their players felt slightly bored, a little bit niggly, flat with no buzz about the place. Here were Wimbledon, nine years later, and the same thing was happening to us.

I spoke to granddad: 'Just be with us, please get us through it.'

But even that was different. I sensed a change and that he, for once, was saying to me: 'You can't just get in touch and ask me to go and buy you a lottery ticket.' Maybe that added to the flat feeling. I had the impression he was holding back and telling me I had to do it by myself on the day. I felt as though I was being tested and I sensed it all the way to Highbury on the coach, during the warm-up and in the dressing-room before the game.

We were all crap. I can't explain why, but we didn't have a run in us – any of us. The preparation had been superb, the approach to the game had been great. Joe had given everybody the chance to be flying that day but we never looked like raising our game. We even started off by rowing among ourselves. Chelsea began with Roberto Di Matteo as a forward midfield player and we started by bollocking Oyvind Leonhardsen because he wouldn't sit-in and do the job that was expected. He eventually knuckled down and we didn't do too badly for a while but the outcome was always inevitable and nailed down by a brilliant goal from Gianfranco Zola and another from 'Sparky' Hughes.

Back in the dressing-room we knew we had all let ourselves down. There was no ranting or raving. Even at the end of the game we couldn't get ourselves worked up. I couldn't get upset with myself. That was unheard of, a unique situation – Wimbledon of all teams sitting on a coach having been ninety minutes from Wembley and not able to get upset about losing. It was something I will never be able to explain.

Our coach was immediately behind Chelsea's as we prepared to leave Highbury. We were sitting in virtual silence. I looked out and saw Ken Bates full of himself, really bubbling, and I couldn't get angry at that, either. I was sitting there, captain of the beaten team, asking myself any number of questions and I couldn't provide an answer to any of them.

Chelsea had provided me with a memorable moment, though. It was at Stamford Bridge in a league game a couple of seasons before and we were two-down. I had the ball inside our penalty box when Glenn Hoddle, then player-manager with Chelsea, came to close me down. I just popped the ball through his legs – yes, I actually nutmegged him – ran round him and passed it. Probably straight to an opponent! As Glenn wandered past me, he smiled and said: 'I like that.'

Dennis Wise told me that when Hoddle took over at Chelsea Glenn had told him: 'It's a shame Vinnie has left because I would have liked to have worked with him.' For me, that was the highest praise anyone could have offered because, in my book, Glenn Hoddle the player was The King, probably the best footballer in the world for vision. He wasn't a grafter like Bryan Robson, or an engine-room player, but if he'd had some of my strong points I believe he really would have been the best player on earth.

There were times when Hoddle wasn't in a game at all but a couple of those glorious long passes made up for it. I have met him on several occasions and, although nobody needs telling that we are different characters, I admire his personality. I sat behind him at the 'Sports Personality of the Year' function at the BBC and he talked to me, man to man. It gave me a real glow to know that he was prepared for other people, all those prominent figures in sport, to see him talking with Vinnie Jones.

He was my hero as a kid and I used to try to do what he could do. I could play one of his passes but not as many or as often as he played them. I don't kid myself. Even if I had been blessed with his wonderful skills my temperament would have let me down. I'm not the first and won't be the last to have temperament trouble. Ian Wright is a classic case –

brilliant striker, record goal-scorer at Arsenal and such enthusiasm for the game. But it's his temperament, his tendency to snap, that has landed him in so much trouble.

Why does Gazza do such things on the pitch? Somebody should have said to Paul years ago: 'Don't tackle anybody. Hustle them, shut them down but don't try to tackle.' In that case I think he would have been a far better player but his character and his personality take over. Just look at the challenge that knackered his knee in the 1991 Cup final. It was needless and reckless; he had been completely carried away by the occasion.

What people really wanted from Gazza during his career – those who managed him, those who played with him and the fans who loved him – was for him to go past an opponent, sometimes two, play it and get it back and have a go at goal. But he has to go and get himself involved in so much more. Having said that, I can identify with Ian Wright and Paul Gascoigne more than I can with Gary Lineker and Glenn Hoddle. I don't understand why some people can stay so cool and not seem to get irate or worry too much about losing.

Wimbledon did plenty of that, losing, at the start of 1997-98 – my final season with them. Once again we were among the favourites for relegation, according to many of the so-called experts, despite the likelihood that all the promoted newcomers – Barnsley, Bolton and Crystal Palace – were going to struggle. To be honest, though, I and a few others at Selhurst Park had a feeling that Wimbledon were going to have a difficult time.

The old spirit and defiance proved strong

enough yet again, although I was to find myself involved in a fight for survival one division lower, having moved to Queens Park Rangers with a few vital matches left and needing points to avoid the same fate that took Manchester City down to the Second Division. It still takes some believing that a club of their size and potential is now operating at the same level of the game as Macclesfield!

Of course my departure from Wimbledon left a lump in my throat for a while, but it was a great move for me, offering the chance to learn the ropes of management before, eventually, becoming the gaffer in my own right. Going to Loftus Road as player-coach – and thankfully surviving those last few matches to stay in the First Division – has given me the perfect chance. Manager Ray Harford was involved in the talks when I signed and I was told: 'Look, we're in the shit. We need a couple of strong men, sound characters in the side. We've a chance of getting Neil Ruddock on loan and we think that with you in the middle we should just about scrape through.

'In addition, we know you want to get into coaching and management and we can offer you the chance to come in with Ray and learn everything.'

Ray was good enough to tell me: 'You pick my brains. It might take twelve months, it might take twelve years, but I'll teach you all I can.'

I had no hesitation. Ray Harford is a man's man – I like everything about him. I love standing up there alongside him and I would like to think it could become a healthy and successful partnership on the lines of Brian Clough and Peter Taylor, Joe Kinnear and Terry Burton, Howard Wilkinson and Mick

Hennigan, Don Howe and Bobby Gould.

The dread of being finished in football, ending my career as a player with nothing to follow on, became as intense with me as my fear of dying. Every week that passed at Wimbledon the more I knew I would have to stay in football for the sake of my life and soul. If I hadn't become a player, or if I had looked beyond gamekeeping for a living, I would have joined the army. I need people around me. I have to be organising things. Eventually, if I ever become disenchanted with the game or it rejects me from the management ranks, providing I have enough money I will probably set up my own game farm.

But management it is, or will be when I've graduated from player-coach, and when I do become one of the bosses of the game I will make sure I treat players as men. They'll still need to be told what time to be down for dinner, what time the coach leaves and even what time we kick off, because that's how footballers are – so many things, maybe too many things, are done for them. But I have mostly been treated like a man and because of it those responsible have always had my total respect.

If one of my players is sent off, rightly or wrongly, I will have someone walk with him to the dressing-room. Not the manager or assistant manager but somebody from the touchline, maybe the kit man. I believe it is important that a player, even in a moment of personal disgrace, is not made to feel he has been disowned. In the privacy of his own dressing-room yes, nail him by all means. Slaughter him if necessary. But not in public because that can create cracks.

Have your house painted and it looks lovely.

But after the sun, the rain and the frost have got to it the marks and the cracks appear and it starts to look grubby. It doesn't matter how nice and cosy it is inside, from the outside everybody can see it is scruffy. That is why it is vital to show the outside world, whatever the circumstances, that you are closer than close, everybody is pulling together. Sam Hammam has taught me that.

I spent all those years at Wimbledon learning the true value of collective spirit and the will to beat the odds. That club had to stay in the top division if they were to survive and remain in business. It was as if we were in the middle of the Atlantic Ocean clinging to a plank of wood. If we ever let go we were going to sink and drown. My feeling, while there, was that if ever they did go down I'd finish playing altogether.

But I'm looking at new horizons now, and I'll take much of the Crazy Gang mentality with me. I'd rather have all of it and control some of it than have none of it and have to create it. I don't want people to label me with the old long-ball Wimbledon methods but I know some will lumber me with that, whatever I do. But I've most enjoyed games of football when I've played well. They are the best times. At Leeds, playing good football under Howard Wilkinson. At Wimbledon playing good football under Joe Kinnear. Passing the ball – you've got to pass the ball. Journalists tend to create that long-ball stigma as a negative thing but they should realise that a good pass doesn't have to be over four or five feet or five to ten yards. For me, the great Liverpool side with Alan Hansen and Mark Lawrenson played the long-ball over the top and perfectly.

My teams will play football in the right areas. There'll be no lumping it and chasing it and 'getting it in the mixer'. I won't ask for total effort and commitment, I'll demand it. When players come in for training at eleven o'clock I want them out there and ready to start at eleven o'clock. The late Bill Shankly used to say that any player who gave less than his absolute maximum at all times was guilty of an imprisonable offence. And that's the way I see it.

reflections, predictions and a score settled

I didn't have a wardrobe before I became a footballer. I didn't have a suit; now I have them made. I buy my shirts and ties from Jermyn Street and have my shoes hand-made. I used to have one gun, now I have fourteen for all the different types of shooting.

When we first moved into Oaklands there was a pond and a rockery but Tanya sent me off to buy a paddling pool for the kids. I asked for the biggest one they stocked but while I was looking round I enquired how much it would be for a swimming pool, and I bought one of those instead! I'm not a millionaire, yet. I don't know how close I am to seven figures because my money has been put to work by Steve and me in two companies: Golden Apple that handles all our promotional work, plus a significant investment in a company in the information technology field. I'm very excited about that – watch this space!

I have put my money into property whereas most players put theirs into pensions. My life and career have been a fight and a struggle, but I think I've come out on top. I've got the vehicle of my dreams, a top-of-the-range Range Rover, Tanz has a brand new BMW. I've also got a Toyota truck and my new Merc comes with the job at Queens Park Rangers.

I've bought houses for Nanny Ann, in Abbots Langley, and for Tanya's nan, Ella. Mum, Dave and my sister live in a house I own down the road in Hemel Hempstead and the one next door but one is mine as well. I've bought my sister two or three cars over the years and Dad has had a Jeep. I put money into my nan's account every month plus any odd cheques, here and there, and I've just spent about £20,000 doing the house up for her.

We moved to Box Moor in July. There I was, technically two years away from official retirement, spending heavily on a new house. There is an unfortunate story behind the move: difficulties with the neighbours, as you might have read! I had never before experienced the combination of depression and fear that grabbed hold of me during and after the court case that followed my bust-up with next door neighbour Timothy Gear. One night in the police cells after my arrest was bad enough, but what followed was a total nightmare. And there was nothing I could do to ease the anguish.

I always felt confident that I would be cleared of the charges – actual bodily harm and criminal damage – and that was still my feeling when I arrived at the St Albans Magistrates Court at the beginning of June, accompanied by Tanya, my sister Ann, mum and dad, mother- and father-in-law, and Steve Davies. You can feel what you like but, in those circumstances, you can never be certain of anything.

After the evidence had been heard – Gear had had his say, I'd had mine and the prosecution and defence had done their stuff over two long days – I was still sure I'd be cleared. When the magistrates retired to make up their minds even one of the policemen involved in the case said to me: 'You must be very confident of the outcome.'

The magistrates, a man and two women, were out for about a couple of hours, although for me it seemed more like a couple of weeks. It must have been a pretty close call. I was worried as the time dragged by, but there was also the reassuring feeling that, apart from the verdict, nothing bad could happen to me that day. There wouldn't be a sentence, there and then, so whatever the decision at least I knew I would be going home. So that knowledge softened the blow quite a bit when the magistrates came back into court and announced they had found the charges proved and declared that I was guilty.

It was the next stage that drove me crackers. We were moving house, from Redbourne to Box Lane on 1 July. I was to return to the court on 2 July. I had a month to wait before learning of my fate, during which time I had to put up with a lot of mickey taking from my mates. In a way, that helped a little bit because I could tell they were concerned as well. I was trying to put a brave face on it, but I was also becoming convinced that they were going to put me away.

Maybe it was the fear of it, maybe I was trying to accept the worst possible consequences, but I eventually became resigned to the prospect of a six-month prison sentence. Even with a reduction for good behaviour, that would have meant three months inside. I knew I could have coped with prison. People who have done time have told me, 'The first night is the worst but after that, it's all right.' I would have adjusted to the routine and got on with it, and I might even have come to enjoy parts of it. That's me, I muck in and make the most of any given circumstances.

But it was no longer about me, alone. It was about Tanya and the kids and the rest of the family, who I knew would stand by me. It was about the people at Queens Park Rangers, who had made me assistant manager and offered me the first chance to extend my career into that side of the game. I spoke to chairman Chris Wright and chief executive, Clive Berlin. They both said they were fully behind me but I couldn't know exactly what that meant and I daren't force myself to ask the big question: 'But if I'm put away, will I be sacked?'

It was all a nightmare for Tanya, as well, because she was having to see me in a deep and constant depression for the first time. The days dragged on. Then the hours and minutes dragged until I didn't really care what I was doing over that bloody terrible month. I had given up.

I drank more in those weeks that I have ever done in my life. I seemed to live at the Steamcoach in Hemel Hempstead with the boys. I was drinking for company, drinking to forget. And I did forget for a while, but only for as long as the effect of the booze lasted. Back home I would sit and read a newspaper or magazine without consciously taking in a word of it. I'd stare at the television without seeing what was on the screen or hearing what was being said. Even in the comfort of my own home, I was frightened.

Can you imagine what it was like to move house the day before I had to go back to court to learn of my fate? We arrived at Box Lane for our first night in our new house knowing that it could be my last night there for months. Hardly the time for a party!

So we trooped off to court again on 2 July. The same little group of family and friends offering reassuring words to one another but with me still fearing the worst – a prison sentence – feeling that anything less would be a fantastic relief, and for some reason thinking to myself as I always do: 'Whatever happens in my life, something good always comes out of it.'

Maybe it was because, in the early stages of the case, I managed to joke with Sam Hammam and Joe Kinnear: 'If I go down and QPR fire me you'll be able to get me back for nothing!'

Suddenly I was called. I stood next to my solicitor Reid. He began addressing the bench, talking about my personal circumstances, job and so on when the chairman of the magistrates leaned forward and said quietly: 'Mr Reid, we are not considering a custodial sentence.'

When I heard those few words I disappeared. It was as if I just floated away. It was no longer me, Vinnie Jones, standing there in that court room. It was just my empty suit – I had dropped out of it through the trouser-legs. I daren't look at anybody. Not at Tanya or my sister or anybody. I was fixed to the spot, elated inside but frightened to death to move a muscle or show any kind of facial expression. But I knew that any punishment they were to hand out, now, would be completely acceptable. It turned out to be 100 hours of community service, with a fine and costs amounting to £1150.

Afterward we took our legal team back to Box Lane and drank champagne. Despite my disappointment at being found guilty in the first place, I still had reason to celebrate because, thank heavens, those worst fears proved to be unfounded. We had a late lunch at the Steamcoach where Steve Davies put £500 behind the bar on the Thursday and the phone never stopped ringing. All my old mates arrived, even people who didn't drink in there had said they would come and celebrate with me if I wasn't put inside, and they were true to their word. At times there must have been upwards of 150 people drinking with us and, although I went home each night, I spent virtually all of the Thursday, Friday, Saturday and Sunday in the Steamcoach.

I had hoped I could do my community service coaching kids, possibly under-privileged kids. I hadn't assumed that would be the decision of the probation service, but I thought there would be a decent chance of it seeing that was how Eric Cantona fulfilled similar punishment for his 'Kung-fu' dust-up with the bloke who bad-mouthed him at Selhurst Park. But, for some reason, it was not to be. The probation officer picked me up from the house, took me to an old people's home and told me: 'This is what you will be doing. The place needs decorating.' That was my task – painting, Sundays and Wednesdays.

Somebody, somewhere had decided against letting me carry out the community service by helping youngsters. I was devastated when I heard suggestions that it would be 'inappropriate' or 'unsuitable' for me to do so. That hurt, particularly as I have done so much for needy youngsters, and am proud of being a patron of the SPARKS charity.

Apart from the conviction itself, the stain on my record, the worst outcome of the court case has been the loss of my shotguns. They were confiscated by the police on the night of my arrest. My licence was revoked and they gave me twenty-one days to appeal. I had to appeal – it wasn't a matter of choice but necessity. Having read this far you won't need me to explain any further the importance of those guns in my life. They are my life – at least the part they play in my love of the outdoors, the country pursuits that keep me sane. I had to do everything possible to get them back because life without them would be no proper life at all.

There was even a dispute over my community service after a mysterious note was put through my letter box from a woman asking me to get in touch because, she said: 'You should know what's going on.' Steve rang her to be told: 'Look, I've been pressured into giving information to the probation office dealing with Vinnie's case. They're allegedly tipping off the papers about where he's doing his work. I'm getting very scared and I want out.'

A picture of me painting appeared in the *Daily Mirror*. Steve and I were amazed at hearing all this. The police became involved and two women were arrested. I felt betrayed. Surely there is a code of practice in organisations like the probation service and I said: 'Right, let's take them on.' It was probably the wrong attitude but an easy one to take on the spur of the moment, tarring everybody with the same brush. That part was wrong because, in the end, I actually got on well with the people who dealt with me.

I was taken back to court and accused of breaching my community service. Tanya, Steve and I had all been involved with giving statements to the police. I had done one day of service but felt betrayed by the fact that the press knew where I was working and, in the circumstances, thought the whole thing had to be reviewed. I believed it was all so insensitive when the probation authorities put me back in court – more expense, as well, with solicitors and a barrister – especially as, on the three occasions I was accused of not turning up, my solicitor had informed them why I would be absent. Despite the fact that I regarded my explanations as completely valid they found me guilty on two of the three counts and extended my community service by forty hours. From 100 hours to 140 hours plus all the costs. I thought: 'Sod this – I'm not having it.' So I appealed against it.

A woman from the probation office had been sacked and there had been so much controversy that my solicitor told me: 'We'll appeal against the extra forty hours. Get as much done and under your belt as you can before we go back to court.' I actually completed ninety-one hours before the appeal.

I went to the Crown Court in St Albans. I was taking on the Hemel magistrates and it took all day to have a change made on the bench. We objected because of local authority connections and succeeded but by this time I had upset just about everybody. My barrister had to announce, before the change was made, that 'my client has no confidence in the court'. I was brassed off. By that stage I was ready to pay my fine and complete the extra forty hours and told them so. They had never heard anything like it, but I felt I had taken away the satisfaction they would have enjoyed saying: 'It is our decision that you will do the extra forty hours.' This way, it was my decision and I enjoyed the moment, even though they stuck me with a grand for costs. Six weeks previously it was half the price. I think they must charge £500 on Mondays and £1,000 for Wednesdays!

Eventually I resumed my service saying: 'Let's get it done. Get the lot out of the way as quickly as possible.' The probation people agreed I should stop the painting and decorating and work on the move in a van so that the press couldn't get to me so easily. I worked for the local health authority delivering medical supplies and equipment – beds, mattresses, commodes, hoists for old and disabled people. Usually there were three or four of us in a team and some of it was fairly heavy graft. We also delivered furniture to a warehouse on behalf of the social services, where people such as single mothers could buy, and then we distributed it. There were so many rules and regulations laid down for community service, such as a strict ten-minute tea break. But the reality of it was that if you were a good lad and worked hard it was so much more relaxed that I can say now that I really enjoyed it. One probation officer had said to me: 'You've got all these hours to do and there are so many people saying you won't manage it, you'll end up back in court', but I really got stuck in.

It was hard going. The medical delivery part of it could be uncomfortable, seeing old people just lying there with no family or friends around them. And clearing out houses soon after people had died there. It wasn't without its funny side, though, although I have to say the humour was generated by the nature of the work. Like the day one of the lads emerged from a house carrying a commode. It was only when he tried to chuck it in the back of the van that he realised it hadn't been emptied and he copped most of the contents all down his front!

You are allowed to do only twenty-one hours' community service a week so I worked two days, sometimes three. Despite the goodwill that builds up among groups of blokes in those circumstances, you do need a break and a contrast. So I was even more grateful for my involvement with charity events such as the SPARKS charity ball, the annual dinner where, if you read the papers at the time, I danced with Princess Michael. She is the head of that charity. I had met her a couple of times before, as Tanya and I go to the ball every year – it is a 'thank you' occasion for all the celebrities who do such hard and valuable work. Someone tells you Princess Michael would like to thank you personally for what you have done over the previous year and this time we chatted about the film I'd made, about football, her kids and one thing and another. Because of the success of *Lock, Stock* I somehow felt on a level with her and we got on great.

After dinner I walked through a door and Princess Michael happened to be standing there with her husband. The music was playing and I just said: 'Do you want to dance?' No fancy angle to it or anything. We got out there and had two or three dances – I can't remember the exact music but I think it was a bit of rock 'n' roll. I wasn't conscious of dancing with royalty or feeling any sense of awe because, with me, it's a case of what you see is what you get. I'd only have let myself down if I'd tried to put on any airs and graces. When people meet me they seem to like me for what I am, not for something or someone I'm trying to be. I was just myself. We didn't talk a lot because we were dancing. And, anyway, the music was playing full blast.

She thanked me very much and I thanked her and took her back to her husband, then I went and danced with Tanya. Next morning I was back on the van, probably shifting commodes – having first made sure they were empty. The community service was eventually done and dusted, we were in our new house and away from the place that had once been so happy for us but had gradually turned sour and ended with the incident that landed me in court.

All this belongs to an episode that is now over. A bad memory of the place that began with so many happy ones. Redbourne . . . the place where Tanya and I were married and set up home and haven for the kids, but sadly that dream turned sour. When we were pulling out for the last time, driving off to Box Lane, Steve told me to remember one thing – to look in my rear-view mirror and see Redbourne disappearing behind me.

I didn't forget. I looked in the mirror of my pick-up truck not once but twice. I was glad to be out of it. It was like taking off a wet overcoat. Yeah, it was a really good feeling.

I used to open shops and appear at various functions for fees between £500 and £1000 but I don't any more, because there wouldn't be enough time in a week. Since Christmas 1997 we have decided that if I'm going to do anything in that field it's a three grand minimum. Charity work gives me a lot of pleasure. You do it for nothing, of course, and there are times when it actually costs you money. I was at a SPARKS function – just to be photographed with other celebrities – and ended up buying a golf day for my father-in-law, which cost me £1000 in the auction. I shelled out £700 at one of Frank Bruno's events for the President's charity but you can imagine the satisfaction there is in knowing you are helping underprivileged kids.

I am extremely proud to be made a patron of SPARKS. That has given me the biggest thrill of all my charity work. I regard it as a 'thank you', real recognition, with my name included alongside such stars as Jimmy Tarbuck, Jimmy Hill, Henry Cooper, Sean Connery. It's an example of being wanted, feeling wanted, in the nicest possible way.

We always say Christmas Day is for children and it is a wonderful privilege for me to be able to spread a little magic every Christmas morning.

For five years or more, Steve and I have taken toys to Hemel Hempstead hospital and distributed them among the kids. Board games, Disney products, cuddly toys – a cross-section of gifts for the various age groups. We try to check, four or five days before Christmas, how many children and what ages will be there. Some are allowed home for Christmas Day but ones who are not tend to be those with real problems. One of the real delights of Christmas is seeing your own kids opening their presents but there is something about the faces of children in hospital that morning.

I've never checked on how much I spend, because it doesn't matter. I just love being there, seeing those faces. Since we began, we've only missed once – that was the occasion when Joe

Kinnear had us in on Christmas morning for extra training!

I have some of my fondest memories from that short time with Leeds United. I helped raise a substantial amount of money for the local kids' home. Trouble was, the kids used to run away and head for my home. There were many occasions when I had to phone up and return them, after giving them a bloody good meal.

Every time I ran out on match days at Elland Road the first thing I did was to go and talk to the large group of disabled people in wheelchairs. For me to go and spend two or three minutes of my time with them was no hardship and maybe players, generally, might bear it in mind. It lightened up the hearts of those people and suddenly their life didn't seem too bad for a little while. The first couple of times I did it I received such a response from them that I had to keep it up, every home game. The crowd always burst into applause so, who knows, maybe it encouraged one or two others to spend a little time and thought for the handicapped.

When I left Leeds the handicapped members of the supporters' club all chipped in and bought me a lovely painting of a countryside shooting scene. It is among the possessions I treasure most.

Fame, such as it is, has its irritating aspects if you happen to be in the wrong place at the wrong time but I wouldn't really be without it. How else would I have landed my own TV chat show? One of the Sky channels gave me a slot on their 'Men and Motors' show – going out interviewing virtually whoever I liked. I had the bright idea of interviewing Mike Tyson at his home in America and although you might think I was off my head there was a stage when a chat with Mike looked 'on'. Instead, Steve suggested I went to see Charlton Heston!

'I can't interview Charlton Heston,' I said.

"Course you can.'

'Right, let's have a go, then. Let's do it.'

A meeting was arranged at the Dorchester Hotel. He was over here for a film premiere and it was made clear to me and the TV crew that we'd get no longer than three or four minutes. He gave us fifteen minutes and later a lady from his party came to me and said: 'Charlton would like me to tell you how much he enjoyed that.' Charlton . . . he'd enjoyed chatting with Vinnie Jones! Was I made up, was I a tiny bit thrilled or what? Others followed, Damon Hill, Mickey Duff and a great laugh with Peter Stringfellow at his club.

The idea spread. We wanted a football chat show but the budget was hopeless, so the thought occurred: 'It's Men and Motors so why don't we give them what they want – a blokey item filmed in pubs just as if we're sitting chatting with the boys?' So we did – chatting with the likes of Terry Neil, the former Arsenal manager and referee David Elleray. Successful? I was only voted 'New Presenter of the Year' at the Sky awards, that's all!

And then a film. A proper film. The part of a tough-guy debt collector, Big Chris, in *Lock, Stock and Two Smoking Barrels* scheduled for release this autumn. It all began with a phone-call from Guy Ritchie, who wrote and directed it, and Matthew Vaughan the producer. Apparently the notes about Big Chris had described the character as: 'Very cool. An aura about him. Respected but you wouldn't

want to cross this man. If he loses it, he loses it —
similar to Vinnie Jones the footballer.'

I'd once had a walk-on part in the TV programme *Ellington* and Matthew and Guy had seen it,
so when they were casting the film Matthew suggested they ask Vinnie Jones to play it. We had a
meeting at Stoke Poges Golf Club and the next
hurdle was a screen test for the woman who was said
to have discovered Arnold Schwarzenegger. Guy
told me: 'The part's yours but you'll need to get past
her first.' Panic! I began by doing the part of the
script I'd memorised but she said: 'That's OK, it's
pretty good, but now do it as yourself. Not as Big
Chris, do it as Vinnie Jones.' And they were over the
moon.

The movie was hard work. We were well down
the road when everything stopped and seemed to
have gone down the pan, but it was picked up again
and eventually took nine weeks of filming. I was
standing around all day and acting for about five
minutes but I really enjoyed it. They were great
people to work with and it gave me the taste for
more but only if it's big-time.

I've always been a believer in luck money. If
you buy something from a traveller they usually
give you a few quid back — money for luck, they call
it. My money from the film was substantial, paid in
stages. I have left all mine in, so that eventually
there will be one cheque. And it will all go to
Harefield hospital.

There is no way I can repay them for help they
have given and still provide for Tanya. If ever you
went to Harefield for a day you would understand
why I wanted the money to go there, in addition to

money I have sent them before. The dedication of all those who work at that place is phenomenal. All I can do is make a little gesture of my personal gratitude.

I'm still thankful for my love of the outdoors. It clears the head, relaxes the mind and brings you down to earth. We had dogs when I was young but they were dad's dogs. So when we moved to Oaklands I was able to have the Alsatian I always wanted. We bought Ben as a pup from kennels in Bedmond and he's a great fella. My mate Click then gave us Tessie the Jack Russell for Kaley. The first thing I did was build a big pen on part of our three acres and bought a load of chickens. Then a load of ducks, geese and guinea fowl. Then a load of partridges and pheasants – wild, not penned, and it's lovely to have them around. When we arrived at the house there were only crows and magpies, so I introduced some wildlife to the wildlife.

I hate bloody magpies, though, I'm really super-stitious about them. One for sorrow, two for joy, they say. If I leave the house and see only one I have to say: 'Good morning Mr Magpie, good morning Mr Magpie, good morning Mr Magpie.' And then I have to find another one to be able to say 'Two for you.' I know they are common but it's amazing how long it takes to find one when you need one. I've been known to drive around for bleedin' miles!

Despite the superstition, I do shoot them. They are vermin. A lot of golf courses and the countryside suffers because all the songbirds are being reduced by the vermin like crows, jays, magpies, squirrels, foxes, stoats and weasels. They are all becoming too dominant. A magpie can clear an entire hedge of chicks, stealing them from their nests. I shoot all vermin.

Shooting has taken me to places and introduced me to people I would never have known without it. Duck shooting, pheasant shooting, partridge and grouse as well as clays. I go with lords – Lord Fisher from Thetford and his family have become particularly good friends – as well as many others – Allan Lamb the cricketer shoots with me. And then there is the fishing – glorious quiet hours on the edge of a lake. My ideal lifestyle would be living on the edge of a lake.

Other livestock was quickly on the scene at Oaklands. When I think of something, I have to have it so I went and bought five cows – a Charolet, a Hereford and three Friesians. They were a disaster – they kept getting out and running down to the main road. Twenty sheep came next, and caused another nightmare. It's all right at first but when the novelty wears off and little lambs turn into big sheep . . .

The pot-bellied pigs arrived. So did the brainwave that told me it would be a great idea to have a male in there and some baby pot-bellied pigs. As luck would have it, a mate of mine gave me a wild boar, Horace. So now we have thirty-eight pot-bellied pigs as well as Horace.

It's a good job we've got Bill as well. Bill Ireland looks after the animals and the garden and the various odd-jobs around the place. I was in The Bell one night and mentioned to somebody that I was wanting a partition, a trellis behind the swimming pool, and about half an hour later a bloke came up to me and said: 'I would like to do that job for you.' He came and had a look, gave me a price, got all the wood and said: 'Do you mind if I stay up here 'til I've finished the job?'

'What do you mean?' I couldn't imagine he was wanting to stay with us.

'I live in a little tent near my sister's place in the village, you see. And I could set it up in your field and get the work done.'

And he did. He put up his one-man tent and he did us a terrific job. But it was winter and I couldn't be thinking of him going off to live in his tent or even living in it at my place alongside the straw bales so I told him: 'Why don't you clear out my 8 × 10 shed and get yourself in there?'

We put a calor-gas heater in there for him, eventually connected the electricity supply, carpeted the floor, got him a telly and a little fridge. And he stayed. 'You live here, I'll give you a bit of pocket money and you can look after the garden and the animals,' I said. He was delighted. He was even more pleased after decorating the inside of that shed and after I had it all insulated and found him a two-seater sofa!

There have been occasions when I have returned at five in the morning and called in at Bill's cabin to share a beer with him. He's been a godsend, really, he's a diamond, old Bill and now he's living in proper luxury. I bought him a caravan with its own shower and toilet. Sadly, Bill became ill during 1998 and Tanya's been taking him to Harefield. He's one of us, and there was a caravan behind the removal van when we moved the ten miles or so from Redbourn to Box Moor.

I still have the sensation of being in a goldfish

bowl when I'm out but not when I'm in the country-side with my shooting pals. I'm just Jonah. We never ever talk about football. What I also enjoy is the fact that I'm good at ferreting. I'm good at 'lamping' and 'squeaking' foxes at night. I go out with my truck with the bright lamps – I know it's frowned upon but everything is frowned upon by somebody these days. I frown upon the times when, after spending hours and hours tending my chickens, geese or ducks, the fox comes along and creates carnage. I shoot foxes for a reason. I lost two of my chickens the other night and I can live with that. It's nice to have one fox about but I can't have three. I remember letting the pheasants out at my old man's place, once. The young birds go in the long grass and jump up for the seeds. It's called 'jogging'. We bring them in later to feed them. That day we found over 400 dead chicks on that rearing field – the work of two fox cubs. They have to be controlled.

I don't believe the argument that hunting with hounds controls them. I think the only way, the most successful way, is lamping them at night with rifles. It is also probably the most humane way. I put a red filter on the lamp that lights up their eyes. Then the 'squeak': with your mouth and your hand you pro-duce the sound of a distressed rabbit. The fox is an inquisitive creature and will move towards the sound. But for every one that comes closer, three don't.

I've been known to go out at dusk and not return until dawn, especially in the summer. Farmers ask me over to do the job for them. There is a friend at Aylesbury, I've been to farms in Northampton-shire and other places dealing with the fox problem.

The most I've ever killed in one night was thirteen. People are phoning me all the time, asking me to clear their land of vermin. For a farmer, it can be an expensive business.

Looking back on it all I know I'm not a bad footballer but realise that my real expertise is applied to the shooting and the fishing – the country life. I have made mistakes but I've enjoyed most of what has happened to me so far. Even now, if I see Elton John, I can have a proper conversation with him, but, to this day, I still can't put myself in that stardom category although they call me a celebrity. For whatever reason, right, wrong, my fault or someone else's, I am a name. I am instantly recognisable and, know what, when I was at Chelsea John Major and his son actually asked to meet me. I've been known to sit next to Tony Blair and natter away with him no differently than to the lads at the local.

I have friends who are lords and friends on the dole, and I've managed to keep a balance between the two. It's wonderful to be able to go out and buy a swimming pool and motorbikes for the children – the kind of things you dreamed about as a kid. I used to think it was a dream – all of it – and that it might end at any time. But not now, it's there and I have to deal with it all and I've moved into a different stage of my life.

This is a good time for my autobiography to be published because I would say I have grown up a bit. I can no longer say 'Well, I'm just a youngster and I'm mad.' I still do the odd, unwise thing – the Bedmond Green estate still comes out in me. That's not a bad thing because I don't want to be a total celebrity. I am still one of the chaps from Bedmond and it's nice to go down there every now and then and hear them say: 'Great to see you.'

I have to admit that Vinnie Jones has been a thug at times, on and off the field. I cannot sit here and say 'I'm whiter than white'. With me, whatever the subject, needlework or fighting someone, I'll always have a go. I cannot be defeated before I've tried. I feel that I have been honest with myself, with my family, my managers and team mates, with my animals and with my friends. I do not look back and feel that I have deceived anybody.

Thuggery has been part of my character, my upbringing, my life. And one thing I would never do is try to hide my past. It is there for all to see.

My future, or so it seemed then, was with Queens Park Rangers where one official said to me: 'You are now representing QPR and Ray Harford.' I knew I was also representing my family and what I had achieved. What I couldn't foresee were the events that were about to change everything at Loftus Road.

We played at Oxford on a Saturday towards the end of September and were trying to do anything to get the boys going. It was a familiar story for me – I'd played for the reserves against Swindon a week or two earlier and been sent off. The referee had called it an off-the-ball incident, but it was much ado about not a great deal with one of their blokes and we were both sent packing. I wanted to play in the Oxford game but Ray Harford said: 'We'll leave Peacock and Murray in midfield. Let them get on with it.' Oxford got on with it a lot better than QPR did and beat us easily.

That was to be the last time I saw the lads. I really pointed the finger afterwards, and had a right go at them in the dressing-room. There was absolutely no will to win and I told them straight, the way Vinnie Jones has always done it, and let them know that things had to change. I thought two or three of them were out there playing just for themselves rather than for the team. Too many players at that club at that time just weren't being genuine. And that kind of attitude was completely alien to me. I found it unacceptable and blew my top. After fourteen years in the pro game I felt disillusioned within four months of switching to QPR. There was a lack of professional pride, there was tittle-tattle throughout the club – it was a complete and utter mess.

It was all quiet inside the coach on the way back and chucking it down with rain outside. When we stopped at Wycombe for Ray to collect his car his miserable day was completed by the discovery that someone had broken in and nicked the stereo. 'What else can happen?' he wondered, wearily. Somehow, as he drove off, I knew that was that. I remember thinking: 'This bloke can't take any more.' I just sensed it. The team was struggling, the spirit was low and the following day I told Tanz that I was expecting a phone call from Ray. I wasn't around for most of that Sunday but, sure enough, I had about forty missed calls on my mobile, the first one from Nick Blackburn, Chris Wright's right-hand man, saying: 'Phone me urgently.'

He told me Ray had resigned but he wasn't saying anything I hadn't anticipated already until he announced this: 'We're putting Iain Dowie in charge. Because of your commitments and one thing and another we had a meeting and put Iain in charge.'

'What do you mean "in charge"?' I asked him.

'We've made him manager.'

So I had gone from assistant manager, Ray's No 2, to a position where Dowie, the No 3, had been promoted over my head. My understanding had been that had Ray left the club I would be the first to be considered for the job of manager. I thought they would have discussed it with me at the very least. Ray and I had had our hands tied behind our backs. We couldn't get players in or players out because there was no money. Wright had told us from pre-season that we needed to sell £3,000,000-worth of players by Christmas. We would have struggled to raise 300,000 let alone 3,000,000.

There had been seven games to go in 1997-98 when I joined QPR. Relegation was a real threat but we stayed up. Brilliant . . . saved the day . . . right, now let's rebuild this club. But as we tried to build the wall it was being kicked down and every time another brick tumbled they kept saying: 'We need three million by Christmas.' No wonder, when I phoned Ray, he told me: 'I can't take any more. I don't need all this at my age.'

I met Chris Wright and the other officials on the Monday. I've got to be honest – I felt that what had happened was disgusting. They can all say what they want but I was thirty-four years old and I wanted to have a go at management – my way. It's my biggest regret, and, even now. I'm really gutted that they didn't give me my chance. They booted me right in the teeth and gave it to Dowie. They said that the decision had been made because of my other commitments – I suppose they meant the film. QPR is a fantastic little club that just needs sorting out and all I needed, right then, was the nod and the trust. As much as I pleaded with the chairman and Nick Blackburn, and told them I could commit myself completely to the job, the QPR chapter in my life was as good as over there and then.

I had pleaded with them, begged with them but it all met with the same reply: 'No, sorry.'

'Right,' I said, 'so where do we go from here?' They told me that, although Iain Dowie had been put in place for the time being, they would advertise the job and invited me to apply! They even said I would have a good chance of getting it if I had a senior partner, a kind of guru. I thought about it for a while and wondered about people like Peter Shreeves.

You should never make decisions hastily, and I took about a week to consider my options. I woke up one morning and thought: 'Who the hell do they think they are? I am the No 2 and they've gone right over my head. It's a bloody insult.' I had done all my begging at the Monday meeting, so I rang the club and told them: 'I won't be applying for the manager's job, I'll just come back as a player.' And that's where other complications set in. I realised that the new manager, whoever he was to be, would either get rid of me – in which case I should receive a pay-off – or keep me on.

They appointed Gerry Francis, the boss who did so well for them between 1991 and 1994, and I told him: 'I've upset one or two people here. I've ended up as the No 2 working for the No 3 and I can't operate under conditions like that. You can sell me or give me a free transfer.' But the club wouldn't give me a free.

Gerry explained: 'The reality of it is that I'm bringing in my own man as No 2. You can come back as a player, but I don't expect to use you all that much. I have to try and bring money into the club and with all due respect you are not going to be worth a million.'

'Fine. Fair enough. But where does that leave me?'

'Let's try and sort it out with the board.'

'But don't expect me to be in here training. I've been kicked in the teeth by everybody and trodden on, and I'm the innocent party.'

Bear in mind I'd helped keep them up the previous season. I had come from being captain of Wimbledon, played a handful of games with QPR and suddenly it was all over. And their only excuse seemed to be my involvement with the film, which was over and done with by then. Gerry told me to try to find another club, but it all dragged on for weeks and weeks. They could have sacked me and paid me off, but that would have been difficult struggling for money so they just continued to pay my wages. I did try to find another club, and there was quite a lot of interest, but it came from the lower divisions – Burnley, Wycombe, Blackpool, Rushden and Diamonds. They all wanted me to go in and liven the place up and get them going. But I'd been at top level for so long that if I'd dropped down I know that many people would have said: 'Look . . . told you he'd end up in the lower leagues.'

A few years ago there was an article in one of the papers forecasting that Vinnie Jones would eventually sink, finishing up at the lowest level, trying to earn his last few desperate quid from the game. I remembered that article and began thinking of what it would be like playing in the Third Division or non-League, of how everybody would be trying to wind me up and how I was almost certain to be sent off again. Everything I had achieved would go out of the window and I couldn't bear that. There were whispers that I might join Watford, and I was hoping that that would happen, but no contact was made.

This autobiography came out in hardback in October 1998 and there were stories in the papers saying that supporters were complaining that QPR was struggling while Vinnie Jones was out doing book-signing sessions. What was I supposed to do – sit at home? I was advised by my solicitors not to hit back. I just kept my gloves up and resisted the temptation to get sucked in. I didn't once feel bad about picking up my wages, good wages, no sense of guilt whatsoever. Their decision finished my football career, so, as far as I was concerned, QPR had a lot to answer for.

I suppose it worked pretty well for me in a way because, not having to go in to training, I was able to promote my book and the film. I was accessible and available – personal appearances, opening shops, earning bundles. I even flew over to New York to see the Lennox Lewis/Evander Holyfield world title fight fiasco. I was having a whale of a time but always waiting for the phone call and eventually it came. It was to change the future completely, as you'll see in the next chapter.

Meanwhile, I received a letter from the club effectively saying I had to give up my claim to be paid the rest of the money due on my contract or go back to training. I thought they were trying to call my bluff so I told them: 'Right, this is what I'm going to do. You pay me until the end of the season and I'll let you off the next two seasons of my contract.' I said: 'I'll give you time. Give me four months' money, pay me to the end of the season and I'll walk away. Give me my registration and I'll let you off two years' money.'

The first thing I saw after that was an article in which Chris Wright complained that the signings of Ray Harford and me were the biggest mistakes he had ever made. And I'd just let them off with two years' dosh!

But, in the end, looking back on my football career, I am happy with what it has brought me.

I like it when people come to my house, look round and say: 'Bloody hell, you've done all right for yourself.' It gives me a great feeling when my mates pop round and there are famous people sitting there and we all sit with a glass of wine while the barbecue is catching light and the kids are in the pool.

I will have made some enemies along the way. Gary Stevens blames me for finishing his career. Steve McMahon probably wouldn't have a good word to say about me. Rightly or wrongly, if people don't like me I dismiss it as some form of jealousy. None of my childhood mates behaves like that. It's only people I have met since becoming a player who have looked at me through green eyes.

We've got all the family together and we all look after nan. There is also Mylene and Steve Terry. I have Tanya's family, too. I like putting smiles on people's faces. I know I've hurt people on the field and off the field but it's great to have that warm feeling, that sense of pride in myself when I realise how far I have come since packing my life into a plastic bin-liner and washing pots and pans for a few bob. I look back on my childhood, now, and understand more than I did at the time. The scars are not with me any more. For the first time in my life, over the past year or so, the scars of a lot of wounds have finally faded.

They may be beginning to fade for John Fashanu by now. I have purposely left until last the scandal that burst over English football during my last couple of years at Wimbledon – the match-rigging allegations that put Fash, Bruce Grobbelaar, our former keeper Hans Segers and a businessman from the Far East in the dock. No, Fash has not had the best of times in the late nineties. First the awful allegations and then, in 1998, the suicide of his brother Justin in a London lock-up garage.

My first reaction when the scandal hit the front pages was shared by most Wimbledon players. I immediately thought back to our last game of the 1993-94 season at Goodison Park where Everton needed to win to keep their place in the Premiership. We were cruising, leading 2–0 until the game was suddenly and dramatically turned on its head with Everton snatching one of the most important victories in their history, 3–2.

As we trooped into the dressing-room after the

final whistle Joe Kinnear was going cra.
turned to Segers and said: 'If I didn't know bet
have thought you'd just thrown that game. I'd
thought you had a bet on it.' It was just Joe blasting
off in the fury of the moment, remarks that are
probably made by other managers to other goal-
keepers in similar, disappointing circumstances.
Once the temperature had cooled, nobody thought
another thing about it. Until scandal hit the papers
almost a year later.

People in this country, especially well-known
people, seem to be guilty before they are proved
innocent. Any slur and it's jumped on and slurred a
bit more. As the first trial for taking bribes
approached, everybody was talking about it and I
can remember, now, thinking it had been decided
before it started – there were so many jumping on
the bandwagon, their minds already made up.

With Fash and me, when one of us is in trouble,
the phone rings. Like with the death of Justin. I left
it for a day and then rang John and the first thing he
said was: 'I was waiting for this call, Jonesy.' If it's
me in bother, leave it a day and Fash will be on the
line. We reassure one another about what we've
done, where we have come from, a 'we shall overcome' sort of attitude.

I was at Towcester races with Steve when we
learned that the match-rigging story had broken.
We were on a mobile phone and were told to ring
back a newspaper on a land-line. They offered me
£100,000 – just for an interview saying I believed
the allegations, that the people mentioned could be
involved in such a thing. They told me exactly the
type of things they wanted me to say. I promptly

put down the phone and called Fash, there and then.

'This is the situation,' I told him. 'I've been offered a hundred grand to do a piece saying "I think my mate could be involved . . . and I'd be gutted, etc etc." '

If he had told me he was guilty, I would have been on the floor.

'I'll tell you what I'll do, Fash. If something has happened and they are going to screw you, we might as well do the story and at least I can give you some support in the paper. We'll split the make down the middle.'

'Jonesy,' said Fash, 'I was just about to give you my word that I am not involved. But I don't think we need to do that, you and me, do we?'

'Fair enough, boy,' I said. And put the phone down.

I contacted the newspaper and told them: 'Thank you for the offer. But no thanks.'

I could have taken their money and done a story that Fash could have read on the Sunday but I'd have felt I'd have betrayed him. Not even £100,000 could have bought me what John Fashanu gave me in help and support over several years. I have spoken to him many times since. Wished him good luck on his way to court and even if they had found him guilty I would still have believed him when he said he wasn't. That was the strength of our friendship. In the battle between the devil and the angel on my shoulders, the angel won through.

Our relationship was tested to the tune of £100,000 but if it had been £1 million I would have done exactly the same. I'd say 'No' to this day because if a judge had decided they were guilty I would not have accepted it. Of course, they were found not guilty in the end.

CHAPTER 25

vinnie goes to hollywood

Times have changed dramatically for Vinnie Jones since that awful, unforgettable day I told you about when all this started – the day my parents discovered I had been nicking money from my old man's desk. They've changed for the better – better than anyone could imagine, let alone a seven-year-old who had just done something he would remember and regret for the rest of his life.

It had been quite a journey from petty thief, a washer-up of pots and pans with his life in a plastic bin liner, then working on building sites carrying hods, to fourteen years as a professional footballer, becoming captain of Wales, playing at Wembley and gaining an FA Cup winner's medal and no end of dog's abuse and resentment along the way. And eventually to a home address in Beverly Hills. Vinnie goes to Hollywood – if somebody had made all this up nobody would have believed it.

That first film part in *Lock, Stock and Two Smoking Barrels* has changed the nature and direction of my life. I didn't make much of it earlier in the book simply because I had no idea of the impact it would make. It was just something I was invited to do, something that appealed but I never anticipated what would happen once it was in the cinemas. I first saw it at the wrap party – the celebration held at the end of filming for all those involved in the production, from the cast and directors to the tea girls and truck drivers. When I saw myself up there on the big screen it hit me right in the stomach. It felt like I had just swallowed ten jars of butterflies. But, my God, I felt so proud by the time the credits rolled. Even then, despite the satisfaction of believing I'd done a decent job for a first time effort, it wasn't until later that I began to think I might have something of a future in this game rather than the one in which we booted a ball around.

Those thoughts began at the London premiere. Dustin Hoffman was among the big names present. I had a picture taken with him and he mentioned something about 'the new Bruce Willis'. Maybe he was just being kind, but as we chatted I turned round and saw my dad with tears of pride streaming down his face. The flood gates had opened again. Tanya's emotions showed themselves in giggles. What was nice, too, after receiving so much criticism and ridicule as a footballer, was picking up the papers and reading: 'Vinnie Jones's contribution to the movie was impressive.'

Everybody congratulated me. All the old pals from Bedmond and around, those from the Under-18 football team, all of them said: 'Well done, cos we remember where you came from.' And so do I. Nothing has changed in that way. My mates are still my mates and always will be. When the success of *Lock, Stock* hit the headlines, I looked through the window one morning at the builders working out-side our new house. I looked at Paul Hobbs who was with me in the Watford boys side and thought: 'Yeah, Paul looks as happy as a king as well. He's gone on to be a great brickie.' No difference, really. We still treat each other in exactly the same way.

We flew out to Los Angeles for the American premiere of the movie. We went early so that I could be introduced to people, casting agents at Paramount and Warner, and I began to think that this was going to be my living because everyone was saying how good I was and a couple of scripts arrived. Flown around all over the place, first-class, limousines here there and everywhere, private jets to Las Vegas and back for lunch. I was winning awards – the Empire Variety Club of Great Britain, the Odeon Cinemas award. The film was winning them as well. I was going to all the functions and becoming friends with people like Michael Caine, Bob Hoskins, all the big-hitters. I found myself accepted by them.

All of a sudden it was as if the big movie stars, Kate Winslet included, wanted to meet me. They were my new pals! Remember, earlier in the book when I used to run when I wasn't wanted? Well, I found myself in another gang and felt at home and comfortable among them. I became aggressive towards football and the people in it. I get angry and frustrated with some of the TV pundits like Alan Hansen and Trevor Brooking on BBC. I think some of the things they come out with are a disgrace. For example, Brooking was hosting a golf day last year, and John Hartson and I took part and we had a lovely day. But when Hartson signed for Wimbledon last season Brooking slaughtered him. Little wonder that when his secretary rang to ask if we would play in Trevor's golf day this year we both told him to get stuffed.

The criticism centred on the £7 million Wimbledon paid to West Ham. Some think Johnny is worth it, some say he isn't. But he's a young boy. At twenty-four years of age who knows what he's going to be worth? People said Alan Shearer was overpriced when Blackburn bought him for £3.5 million. Why is it that some so-called experts seem to be so ready to criticise? I listen to them on television, all channels, and it makes me cringe now – it really, genuinely, makes me cringe.

I believe the honesty has gone out of football. It is over-hyped. Some of those doing the criticising have never been managers because they don't have the bottle; many others haven't even played at the top level. Let them try it and succeed or fail and then I might listen with more belief to their observations on the efforts of those with the courage to take on the most difficult job of all. Fortunately, football still produces great individuals.

When I have a day at the races and meet Alex Ferguson or Joe Kinnear, I know I am in the company of real men, proper people. Harry Bassett is another. Then I think, for instance, of Andy Gray who tells the world and his dog what is right or what is wrong with every team in the land through his Sky TV microphone. He had the chance to be manager of Everton but chose to stick with Sky. I know you don't need to be an egg to make an omelette but you need to have beaten a whisk to find how much it can make your arm ache!

I had some fantastic times in football, particularly at Wimbledon, Leeds and Chelsea. But after what happened to me at Queens Park Rangers I think people can understand when I say, 'Sod you, now. I no longer need you lot.'

I didn't rule out a return to the game as a coach or manager eventually and still don't. But it is going to depend on what happens to me in the film world from now on. They've given me the taste and I like it. I jetted all over the place promoting *Lock, Stock* – Norway, LA, Vegas. I was thinking 'This is all right, but am I on an escalator going up or an escalator going down?' You can only be on an escalator for so long. Once you are at the top, if you don't step forward, you fall over.

There was a chance of me joining the Gladiators television team, but I just missed out – hit the post. But I have earned a lot of money since I've been out of football through promotional work, personal appearances, that kind of thing. Yet always there is that nagging thought that the phone might stop ringing and everything will dry up. You know me . . . I have to have something that terrifies me!

I did make one important change. From the beginning of 1999 Peter Burrell took over from Steve as my agent. Steve needed to take more of a hands-on role with the computer company and is now full-time with that. Peter has represented top jockey Frankie Dettori since he was sixteen years old and has done a fantastic job for him. I had done a bit of asking around, met Peter, spent quite a bit of time in his company and regard him as just the nicest man ever. He was very well educated at Harrow. His grandfather was a prominent racing man with a stud in Newmarket and the value of Peter's expertise has been immediate. Like Frankie,

I now have a lucrative sponsorship deal with Yves St Laurent who clothe me from head to toe, casual and formal. I also endorse Slim Jims, the American snack company, and Penny Black aftershave.

But back to that phone call. It was a Monday evening and I was sitting at home at around ten o'clock at night. It was my agent in America (well, you have to have one, don't you!), Nick Styne, whose company looks after the interests of Cameron Diaz, Anthony Hopkins, Jimmy Nail, people like that. I was lucky they took me on. You can't just tell people like them to be your agent – they have to want you and, after *Lock, Stock*, they wanted me. Anyway, Nick rang to say Jerry Bruckheimer, the man who produced *The Rock*, *Top Gun* and the like, had been on 'and would like to meet you on Wednesday'. I had to be in Hollywood by three o'clock on Wednesday!

'Well, how do I manage that?'

'There's a first-class return ticket waiting for you at the airport. The noon flight tomorrow.'

First-class return flight. I'd have bloody well swum the Atlantic for the chance of a part in a blockbuster, but I didn't let them know I was that keen exactly. Not until I'd heard what they had to say. Peter assured me: 'If they're not ninety-nine per cent sure you're what they're looking for they wouldn't send you a first-class return ticket. But you haven't got the part yet. They want to chat with you first.'

Funnily enough, Tanya was in the States at the time. I'd sent her to Gracelands for her birthday. She was so excited, we both were, and I needed that part because we didn't know what the future held. Strangely, Tanya was flying back from America at the same time as I was heading out there. I arrived on Tuesday night and was taken by limo to the Sheraton Hotel, Santa Monica.

I had received the script about three weeks earlier – a $100 million production of *Gone in Sixty Seconds*. I had read it over and over but I read it again next morning and it took me around three hours. The part proposed for me does not involve a lot of dialogue. It is all in the strength of the character until, at the end of the movie, he comes out with a big speech that stuns everyone.

The limo took me to Bruckheimer's office in Santa Monica – an ordinary-looking place from the outside but massive inside. I was told to wait and sat there looking at all the credits around the place and the discs for the soundtracks. I then met Bruckheimer and Chad Omen, his right-hand man. They were behind the biggest desk I'd ever seen – it must have been twenty feet long. This was no casting, they were just asking me how much I enjoyed doing *Lock, Stock*, how many takes I needed, asking general questions. I sensed that the director was quite excited and so Jerry just looked across and said: 'Well, do you want me to hire him?'

'Yeah, yeah, get him on board.'

'Welcome aboard,' Jerry said. Just like that. It took maybe half an hour.

'Thanks very much, Vinnie, we'll be in touch,' they told me. 'We'll be in touch. We'll speak to your agent, Nick. He will send your lawyers in during the next few days and we'll do the deal. We'll sort out a house for you out here in Beverly Hills or wherever you want it. Just come out and have a look.'

Out . . . limo . . . airport . . . phone everyone and

their aunt from the first-class lounge. Once on the plane, even though I was absolutely knackered, I want to run up and down the gangways telling everyone who was prepared to listen. But I tried to stay cool. Then the fear hit me.

In the first place, the contracts hadn't been signed. Secondly – it just occurred to me – I hadn't asked them what the money was. I hadn't even thought about what it would earn me, although I did know the star of the movie, Nicholas Cage, was reckoned to be getting $20 million. Me? It might be a couple of million, I said to myself. Maybe one million? Well, half a million at worst. It was all whirring round in my head. What would I need to live out there for six months? I spent eleven hours wondering, not a minute's kip. I only saw Tanya for three hours when I got home because I had an appointment in Wales. So we celebrated a couple of days later – with a night in Walthamstow Stadium, watching the greyhounds.

That's another thing. I own greyhounds now. I paid £2,800 for one, called her Smoking Barrels. She's two years old now, and she became the best stayer in the country attracting three offers up to £25,000 but I'm not selling. We want to win a Classic with her, the TV Trophy or St Leger. It's the prestige, the fun of it that appeals. People say you should sell a dog when the right bid comes along, but with me it's the winning that is far more important than the money. Take Joe Kinnear – I bought him a grey-hound as a present and called it Joe's Vinnie. It won at Walthamstow, his first trophy, but poor old Joe wasn't there to see it. He'd been going to that track for thirty years but missed his own winner!

Everything seems to have taken off for me since *Lock, Stock*. The phone never stops. I could probably do ten things a day for one or two grand but it's far better to do two or three a week for the rates I'm being paid.

Once my mates heard I was off to make a film in the States, they told me to make sure I took a big house because half of Hertfordshire is looking forward to a holiday in Beverly Hills. It's a six-month contract but they say the filming, with a lot of outside work including car chases, should take about four months. I'm playing a gang member called the Sphynx. It's not a brutal or hard part, but I'll need to act more because I'm on screen a lot. The Sphynx had been involved in a car smash four years earlier and hadn't spoken since, not until he makes a big speech at the end, that is. Much of the part is mute so it's body language, facial expressions.

As far as the wages go, I am not going to be a millionaire overnight, but it will help. It's a $100 million movie with Nicholas Cage and Robert Duvall for Christ's sake – what a chance! The biggest movie of summer 2000, I would have done it for nothing – it's such a big step on the ladder.

And when it's done, when I'm back home again, a third film has been more or less rubber-stamped already – a remake of the Burt Reynolds movie *The Mean Machine* with the team who produced *Lock, Stock*. There is also serious talk of my life story being filmed for television on the same lines as the recent two-part documentary on Diana Dors.

I've really taken to people in the film industry. I've no time for those who knock anything and condemn the stars of the big screen and TV as luvvies. A lot of them are very well educated so they speak very well, know their manners, know about the theatre and Shakespeare. I find them super people, despite accusations of it being a dog-eat-dog world. You can't get more two-faced back-stabbers than exist in football, so I have been well-primed.

To go back into football would be a desperate measure for me, if I hadn't any more work as an actor. I still harbour distant thoughts of being a manager or coach, but the longer I am out of the game the harder it will be for me to return. To say I enjoyed football on the way to Hollywood would be an understatement. You can't condemn a whole sport on the basis of a few bad months in a fourteen-year professional career. I don't have a chip on my shoulder, I have a dislike of the people who ran QPR. But the sourness of that will never ruin the sweetness of what I enjoyed and achieved all down the line. If I'm on a train somewhere, or a plane to America, most of my thoughts go back to Wimbledon and the tours to Portugal for preseason, the Crazy Gang and the pranks, Harry Bassett's bedroom perfectly rearranged outside the lifts. It was brilliant.

All the criticism I got from the press was hard to endure. I don't know whether I was taken seriously enough. The people I worked with took me seriously. Still, what the hell, I am bigger now than any of those people who took delight in hammering me. You don't get much bigger than a $100 million movie. I'm not gloating, though. My biggest concern is finding a house in Beverly Hills with enough bedrooms to accommodate half of Hertfordshire.

I know somebody who will be looking down on all this with a satisfied smile on his face. I still talk to Granddad Arthur on a regular basis, whenever I feel the need. When that phone call came through telling me of the first-class plane ticket to LA I had another quiet word. I never forget to say thank you. It's been a great journey until now, but I've still got a lot of miles to travel. So far it's been emotional.

index

Lock, Stock and Two Smoking Barrels

GUY RITCHIE

Streetwise charmer Eddy walks into the biggest card game of his life with £100,000 of his own – and his mates' – money. But the game is fixed and Eddy ends up owing half a million to porn king and general bad guy Hatchet Harry. Eddy has a week to come up with the money before he starts losing his fingers to Harry's sinister debt collector, Big Chris – unless he can persuade his dad to hand over his beloved bar instead. Or maybe Eddy and his mates can come up with a better plan . . .

'a hilariously twisted, razor-sharp, comedy gangster thriller . . . *The Long Good Friday* for the *Trainspotting* generation' FHM

'Mixes the authenticity of *The Long Good Friday* with the jet-black humour of *Reservoir Dogs* and the intricately plotted wit of *The Italian Job* . . . one of the funniest films I have seen in years' Neil Norman *Evening Standard*

NON-FICTION / CINEMA 0 7472 6205 5

If you enjoyed this book here is a selection of other bestselling sports titles from Headline

A LOT OF HARD YAKKA	Simon Hughes	£6.99 ☐
DARK TRADE	Donald McRae	£7.99 ☐
TO WIN JUST ONCE	Sean Magee	£6.99 ☐
ATHERS	David Norrie	£6.99 ☐
LEFT FOOT FORWARD	Garry Nelson	£5.99 ☐
FERGIE	Stephen F. Kelly	£6.99 ☐
RED ARMY YEARS	Richard Kurt and Chris Nickeas	£6.99 ☐
DERBY DAYS	Dougie and Eddy Brimson	£6.99 ☐
TEAR GAS AND TICKET TOUTS	Eddy Brimson	£6.99 ☐
MY TOUR DIARIES	Angus Fraser	£6.99 ☐
MANCHESTER UNITED RUINED MY LIFE	Colin Shindler	£5.99 ☐

Headline books are available at your local bookshop or newsagent. Alternatively, books can be ordered direct from the publisher. Just tick the titles you want and fill in the form below. Prices and availability subject to change without notice.

Buy four books from the selection above and get free postage and packaging and delivery within 48 hours. Just send a cheque or postal order made payable to Bookpoint Ltd to the value of the total cover price of the four books. Alternatively, if you wish to buy fewer than four books the following postage and packaging applies:

UK and BFPO £4.30 for one book; £6.30 for two books; £8.30 for three books.

Overseas and Eire: £4.80 for one book; £7.10 for 2 or 3 books (surface mail).

Please enclose a cheque or postal order made payable to *Bookpoint Limited*, and send to: Headline Publishing Ltd, 39 Milton Park, Abingdon, OXON OX14 4TD, UK.
Email Address: orders@bookpoint.co.uk

If you would prefer to pay by credit card, our call team would be delighted to take your order by telephone. Our direct line is 01235 400 414 (lines open 9.00 am–6.00 pm Monday to Saturday 24 hour message answering service). Alternatively you can send a fax on 01235 400 454.

Name ....
Address ....
....
....

If you would prefer to pay by credit card, please complete:
Please debit my Visa/Access/Diner's Card/American Express (delete as applicable) card number:

Signature .... Expiry Date ....